# Cry Scandal
# The Root of His Evil

## WILLIAM ARD

### Introduction by Nicholas Litchfield

**Stark House Press • Eureka California**

CRY SCANDAL / THE ROOT OF HIS EVIL

Published by Stark House Press
1315 H Street
Eureka, CA 95501, USA
griffinskye3@sbcglobal.net
www.starkhousepress.com

CRY SCANDAL
Originally published by Rinehart and Company, Inc., New York, and copyright © 1956 by William Ard. Reprinted in paperback by Popular Library, New York, 1958.

THE ROOT OF HIS EVIL
Originally published by Rinehart and Company, Inc., New York, and copyright © 1957 by William Ard. Reprinted in paperback by Dell Books, New York, 1958, as *Deadly Beloved*.

All rights reserved under International and Pan-American Copyright Conventions.

"Timothy Dane: A Hardboiled Combination Of Toughness, Compassion, And Quiet Humor" copyright © 2022 by Nicholas Litchfield

ISBN: 979-8-88601002-2

Book design by Mark Shepard, shepgraphics.com
Cover design by Jeff Vorzimmer, ¡caliente!design, Austin, Texas
Proofreading by Bill Kelly
Cover art by Robert Maguire

PUBLISHER'S NOTE
This is a work of fiction. Names, characters, places and incidents are either the products of the author's imagination or used fictionally, and any resemblance to actual persons, living or dead, events or locales, is entirely coincidental. Without limiting the rights under copyright reserved above, no part of this publication may be reproduced, stored, or introduced into a retrieval system or transmitted in any form or by any means (electronic, mechanical, photocopying, recording or otherwise) without the prior written permission of both the copyright owner and the above publisher of the book.

First Stark House Press Edition: December 2022

## 7
Timothy Dane:
A Hardboiled Combination Of Toughness,
Compassion, And Quiet Humor
by Nicholas Litchfield

## 15
Cry Scandal
By William Ard

## 115
The Root of His Evil
By William Ard

## 224
William Ard
Bibliography

## CRY SCANDAL

It all begins when Timothy Dane's former partner goes missing. He and Barney Glines had been private investigators but had parted company over Gline's shady tactics. However, Gline's secretary is worried, so Dane starts to dig. The more Dane uncovers, the dirtier Glines begins to look. He's been working with a sleazy magazine called *Info* that specializes in celebrity gossip, taking their dirty secrets and dealing a little blackmail on the side. Soon Dane is working for a group of theater producers who want *Info* shut down for good. Then it becomes personal when Dane falls for a Broadway starlet who is next in line for the *Info* treatment. It all leads back to Barney Glines—who is nowhere to be found.

## THE ROOT OF HIS EVIL

Johnny Cashman is trying to put together the deal of a lifetime by investing in a Latin American general who is willing to trade arms for his country's gambling concessions in a takeover bid. But to make this happen, Cashman needs cash. So he starts to pull in some gambling debts, including the $200,000 that singer Buddy Lewis owes him. Buddy can only scrape together $100,000 but it's enough to send Timothy Dane down to Florida to trade the cash for Buddy's markers. Trouble is, the current Latin American regime doesn't want a takeover, and are prepared to do whatever is necessary to stop Dane. And if that weren't distraction enough, there's Lissa, Cashman's girl—one hell of a distraction.

# TIMOTHY DANE:
## A HARDBOILED COMBINATION OF TOUGHNESS, COMPASSION, AND QUIET HUMOR

by Nicholas Litchfield

Popular but long-forgotten novelist William Ard (1922—1960), considered one of the best writers of private-eye detective fiction during his lifetime, produced a large and significant body of work over the course of his startlingly short career. Utilizing four pseudonyms, as well as his own name, he wrote at least thirty-six works of fiction (Contemporary Authors, 2003) and found success with various aliases. Many of his novels were published in several foreign languages, and he also wrote television scripts and, purportedly, the movie screenplay for one of his books, *Buchanan Rides Alone* (Buck, 1960), although, contradictorily, Charles Lang is credited with having written it. Curiously, Oscar "Budd" Boetticher Jr., a director of several low-budget Westerns hired to film this one by Producers-Actors Corporation for distribution by Columbia, insists that Burt Kennedy rewrote Lang's script but that he allowed Lang to take the screen credit as the writer needed the money (Nott, 2018).

While best known for his string of "Buchanan" books (written as by Jonas Ward), Ard was essentially a writer of hardboiled fiction. Set apart from the emergent crowd of tough-guy mystery writers, his novels were crisp, lively, and highly readable, with fairly convincing characters and credible action. As journalist Maurice Richardson put it, Ard's stories contained "unusually verisimilitudinous gangsterism" (Richardson, 1954).

Ard's unfaltering rise to prominence was particularly swift. Having graduated from Dartmouth College, mentored by distinguished writer Sidney Cox (a close friend of Robert Frost), he spent two years with the Marine Corps, then worked as a copywriter for an advertising agency and a publicity writer for movie corporations. (Buck, 1960). For three years, he was employed by Warner Brothers Studios and for four years by Paramount Studios.

He established himself as a novelist while still in his twenties. Considered "above average" from the moment his first story appeared, he improved with age "like whisky in a charred keg" (Badger, 1953). He was "ever-dependable," always satisfying his legions of mystery fans and "consistently carving top-notch yarns" (Badger, 1956). The novels bearing his real name and the Jonas Ward pseudonym were massively popular, but his minor nom de plumes also gained a keen fanbase. Case in point, Ben Kerr. There aren't many reviews of the Kerr novels—or, rather, information isn't readily available—but Ard's pseudonym was prosperous enough in its day. Publishers like Henry Holt & Co. and Popular Library released half a dozen Kerr mysteries throughout the 1950s, each with striking covers. Court sessions, real-life situations, and famous criminal cases helped inspire the plots of these novels (Buck, 1960). With his first serving, *Shakedown*, he cooked up "a smooth blend of slugging, sleuthing and sex" (Ottenberg, 1952). Book critic Edward Badger of *The Birmingham News*, seemingly a big admirer, had nothing but praise for the author's writing style. Here's Badger's verdict on *Shakedown*: "Ben Kerr might well become the successor to Mickey Spillane now that the latter has retired from the mystery novel field." (Badger, 1952). Evidently, Badger was unaware that *Shakedown* was not the author's first effort as a mystery writer: "He should try again, for he has done a good job with this one."

It's worth noting that, in spite of the mass appeal of Mickey Spillane, for some, the whiff of Spillane was far from welcome, and comparisons with Spillane recurrently dogged Ard. "If Kerr kicks over the Spillane traces, he'll probably turn out some good stuff," thought famed crime writer Dorothy B. Hughes (Hughes, 1952). Nonetheless, despite the usual cops, criminals, dames, and irresistible private eyes, "his brave attempt to freshen these ingredients" was duly noted (Hughes, 1952).

Another writer who loathed the Mickey Spillane school of savage, sleazy storytelling was Anthony Boucher, the influential *New York Times* critic. Curiously, his and other journalists' critical assaults on Spillane had no impact on the author's rising popularity. To Ard's credit, though, there's rarely any hint of Spillane in the books bearing his own name, and Boucher made a point of saying that he greatly preferred Ard's gal and gore approach to crime writing as opposed to Spillane's unreadable drivel. Regularly expressing appreciation for Ard's "extraordinary technical skill" and "complexity of plot and counterplot" (Boucher, 1955a), he enjoyed his "vigor, pace and economy" of words (Boucher, 1957), valuing that his novels were "gratifyingly distinct from each other, and each one better than the last" (Boucher, 1953). While each of his Timothy Dane novels was, in essence, "standard tough stories," unlike other hard-boiled writers, he approached "each book on its own merits, free from formula," and gave it "its own fitting plot, construction and flavor" (Boucher, 1953). In his opinion, Ard was "just about unmatched for driving story-movement and acute economy"

(Boucher, 1955b), and his "sound and credible operative, Timothy Dane" (Boucher, 1954) was "one of the best private detectives in the business" (Boucher, 1955b).

As with Boucher and Dorothy B. Hughes, Drexel Drake (real name Charles H. Huff), another of those top-tier reviewers well-known for their crime fiction, also enjoyed Ard's familiar yet noteworthy tales. Drake relished the shrewd plots, the captivating style, the "precision action" (Drake, 1955), and the fact that Ard's hero sleuth didn't sing his own praises (Drake, 1952). It was an opinion shared by many others. The author's appealing, "fast-moving and entirely likable" (Quick, 1955) prose made his gritty yarns more agreeable, and his singular characters, "whose actions are entertaining without leaving a morbid memory of the book," were judged "even likable" (E.F.L., 1955).

Concise storytelling, rapid action, and an empathetic lead were the key ingredients, and it helped that Ard's secondary characters were reasonably well-defined and "carefully considered" (Hughes, 1955). And while his crime fiction was, as modern critics like Kevin Burton Smith note, "very much of its time: crooked cops, corrupt politicians, treacherous women, and murderous thugs pitted against a big-shouldered detective with a smart mouth and a Colt .45" (Burton Smith, 2020b), in contrast to his contemporaries—the writers of hard-bitten characters like Mike Hammer and Shell Scott—Ard "showed a compassion and sensitivity rare for the time in detective fiction, recalling Ross Macdonald's later Lew Archer novels, or perhaps Thomas B. Dewey's Mac" (Burton Smith, 2020b).

Of all Ard's novels, Timothy Dane stands front and center, his chain of stories extending to nine adventures. Despite not being his greatest achievement, he was the author's passion, his first baby. *The Perfect Frame*, which marks his entrance into the literary world, brought the writer immediate success. Some, like prominent reviewer Avis DeVoto, dismissed this early attempt as having an "extravagantly silly plot" (DeVoto, 1951), while others drew attention to the energetic, brash young protagonist, full of "nerve" and "charm" (Pottsville Republican, 1951), declaring the book a "hard-hitting, fast-moving story" (L.S.Q, 1951).

*The Perfect Frame* would become the first in a series featuring the "high-minded" insurance investigator (Toledano, 1955), who is "personally likable and professionally believable" (Boucher, 1952). Habitually employed by an insurance company specializing in risk capital, Dane "fancies himself as a great lover and a man who never crosses a busy street to avoid a fight." (Johnston, 1957). He's also a handsome, honest man, "albeit a rough one," who is "catnip to women" (Johnston, 1953).

In the age of gimmicks, where mystery writers concocted elaborate plots and eccentric gumshoes, Ard maintained a recognizable framework but initiated nonstandard assignments for his private eye. For example, in *Don't Come Crying to Me*, there's a mystery concerning which of three men sired an infant, and in "the long-to-be-remembered" (Profilet, 1952) *The Diary*, Dane must solve the theft of an eighteen-year-old's diary. In the final two series entries, both included in his collection, Dane has equally interesting yet dissimilar errands.

In *Cry Scandal*, published in July 1956, Barney Glines, Dane's problematic former business partner, has gone missing. Despicable, incorrigible, and habitually flouting the law, Glines' penchant for embezzlement, blackmail, and shakedown eventually brought an end to their partnership. Having broadened his reputation as a lying, swindling, womanizing rogue since the two detectives went their separate ways, Barney isn't short of enemies. In fact, his secretary—Barney's latest sweetheart—is about the only person interested in seeing him again.

Though hesitant to get involved, Dane's curiosity and sympathetic nature allow him to be persuaded to investigate his old associate's disappearance. And while accessing the man's case files, uncovering more of Barney's shady practices, he comes across a provocative magazine titled *Info*. It's a vulgar, salacious publication focused on sex, smut, and public scandal. While pimps, peddlers, prostitutes, and other slimeballs stand to profit from its exposés, those in the limelight stand to have their careers greatly tarnished. Widely read and highly profitable, it's a puzzle however, to determine exactly who finances the lurid rag, who produces the sensational stories, and how it gets distributed. It is puzzle television executives and movie agents are keen to throw money at in the hope of getting answers and, hopefully, putting the journal out of circulation.

Expedient digging into Barney's private affairs turns up more than Dane bargained for, and his colorful recollections of Barney's many misdemeanors during their time as partners enhance this fast-moving tale of greed, disloyalty, extortion, and murder.

In the equally enjoyable subsequent tale, *The Root of His Evil*, published in July 1957 and reissued by Dell as *Deadly Beloved*, Dane is hired as a courier to deliver $100,000 in cash to Johnny Cashman, a shady entrepreneur. Big, bluff, arrogant, and ambitious, Cashman, owner of a very successful nightclub in Miami Beach, is also a bookmaker looking to gain control of the gambling racket in parts of South America—everything from the lottery, horseracing, casino tables, and crap games on the docks. His powerplay hinges on a gun-running operation and a political coup. Unfortunately, a lack of capital requires him to call in debts pronto, but one of these borrowers, a famed nightclub singer in New York City, can't come up with the cash. Having borrowed half of what he owes from the bank, he then hires Dane to deliver the money and collect his markers. Unsurprisingly, the straightforward assignment is anything but simple, and Dane's journey to Miami becomes a rough, breathless experience fraught with danger and major complications.

Although remarkably compressed, with a lean, unconvoluted plot, Ard packs his high-speed tale with a surprising quota of action and excitement and puts the hero through an excruciating forty-eight-hour crusade. With umpteen enemies on his trail, keeping hold of the cash long enough to get it into Cashman's grasping hands is a challenge even the mighty Timothy Dane may not quite be able to achieve.

Alas, *The Root of His Evil* signaled the end of the line for Timothy Dane. Ard focused on other protagonists in his final years, and he was creative and prolific right up to the end. When he died, he was at the very height of his career. *Buchanan's Revenge*, published by Fawcett, had just hit the shelves in January 1960, and while in the process of penning a new Buchanan novel (untitled), he fell ill. Diagnosed with cancer, he died soon after, within a matter of days, in fact, aged only 37 (Buck, 1960). His career as a novelist spanned a mere ten years. Apparently, he "longed to produce more serious novels, but was kept from this goal by the pressures of the popularity of his western novels and mysteries" (Buck, 1960).

Interestingly, some of his characters continued to thrive despite his death. His "Lou Largo" series prevailed, with new adventures ghostwritten by Lawrence Block and John Jakes (Burton Smith, 2020a). Likewise, his "Buchanan" Western series, written under the Jonas Ward pseudonym, was so commercial that it lasted well into the 1980s, with Brian Garfield and William R. Cox providing new tales. And when Arthur Silber acquired rights to *As Bad as I Am*, intending to turn it into a big-budget motion picture (Lipson, 1960), "Danny Fontaine" looked poised to be more than merely a two-book series. Alas, no movie materialized.

Surprisingly, the blithe and youthful Timothy Dane has aged remarkably well in seventy-five years. Droll and engaging, his tough, compact, adrenaline-fueled narratives move with vitality, pace, and purpose. Neglected for decades, these top-tier tales make a welcome return to print.

—Aug 2022
Rochester, NY

## Works Cited:

Badger, Edward. "Here's mystery novel with spice a-plenty." *The Birmingham News*, Jun 8, 1952, p.88

Badger, Edward. "Private eye Dave fights labor leeches." *The Birmingham News*, Jul 26, 1953, p.74

Badger, Edward. "Timothy Dane in seventh success." *The Birmingham News*, Sep 9, 1956, p.89

Boucher, Anthony. "Criminals At Large." *New York Times*, Mar 9, 1952, p.BR24

Boucher, Anthony. "Criminals at Large." *New York Times*, Jul 26, 1953, p.BR17

Boucher, Anthony. "Criminals at Large." *New York Times*, Jul 4, 1954, p.BR11

Boucher, Anthony. "Criminals at Large." *New York Times*, Jan 23, 1955, p.BR26

Boucher, Anthony. "Criminals at Large." *New York Times*, Jun 26, 1955, p.BR21

Boucher, Anthony. "Criminals at Large." *New York Times*, Aug 4, 1957, p.BR10

Buck, Bill. "William Ard, Noted Mystery Author, TV, Movie Script Writer, Dies At 37." *Tampa Bay Times*, Mar 13, 1960, p.33

Burton Smith, Kevin. "Lou Largo." Thrilling Detective, May 17, 2020. *Thrilling Detective*, May 17, 2020. https://thrillingdetective.com/2020/05/17/lou-largo/

Burton Smith, Kevin. "William Ard: He Coulda Been a Contender." Thrilling Detective, May 17, 2020. https://thrillingdetective.com/2020/05/17/william-ard/

Contemporary Authors. "William (Thomas) Ard." Gale Literature: Contemporary Authors, Gale, 2003. Gale Literature Resource Center.

DeVoto, Avis. "Thrills and Chills Dept." *The Boston Globe*, Jul 8, 1951, p.65

Drake, Drexel. "Keeping Tab on Murder." *Chicago Tribune*, Oct 12, 1952, p.212

Drake, Drexel. "Keeping Tab on Murder." *Chicago Tribune*, Feb 20, 1955, p.186

E.F.L. "For the Mystery Fan." *The Herald-Sun*, May 8, 1955, p.41

Hughes, Dorothy B. "Shakedown." *Daily News*, Jun 14, 1952, p.8

Hughes, Dorothy B. "Report Card of Crime." *The Albuquerque Tribune*, Jan 21, 1955, p.18

Johnston, Ben B. "Labor Union Rackets." The Times Dispatch, Aug 9, 1953, p.88

Johnston, Ben B. "Mystery and Intrigue." The Times Dispatch, Sep 1, 1957, p.59

L.S.Q. "Mysteries." *Dayton Daily News*, Jul 15, 1951, p.47

Lipson, Larry. "Valley Ramblings: Arthur Silber Reports Plans on Production." *The Van Nuys News and Valley Green Sheet*, Dec 30, 1960, p.12

Nott, Robert. "The Films of Budd Boetticher." Jefferson, NC: McFarland & Co., 2018. p.129

Ottenberg, Miriam. "Crime—." *Evening Star*, Jun 1, 1952, p.58

Pottsville Republican. "About Books and Thereabouts." *Pottsville Republican*, Jun 23, 1951, p.7

Profilet, Fay. "Crime Corner: Murders and Mysteries." *St. Louis Post-Dispatch*, Oct 5, 1952, p.36

Quick, Dorothy. "Quick Look At Things." *The Central New Jersey Home News*, Jul 23, 1955, p.4

Richardson, Maurice. "Crime Ration." *The Observer*, Sep 12, 1954, p.10

Toledano, Nora de. "Crime and Thrillers: MacInnes 'At Peak' As Real Spell-Binder." *The Knoxville Journal*, Feb 20, 1955, p.36

Nicholas Litchfield is the founding editor of the literary magazine *Lowestoft Chronicle*, author of the suspense novel *Swampjack Virus*, and editor of ten literary anthologies. His stories, essays, and book reviews appear in many magazines and newspapers, including *BULL: Men's Fiction*, *Shotgun Honey*, *Daily Press*, and *The Virginian-Pilot*. He has also contributed introductions to numerous books, including fourteen Stark House Press reprints of long-forgotten noir and mystery novels. Formerly a book critic for the *Lancashire Post*, syndicated to twenty-five newspapers across the U.K., he now writes for *Publishers Weekly* and regularly contributes to Colorado State University's literary journal *Colorado Review*. You can find him online at nicholaslitchfield.com.

# Cry Scandal
## WILLIAM ARD

## ONE

At eleven o'clock that bitterly cold morning, Timothy Dane got a call from Barney Glines's secretary.

"I can't find him," the girl said anxiously. "Barney is missing."

"I wouldn't worry about it," Dane said.

"Will you be right over?"

"What for?"

"What for ...? To help me find him. Barney's your best friend."

"He is?"

"There's another call coming in," the girl said, her voice edged with panic. "Please come quickly."

Click. Dane cradled the phone, frowning as though he had been bitten by it. *Barney Glines is missing.... Will you be right over ...?* She was kidding. She had to be, to call him about any grief of Barney's. It was so laughable that the big man all but brushed the phone off his desk to make room for the folders full of his own work. The first, certainly, was familiar enough—the embezzlement of nearly a hundred thousand dollars by a department store's chief accountant—and Dane had only to write his final report and tot up the bill for the six months' work on the case. The evidence was in the folder and the report would write itself. Inexplicably, it didn't. His mind wandered and he kept hearing the voice on the telephone.

*Barney Glines is missing.* So who gives a damn? Nobody. Nobody in the whole wide world. Dane slammed down the cover on the typewriter, shut the folder and stood up angrily from the desk. Ten minutes later he was entering the outer office of something called *Investigations Unlimited—Barney Glines, Investigator-in-Chief,* and gazing into the harassed eyes of a shelf-bosomed, round-faced brunette in a skintight knit suit.

"I hope you're Timothy Dane," she said.

"Yes. What's wrong with Glines?"

"I don't know," she said. "He's not anywhere around. I'm Eloise King," she added and Dane nodded. He knew she was Eloise King.

"The last I saw or heard of Barney was Friday night," the showgirlish secretary went on. "He took me to Sardi's for dinner and then to a show ..."

There was a lagging pause. *And then to bed,* Timothy filled in mentally, without malice. Aloud he asked, "Was he supposed to be in town this morning?"

"Supposed to be? He *has* to be here on Monday."

"Pretty busy, is he?"

"It's a madhouse. God, you'd think there wasn't another private detective in New York—" Shapely Eloise stopped and smiled lamely. "I didn't mean that the way it sounded," she said. "Barney's told me how well you're doing."

The hell he had. It wasn't possible for Barney Glines to speak good of anyone, and anything he had to say about Timothy Dane would be delivered with the curled lip. Just as a month ago, when Dane had run into him at lunch, he had debased this girl who was his current mistress.

"I got a live one, kiddo," Barney had said in his loud, overbearing voice. "I got a gahdamn animal. Lemme tell you about last night up at her place …"

And on and on, blow by blow. There was no shutting him up. He'd had three martinis, his words carried throughout the small restaurant, and two dozen strangers had been given a gratuitous account of the intimate affairs of Barney Glines and Eloise King.

So now, as the girl led him into Glines's private office, Dane smiled away the girl's discomfort. Nothing that Barney would say of anyone was of any consequence.

"Where have you looked for him?" he asked.

"Everywhere. I've called his apartment, his bars, his club—"

"What club?"

"It's downtown," she said a little vaguely. "He gets a steam bath, and plays handball. You know how he likes to keep in shape."

Dane knew no such thing. In the last few years Glines had run to fat, hog fat and jowls.

"How about the airlines?" he asked. "The railroads?"

She looked offended. "Barney wouldn't take a trip without telling me," she said. The telephone rang and she crossed to answer it with an attention-getting, hip-swinging gait. Crossed a room that was huge and expensively decorated, soundproofed, deep-carpeted—elegant. Dane studied the room, and the girl in the tight knit suit, and he wondered how Glines got anything done in such surroundings.

"… I know how late it is," Eloise King was saying to the caller. "But Mr. Glines hasn't come in yet. Yes, I'll have him call you first thing." She replaced the phone and made a notation in the daybook on the desk. Almost immediately the phone buzzed again, and again the secretary made her excuses. This call was also dutifully logged.

An animal, Barney had called her. But efficient enough. "I'm going crazy," she said to Dane. "Everybody wants to talk to him."

"What was he working on as of Friday?"

"He had an assignment from Max Lowe," she said. "That was one of the calls just now. And Credit Incorporated had a batch of new cases for him."

"Did he have anything personal?"

"How do you mean?" she asked, bridling, making some sex inference of the question that Timothy had not intended.

"I mean any job that came to him directly," Dane said. "Work that wasn't referred by Lowe or that collection bureau."

"Oh," she said, lowering her breasts to a less belligerent angle. "Well, there were people coming in and out of here all last week. What they talked to Barney about I have no idea."

"Mostly divorce, isn't it?"

"Barney helps a lot of people who aren't happy," she said defensively. "After all, if he doesn't somebody else will."

"I guess. Let's see his current file."

Eloise King's eyes flashed a caution signal at his request and Dane laughed. "It's safe with me," he told her. "I won't steal any of his clients." He wouldn't take them, in fact, as a gift.

"I guess it'll be all right," she said, taking a key from the desk and crossing to a locked file cabinet. "After all, you are about the best friend Barney has."

It was in Dane's mind to qualify that, to make it clear that what had once been a friendship no longer existed. But what would be the point? Instead, he took the folder from her hands and sat down with it at the low, ultramodern, ingeniously uncomfortable desk.

"I'll take the calls outside so you won't be disturbed," Eloise said. She opened the connecting door and paused there for a moment. "And thanks for coming over—Timothy. I know everything will be all right now."

"Not necessarily."

"What do you mean?"

"Nothing." The telephone rang and the girl left the office to take the call at her own desk. Dane opened the folder without enthusiasm, almost as though he were prying up a sewer cover, and saw that the topmost item was the carbon of a report mailed Friday to Max Lowe, Esq., Attorney-at-Law. Timothy read:

Re: Your file #56-042, countersuit, Huntington vs. Huntington.
Report for full week ending 22nd.
Dear Max:
This is not going to be easy. The lady leaves the house eight thirty A.M., delivers the kid to a nursery school, then checks in

at a modeling agency. She has a lot of assignments, mostly in the clothing district, and is really built for the work. Eats lunch alone or with other girls. No drinks. Picks up the kid at four P.M. and has dinner at home. Goes to bed before eleven. Contacted cleaning woman who claims there's no boyfriends or telephone calls. No liquor in the house. She's obviously behaving herself, Max, and possibly suspects an investigation is going on. Here's what I suggest: I'll put a girl onto her, a model who's worked for me before. She's a real con at chumming-up and will get our subject into her hotel room on some pretext. Leave the rest to yours truly. Await your instructions. Sincerely, Investigations Unlimited, Barnard J. Glines, Investigator-in-Chief.

There it was, pure Glines, the master at work. "Leave the rest to yours truly." Direct, simple, right to the point. But it wasn't going to be easy, and Timothy hoped that was right. For Mrs. Huntington, an attractive mother, was working hard and behaving herself. And she was either legally separated from Mr. Huntington or was suing him for divorce, and all the right was on her side.

How could Dane be sure the lady was in the right? Simply because her husband had gone to the likes of Max Lowe; because Lowe had sicked Barney Glines onto her. And Huntington had money. Timothy would even bet you that the man's money was at the bottom of the whole investigation. He'd bet you that Mr. Huntington had been caught so far off base that he was shaking in his socks about a whopping big alimony coming up.

But Lowe-and-Glines would be in there pitching for him. And the lady had better bolt the doors, draw the blinds and not stir a foot outside from here on in. Because Barney Glines was going to get her into a hotel room, get her there with a man she'd never seen before, so drugged she wouldn't know what they were doing to her or what the cameras were for.

And what was it Eloise King had said? About Barney helping a lot of people who weren't happy? Dane set the report to Max Lowe aside, deciding that Glines' nonappearance this particular morning had no connection with it. Next was the copy of a letter sent to one George R. Brown, 234 Market Street, San Francisco, California. Barney had written to Mr. Brown:

Your latest remittance is overdue. Apparently you don't appreciate cooperation. If a certified check for $3500 is not in the return mail my client is going to swear out a warrant for your arrest for assault and damages as well as take legal action in the civil court. This is your final warning.

Sincerely ...

Shakedown. So flagrant that only Barney Glines would have the nerve to sign his name to such a bare threat. Thirty-five hundred dollars to avoid being arrested? Mr. Brown must not have anything between his ears if he kicked through with so much as a nickel; if he stood still for such intimidation.

But this letter reminded Timothy of another that Barney had written. It had been sent out under the letterhead of the Manhattan Detective Agency and concerned, of all things, a party given in the name of sweet charity. A very prominent society woman in Westchester had become too heavily indebted to a New York bookmaker. Something in the neighborhood of fifty thousands, and in lieu of paying him she had agreed to his suggestion that she lend her name and her spacious country home to a party—a Monte Carlo night for the benefit of the local hospital. The bookmaker supplied the gambling for the lady's well-heeled and unsuspecting friends. He provided loaded dice, geared roulette wheels and marked cards for the twenty-one tables. Along about dawn some of the big losers began comparing miseries, realized they had been outrageously cheated and, when their banks opened for business, stopped payment on the checks they had written.

About seven mornings later Timothy Dane was ordered down to Leonard Street where an angry assistant D.A. showed him a letter written and signed by Barney Glines. It had been sent to the president of a bank, a man who had been one of the cheated guests at the Monte Carlo party, and in it Glines identified himself as the bookmaker's collecting agent. He told the banker to make good on the stopped check, quick, or take the consequences of some very bad publicity.

"We are not fooling," Glines wrote. "Welshing is a very dangerous business."

Dane handed the letter back and shook his head in bewilderment.

"I don't know a damn thing about it."

"You're a partner in this Manhattan Detective Agency, aren't you? You and Glines own it, don't you?"

Timothy nodded, knowing what was coming next.

"And under law," the assistant D.A. said, "each partner is responsible for the acts of the other. You know that, don't you?"

"Yes."

"And you're aware that this is extortion?"

"Yes."

"By the way, where is this Glines?"

"Out of town," Timothy said truthfully.

"He sounds like a helluva partner...."

But it could have turned out a lot worse. Timothy paid a thousand dollar fine and was suspended for thirty days. Glines drew twice the amount and was set down for six months. The young partners had words about the incident, hot ones, and what worried Dane was that Barney did not really understand that he had not only violated his license but had very nearly involved both of them in a crime.

And then there was Joyce Baker. Joyce was a laughing-eyed, stunning-looking woman of forty who had been a call girl in Manhattan since she was eighteen and, when Dane first met her, was managing the affairs of a dozen other girls in the same profession. But on a vacation trip to Florida she had met this army general who was about to retire. They were in love and the marriage was set for the following June. What Joyce wanted was to retire from the field without a trace, and the Manhattan Detective Agency went to work negotiating for the return of autographed pictures, an occasional intimate note, a little black book or anything else that would link her to the past twenty-two years. Fortunately, Joyce preferred gentlemen and there was little if any trouble negotiating the recall of these things or persuading the owners to destroy them.

Joyce married the general and all went well—until Timothy learned that Barney Glines had blackmailed the bride out of ten thousand dollars. Dane had worked out his anger in a short, vicious fight, and from then on had gone his way in the business alone.

Memories. Coming back to Barney's queer business with Mr. Brown, Timothy figured that it was likely that the man in San Francisco neither knew nor particularly cared where Glines was at this moment. Distance lent enchantment, and Dane lifted the letter out of the caseload. In the same moment he had the sensation of looking into the face of a striking rattler.

What lay exposed there was really only the cover of a magazine; the cheap, gaudily colored cover of a cheap, brazenly headlined magazine. Info, it called itself in squat yellow letters against a glossy black background. *Info*, it sneered, *The Lowdown On The High And Mighty*. Beneath the title were four square-cut halftones, two men and two women whose faces even in these off-guard, unflattering photos were still as familiar to Americans as their own in a mirror. The captions were provocative, leering.

*Hollywood's perfect little screen wife*, said one. *But once she was anybody's girl*. Another: *TV's No. 1 star is holding nightly auditions for his nude art collection.* And: *He's what every girl dreams of—but the dream would be a nightmare.* This about a young and recently married singer. The fourth smirked about Lesbianism. *What has she got against men?* it asked of a constantly publicized motion picture personality.

Rough stuff, Dane thought. But big business. The competition for the spectacular material they printed must be ferocious, no holds barred. Made to order for the talents of Barney Glines, in other words, and Timothy understood that Barney might have got into the most profitable deal of his life.

Then a puzzling surprise. Lifting the cover of *Info* he found nothing inside. Not a thing. Just thirty-odd pages of glossy stock paper with nary a line of printed copy nor a single ad.

"Any leads?" Eloise King asked, coming back into the inner office.

"I don't know," Dane said. "What does Barney do for the people who get this thing out?"

She looked at the cover of the dummy magazine, surprise in every line of her brittlely pretty face. "Where did you get that?"

"Right here. Something wrong?"

"No," she said. "Nothing wrong. May I have it, please?"

"Sure," Timothy said, handing it over when she came to the desk, looking up at her quizzically. "What does Barney do for *Info?*" he asked again.

"I don't know, Timothy. I don't know very much about it at all."

"Let's see his file on it," Dane suggested.

"There isn't any," the girl said. "I never kept one."

"Had he worked for any of the people on the cover?"

She shook her head.

"But Barney must have some connection—"

"It's one of the few things he never talked to me about," Eloise said, then smiled down at him brilliantly. "I don't know about you," she told him, "but it's my lunch hour."

"You go on ahead and eat," he told her. "I'll finish with this file."

The smile disappeared as smoothly as it had come and Dane watched appreciatively as the bosom, like a slowly elevating howitzer, assumed the telltale anger angle.

"You don't think much of my staying here all by myself, do you?" Timothy asked good-naturedly.

"It isn't that so much," she said. "I certainly trust you. It's just—well, Barney makes me feel *responsible* for things when he isn't here." She tried another smile on him. "He wants me to be around when things are happening."

"I wouldn't have it any other way," Dane told her blandly, rising so abruptly from the desk that the girl had to back off. "I'll go have a look-see at my own work ..."

"I've hurt you, haven't I, Timothy? You're mad at me."

Timothy marked the new breast line and nearly laughed in her face. "Not a bit," he said. "If you were my secretary I'd want you to operate just as you are."

"But you will help me locate Barney, won't you?"

"I'll drop back later this afternoon."

"Wonderful. Are you looking for a girl?"

"For a secretary, you mean."

"Yes," she said. "I meant for a secretary."

"No," he told her, "I'm not."

"You know," she said then, "I might really have been fishing for a luncheon date with you."

"I'd like that," Timothy said with a serious expression. "But I don't think Barney would."

"Barney doesn't ..." she began, then stopped.

"Doesn't what?"

"I just thought that if he really *is* out of town. And after all, a luncheon date doesn't mean anything. Does it?"

Barney was right, Timothy thought. "A gahdamn animal"—and on the prowl right now.

"I'd be thinking about Barney," he said out loud. "Better leave it that I'll check back here in a couple of hours." She held her ground, made him brush against her to get by.

"I'll be here," she called after him.

Glines's office was in a spanking new building, rich-smelling, with elevators that stopped on electronic impulse and coasted ever so gently and precisely to each landing. Dane strode purposefully through the spacious, luxuriant lobby, turned south on Fifth Avenue and bucked the chilly, snow-threatening wind as far as Rockefeller Plaza. He went west then, but instead of continuing that way to his own building on Broadway, the tall man squared his route and doubled back toward the place he had just left. When he saw Eloise King come out and cross east with the light he went back into the building, ascending in the same elevator. Dane let himself into Glines's suite with the key he had taken from the desk only a few minutes earlier.

But if re-entry had been easy enough, finding Glines's connection with the magazine called *Info* eluded him. There was no reference to it in Eloise King's cross index of the files, nor was it filed with "I," "M" for *magazine* or "P" for *publication*. Dane even searched the "S" folders, thinking of the words *smut, scandal* and *sex*. But there was no short cut, and he went wearily at the dull job of examining Barney's file case by case. It turned up, inexplicably, in a thin folder that seemed to have been slipped almost carelessly in the cabinet with the "T's." There were no carbons of correspondence in the folder, no expense accounts, memoranda, photostats or photos. Only slips of notepaper, scraps of information written in the semi-legible script of Barney Glines.

Timothy deciphered the first: "Lili Storm (Lucy Stern). Call girl. $25. EL 5-4182. Applied for chorus job on Grayson show."

And: "Roland Turner. Bellhop. Fairy. Works NY-Miami hotels where male name stars, celebrities etc. stop."

And: "Frank Rossi. Art store. Expensive pornography. Will sell list of famous name customers-10G." The "10G" was underscored, and Timothy had the impression that the underscoring had been done in anger by Barney Glines.

And: "Donna James. 323 W. 44," and after that a bold check mark. Ten other longhand slips were in the folder, all of them X-ed out and run through with the scrawling word, *used*.

Used? Who had used that check? Timothy glanced through the ten. Such solid citizens as a pimp who recruited teenagers along 42nd Street, a Negro Lesbian, a bartender who would tell the drinking habits in the theater district, a retired cop who had taken graft during the O'Dwyer regime, a bouncer in a Spanish Harlem bordello, more call girls with black books, bellhops and even a male prostitute.

The slime and shame of a city, daring to crawl out from beneath their rocks because now the stinking rottenness of the lives they led could be converted into money. Lots and lots of money. Millions of dollars for the alchemists who published depravity and sold it on every newsstand in the country. Sold it out, issue after issue.

Dane knew that *Info's* competitors had used the material crossed out in the folder. Now he took the four unused slips, closed his eyes and shuffled them until he had lost track of the sequence. The one on top was Frank Rossi, the dealer in pornography who was willing to part with his list of customers for ten thousand dollars.

## TWO

Billy Tyson was a lovable little guy. On Broadway they were very fond of him. He represented something that was hard to find in show business; he was a solid citizen; you could trust him. Just about everybody knew Billy Tyson, and everybody knew he could keep your secrets better than you could keep them yourself.

To the other commuters on the 9:03 out of New Rochelle, Billy Tyson probably didn't seem like very much. In a smoking car full of conservatively dressed stockbrokers, account executives and insurance men he was only a roly-poly, ineffectual-looking little fellow wearing a fawn camel's hair overcoat and smelling faintly of some man's cologne. Not of any distinction on the 9:03, but a real personality in that mile-long world between Madison and Eighth avenues.

That he was a man without an enemy in that complex business was remarkable of itself. But to achieve that and be what he was verged on the impossible. For Billy Tyson was an actor's agent, a ten-percenter, the man-in-the-middle in the endless war between the producer and the performer. True enough, Tyson wasn't the most successful agent on Broadway, but he did have clients who were eating regularly, he was paying an income tax—and he did have the reputation of a man you could trust.

And on the particular winter's morning that Barney Glines was missing from the arena, Tyson was very much present. It was becoming a hectic Monday, too, with an emergency conference at NBC, then rushing to Madison Avenue for contract negotiations at CBS, back across town to check the rehearsals of a musical just on the verge of opening after its successful out-of-town tryouts. And everywhere that Billy went that morning, no matter what his mission was, the conversation invariably came around to the magazine called *Info*.

At NBC, for instance, he had been summoned because his client Franklin Joyce objected to his billing position in next week's *Aluminum Hour* show. The middle-aging Mr. Joyce, whom Tyson had rescued from Hollywood oblivion a year back, demanded that his name appear above Teresa Holm's or he would depart the cast. Miss Holm, naturally, felt the same way about the importance of her name, as did *her* agent, and though the production involved had a rather tender and sentimental theme, the real-life scene in that producer's office was anything but. And then, at a mild suggestion from Billy Tyson, the tempest died and all was sweetness and understanding. Miss Holm's and Mr. Joyce's names would roll side by side across the television screens, equal in height, weight and letter spacing. Everyone prepared to leave, but the producer signaled Tyson to remain behind.

When they were alone he unlocked a side drawer in his desk and lifted out a black and gray photostat of a cover of *Info*.

"Have you seen the latest, Billy?"

Tyson's face had its usual expression of cheerful alertness. Now the mobile features sagged and his eyes were troubled.

"I've seen it, Van," he said. "But it's not the latest …"

"My God—what is somebody trying to do?"

"That's what we're going to find out," Tyson said earnestly.

"That's what *who's* going to find out?"

"We call it FAST—Fighters Against Smear Tactics. We're not too well organized," Tyson explained, "and we haven't got much money. But we have hired a private detective agency to smoke this *Info* crowd out into the open."

"Well, damnit, good for you!" The television executive, Jon Van Ormen, reached impulsively into his desk and produced a checkbook. "What kind of contribution you people asking for, Billy?"

The other man's forcefulness seemed to startle the mild-mannered actor's agent.

"We haven't really gotten around to that yet, Van."

"How much, kid? I want *in* on this deal. Those yellow, dirty-minded sons-of-bitches aren't going to get away with that stuff month after month. How much? Fifty? A hundred?"

"Fifty," Tyson said, abashed by Van Ormen's anger. "Fifty would be wonderful. And you can bet our group will know you're in this with us."

The producer wrote the check, signed it with a flourish. "Here," he said. "And *you* can bet that the boys upstairs know that Billy Tyson's in there pitching for the industry." He handed over the check, took Tyson's hand and shook it fervently. "Keep me in touch, will you, kid?"

"Sure thing."

"And, Billy—shoot me over a stat of the latest one, will you?"

"I don't have one," Tyson said. "All I got was a glance at the dummy cover this private detective found."

"Found where?"

"He wouldn't say. Kind of a closemouthed egg. Doesn't even seem to trust us, and we're paying his bills...."

"Probably trying to make the job seem tougher than it is."

"I guess that's it, Van." Tyson turned to leave "Gotta run," he said, mindful of his appointment at CBS.

"Sure," the producer said, walking with him to the door of the office, linking their arms together. "Tell me—who was getting the treatment on the new issue?"

And Tyson, lowering his voice, spoke the four famous names in hushed tones. Jon Van Ormen looked as though he were going to be ill.

"Good Christ," he said worriedly. "I've got two of them signed for the *Aluminum Hour*. Something has to be done, damnit, and done fast!"

"That's what we call ourselves, FAST," Tyson said.

Van Ormen didn't seem to hear. "Do you think I ought to tell the agency? Alert them in case the client gets a copy of *Info* mailed to him?"

Tyson shrugged his shoulders apologetically. "You're the judge of that, Van. All I can do is keep my own people out of trouble."

"But *would* you call the agency?" Van Ormen persisted.

"You put it like that, Van, and I have to say I would. No reason for you to be holding the bag when they put that dirty rag in circulation."

Billy left then, and though the business at CBS was a routine one about reruns of a projected television series—the exact amounts to be paid his client after the initial twenty-six shows—something of much more importance was on the network lawyer's mind.

It was *Info*, and once again Tyson sympathized with the very serious problem it presented, and again mentioned FAST and what it was trying to do to end the *menace*. The lawyer asked the name of the detective agency the group had hired.

"Investigations, Unlimited," Tyson told him.

"Never heard of it."

"It came highly recommended. Fellow that runs it does a lot of work for Max Lowe."

"That's a recommendation?"

Billy seemed uncomfortable. "Well," he said, "Lowe does come to court well prepared ..."

"So does a skunk, Billy. You ever hired a fellow named Timothy Dane?"

"Fred," said Tyson fervently, "I never personally, hired a private detective in my life. They scare me to death. It was our committee that gave this job to Investigations, Unlimited—"

"Who's putting up the money for all this?"

"It's strictly a personal affair so far. Just a little group of us trying to find out who this Info crowd is. Jon Van Ormen joined in the fight. But we're not soliciting ..."

"What did Van contribute?"

Tyson spread his hands imploringly. "I wouldn't tell you that, Fred," he said. "I couldn't. Believe me, we haven't even discussed ways and means. All we know is that this terrible magazine has to be suppressed—"

"How much did Van give?"

Tyson shook his round head from side to side. "You know Van when it comes to causes," he said. "He's even going to prime the big bosses over there. You know how enthusiastic he can get."

"It's no more than we can get," Fred Marsh said. He, too, produced a checkbook and wrote in it. "A hundred dollars," he said, handing it to Tyson. "Is Jon Van Ormen more eager than that to see this *Info* thing exposed for what it is?"

"No," Tyson said. "And thanks, Fred. It's going to help to know that we're all together in this."

"We've got to be, Billy. And this afternoon I've got a report to read to the board. I'll use the opportunity to let the brass know what you're doing."

"Show business is my life," Billy Tyson said. With a handshake he was gone, west by cab to the Lyceum Theatre where even the guard at the stage entrance knew him well enough to admit him without question to the supersecret rehearsal of *Solo*. This was against Ralph Blodgett's orders about outsiders on the premises, but Tyson's selfless devotion to *Solo* was a Broadway legend aborning, and no one who had watched it develop had the slightest inclination to do anything but nurture it to whatever finale such an improbable situation could produce.

The columnists, of course, scented something, but it was so offbeat that they were wary of it, suspicious that a publicity man was feeding them baited tidbits. But those who'd been around *Solo* from the time Ralph Blodgett had begun auditioning for his musical drama, the real insiders, knew these to be the facts:

A year ago, Billy Tyson had turned his back on the New York winter and flown to Florida. But not to Miami, where he could have written off the vacation as a business expense. Tyson had gone instead to west Florida, to the quiet, sunny little town of Dunedin, where there were no night clubs, no working clients—nothing but the unruffled waters of the Gulf of Mexico and a hotel that asked him to keep his room radio turned low after 10 P.M. "in consideration of our other guests."

Being Billy, he watched the volume of his set scrupulously, had his breakfast before 8:30 so as not to inconvenience the waitresses, learned to play shuffleboard, and comported himself in general so as to be unnoticeable. And it was so motiveless as to be almost chance that he was in neighboring Clearwater for the day of the "Fun and Sun" parade, and to be looking that way when the "Goddess of Sunshine" was carried past on her extravagant float.

The Goddess was a tanned, leggy blonde, a bold-breasted nineteen-year-old who knew exactly how dazzling she looked on her high dais above the admiring throng. But her glance never met Billy Tyson's, and the beauty-wise, talent-conscious eyes of the little man from Broadway passed over the Goddess in an instant, to settle wonderingly on another young girl aboard the float. She was one of the half-dozen "Attendants" to the Goddess of Sunshine, well set up physically, but in comparison to the blonde she was an undistinguished brownette with a saddle of freckles across the bridge of her nose that was visible at sixty feet. What went straight to Tyson's heart was the expression on the girl's face, the look of absolute boredom, of hypersophistication, of complete aloofness to the whoop-de-do of the marching bands, the splendor of her surroundings, the hand-clapping and whistling of the crowd that so thoroughly enjoyed the bathing-suited beauty on display.

Billy Tyson felt a stab of sympathy with this girl that was nearly unbearable. She had the detachment of a Grace Kelly, the disdain of a Katherine Hepburn—but with a face and figure and distinction that was very much her own.

Her own, Tyson thought, and marketable. Warner Bros., he thought. Warner's would see her specialness as immediately as he had. But maybe TV would be better. Safer, Billy thought. The boys in Hollywood weren't taking the chances they had on new talent; the build-up for newcomers was out. But television was still wide open, still hungry for talent, and that's where he'd spot her.

This was all very objective thinking on Billy Tyson's part. She would become a success and he would collect his rightful ten percent. To no one, on that day or this, would the little man admit that he had fallen in love with Dorothy Jenkinson, aged twenty and now rechristened Donna James. His motives, he insisted, were professional, unemotional, but when the showfolk observed the long hours and hard work—and money—that Billy expended on the girl during the next six months, they were certain that he was moved by something more than his future commissions.

Donna, herself, worked very hard, learning to walk without a sway, to talk without a drawl, to pose for portraits, to model clothes, to hold a glass, to inhale a cigarette, to memorize the ridiculous lines from some impossible drama and give them back as the most natural thing in the world. She worked, and did as she was told to do, and was agreeable and cooperative and, in her fashion, grateful. For the truth was that the girl was just as bored by show business as she had been by beauty contests and parades in Florida. There was no hunger in her for success, no driving determination, and so it came as a very sharp surprise to some people when *Variety* carried the brief announcement that Donna James was being represented, henceforth, by World Wide Artists, the huge, sprawling talent agency that was, literally, worldwide.

What had happened between her and Billy Tyson?

"Nothing happened," Donna said. "I was rehearsing this little television part I had and this fella asked me was I under contract to anybody. I told him no, and he asked would I sign a contract with him." Here Donna shrugged her shoulders. "So I signed," she said. "That's all there was to it."

Tyson was equally vague. "Donna owes me nothing, now or in the future. Actually, you know, I couldn't possibly do as much for her career as World Wide can."

That, said his friends, was typical, for at the moment that Donna was signing with the big agency Billy Tyson was working night and day persuading Ralph Blodgett to cast the girl for the part of Marion, the streetwalker in *Solo*. Blodgett had liked the girl's reading a week before, but he would have been inclined to give the part to a more experienced actress had Tyson not convinced him that Donna *was* Marion. In a second, more probing audition the director decided that Tyson was right, but negotiations from then on were conducted with Hal Neff of World Wide. Billy Tyson was abruptly on the outside, looking in, and when instead of folding his tent and stealing away he proceeded to follow the rehearsals and tryouts of *Solo*—at whatever inconvenient hour or place—Broadway suspected the man of carrying the biggest torch of the decade.

His relations with Donna were as friendly as ever, and they dined together on occasion, but it pained Billy's friends to watch. For Billy, they said, must know that the wolves were in full pursuit of the girl and that in *Solo's* frequent love scenes, star Mike Carhart was doing very little acting.

And that, very briefly, is the story that Winchell, Kilgallen et al, didn't print for the very simple reason they didn't believe it. It was easy to believe that Mike Carhart was turning on his considerable charm again, and that the boys from El Morocco and the Stork were laying siege to the town's newest female attraction, and that Donna James looked like good copy for some time to come—but they couldn't digest the Billy Tyson angle. It was too pat, too uncomplicated. And besides, how does the sad little story end?

If Tyson knew he gave no indication of it as he sat in the empty balcony of the Lyceum Theatre and watched his discovery perform on the bare rehearsal stage. The full orchestra was there, and so was the lyricist, for this was a special morning. Donna's part was being padded—an extra scene with Sylvia Hall, the leading lady of *Solo*—and she was to be given a song of her own to sing. The girl's voice was not a strong one, but it was plaintive and she seemed to have a good sense of tempo and harmony in the passage with the string section. Tyson also noticed a difference in Donna's Act Two costume, more cleavage in the bodice, higher hemline in the skirt, and he guessed correctly that Blodgett had instructed Wardrobe to concentrate on the girl personally.

Now her song was interrupted, and there was a quiet conference between the arranger and the conductor.

"What are you doing up here, Billy?" Ralph Blodgett asked good-naturedly, and the agent turned to look up at the other man standing in the aisle beside him.

"I wanted to be sure she projected this far."

"Does she?"

"Yes."

"And if she hadn't? What were you going to do about it?"

"Send you an anonymous note to speak to her."

"Another note?" the director said, smiling. "Do you really think I read all those amateur suggestions you mail me?"

"I haven't any idea what you do with them, Ralph," Tyson said.

"I heed them very carefully, my friend," Blodgett told him, and then casualness passed from his strong-jawed face and he looked very serious, even troubled about something, although you would guess that life held very few fears for Ralph Blodgett.

"I also heed this very carefully," he said now, sitting down beside Tyson and handing him a folded piece of notepaper.

Unfolding it, Tyson read: "Personal Memo From The Editors of *Info*." This was printed across the top, with *Info* appearing in the same yellow-on-black logotype as the magazine cover. Below was the typewritten message: "We are about to go to press with Issue No. 4, and as your play will have opened before our publication date you will be especially interested in one of our cover stories. It is the inside—everything—about what goes on between M.C. and D.J. when their play-acting is done for the night. Anticipating your professional and financial concern, we have put you on our special mailing list for a prepublication proof of the cover." There was nothing more on the slip of paper.

"What do you make of it, Billy?"

"I don't believe it," Tyson said in a low voice.

"Don't believe what? That my actors sleep together? Or that this filthy little gutter crowd are going to make a dirty joke out of a rather boringly natural situation?"

"I can't believe they would print anything like that. I just can't believe it...."

"What are these guys trying to prove, anyhow? I've seen two issues of this *Info* and I'm damned if I get the moral. And who are they, Billy?"

"That's what we're trying to find out."

"So I heard," Blodgett, said. "That's why I gave you that memo from them. Maybe they can be located through the typewriter, or the watermark in the paper—anything."

"Say, that's a good idea, Ralph. I'll give it to this agency we hired." He put the memo in his jacket. "Have you spoken to Donna about this?"

"Hell, no. The kid's got enough to think about with an opening next week."

"But you do think—well, you're pretty certain that she and Mike are serious about each other?" Tyson asked the question tentatively, as though he really didn't want a truthful answer.

"I'm pretty certain that they're not *un*friendly," Blodgett said in his blithe fashion. "And having worked with Mike Carhart in two other shows, I know that he has a way of making friendships ripen with really blinding speed. I've accused him of spiking their Postum, but he won't give out his magic secret."

Billy Tyson hardly seemed to be listening, and now he arose and made his way into the aisle.

"I've got a date for lunch," he said. "So long, Ralph."

Blodgett almost called him back, to remind him that the luncheon date was with him. But then he remembered their conversation and he began to wonder if he understood the relationship between his friend and Donna James. Certainly Billy took a very keen interest in the girl's career, but the producer never suspected until this moment that there was anything in the way of love and jealousy between the two.

He could not believe there was anything like that to it. Why, Billy had known dozens of beautiful women through the years, sophisticated, glamorous, tremendously exciting personalities. If he had avoided matrimony or any other sort of entanglement with those, how could he be affected by this kid?

Even as Ralph Blodgett was thinking that, his attention was directed to the resumption of activity on the stage below. The kid named Donna James was singing again, speaking the words as the voice coach had instructed her to speak them, moving around the stage, stopping, moving again as Blodgett had told her to move. But for all that she should have been just another raw ingénue going through the motions, the man in the balcony felt a tremendous impact from what he was seeing.

For the thousandth time in his long career, the man was asking himself to define the difference between a very good performance and a star performance. Why could there be only one Gertrude Lawrence? One Ethel Merman? How could a song be sung over and over and yet never really be heard until Mary Martin sang it to you?

Blodgett didn't know the answer. All he could do was point to the young girl who was giving a star performance at this moment. Then Donna was finished and there was a very curious silence in the place until a prop man, of all people, began applauding. In the next moment the entire company was clapping and shouting, and Ralph Blodgett was a little awed and frightened by what he had helped create.

## THREE

Midway through his second call, Timothy Dane discovered that he would never make a living as a confidence man. First it had been A. Frank Rossi, dealer in art, antiques and you-name-it. Dane had not only named what he wanted, he had spelled it out, but to every reference to pornography Frank Rossi had rolled his flashing brown eyes, shaken his head and spread his hands palm up as proof of his innocence.

"In other words," Dane said, "you already sold the list."

"List? *List?* What is this list? A man has customers. If he doesn't have customers he doesn't have a business. Is that right?"

"Frank, all I want to know about is the list of people who buy your lewd stuff. When did you last see Barney Glines about selling it?"

"For the last time," Rossi said, shaking a finger up into Dane's face, "I never heard of this Glines."

"Or *Info?*"

"Or *Info*."

Dane sighed, then reached toward his inside breast pocket and withdrew a wallet. "You're a hard man, Frank," he said. "But the boss told me to get that list before *Info* did. Ten thousand, right?"

Frank Rossi caught his breath, involuntarily. His eyelids swept down, then up again, and it was obvious that a great sadness had come to him.

"I sold the list to Glines," he said.

"When?"

"Friday afternoon."

"You're sure it was Friday?"

"Sure I'm sure. And for a lousy thousand bucks—the sonnabitch!"

Timothy laughed in his face and left the place. Left with the hope that Frank Rossi had a nice liver attack as he worried over the nine thousand dollars he had missed out on. There was nothing more to be gained from the pornographer, nothing to indicate that he knew where Glines was. Barney, after all, didn't *have* to be missing. The character could be anywhere—incommunicado in a hospital with a well-deserved broken jaw, chasing down a lead for *Info* in Bermuda, on one of his fabulous binges, shacked up. Anywhere.

The hell with him, Dane thought. *Why am I giving up a day's pay for that good-for-nothing bum?* He remembered his ex-partner's aversion to legwork, to any exertion at all where there was no hundred-dollar bill involved. *Imagine that you're missing. Imagine that you've got a secretary!* She calls Glines, all out of breath. Glines says: "You got the *wrong number, doll. This ain't Missing Persons...."*

The hell with him. He dug into the pocket of his overcoat for cigarettes, pulled out both the package and the list of names he had written down. Number two after Frank Rossi was Lili Storm, the prostitute. Timothy lit the cigarette, tossed the match to the gutter angrily and hailed a cab to take him to the apartment on 59th Street, just west of Eighth.

It was a four-story walk-up and he knocked on the sorry-looking door gently, not wanting to startle Lili into thinking this was a raid. But there was no answer and he had to knock again. Then a third time. He laid his fingers around the knob and it twisted quite easily in his hand. The door swung open and he stared into chaos.

It was a living room, but the couch had been turned on its back, upending a lamp and a table en route. Another lamp was still erect, and draped over its shade, pathetically, was a torn brassiere and one nylon stocking. Timothy crossed the threshold, stepping over a whiskey bottle that had added a fresh stain to the rug and avoiding the scattered fragments of what had once been a champagne glass. Beyond the rug was a second stocking, its toe pointing symbolically toward the bedroom, and on the floor beneath the closed door to that room a pair of black silk pants.

With a feeling of being foolish, Timothy knocked on that door, too.

"I don't want any!" cried a voice from within and Dane pushed the door open. This was just as riotous, but more active. A chesty, square-hipped bottle-blonde leaped all naked from one side of the tousled bed and advanced on him menacingly.

"Get out!" she shouted. "Enough is enough...."

Dane circled to his right, drew close to the blanketed figure on the other side of the bed and pulled back the covers. There was a man there, sleeping heavily, but the man wasn't Barney Glines.

"If he belongs to you," Lili Storm said, "then take him the hell out of here."

Dane shook his head. "I'm looking for Glines," he said.

"*Glines!* Just let me get my hands on that miserable four-flusher—"

"Gently, honey," Dane said. "Gently."

"Who the hell are you, anyhow? Whatta you want?"

"Just a guy looking for Barney Glines. But keep your voice down before you wake your friend."

"You couldn't wake that slob with a brass band. What day is this, anyhow?"

"Monday."

"Oh, no ... What happened to Saturday and Sunday?"

Timothy shrugged sympathetically. "When did Barney leave here?"

"Leave? He hasn't been near me for a week."

"You sure?"

"This is Monday? Then the last I saw of that louse was a week ago tomorrow. When he took the pictures."

"Pictures of what?"

"Of me, what do you think? For the story in the magazine."

"The story about you and Mickie Grayson?"

She laughed. "What a crazy idea. I go down there and try out for a job on the show. They turn me down. Then Barney shoots a lot of cheesecake of me and ties in the pictures with Grayson. I never even saw the guy.... Hey! How come you don't know the racket if you're looking for Barney?"

She went one up on him there, Dane conceded, conceding also that she had been plying her trade over the weekend and hadn't seen or even heard from Barney since the day she said she had. So, smiling faintly and murmuring his apologies, he made his way to the door and a quick departure.

It had not all been on the loss side, either, for at least he was certain now which side of the street Glines had been working regarding the magazine. But the publishers of *Info*, or Barney, must be getting desperate for material when they tried to embarrass a celebrity with such a phony story as Lili Storm had outlined. And as he proceeded to the next name on the list he had no idea what he would ask or what he'd be told. For there were no explanatory remarks beside "Donna James," only a check mark.

To make the interview even more confusing, the door to Donna James's apartment was opened to Dane by a man. And quite a man. Fully as tall as Timothy, with a leonine head of glistening black hair, a long, heroic face, a jaw that seemed to have been clefted with a sculptor's chisel, and all of it dominated by a nose that hooked aristocratically and was now pointed at Dane like a dagger.

"You're late for your appointment, my friend," he said in a vibrant baritone, lips parting to show strong white teeth set in an ominous smile. "You're very late," he repeated, "but come in anyhow."

"Thanks," Dane said, hiding his confusion and crossing the threshold of the neatly decorated little apartment. The door was closed behind him, then locked, which surprised him. So did the presence of two other men in the place, two husky men in workmen's clothes but otherwise undistinguished. And it was not so much their presence that was curious but the set expressions in their faces, the way they stared fixedly at him. There was hostility in this room and Timothy turned to the one who had asked him inside.

"What gives?" he asked.

"You," was the cryptic answer. "Till it hurts." Beneath the man's short-sleeved silk sport shirt powerful, well-trained muscles flexed in agitation, and with the easy grace of an athlete he moved away from the door at the same time picking up some object from the table at his side. It was happening very fast, and Dane's first impression was that it was a stick. But then a *crack!* split the air, sharp as gunfire and what the man held was a whip with a knot at the end of its leather thong. His wrist flicked again and a second pistol shot resulted, this one inches from Dane's ear.

"Old fashioned but effective," the man was saying. "And exactly suited to the offense."

"You don't think you're going to use that thing, do you?"

"Think? I know I am."

A strong arm circled Dane's neck from behind, had his throat in a vise almost before he was aware of the movement. The second man came around front and began pulling off Dane's overcoat and jacket. His tie was unknotted and his shirt literally ripped from his back, and when he was bared to the waist the punishing grip on his windpipe was released and he was left to stand alone.

"You deserve this, Glines. Don't think you don't!" There was no time to set the thing straight. The whip was already lashing out, striking and creating an exquisite pain in his collarbone. It came at him again, across the chest, and again. Four times in all before Dane caught the swift rhythm of the whip's movement. Then his own arm moved, and his fingers locked around the man's wrist as it recoiled for the fifth strike.

"*The hell you do!*" the whipper roared, and seemed mystified a moment later when he had not freed himself from Dane's grip. And more than that as Dane drove his free fist into the other man's stomach and wrenched the whip loose. He turned with it in his hand, catching the first of the on-charging pair flush on the mouth with the whip handle. The second man caught him from the side with an awkwardly effective tackle that sent them both plunging heavily to the floor. It was a pile-on then, with Dane outmatched and losing badly until an incongruous sound—the voice of a woman—brought an abrupt end to his punishment.

"It's not him!" she was saying. "Stop! It's not *him!*"

Timothy was the first to stand, and he and Donna James looked each other over quite frankly, as though they were alone in the room. Dane was obviously intrigued by the person who had materialized from a name in Barney Glines's folder, and mentally he added a second check mark.

She broke the glance when she turned in answer to a question from the black-haired man.

"Then who is he?" There was no chagrin in that resonant voice, no hint of an apology to come, and for the first time Dane felt anger at him. He could understand being horsewhipped for Barney Glines, but now it was being put in a different light.

And the girl seemed to sense his mood, intuitively. "I'm sorry this all happened," she said, laying her fingers on his arm as though to restrain him. "And I'm sure Mike is, too...."

"Oh, sure," Mike said. "You bet." He extended the hand that had been holding the whip moments before. "Sorry as hell, fella."

Dane accepted the apology, shook the hand noncommittally. In the same instant a puzzle solved itself in his mind. Timothy pegged this character as an actor, and actors couldn't be held responsible for anything they did or said.

"Mike Carhart's my name," the actor said, smiling away all the recent unpleasantness.

"Timothy Dane," the investigator said, unbeguiled. "And you ought to shelve that ten-twenty-thirty routine with the whip."

"I said once that I was sorry, friend. If that doesn't satisfy you ..."

"Then what?" Dane asked when the rest of the threat was left trailing.

"What exactly are you here for?" Carhart said, taking another tack. "What's your game, anyhow?" There was something between them now that had nothing to do with past actions. It was a clash of personalities, as natural as the enmity of bull mastiffs meeting unexpectedly, and somehow it was the presence of the girl that fired it.

And she sensed that, too, for when she spoke to Dane there was a huskiness in her tone, an acknowledgment of the physical attraction.

"What did you want to see me about?" she asked.

"About Barney Glines."

Mike Carhart's head shot back. "Then maybe I didn't make any mistake," he said. "Any friend of that bloodsucking bastard deserves just what he gets—"

"Mike, stop it. What about Glines?" she asked Dane. "Did he send you here instead?"

"No, he didn't," Timothy said unevenly, his mind full of Carhart's arrogance and about to spill over. "Barney doesn't know I'm here."

"Then what—"

"I don't know 'what,'" he cut in. "But I'd like a talk with you. Alone."

"The hell with that!"

"It'll be all right, Mike," she told him. "And thanks for everything. I'll see you at rehearsal later."

"I'm not leaving you alone with this guy ..."

"Yes you are, honey," she said definitely, but with a note of easy familiarity that Dane found irksome. She turned the glowering Carhart around and guided him to the door. The two other men, propmen from the theater, Dane guessed, followed along. They seemed happy to be quitting the place.

The girl came back to where Dane waited.

"Now what?" she said, not belligerently, but with a light touch that brought a smile to Dane's eyes. She has something on the ball, he was thinking. Something special that marked her as an individual. But it was elusive, too; not easily caught. He wondered if Carhart had.

"Are you in show business, Miss James?"

"So they tell me. But I may be out of it," she added, in a voice that said it didn't much matter. "The show I'm in is going to open right soon." She settled herself onto a small couch, crossing slim legs that were sheathed in tight-fitting toreador pants. Above them she wore a long-sleeved candy-striped blouse. "What's your business?" she asked.

"I'm an investigator," Timothy answered. "Like Glines."

"Just like him?"

She'd thrown that one back at him high and hard, and the tall man's face was speculative for a moment. "I'll put it this way," he said. "Barney Glines was once my partner. He isn't anymore."

"Which one got the divorce?"

"It was more like an annulment."

"I like your voice," Donna James told him unexpectedly. "Come sit down and tell me what you're here for."

Dane chose an armchair facing her. "I'm trying to find Glines," he explained. "When did you see him last?"

"Friday," she said.

"And he was supposed to come again today?"

"Yes."

"Are these visits personal?" Dane asked abruptly.

"Very," she answered without hesitation.

Dane got up. "He picked a good time not to show up," he told the girl. "When I find him I'll tell him to beware Carhart."

"Is it so important to find him?"

"I guess not," Timothy said. "But I just have the idea that if I don't go out and look for him nobody else will."

"Where do you go from here?"

"I have a little list of names...."

"Oh. Was my name on the list?"

"Apparently by mistake. These others are people he had business with.

It wasn't personal."

"It wasn't a mistake," she said. "He was coming here on business, too."

"I see. Well, I'll be on my way …"

"Wait a minute," she said, slipping to her feet. "What's wrong?"

"Not a thing," Timothy said and started for the door.

"But there is," she called after him. "You seem disappointed or something. As though it were my fault."

Dane swung his head around. "I don't know what it was you intended to sell him," he said, "and apparently you changed your mind. But I've just about had a bellyful of that peephole magazine and everybody who supplies it—"

"*You've* had a bellyful? What about *me?*"

"What about you?"

"Come here," she commanded, her face stormy. She turned and walked directly into the bedroom. Dane held back, but when the girl summoned him a second time he went to where she waited. She was taking a metal strongbox from a vanity drawer and now she set it on the bed and opened it.

"Which picture is *Info* going to print?" Donna asked him, taking three seven-by-ten photos out of the box and handing them to him with a kind of defiance. On top was a nude, a snapshot, not a professional job, and it was a three-quarter view of Donna James apparently sleeping on some sunny beach. It was not the same mature-bodied girl standing beside him and Dane guessed that the picture was three or four years old.

"I didn't pose for that, incidentally," she told him. "A girlfriend and I were sunbathing and she snapped it."

"Glines has a print?"

"He's the one who gave me that copy."

"Where did he get it?"

"God only knows. I certainly never had anything to do with him down in Tampa."

Timothy was looking at the second photo, unhappily. It was a police identification picture of a teenaged girl, a very frightened, hungry-looking kid with a vast emptiness in her eyes. She was clothed in a prison smock that hung limply from her thin shoulders, and across the lower lefthand corner was a stark six-digit number.

"Come on, laugh it up a little," Donna said at his side. "You're looking at Dottie Jenkinson, the dangerous criminal."

"This happened after the other picture?"

"About a year. My mother got married again," she added, "and my stepfather thought it was some kind of Mormon arrangement. It got so bad that I had to get away. They arrested me in Jacksonville, in a bus station where I was sleeping. Sleeping in a bus station, so they charge me with 'loitering.' God, what a nasty word that is. They don't dare call you the other thing so they hang 'loitering' around your neck and let everybody fill in their own definition."

Dane turned the police photo facedown atop the nude. A moment later there was anger in his face as he stared at the third print.

"Frank Carlo is a friend of yours?" he asked curtly.

"I never met Frank Carlo," she said. "I never said two words to the man in my life."

From the glossy, nightclub photo in his hand it was difficult to take the girl at her word. Sitting beside her, grinning wolfishly, was the hoodlum and killer, extortionist, white slaver and dope peddler named Frank Carlo. Every city had some kind of personal file on the man, yet it was a wonder that out of fifty-odd arrests Frank Carlo had served less than ten years in prison. Dane recalled that even now he was out on parole, some recent incident involving a bar brawl and someone stabbed to death.

He had a charmed life, this Carlo, and if some of the things that were rumored about it were true then the unpublished portions were even more fantastic than what the newspapers had already written about him.

"Don't you believe that I don't know him?" the girl asked, misunderstanding his concentration.

Dane nodded. "Is this the picture *Info* plans to use?"

"Yes."

"And how much not to?"

"Ten thousand dollars."

Timothy whistled softly. "Glines was coming by today for the money?"

"For an installment. Naturally, I don't have anything nearly like that. And when I tried to borrow some from Mike he made me tell him the whole story. Mike said there was only one way to deal with a blackmailer."

"He might have been right," Dane said. "And there's also the chance that Barney saw him and the other two coming in here."

"What will he do now?"

"Get a little nastier. A little tougher. Or maybe run the picture."

She looked dismal. "I don't care about myself," she said. "But when I think of all the work Mr. Blodgett has done, all the money involved in the show...."

Dane was moving away from her, going to the telephone beside the bed. He dialed a number, waited for an answer, and when it didn't come he replaced the phone. "What's the matter?"

"She's still out to lunch," he said. "Glines' secretary. I was hoping the louse had turned up back there."

"How long has he been gone?"

"The girl was with him Friday. And Friday is as far as anyone else I've talked to has seen him." His face showed another thought being born. "I'll check back with you," he said.

"Where are you going?"

"To his apartment...."

"Give me ten seconds to change. I'll go with you."

"Why?"

"Because I want to," she said, already unbuttoning the striped blouse. "You go mix yourself a drink and I'll be there before you've finished."

Dane was a man partial to fine breasts, and now he stood intrigued by the promising swell beneath the parted blouse. On his face was the rapt expression of a collector who is about to see some object for the first time, and it was only after many moments had passed that he was aware of the utter silence. He lifted his eyes to her face.

"Don't you think it would be better if you waited outside?" she asked softly, without recrimination.

"I guess it would."

He left her alone in the room and wandered thoughtfully to the bar. He still thought of her as elusive, as quicksilver. But he also had the feeling that for an instant in there he had trapped a small part of it, caught it in a jar.

As Donna had said, she was ready before he had finished the drink. In fact, he had hardly tasted it.

## FOUR

If Timothy Dane had been burned by his brief exposure to Donna James, then Mike Carhart, after three intensive months, was hopelessly addicted. And now, with his massive arms spread along the bar at Sardi's, the prizefighter-turned-actor brooded morosely about the frustrating turn of events back in the girl's apartment.

A veteran of a hundred fights and five marriages, Carhart wondered if he had really learned anything in the ring or the bedroom. The thing up in Donna's should have gone off like one of Ralph Blodgett's scenes. Enter the heavy. Exit the heavy. Exit the stagehands. Donna smiles. Down come the blinds. Curtain. Instead of that he ends up feeling like an overgrown slob. Donna kicks him out. And the dark-haired guy, Dane.

Too goddam sure of himself, that baby. And can hit. Hits as if he knows something about it.

"Another one, Mike?" the bartender asked.

"Put something in it this time."

The man in the red jacket shrugged, poured out a *double* double Scotch, found he had no room for soda and set it down as is. Actors ... "Where is everybody?" Carhart complained then. The barman looked at him, then along the crowded bar, then into the crowded restaurant and the jammed lobby, and back to Carhart.

"I don't know," he answered neutrally.

"Merle Wilson ever come in anymore?"

"Every day. Mr. Sardi just seated her."

"Where?"

The bartender pointed to the most prominent table in the big room. Most prominent at the table was a striking silver blonde, tanned the color of cocoa and smiling dazzlingly at everyone but the three men with her. They didn't seem to mind, especially. One was a pinched-looking, owlish little fellow who looked out on the world from behind huge, horn-rimmed glasses. He was Larry Kaye, a publicist who worked in the New York home office of the same studio that employed Merle Wilson. He was troubleshooting today, seeing to it that the blonde kept away from both vodka martinis and those unquotable remarks that columnists were always quoting. Next to him was the columnist Kaye's boss was buttering up today, and the newspaperman was becoming more and more annoyed at Kaye's adroit parrying of every leading question put to the free-wheeling actress. The third man was a chunky, glowering character named Sonny. He had traveled from Hollywood with Miss Wilson, accompanied her (in the close background) to each of the three premieres of her new picture, had an adjoining room in the same hotel and seemed to be always present. Sonny appeared on the studio payroll as a "Unit Man"—supposedly supplying the fan magazines with publicity on a picture while it was being filmed—but he was actually a private employee of Mr. Gregory Proctor, the studio's executive producer, and it was Sonny's current project to keep Merle Wilson inviolate until Mr. Proctor's wife left for Palm Springs with the children and Gregory could join Merle for a winter sojourn in the Catskills.

"Merle, baby!"

"Mike, darling!"

Carhart's booming voice seemed to rattle the dishes on the table. Fifty heads swiveled around to locate the source of the explosion. And they weren't disappointed. Mike lifted Merle Wilson out of her chair, swung her around and kissed her as though they were standing in a very narrow closet. Sonny started to his feet, gazed bleakly at the awesome dimensions of the other man and sank back down in his chair. Larry Kaye observed that and permitted himself a rare smile. The columnist looked as though the bright sun had just burst from behind an unpromising cloud.

Carhart ended the embrace and the blonde, slightly disheveled, sat down again a little shakily.

"Gee, you're looking swell!" Mike said, staring unabashedly into the depths of her low-cut gown. "You haven't changed a bit."

"You either, Mike," she told him.

"Sit down, Mike," the newspaperman told him urgently.

"There isn't room," Larry Kaye said. "See you around, Mike."

The columnist reached over and commandeered an unused chair from the table next to them.

"Put it there, Mike," he said. "Good to see you."

Carhart wedged himself between Sonny and the girl, turned his broad back to the man and draped his arm around Merle's bare shoulders.

"Whatta you drinking, you gorgeous beast?" he asked her.

"A martini, lover. With vodka."

"I don't think you really want one, Merle," Larry Kaye said.

"What the hell do you know what she wants?" Carhart growled, leaning away from the girl to scowl at the publicity man.

"You tell 'im, Mike," the columnist said happily. "Give the lady a double martini," he told a hovering, worried-eyed waiter.

"With vodka," the lady reminded and the waiter departed for the bar.

"Remember those martinis last Christmas?" Mike said.

The movie star giggled. "You dirty dog," she said.

"Where was this?" the columnist asked.

"We're late for our date with the *Life* photographer," Larry Kaye said, getting up. "Mr. Proctor considers that a must this trip—"

"That's tomorrow," the girl told him. "All I've got on for today is the Steve Allen show."

"And that's tonight," Carhart said with a deep chuckle. "So all you got on is me."

She giggled. "You dog," she said.

"Why don't you two get married?" the columnist suggested.

"What for?" Carhart asked, his voice plainly wondering.

"Yeah," Merle Wilson said. "Why spoil a beautiful friendship?" Larry Kaye closed his eyes, looked ashen. He opened them to see the waiter set down a crystal-clear martini in a champagne-sized glass. Paramount, he recalled, was looking for a man in their publicity department. And he could probably go back to promotion at Macy's. Meanwhile, the howitzer voice of Mike Carhart was sending salvos to every corner of the room.

"What's with you and old man Proctor, baby?" he asked. "Next thing I hear you'll be doing benefits...."

"Gregory is very nice to me," she said, draining half the glass. "A girl's got to do what she's got to do."

Sonny shifted in his chair, made desperate by the mention of that feared name.

"If I were you," he said to Carhart, "I'd blow on out of here."

Carhart looked at him over his shoulder. "If I were you," he said, "I'd take a pipe. Get lost."

The watchdog didn't know what to do. The overeager fans he could handle. The nightclub wolves were no problem. But this behemoth was something Mr. Proctor had never told him about.

"Get lost," Carhart told him again. "You bother me."

"Now don't start a fight, darling," Merle said. "You remember how sorry you were when you beat up that other poor man last year."

"When was that, Mike?" the columnist asked and Sonny took the opportunity to get out of his chair and move away from there.

"You're really mistaken about that *Life* appointment," Larry Kaye said before Carhart could answer. "We're late right now. *And you remember how angry Mr. Proctor can get.*"

"Another martini," the columnist shouted to the waiter. "Quick!"

"I don't guess I'd better," the girl said, her eyes held by the publicity man's unwavering stare. Her whole easygoing, lighthearted personality seemed to leave her in those moments. It was as if a bright light had been turned off.

"Come off it, Myrt," Carhart said, calling her by her real name. "Let's have an old-fashioned ball."

"Maybe some other time, Mike," she said, and at Kaye's signal she arose from the table. "Right now I—I've got things to do."

"Your career," Carhart said.

"My career," she said, smiling up at him wanly. Larry Kaye took her firmly by the arm and led her out of the restaurant.

"Was she good, Mike?" the columnist asked.

"A lot of fun," Carhart answered, watching her leave. "But I guess that's all over now. What the hell's the matter with everybody, anyhow?" The newspaperman, out of gratitude for the material just handed to him, offered to stand a drink. Carhart brushed him off, settled his own bill and left. He walked in the direction of Eighth, wandering aimlessly, his mood depressed again. On Eighth he turned right, and four blocks later he had left the theatrical world and was entering another. Up ahead was the Garden, and though the marquee advertised basketball and hockey, he crossed the street to the arena, drawn there by a memory.

Carhart had fought in the Garden six different times, winning four by knockouts but losing the last two the same way. He realized now that he had been brought along too fast during the postwar free-for-all to take the aging Joe Louis's crown. If he'd had somebody like Al Weill to handle him, somebody to bring him along nice and easy the way Marciano had.... Carhart stood looking up at a poster of the champion now, a fighting pose, and his own body shifted instinctively into a defensive position.

If he'd only had the right manager, he thought, and then broke out into laughter. No manager in the world could do anything about a glass jaw. Ah, the hell with it, anyhow. Singing and acting on a stage was the softest racket ever invented. Who wanted to be champion of the world only to have the next crop of hungry young tigers come along and scramble your brains?

Still, fighting was in his blood. He loved nothing on earth better than a brawl, and if he had his whole life to live over again … For one thing, he told himself, he'd stick to his church. Give him back fifteen years and he'd stay married to his first wife come hell or high water. He missed the confessional, he realized with surprise. Missed it very much. But he couldn't go back now. Not after fifteen years and all the helling and whoring. Besides, he wasn't so sure he really repented *every*thing.

Then he brightened. Maybe he didn't have a father-confessor, but he had the next best thing. Carhart hailed a cab and had himself driven over to Billy Tyson's office.

## 2

It was just as well that the girl had come along. The superintendent of Barney Glines's building, a phlegmatic, unshaven Scandinavian, was flatly opposed to Timothy's entering the apartment. But Donna's attraction seemed to reach out to all men, and after several moments of some earnest and private conversation, Nils Larsen unlocked the door.

"How did you do it?" Dane asked when they were inside.

"I just *told* him," she said simply. "I just told him we had to get in. But I wouldn't want to do it again. Not with those eyes of his looking me over. There's something creepy about that old man."

"Forget him," Dane advised her, looking around Glines's apartment much as he had the office earlier in the day. Tim's entire 53rd Street diggings would fit inside this living room; his yearly rent wouldn't pay for the furniture.

"Where are we," Donna asked, "in an opium den?"

"Not very cozy."

"Not very. Where do we start looking for things?"

"The bedroom," Dane said. "It's a more likely hiding place than out here." He followed her out of the living room, then stopped short when she did.

"Holy Hannah," he murmured, looking over her shoulder at the shambles of Barney Glines's sleeping quarters. The contents of dresser drawers were spilled over the rug, both chairs were overturned, their insides split open. The bed clothing had been stripped away, the mattress slashed in a dozen places. A large mirror had not only been lifted from the wall but methodically dismantled. So had a standing lamp and both bed lamps, even to unscrewing the bulbs.

"I guess that takes care of that," Donna said, calmly accepting a situation that Timothy found disturbing. Not only the question of the room being taken apart, but the fact that someone else had got around— or past—the super. He slipped by the girl and went farther inside, seeing on closer inspection that even the valances at the windows had been torn loose in the thorough search. He went over to a closet that ran the length of the wall. Expensive suits had been gone through and thrown to the floor, ties on a rack were turned inside out. In the back of the closet stood a squat safe, its door ajar.

The safe had been emptied, but on the closet floor were scattered a dozen or more photos as well as some legal-looking documents. Timothy bent down, examined them without touching them.

"What are they?" Donna asked, stooping beside him. Suddenly she straightened. "Those people are naked," she said.

"Divorce evidence," Dane said. "Illustrated adultery, produced and directed by Barney Glines. These other things are sworn affidavits. People swearing to something that nine times in ten never happened...."

"I think I need fresh air," Donna said disgustedly, moving out of the closet. Timothy stuck his arm inside the safe, began sorting out other pictures of undressed men and women, some actually embracing, others reaching frantically for bedsheets or some other covering. He rapped his knuckles against the sidewalls of the safe, found them solid. He rapped against the roof and dislodged a rectangular section in the rear. He got his fingers on the piece, brought it out. There, Scotch-taped to the other side, was a packet of negatives. He ripped it loose.

"*Timothy!*"

He was erect in an instant, moving swiftly in the direction of the girl's agonized outcry. He found Donna standing in the entrance to the bathroom, her body frozen, eyes staring straight ahead. Then he saw it, pulled her back into the hall and went in, shutting the door at his back. Eloise King floated face downward in the filled tub, a pathetic figure communicating lifelessness.

But even so, Dane got his arms beneath her, lifted her out of the water and lowered her to the mat. With his ear pressed beneath her breast he listened fruitlessly for a heartbeat. The door was reopened.

"Tell me what I can do," Donna said to him, fighting to hold her voice even.

"Get the police emergency squad on the phone. Just tell the operator. Then leave."

"Leave?"

"As fast as you can. And take these with you," he said, tossing her the packet of negatives.

She went, and for himself Dane worked to induce breathing in what he knew was a corpse. Donna came back.

"I'm not going," she said.

"Your case is special," he said without pausing to look at her. "You had nothing to do with this. All you can get here is a bad dose of publicity. Go on home."

"But what about you?"

"You'll be hearing from me."

"I'd better, Timothy." It was almost a warning. Then she was gone from the apartment and Dane was still trying to bring off a miracle when the police arrived. A machine relieved him, and afterwards an assistant Medical Examiner declared Barney Glines's secretary and mistress officially dead.

But by that time Dane was seated in the living room, repeating details of his knowledge to a professionally skeptical trio from Homicide East.

"That's a pretty straightforward story, mister," said a detective named Boros.

"Thanks."

"Except that it doesn't hold much water."

"How do you mean?"

"Well, you keep telling us about coming up here with a woman. When the super tells us about her he describes a girl. How come you want to tout us off her like that?"

Timothy spread his hands. "I'm not accusing the super of anything," he said irrelevantly.

"Come again?"

"If everybody looks like a girl to him, that's not my business."

Boros and his partners looked once around at each other. The detective named Pat Herman spoke up. "This woman—this girl. When she hired you to contact Glines why wouldn't she give you any name but Mary Smith?"

"What name would your wife give me if she were being shaken down …?"

"*My* wife?"

"No offense meant," Dane said. "But she wouldn't tell me her real name, would she?"

"Now, listen," Herman said, losing the thread of his questioning. The third detective, Carson, took it up.

"So you've been looking for Glines all day, and when you couldn't raise him around town you and Mary Smith came up here for a try."

Dane listened attentively to the playback of what he had told Lou Carson. Now he nodded. "Between you and me," he said, "I got the idea this woman came from out of town. I think she had to get back before her husband missed her."

"And you got some money to make out of the lady's trouble?"

"You could say that."

"So you come up here with the idea of looting the place?"

"I don't think that was the proposition. I'd rather put it that Mrs. Smith was recovering some letters she'd written a third party. Glines had no business holding them."

"No matter how you tilt it, friend," Carson said, "it's still breaking and entering."

"No kidding? When the man lets us into the place …?"

Boro's voice cut in. "So you look in the bedroom and find that somebody else beat you to it?"

"Right."

"And you look in the john … Tell me, how would you describe that one? A woman or a girl?"

"That was a girl," Timothy said positively.

"And while you're lifting her out of the tub, Mary Smith lams out of here."

"Like a shot."

"And you don't know where to start looking for her?"

Dane paused. "From the way she spoke certain words," he told them, "I'd put her down as coming from New England. Maybe even Boston."

"Oh, fine."

"When you locate her," Dane said, "I'd appreciate your letting me know."

"Hurts, doesn't it," Pat Herman said, "to put in all that time for free."

"You said it," Timothy said and stood up.

"Let's get that super back in here," Boros said. "You go on about your business," he told Dane. "We'll feed this bushwah to the D.A.'s office and I'm sure he'll be in touch with you."

Smiling gamely, Dane left them to their work, silently agreeing that some Assistant District Attorney would want to hear the story for himself. It had been an exercise to remember the particulars of the fable he had spun and only now, stepping into the bitterly cold dusk at Washington Square, was he able to do any guessing at all about the actual events.

He began with the top of the day, and he saw Eloise King in a different light, found a new motive for her words and actions. Instead of the loyal secretary guarding Barney's confidential folders, the girl's main interest had been to empty him out of the office. That had been immediately after he located the dummy issue of *Info*. He wondered what her movements had been then, and all he could figure was that she had spotted him leaving the place after the second visit. But instead of wasting time with pornographers and call girls, the secretary had gone straight to home base.

To protect Barney's cache? A noble gesture, and Timothy wished he could credit her with it. But what he really suspected was that Eloise had tried to convert some of Barney's blackmail material to her own use. For if something had happened to Glines, his business was up for grabs. And, of course, Eloise had been joined by someone else—someone who had persuaded her to undress, for if Dane was sure of anything it was that Eloise King had not been given the chance to fight for her life.

And where the hell was Barney Glines?

## FIVE

Like a lot of other people he knew, Timothy was cutting down on his drinking. *Down*, not out, and he was an appreciative spectator as Ernie the barman mixed six of the one with hardly any of the other, stirred briskly and poured out the chilled, crystal-clear masterpiece into an outsize cocktail glass. That one tasted like another, and with the second martini came relaxation, an unwinding of nerves that he hadn't realized were stretched so taut.

Professionally, he wrote the day off as a loss. He had accomplished nothing, earned nary a dollar, arrived twice at the right place at the worst possible time. His back still reminded him of the encounter with big Carhart, but aside from the man's general belligerence he couldn't really be angry at the mistake in identity. Taking a whip to Barney Glines would have been a theatrical gesture, but fitting, somehow. If Carhart had used his fists it would have been punishment, but an honorable one. Just as in old military law a soldier shot by a firing squad died a prouder man than the one who was hanged. There was a stigma to being whipped that was still there after the wounds had healed—but knowing Barney as he did, Dane was certain that Mike Carhart would have paid for his gesture with his life. For all the larceny and dirty-dealing he was capable of, Glines also had guts and a kind of foolish recklessness.

Timothy turned the long-stemmed glass in his fingers and in the liquid he could see again the nude and lifeless Eloise King. He still felt as he had this afternoon, that her nakedness was important. Supposing that it was, then who would she have undressed for of her own will? If what Barney had said about her that day at lunch was even partly true, then the girl was ready for a party at anytime, anywhere. He recalled the halfhearted pass she had made in the office, but by that time she was thinking of the *Info* file and it could have been merely a diversion.

And what was she doing in the tub? Had Eloise been the courtesan type who came to bed bathed and scented? It was useless to sit here and try to guess at the libido of a dead secretary. Much pleasanter to guess about the live and lively Donna James. For nonprofessionally the day showed a profit. Touching the world of the mercurial, mixed-up actress was a credit that almost struck a balance.

And certainly would after one more of Ernie's efforts with the Dixie Belle and vermouth. But midway through the third one and he would be on the phone, inviting her over to meet the world's greatest bartender and bite into one of Manhattan's best tasting sirloins. And after dinner a stinger or two, and let the chips fall where they would.

Instead, Timothy set what was left of the present martini out of reach and proceeded to order a lonely steak for one. *Asking her to dinner!* After lying his head off to keep her out of the mess, then all but handing her over to the D.A. and the newspapers. You can't go near the girl, he told himself moodily. You lose by default to that beautiful bastard of a Carhart....

"Anything wrong, Tim? Drink all right?"

Ernie's voice and Ernie's sad face made him laugh aloud.

"I was just talking to myself," he explained. "One jackass telling another one."

"Bad day, pal?"

"Bad day." The waitress beckoned that his table was set up and he slipped from the stool. "But it's only Monday, Ernie."

"That's right, Tim. Blue Monday."

"Tuesday is bound to be worse."

But the meal made it right again, coffee and a cigarette put him back on his even course, and when he left the restaurant he was mentally fit to roll with any punch Tuesday might throw.

Snow had been threatening all day and now it was here, a sleeting, bone-chilling downpour slanted by a cutting wind. Taxis, a plague on the city in fair weather, had mysteriously disappeared with the first snowflake, and Timothy bent his long body against the miserable night and trudged the half mile to his apartment. Turning into 53rd Street, with head down and feet wary of the increasingly slippery surface, he swung toward his own building entrance without even seeing the black shape of the Cadillac parked at the curb.

"Hey, you! Dane!"

If he'd slapped Dane in the face, Mike Carhart couldn't have irritated the investigator more than with that arrogant summons. Dane turned to see the actor beckoning to him from the rear window of the car. Behind the wheel was a uniformed chauffeur and beside him another man. Someone else was in the back with Carhart, huddled in the far corner, and he didn't recognize Donna James until he had crossed the sidewalk.

"Now what?" Timothy asked.

"This is him, Ralph," Carhart said to the man up front and Ralph Blodgett leaned forward.

"I want to thank you for taking that rap all by yourself this afternoon," he said. "It wouldn't have done Donna or our show any good to be stuck with anything as messy as that."

"Sure." Frozen-toed, soaked through to the skin, Timothy stood there and fought to keep his teeth from chattering. "Sure," he said again. "Better not hang around here though—"

"Ralph has a proposition for you, buster," Carhart told him patronizingly.

"For God's sake, Mike," Donna protested, "open the door and let Timothy in out of the blizzard."

"Oh, yeah. Yeah, sure." But he moved slowly, obviously not too anxious to get his own expensive clothes wet.

"Why don't we go into your place and discuss it?" Ralph Blodgett suggested.

"Anything," Timothy said, meaning it literally. Anything to get off this gale-swept street. The three of them followed him into the undistinguished brownstone and down the hallway to his apartment.

"Got anything to drink, Dane?" Carhart said.

"Mix yourself what you want," he said, pointing to the portable bar.

"You get out of those wet clothes," Donna told him. "I'll go run a hot shower for you."

"Let him run his own shower," Carhart said, but the girl was already entering the bedroom. Timothy followed and moments later heard the welcome sound of water cascading from the bathroom beyond. Donna came out and pulled the soaked overcoat from his shoulders.

"Thanks," he said.

"You're welcome, Timothy. I thought you were going to get in touch with me."

"There wasn't any reason to," he said and she looked up at him quickly.

"There wasn't?"

"Well—I almost asked you to dinner," he said. "But it isn't a smart idea for you and me to be together."

"You mean because of the police?"

"Yes."

"But you did have an impulse to ask me out …?"

Mike Carhart's voice broke among them. "You taking a shower, Dane, or what?"

"I'll be with you in a few minutes," he said and Donna left the room. Dane came back to them disguised as a country gentleman—Pendleton shirt, flannels, loafing shoes—and the effect was marked on the three who waited. Donna sat perceptibly straighter against the cushion of the couch and Carhart threw a protective arm across the top of her shoulders. Ralph Blodgett stared appraisingly at the capable-looking, quiet-eyed young man who had been only a faceless blob out on the sidewalk.

"That looks like a complete recovery," the producer said heartily.

"It is."

"Feel like talking a little business?"

"Sure."

"I'd like you to do some work for me, Dane. I want all the information I can get about this magazine called *Info*. Who publishes it, how it's distributed—the works."

"Doesn't anyone even know who gets it out?"

Blodgett shook his head angrily. "Somebody is smart. It isn't registered as second-class mail, it isn't even offered for sale. An issue gets printed—and presto!—everybody in the business appears with a copy."

"Where do you get yours?" Dane asked him.

"My secretary handed the last one to me. I asked her where *she* got it and all she had was a blank look. She didn't know where. It was just in her basket when she came back from lunch."

Dane glanced toward Mike Carhart. "Where do you get a copy?"

"I don't. I go over to the Lambs and there's half a dozen hanging around."

"Same thing down at the Players," Ralph Blodgett added. "And in every bar between Lexington and Eighth. But the bartenders don't know who left it behind."

"Is it confined to New York?"

"It seems to be. But a friend of mine told me he found a porter on the Super Chief reading a copy."

"If you get the information," Timothy asked him, "what do you plan to do with it?"

"Do with it? Hell's bells, man, I'm going to shout it from the housetops! I'll take an ad in every paper in town— What's the matter?"

Dane was shaking his head. "There'll be a lynching," he said. "Too many people are too mad about little *Info*. I don't want any part of the excitement."

"What kind of a deal would suit you?"

"A confidential one. That I put this rag out of circulation and no questions asked or answered."

"You seem to have some ideas about who's running it already."

"I think I know someone who's pretty close to the operation."

"I see. A friend of yours?"

"No."

Donna James said, "He's talking about Barney Glines, Mr. Blodgett. They were partners once and I think he did something to hurt Timothy."

"Glines?" Blodgett said. "Wasn't it his apartment where the two of you found that murdered girl?"

"His secretary."

"But I don't get it, Dane. If he's no friend of yours, if he's done you dirt, then why do you want to protect him?"

Timothy seemed about to explain, but then he shrugged his shoulders.

"That's the only way I can work on this thing, Mr. Blodgett," he said without enthusiasm.

"The hell with that, Ralph," Mike Carhart exploded. "Billy Tyson's outfit is going to bust this thing wide open any hour."

"What do you know about it?" Blodgett asked him.

"I was talking to him this afternoon. They got a hot lead on the printer, some little plant up in White Plains, and a real tip that the guy running the whole thing was fired in that last big shake-up at NBC."

Blodgett didn't seem impressed. "I'll take you on your terms," he said to Timothy. "Okay?"

"Fine."

"Maybe you can work with this other group Mike mentioned. Go talk to them and compare notes."

"What group is that?"

"They call it FAST. A nice little guy named Billy Tyson organized it and they hired an agency."

"Do you know the agency?"

"Something about investigations," Blodgett said thoughtfully. Then his face cleared. "Investigations, Unlimited," he announced. "Know them?"

Timothy looked hard at Blodgett, then over to Donna. Neither one connected that name with Barney Glines and he thought how surprised Barney must have been to be handed the assignment to investigate *Info*.

"Yes," he said aloud, "I know the agency."

"Then we ought to get some results," Blodgett said, standing up and extending his hand. "We've got to get back for a rehearsal, Dane. Good luck to you, and thanks again for getting our girl out of that scrape today."

"If your girl wants to stay out of it," Dane said, "she'd better keep out of this neighborhood."

"The police are looking for her?"

"They should be. I was certainly no help to them this afternoon."

"You stay away from this fellow, Donna," Blodgett said sternly. "Stay far away from trouble."

Donna and Mike Carhart had risen from the couch and crossed to the door. Dane held it open and they went out. Almost at once there was a soft knock and he opened it again. It was Donna.

"I forgot to say good night."

"Good night."

Her arms rose and her face came toward him all in the same unexpected motion. Their lips brushed, fleetingly, and then Dane had her close against him and kissed her the way he wanted to. Even so, she lingered, and the tall man kissed her again.

"That's what I wanted to know," she said, slipping away from him, like mercury, and escaping down the hall. Timothy watched from the window as she reentered the Cadillac and was driven away. Then, because of the job he'd just accepted, and the puzzling information he'd been handed, Dane prepared to go back into the cold night again himself.

## 2

Frank Carlo had one car between himself and the unmarked pickup truck he was following when they both entered the Lincoln Tunnel from 46th Street. Pursuit was second nature to him, he had been born furtive, and he kept that arrangement with the truck until they were well out of the tunnel and into New Jersey.

It was sleeting hard now, cutting visibility sharply, and when the truck squeezed off the main route and took a southwesterly course through icier, less used streets, the gangster fell in directly behind and swore bad-temperedly at the force of circumstances that had brought him on such a perilous trip. He cursed hardest of all at the driver ahead, whose obvious inexperience under the conditions threatened to involve them both in a skidding crash.

"Lousy, double-crossing son-of-a-bitch," he said aloud at one point, clearing the inside of the windshield furiously with his gloved hand. "Dumb bastard, can't even drive!" he exploded as the truck's rear end glided sideways on a turn and Carlo had to maneuver his own lightweight coupe frantically. He would have killed the other one then if he had him in his gunsights or at knife point, killed him in one of those blind, maniacal rages that had kept even the likes of Capone, Madden and Lepke uneasy in his presence. Carlo had known them all, worked for them as a *trooper*—a triggerman—but they all mistrusted the sudden, unbridled fury that lurked in his brain. "Crazy Frank" he had come to be called, and he lashed out murderously at friends and enemies alike, at mistresses and wives, until finally he was cast out from the organized mobs and made to go it alone.

Like "Legs" Diamond, "Dutch" Schultz, "Mad Dog" Coll—"Crazy Frank" Carlo had to get what he could out of the rackets without protection from the Mafia or the other, smaller syndicates. And the way he got by was a mystery to the police and city desks of Chicago, New York and Los Angeles. It was known that Carlo had been sentenced to assassination at least six times by the mobs he had raided and scavenged from. And six times he had saved his skin—by guile, by bluff, by the very elusiveness that made him special among those who ran against the law.

Now the panel truck up ahead was turning into Bergenline Avenue, skidding amateurishly across the cobblestones and trolley tracks. This was hapless Union City, and as they passed one of the side streets Carlo's eye was caught by the flickering lights of the Hudson Burlesque.

So strong was the memory that for many moments he forgot the truck he was following.

"Tough" Tony had arranged the party at the burlesque house that night, but everybody knew that "Mr. C." was paying the bill. The theater was all theirs, fifty of them, and there were fifty girls in the chorus, without a stitch of clothes among them at the finale, and all the wine and whiskey you could drink in a week. Frank Carlo was only twenty-two then, but Mr. C. liked him and was trying to calm him down and bring him along in the organization.

But there was one of the girls he'd been watching all through the show. A big tall blonde, and when they went backstage for the party some punk named Gino-something had his arm around her bare waist. Crazy Frank had gone crazy—berserk in that instant—and all he knew was what they told him about emptying his gun into Gino's body. Whoever Gino was. He tried to explain to Mr. C. next week that he was drunk, that he didn't mean it, but he did no more work for the organization and was invited to no more parties.

They left Union City, the panel truck and the coupe, went through Weehawken and came upon the smooth street of bustling little West New York. Here was The Boulevard, overlooking the river, gazing into the Manhattan skyline. This was where the big guys had fled, first from Dewey and the job he did on Luciano, then from LaGuardia when he swept the city clean. That was when the organization almost came apart, when Lepke got stuck and Mr. C. started to lose his control. And when Frank Carlo and the other jackals had been able to wheel and deal with impunity. How could the organization check them? What could Mr. C. do when even Tony was hiding from O'Dwyer and every cop in New York? Carlo had moved in on the chaos among the racket bosses. He was a one-man operation, always moving, always shifting around, paying off cops beat by beat instead of precinct by precinct, cleaning up in numbers, girls, marijuana and heroin for eight big years before the war came and the organization moved back in.

Then, for the first time in his life, he had accepted the facts of life. He'd come over here to Jersey with his money and retired. Only six short blocks from where he was driving at this minute was the sprawling apartment house development he had invested in. Franklin Arms, he called it. Eight stories in the air, the Hudson River at its feet, orange brick and black cornices, fully rented and 100% paid in full. It was Frank Carlo's smartest move. He'd gone legitimate and secured himself against the future.

The icing on his cake was Gloria. Carlo had buried one wife, married a second and deserted her after a brutal beating. He didn't want anybody poking around into the records of that marriage, so when Gloria came around all he could offer her was jewelry, mink coats, a convertible and the big house overlooking the Palisades to run as she pleased. But not marriage.

He certainly thought of the young red-haired girl as his wife, but apparently she didn't. For one New Year's two years ago, in a Jersey City night club, he'd found Gloria kissing one of the musicians behind the bandstand. Carlo had gone into the kitchen for the knife. All at once there was a terrible screaming all around him, Gloria pulling at him, and on the floor at his feet was the musician with the knife buried deep in his chest.

Murder in the first degree was the initial charge. But the lawyer had got that reduced to homicide without intent. The deal had cost him all his ready cash, fifty thousand, every last cent. For the first time in his life, Frank Carlo wanted to go to trial. The lawyer talked him out of it, said that the state prosecutor would crucify him on the stand about all those other killings. The jury wouldn't even think about this case, they'd throw the book at him for the rest of them.

So he listened to the lawyer and copped a plea. And then the big double-cross, but whether it was the state prosecutor who worked it or his own lawyer, Carlo never knew. He did know that the fifty grand was supposed to include the judge—but their judge wasn't sitting there at sentencing time a week later. Ten to twenty, said the one who was there. He even read him off about his record, called him a habitual criminal and a parasite. Ten to twenty, he said.

So he got another lawyer. This one came back with a different deal. He could buy him a parole after three years. The cost? The apartment house, Franklin Arms. The lawyer would sell it and make the payoff in cash. It was that or the whole twenty years. So what else could he do? That deal took—but now, tonight, he was broke and hungry. Flat busted and friendless, and mad enough to kill the driver of the truck ahead. He was being double-crossed again.

They were soon out of West New York and into the tiny town of Guttenberg, and without warning the truck swung off the lighted avenue into a maze of dim and twisting side streets. Carlo cut his driving lights instinctively and hung a full block behind. They turned, turned again, and finally the pickup came to a stop. It was before a two-story frame house, fronted by a double garage, and Carlo's lined, rock-hard face curled contemptuously as he watched the clumsy efforts to back the truck into the driveway.

Meanwhile the garage doors were being swung open from within and the truck halted between them. Someone standing on a platform unlocked the rear of the truck and began loading three bulky packages into it. There was a brief conversation between that one and the driver, the doors were locked again and the truck pulled out.

Carlo let it go by him, picked up the trail again smoothly, and though he had never seen this operation before he was not surprised that their little procession was returning to Manhattan by another route. It was the Holland Tunnel this time, and the truck's destination was a small, grimy warehouse on Canal Street.

Now the driver unloaded his packages, carrying all three to a steel locker. But before depositing the last one and padlocking the cabinet, he severed the cord and pulled loose a dozen-odd magazines from the several hundred that were there. He left the truck in the warehouse, flagged a cab and had himself driven to a shabby hotel west of Seventh Avenue.

Minutes later Frank Carlo entered the musty, threadbare lobby and made his way to the desk with a stealthiness that was natural with him but ominous to watch.

"The one who just came in," he said in a flat, toneless voice. "What room?"

The little man behind the desk had seen enough grief in his sorry lifetime to recognize how close he was to real danger right now.

"Two-ten," he answered hoarsely, his fingers gripping the counter. Carlo turned without another word, made his way to the staircase, and even from the rear the clerk was assailed by the threat of violence in that chunky, bullnecked figure. Carlo ascended to the floor above, moved unerringly to room 210. His fist rapped sharply on the thin panel.

"Who—is it?"

"Carlo. Open up."

There was a brief hesitation before the door was unbolted and pulled ajar. Billy Tyson stood in the opening, his round face pale with fear, his shaking hand holding the new issue of *Info*.

Carlo shoved him backwards into the room, strode inside and slammed the door shut.

"I thought we were partners?"

"We are, Frank. We are—"

"Then how come you go for the books tonight? You said we both go get them tomorrow."

"Something happened. I had to move them from the printer's house before he got worried."

"Worried about what?"

Tyson blinked. "He knows Barney Glines," he said.

"So?"

"Didn't you see the news on television? About Glines's secretary?"

"What's the matter with her?"

"She's dead," Tyson said, almost whispering it. "They—the police are holding the superintendent of the apartment."

"Then what are you so scared about? What's it to us?"

Tyson's short arms spread outward in a helpless gesture. His lower lip began to tremble and no words came from his throat.

"I said, *what's it to us?*" Carlo shouted in his face. Then a look of cunning appeared in his eyes. "It was you," he said. "The reason you're so jumpy is because you did it."

"I want to get out of this thing," Tyson blurted with desperation. "Glines—Glines and you. You've changed it from what it was. All I was doing was something personal. Then you two came along and changed it—"

"Why did you knock her off?" Carlo asked him. "What happened?"

"You're just guessing …"

"Give," Carlo persisted. "What'd she do, start asking questions about Glines?"

Tyson's head nodded, almost of its own will. Then he began speaking. "I've known Eloise for some time," he said. "I'd gotten her a few chorus jobs when she first came to town. But she was always having trouble with the girls she worked with, making up to their boyfriends, starting fights. I didn't even know she was Glines's secretary when I hired him to get material for the magazine."

"So what, so what?" Carlo asked impatiently.

"She called me this afternoon. Around lunchtime. For some reason—I still don't know how—she seemed certain I knew where Glines was. Then she told me that she also knew all about the work he was doing for me. She said that Glines had a lot of material I didn't know about. She said he was running a private blackmail business on the side—"

"Which you already knew. So what?"

"The girl told me that if anything had happened to Glines she could get the material he was holding out. She wanted five thousand dollars for it."

"Five thousand!"

"I said all right and hung up. Then I started thinking about where this material was. He wouldn't keep it in his office, I decided, so I went up to his apartment. I got into the place the back way with that key you found. I was searching the bedroom when she came in—"

"And you let her have it?"

"No," Tyson said. "Not like that. Not like that at all. The last thing I wanted to do was—kill her."

"What are you handin' me? You gave it to her, didn't you?"

"But not like you would," Tyson said, his voice rising. "Not for your reasons."

"Then what reasons?"

"She surprised me in the bedroom. She was very angry. She asked me what I would have done if Glines had caught me. I told her Glines couldn't catch me. I told her too much ..."

Carlo shrugged. "So you killed her to shut her up. What's so special about that?"

"No," Tyson said. He put a hand over his eyes, as though to shut out the scene his mind was resurrecting, "When she knew Glines was dead a complete change came over her. She—she became very amorous, very suggestive ..."

Carlo sniggered.

"She began to undress," Tyson went on, speaking now only to himself. "I struck her from behind and she fell down. I got her into the bathroom and filled the tub...." His eyes cleared and he looked at Carlo, seeing him. "I've got to get away," he said.

Carlo studied him. "Not now," he said. "Not when we're even."

"It's gone too far. I've got to get out!"

"You'll go out," Carlo told him. "You'll go out for good."

Tyson took a step backward, half stumbling over the leg of a chair. Carlo's words seemed to put him in real fear of his life.

"You're *in*," Carlo said hoarsely. "You're in all the way."

Billy Tyson felt like a man going over a high ledge....

## SIX

Dane unlocked the door marked Investigations, Unlimited and stepped inside the darkened suite. He made his way past the desk Eloise King had used and when the door to Barney Glines's inner office was closed behind him he switched on the light.

There was evil in this place, he thought gloomily. A malignance. Nothing that was good or helpful would ever be produced in Barney Glines's office. He began moving around the room aimlessly, touching things, oppressed by the sterile, sepulchral silence and wishing that Glines would walk in the door and set things straight.

The wish sent his mind leapfrogging back to the time just after the war, to the first meeting with Barney at the Donegan Detective Bureau in Brooklyn. A blond, wiry guy, about middle height, with a lazy, lopsided smile and a way of talking out of the side of his mouth that made you think of Alan Ladd.

Maury Donegan, a retired Inspector of Homicide, taught them the do's and the dont's, the ins and the out, and in the deep tradition of the Police Department's buddy system, worked them as a team. And, Timothy thought now, they had worked well together. Divorce business was taboo with old Donegan, and the way things were popping in Brooklyn in the mid-forties the agency never missed it. Hijacking on the waterfront sent Dane and Glines to the docks, shaping up as full-fledged members of the Longshoreman's Union, breaking the back of a mob that neither the shipowners nor the I.L.A. could tolerate.

Donegan had put them to work for the Brooklyn D.A. The Borough's police force had been bought from the top down, corrupted by a two-bit bookmaker whose gambling "concessions" suddenly mushroomed into a multimillion-dollar business, with fabulous payoffs for every cop in on the graft. The District Attorney officially "broke" the case, he brought the indictments to the Grand Jury, but it was the Donegan Agency—and Dane and Glines—who had wormed its way into the gambler's organization, planted the bugs that recorded every damning conversation, taken the pictures that had nailed the indictments down.

And more. Timothy remembered the heist of a warehouse full of liquor. A million dollars, the insurance company put the loss at. And ten percent to Donegan if the cases of 25-year-old Scotch could be recovered. Barney had located a bottle in a very unlikely place for such stuff—a Coney Island bar. Timothy was served a drink in one on Bedford Avenue, near Ebbets Field. They followed their separate leads, came together at a five-tier parking garage in the shadow of the Brooklyn Bridge.

Both men had badly underestimated the size of the operation. Armed hoods appeared from every direction, like soldier ants, and the gunplay was as violent as anything Dane had known in the entire war. They made a break for it, through a high window that looked down on an alleyway. Barney went first and made it. Dane didn't. A slug found him, dropped him in his tracks. He waited, unable to move his cracked arm, while the gunmen moved in on him warily. All at once there was a furious fusillade from behind, from the window, driving the mobsters back in disorder. Glines had returned for him, and now he was climbing back into that hell and dragging Dane toward the window. Barney hoisted him to the sill, stood with his back to their guns while Dane made it safely to the other side. Then he had come out of there a second time.

Remembering it, Timothy realized that he had never forgotten it. Subconsciously that one act outweighed everything else in their relationship, brought Barney Glines into full view. They had worked together well for Donegan, damnit. They tackled every job enthusiastically—ethically—and they earned a good reputation among people who needed honest, straightforward, *confidential* investigation.

Maury Donegan retired, and when he did he gave their new partnership his blessing and his counsel. The old man even advanced the money for the surety bond when Timothy landed their first jewelry consignment work.

But within that one short year the change came over Barney. Something happened to the man. Maybe he looked for overnight success, for tremendous money. They didn't come just by painting *Manhattan Detective Agency* on the door of their tiny office and Barney was quickly disillusioned. He began objecting to the legwork, ducked industrial jobs that were purely investigative, objected to the continued prohibition of divorce work and continually involved them with the bank because of his overdrafts. He argued continually that the only money was in divorce, that faking adultery paid off in big figures.

Timothy was against it and they fought. Wait, he told him. We'll have enough work eventually from insurance companies alone that we couldn't even handle divorces and collections. We've got to grow, Barney. Slowly and carefully, like Donegan.

It wasn't for Barney Glines. He took on a couple of divorce jobs secretly—left himself wide open to a perjury charge—then the threatening letters to the guests at the "charity" gambling party, the blackmailing of Joyce Baker. And during it all a subtle but positive change in Glines's personality. He had always been cynical, but now almost every remark was barbed and poisonous. He drank at the wrong times and could no longer carry his liquor competently. He became sly about his expense accounts and withdrawals from petty cash, and though they were presumably equal partners it was blatantly obvious that one was living on a much higher scale than the other.

But despite the inevitable breakup, and despite the road Glines had chosen to take, Timothy could not forget the night when the man had risked his life to save him.

Impatiently, he quit his reveries of the past and crossed with a purpose to the files. He opened them and removed the very thin folder labeled *Tyson, Billy*. In it was the record of a correspondence that was brief and formal, stiffly businesslike. Glines was hired in the first letter to learn the names of those people who were publishing *Info*. Barney acknowledged that and sent along a bill for one week's work. Then Tyson wrote to inquire about progress, and one line of Glines's reply caught Dane's eyes—"... it is generally wiser, in this type of investigation, not to include too many details in writing …"

All in all, both men seemed to be acting in good faith, and now Timothy set the folder to one side and began leafing through the pages of Glines's call book. Tyson's name first appeared three weeks ago, when he telephoned once. Two days later he called again, and after that his calls became a daily occurrence—even two and three in the course of a morning. These continued right up until last Friday and all but two or three were recorded in Barney's handwriting. The book skipped the weekend, and the calls that had arrived this morning were from Max Lowe's office, the collection bureau, and Mr. Rossi, the dealer in pornography.

It seemed very curious, and then he wondered if it had been the art dealer's call that had sent Eloise on her badly timed scavenger hunt....

There was this small noise, a released breath, and Timothy looked up to see a hand nervously holding a very businesslike Luger automatic. He raised his eyes to the face of the man standing in the dark entrance, a gaunt, high-cheekboned man with such a dedicated expression that Dane knew he must act fast to save himself. He raised his hand in the age-old gesture of peace.

"*You low bastard,*" the man said, and with that the big gun belched fire and roared deafeningly. Dane threw the modernistic swivel chair over backwards, hit the floor with his shoulder and rolled sideways even as the second and third shots slammed perilously close. Through the opening in the desk he could see his assassin circle round for a better target, and now, desperately, Dane risked the plunge for the baseboard socket. His fingers jerked the plug loose, blacking out the room, and where his head had just been a fourth slug tore furiously into the wall.

There was silence of a kind now, except for the reverberations of the gun blasts and the hard breathing of both men. Timothy hardly wanted to take the risk of moving, let alone speaking out, and his ears strained to learn what the gunman was going to do next. If Dane had any advantage it was that the man was certainly no professional killer. Pitched to a high emotional key, hellbent for murder—but driven to it by something very personal. So Dane waited, let the seconds tick by, and at last the tension took its toll.

"I'm not leaving without those letters," the man said in a tight voice. "We can stay here until dawn—"

"Put the gun down on the desk," Dane told him quietly.

"Like hell I will. I'm going to kill you with it."

"You're lucky that you haven't. I'm not Barney Glines."

Deadly blue-orange flame. The thunderclap explosion. But Dane was not where he had been.

"I'm not Glines," Dane repeated, and when the man triggered the gun still another time he came at him from an angle, crouched low. His shoulder passed beneath the Luger, caught the man belt-high and drove him ten feet backwards. The wall stopped their momentum, but the other man took the full impact. He grunted miserably and the gun thudded heavily to the rug. Timothy, coming to a halt on one knee, reached down to retrieve it, then pulled his would-be killer to his feet. There was no fight left in him. There was nothing, and Dane felt no particular triumph.

"That's a hell of a way to ask for something," he said, moving away to find the lamp plug and bring light again.

"It's the only way you'd understand," the man said with a great weariness. "What are you going to do to me now?"

"Give you your letters," Dane said, "if they're here. What's your name?"

"I'm Packi," he answered uncertainly, his eyes wary. "Johnny Packerd. Aren't you Barney Glines? On the level?"

"On the level. Haven't you ever seen him?"

"No. But Ruthie has. He's got her scared half to death."

"Your wife?" Dane asked. He was at the files, looking for but not finding anything under "Packi" or "Packerd."

"Not my wife," Johnny Packerd said. "My girl. *Was* my girl," he corrected. "I just finished a two-year stretch."

Dane looked at him. "And you liked it so much you want to get right back in."

"I have to get those letters I wrote Ruthie while I was away."

"Why?"

"Because she's got her big break," Packerd said as though it were something everyone should know. "Her first picture was a hit. The studio's going to star her—"

"What's Ruthie's name?"

Packerd spoke it, softly, and Dane nodded. It was one of the films even he had seen on a hot day last summer. The girl, a vivacious singer and dancer, had all but stolen the show from the big names featured in the cast. The publicity campaign was just now reaching its full stride. Now Dane went to the "C" files, found nothing. "There's nothing here, Packi," he told him.

"Try Myers," Packi suggested. "Ruthie Myers."

And there it was, a bulging folder of letters, some in envelopes, some not. One was addressed to Mr. John Packerd, Sing Sing Prison, Ossining, New York. Another to Miss Ruth Myers, 22 MacDougall Street, New York City. It had an Ossining postmark.

"Here," Dane said, handing him folder and all, hoping that Glines would come in and make something of it.

Johnny Packerd came forward but didn't immediately take his letters. "I don't know what to say to you, mister. God, I tried to kill you—"

"You didn't figure on the big recoil." He pushed the folder into the man's hands.

"You don't know what this means," Packerd said. "If they'd printed what Ruthie wrote to a con, those crazy letters about the whole thing being her fault and all ..."

"What were you in for?"

"Possession. The two of us were just kind of lost, you know? Couldn't get a break anywhere." He took a breath. "I'm a hoofer, too," he said.

"Were you on the big stuff, Packi?"

"I'd just graduated the night before," he said wryly. "They caught me with my first package of horse. It was hardly touched."

"Ruthie's off it, isn't she?"

"Thank God she never got *on*. All it ever was with Ruthie was a reefer when she was feeling all kicked out. So I got to taking one with her. The trouble was, I was always singing the blues."

"So Ruthie figured it was her fault?"

"Crazy little kid."

"Ever see her anymore?"

"With my rep?" he said. "I wouldn't go near her. She keeps writing to me. She told me all about this guy Glines and his magazine."

"Did she tell you how Glines got the letters?"

"I never asked her. All I know is that I sent all hers back when I read what a hit she was in pictures. I told her how much it had meant getting them so regular, but from now on she'd never even heard of Packi...." His voice stopped abruptly and they both looked toward the outer office. Someone had closed the door there, making no attempt at silence, and in a moment two men entered the room.

"Just hold it right there," one of them said. "Both hands in plain sight."

"Police?" Timothy asked.

"D.A.'s office. Lieutenant Graff. And you'd better be Timothy Dane."

"I'm Dane. What's the trouble?"

"The trouble is I don't like tramping this lousy town for wisenheimers. You knew we wanted to talk to you, why the hell don't you stay put?" The policeman shifted his dark scowl to Johnny Packerd.

"Who are you and what's your business?"

"My name is Packerd. I came up here to get something of mine—"

"Is that it in your hands?" Graff said. "Let's see it."

"No...."

Dane put his hand on Packi's arm, pressured it warningly.

"Let him see your letters, Packi."

Packi handed them over and Graff carried them to the desk. He shoved his hat back on his forehead and opened the folder. Then he glanced up.

"When did you get out?" he asked.

"Yesterday."

"What were you in for and how long?"

"Possession of narcotics. I did two years and one month."

"You're out for good behavior?"

"I've got three years left on parole."

"Make sure you make it, Packerd."

"I will. Can I have my letters?"

Graff shrugged. "There's probably some law or other being broken," he said heavily, "but I take my problems one at a time." He closed the folder and Packi retrieved it, anxiously. Graff gave his full attention to Dane, dismissing Packi with a nod.

"What are you doing here?" he asked as the other left.

"Working. Where do we go now, Leonard Street?"

"As soon as I've thawed out. How come you do your work in this office?"

"Just helping out. Glines isn't in town ..."

"I know. I'm looking for him. And what were you doing in Glines's apartment this afternoon?"

"The same thing I told Homicide I was doing ..."

"Where's Glines, Dane?" Graff asked suddenly.

"I don't exactly know."

"Where's Mary Smith?"

"I don't know that, either."

Graff exchanged a sour glance with the detective he had brought along with him. "There's nothing else for it, Tom. Take him in."

Tom shuffled forward on the balls of his feet, his face expressionless. "Turn around," he said and Dane turned, raising his arms for the search. Tom's fingers lifted out the Luger.

"You've got a license for that, I hope," the Lieutenant said.

"Sure." Behind him he could hear Tom sniffing.

"This thing's just been fired, Fred. Hey, look at the wall there...."

"I am looking," Graff said with interest. "What's the story, Dane?"

"I didn't know it was loaded, or something."

"That's the ticket, crack wise. I'm in a great mood to be kidded tonight."

"I don't think it's his gun, Fred," the other cop said.

"Why?"

"It was in his left coat pocket."

"You left-handed, Dane?"

"Sometimes."

"But you wouldn't swear to it?"

"Also," Tom said, "the safety is still off. You ask me, it was the other guy who used this gun."

"I used it," Dane said.

"What was his name again?"

"I never saw him before. The gun is mine and I used it to shoot holes in the wall. If anybody has a beef, it's Glines. Let him sue me...."

"Tom, put the local precinct onto this. Let's go, Dane."

They left the office in single file, Dane leading, and as they entered the corridor Timothy spied the thin form of Johnny Packerd ducking out of sight. Graff rang for the night elevator, and while they waited Dane voiced the silent hope that the ex-convict had brains enough to keep out of sight until the affair was forgotten. Then they were driving downtown to the District Attorney's office, hurrying so they could wait in an anteroom until one of the Assistants was ready for them. The lawyer was a mild young man named Cooper who didn't offer to shake hands with Dane but seemed friendly enough otherwise.

"Homicide has just booked a suspect in this case, Dane," he said. "But I'm not at all convinced."

"Who did they arrest?"

"It's a material witness charge against the superintendent of the apartment," Cooper told him. "They took him in on the basis of a discrepancy between what he told Homicide and your version."

Dane and the other man regarded each other placidly, but there was nothing but turmoil inside Timothy's mind. Giving Homicide another suspect had been a diversion, a play for time.

"So now I'd like to get your statement down on paper and have you sign it," Cooper said, his clear voice putting Dane into a corner.

"I'd better talk this over with my lawyer," Dane said, stalling. He certainly wasn't going to sign his name to the myth about Mary Smith, or do anything else that was not factual and could jeopardize the superintendent.

Cooper pushed a telephone to him. "Call your lawyer," he said.

"I'd want a little more privacy than that, thanks."

"I don't seem to understand," Cooper said, understanding all too well. "You spoke quite freely to the police at the scene of the murder. I understand from them that you were quite certain of your facts, quite definite. But now you seem to be, well, hedging a bit."

"I'm sorry if that's how it seems," Dane said. "But there are times when it's best to have some legal advice."

"Not off past performance," Cooper said. "While Homicide has been busy checking the superintendent all evening, I've been calling around about you. You've got a pretty clean bill of health in town, Dane."

"Thank you."

"A shame to have to knock a hole in it by holding you down here on a charge of interfering with law officers in their work."

Timothy spread his large hands. "Well," he said reasonably, "if the District Attorney is going to deny me the right of counsel, then there's nothing else for it."

"Call your counsel."

"Sorry. My own client has privileges, too."

"By client you mean Mary Smith?"

"I could mean a Mary Smith," he parried. "I could mean anyone I work for who has absolutely nothing to do with the murder of that girl."

Cooper was about to demolish that line of reasoning when he was interrupted by the softly buzzing telephone. He identified himself, listened, murmured "I see" several times and told whoever was calling that he'd "rather take that up with the boss in the morning." He set the phone down and stared thoughtfully past Dane's shoulder for several long moments.

"I think we'll let it ride for now," he said finally. "You're free to go, Dane."

"Go?"

"It seems our friend the superintendent has a nasty record as a sex offender. It also seems that he's quite willing to confess anything Homicide wants him to—providing there's newspaper and television coverage." Cooper shook his head wonderingly. "You sicked them onto a lunatic, Dane," he said.

Dane did not move to get up. "He must be," Timothy said, "if he killed that girl and then let us into the apartment."

"Unless he had something in mind for you and Mary Smith."

"Maybe," Dane said doubtfully, now rising.

"By the way, where is this Barney Glines?"

"I wish I knew."

"All right. But we'll probably be after that statement, anyhow. I'd take the time to get your lawyer's opinion."

Dane left them there, thinking that if the superintendent of Glines's apartment was really insane it wouldn't matter what statement was signed. A cab took him slowly back uptown to his place, and he went on inside considering the apparently endless eddies set in motion because Barney hadn't come to work this morning.

Timothy mixed a drink at the bar, declining to turn on any light, carried the nightcap into the bedroom and began undressing. He was stripped to his shorts when his hand brushed something foreign, at least in this room on this cold night. It was lace underwear, and in the same moment that he held it aloft a soft voice purred in the dark room.

"Hello, Timothy," Donna said from the bed.

Dane turned on the bed lamp, turned it off again. The girl was propped against the headboard, her hair loose to her shoulders and her body covered lackadaisically by the single blanket.

"How the hell did you get in here?"

"I left the latch off the last time I was here."

"How come?"

"Because I want to," she said in a voice that told him his question had been foolish. "Because I want to spend the night with you."

"How about what I want?"

"I never gave it a thought." Then, surprised: "Don't you want me?"

"Get dressed and go home," he said. "This is the wrong night."

"Not for me it isn't...."

"I say it is," he told her, going to stand by the window as though he didn't trust himself. He heard her slide from the bed.

"Wait," he said suddenly. "Damnit, you can't go." He turned to find her at his elbow, a straight, lithe-figured female, as exciting as he had imagined she would be. But of more importance right now were the chunky, forbidding figures of the two plainclothesmen posted in the street below.

"What is it?" she asked. "What's the matter?"

"Stay back from the window. They've got the place watched."

"Then I've got to stay."

"For a while you can stay."

"Good. Was that ice I heard rattling in a glass?"

"I'll get you a drink."

"Get yourself one. Yours will be better than any you make for me."

He made his way out to the bar, came back inside to find that he could see quite well in the darkness now. And what he saw on the blanket was more disconcerting than he thought it should be.

"Listen," he said plaintively, "aren't you cold?"

"No. Are you?"

He thought he should be cold, too, but he wasn't.

"You know what you are?" he asked.

"Yes."

"You're a foul-up," Timothy said. "You're the fly in the cold cream."

"I'm no damn good."

"I didn't say that," he told her and after his voice died away a long silence stretched expectantly between them. Dane stirred restlessly, turned from the disturbing sight of her and strode to within feet of the window. They were still out there, two poor, cold pitiable bastards standing stolid and frozen, shoulders hunched against the driving sleet. Better men than he was, and what he should do was call them in out of the night, make a steaming pot of coffee, lace it with applejack, show one spark of human decency. And then to be transported back down to Leonard Street, for another session with Mr. Cooper and the prospect of the Women's Detention House for Donna and the Tombs for himself.

"The hell with that," he said.

"The hell with what?"

"Nothing. I was talking to our friends out there."

"They'll be there all night, Timothy."

"It looks like it."

"Then come here to me."

He swung around. "You make it sound very uncomplicated," he said. "So damn simple."

"Not me," she said. "You. You do important things for me like today and you don't even present a bill." She swung her slim legs to the floor and came toward him in the same motion. "I'm dumb about an awful lot of things," she told him when she was inches away, "but I know what happened today every time we looked at each other." Her arms raised upward, encircling his neck, and her body closed against him. They kissed, and all the while there was a thundering on the door.

"Don't!" Donna said vehemently. "Don't let them!"

"They'll break it down." Dane went to the door, wondering about what could have alerted them, what made them so damned insistent. He opened the door a crack and understood. It wasn't the policemen in the hall but a hot-eyed Mike Carhart. He lunged against the opening, throwing the surprised Timothy backward, then pushed by him and stalked toward the closed bedroom.

"Hold it," Dane shouted, but the broad-backed, raging actor sent the door back on its hinges and flooded the room with light.

"Well, ain't she sweet!" he roared at the girl in the bed. "The untouchable—the goddamned vestal virgin! Too good for Mike Carhart, are you? Well, you're nothing but a tramp! A lousy, worthless tramp—"

Dane swung him around swiftly, directly into the path of his hooking right fist. Carhart's knees buckled and his eyes filmed over, but as he started down his arms wrapped themselves around Timothy's legs and both men crashed heavily to the floor. They rolled, upsetting a lamp, hitting out at each other savagely with hands, elbows and knees, and it was anybody's fight when the plainclothesmen broke into the apartment and finally pulled them away.

But Carhart hadn't had enough. He swung without warning at the cop holding him, nailed the man on the point of the jaw and dropped him on the spot. His partner left Dane's side and charged forward with an outraged bellow. Carhart hit him twice, short, chopping blows, and Dane saw to his vast surprise that now both policemen were out of the action.

"You're next, bucko…."

"I'll keep," Timothy told him. "We've got to get Donna out of here fast." He turned to find that the girl had taken advantage of their preoccupation to slip from the bed and cover up her nakedness in an enormous beaver coat.

"You go on with Carhart," he told her.

"I go where you go, Timothy."

"Listen, this is no time for arguing …"

Donna shook her head. "I'm not running out on you anymore," she said stubbornly.

"Oh, hell!" With an eye on the sluggishly reviving plainclothesmen, Dane hurriedly dressed. Minutes later the three of them had left the brownstone and were traveling away in the cab that Carhart had left waiting.

"I guess I blew my stack back there," Mike said. "I got too much damn vinegar for my own good."

"Where'd you learn to hit like that?" Timothy asked him.

"I was going to ask you the same question. You like to have broke my nose…."

"You deserved it," Donna told him.

"I know it. Come on, I'll buy you a drink."

"I'm just dressed fine to go anywhere," the girl said.

"Then I'll buy Dane a drink…."

"No. We'll go up to my place and have one."

Show people, Dane thought happily. There's nothing like 'em on earth. Then they went on up to her place, and after Donna had traded the coat for lounging pajamas they sat around and talked, and listened to hi-fi, and every so often Timothy had to force himself to remember what had happened to the policemen in his own apartment.

It was Dane's second turn to be bartender, and when he returned from the kitchen with ice Mike Carhart was gone.

"Where is he?"

"I threw him out," Donna said, crossing over to him. She lifted the tray from his hands, set it on the small bar. Then she was pressed against him, a very warm woman beneath the thin silk of the pajamas. "Now then," she said huskily, "where were we?"

## SEVEN

The pretty secretary looked down at her appointment book and, then raised her eyes to Billy Tyson's guileless face.

"But I've got you down for ten o'clock," she said. "Mr. Van Ormen has someone with him now."

"I *thought* I was early," Tyson said. "But there's somebody I want to talk to for a few minutes down in casting. Be back up at ten." He reached into the deep pocket of the fawn-colored overcoat, pulled out a small bottle of cologne and set it on the girl's desk.

"You shouldn't do that," she said, beaming.

"Why not, Judy? Someday you're going to be a big star around here. Then, when they're hounding you to sign a long-term contract, you're going to need an agent—"

"Quit your kidding, Mr. Tyson."

"You just wait and see, Judy." He smiled, and the girl smiled back, and as he walked away with the easy walk of his she thought again what a sweet little guy he was. So different from all the other agents who came in to see Mr. Van Ormen.

Tyson, who could come and go in the vast building at will, descended by elevator to the big and sprawling area that served as reception and waiting room for the dozen casting directors of the television company. Comfortable chairs and couches were strung out along the walls, and there were tables covered with the most recent copies of *Variety, Billboard, See, Life* and every other publication that concerned itself with the entertainment world and would help wile away the time for the hopefuls who were here to audition.

There were several dozen of them in the room when Tyson entered and took a seat. But the number was fluid, as first some were called inside to an office and others arrived for their own appointments. They were young and old, short and tall, shapeless and breathtaking. Bright-eyed ingenues sat among tired-faced veterans, sad-looking comedians lent cigarettes to grinning heavies. And the ones who looked the hungriest had never missed a meal in their lives.

Tyson chose an empty chair near a magazine table, picked up *Variety* and held the newspaper spread in front of his body. Then, deftly, he slipped a copy of *Info* from his inner breast pocket, inserted it inside the paper, folded it and set it back down. He sat where he was for another minute, nodded greetings to everyone who happened to pass his way, and with a glance at his watch got up and moved on.

On the floor above he found the men's room unoccupied and deposited a second copy where the porter would find it atop the towel cabinet. He went from there to the office of one of the morning show stars, and, with the knowledge that this was the day that his staff had off, slipped a copy beneath the locked door.

Everywhere he went his movements were natural, neither furtive nor reckless, and anyone coming upon him on any of the floors would consider it a familiar sight and unremarkable. By the time he returned for his appointment with John Van Ormen he had left behind a total of six magazines.

Tyson's business with Van Ormen that morning concerned an option the company was exercising in connection with a dance team he represented. The arrangements were routine and quickly settled to everyone's satisfaction. Then Van Ormen asked what was The Question.

"What have you found out about *Info?*"

"We're making good progress, Van. The detective agency has some very good leads. They think it's being printed up in Westchester."

"I guess you heard that Ralph Blodgett is hiring someone on his own?"

"Oh?"

"I just got it myself. Ralph got word that *Info* was threatening some people in his new show. And you know Ralph when he thinks someone is crowding him...."

"Ralph's one of the real people in this business," Tyson said. "I wonder who it is he hired."

"That I don't know. But with both of you working something ought to turn up pretty soon."

"Yes," Tyson said, then made his good-byes and left the building with a thoughtful, preoccupied face. His next destination was the Lambs Club, where he distributed more copies of the magazine, then uptown to the Colony, back down again to Shor's, the Yale Club and, finally, to 21, where the luncheon crowd was already gathered at the bar. He was not surprised that several copies of *Info* had already preceded him to this mecca from the various places he had left them. Nor that it was Topic A.

"How low can these sons-of-bitches sink?" asked one voice.

"Pretty lousy stuff, isn't it?" someone asked Billy Tyson.

"What's that, Hal?"

"The story in that cesspool magazine about the kid they just signed for the Palmer Hour. The one that's getting all the build-up—"

"You don't mean Buddy Stevens?"

"That's the name. Now this rag runs a big splashy piece about someone named Buddy Stevens who was arrested in Chicago two years ago, on a morals charge. They know it isn't this kid, they don't dare say it is. But, Jesus, the innuendo is about as subtle as a blackjack...."

"It's terrible," Tyson said.

"His agent just went out of here white as a sheet. You know Nat Strom, don't you?"

"Everybody knows Nat. Fine fellow."

"But can you imagine what he's going through right now? The Palmer Company lawyers are probably invoking the turpitude clause while we're talking— Say, didn't you have young Stevens about a year ago?"

"Just for a little while," Tyson said quickly. "I couldn't get him started."

"Did you sell his contract to Nat?"

"It was something like that, Hal. Come on, let me buy you a drink."

The agent stayed in the restaurant until two o'clock, listening carefully to the comments of each new group that entered, observing the stricken faces of the famous and almost-famous whom the magazine had mauled and scarred. He tried to gauge the temper of show business, and what Tyson saw and heard made him nervous. Especially when Ralph Blodgett called him over to his table.

"Well, they did it to us again, didn't they?" the producer said.

"But we'll be onto them very soon, Ralph."

Blodgett nodded impatiently. "I suppose you've heard that I've started my own investigation?"

"Yes, I did. Johnny Van Ormen mentioned it."

"Don't take it as any slight to your group, Billy. But *Info* is getting very personal and I wanted to get into it on my own. You understand that, don't you?"

"Well, I was a little surprised to hear it. You get too many cooks, you know."

"This lad isn't hard to get along with," Blodgett said, "I've told him to trade information with you and work it out together."

"Fine," Tyson said. "That's fine. What did you say his name was?"

"Dane," he said. "Timothy Dane."

"Never heard of him," Tyson said, flicking an ash away.

Blodgett laughed. "Neither have I," he said. "But maybe that's to the good. It seems that the only ones you do hear about these days are either in jail or up to their ears in their own troubles."

"Oh, I wouldn't say that, Ralph ..."

"No? Did you catch that murder in the morning papers? The girl somebody drowned in a tub?"

Tyson laid the cigarette into the tray, ground it out very deliberately. "I did read something of that," he said.

"The apartment belonged to a private detective," Blodgett said. "My paper said he was 'well-known.' Well, let me tell you that he is the s.o.b. who is trying to blackmail a mutual friend of ours. And this Timothy Dane, that nobody knows, is the boy who kept our pretty little friend and my big expensive show from a particularly nasty black eye."

"You don't mean Donna James?"

"I do. Donna was with him when the body was found. But he shooed her out of there before the police arrived. What's the matter …?"

"Nothing, Ralph. Nothing at all."

Then Blodgett remembered his *faux pas* in the theater the day before.

"Incidentally," he said, "I think I gave Mike Carhart credit for a touchdown he didn't score. At least that was the gist of the conversation between them before rehearsal broke for lunch this morning."

"Why do you mention that to me?" Tyson asked in a voice that was strained.

Blodgett looked his surprise. "If it doesn't make any difference to you, Billy, then it certainly doesn't make any difference to me."

Tyson remembered to smile. "Don't pay any attention to me, Ralph," he said. "It's this foul weather."

"And *Info*," Blodgett said. "It's got us all on the edgy side."

Tyson looked into the other man's face. "Yes," he said, getting up from the table. "And *Info*, of course. I've got to get back to my office, Ralph."

The little agent went out of the restaurant, waving busily to all his friends gathered there.

## 2

"How do you want them?"

Dane had been asleep a moment before. Now, in an instant, he was awake.

"How do I want what?" he asked.

"Your eggs, sweet man," Donna answered. "You want them nice and scrambled, or scrambled and nice."

His eyes were plainly critical as he studied her, frankly searching for flaws in the bright cold light of the new morning. But the girl's gamin face was even more intriguing this day than it had been yesterday afternoon. It seemed very alive, very eager, not distant and disinterested. And the conformity of her body beneath the diaphanous nightgown she wore now reminded him of the pleasure he had known the night before.

"And she cooks, too," Timothy said aloud.

"In my fashion," she said, and he noticed that even her speech was relaxed, that she spoke her words lazily, with a drawling sound to them.

"In my fashion," she repeated, her face breaking into a smile, "but you're my first guest for breakfast." She swung away from the bed and walked quickly out of the small room, her high heels beating a happy, busy tattoo on the wooden floor.

The tall man put his own legs out over the bed, took a cigarette from the near empty pack on the night table and while he smoked tried to get his affairs in better order than they were. The girl's arguments, for instance, that he shouldn't return to his place last night didn't hold for today. Today he would have to face the music for the fracas with the police, and the longer he put it off the more annoyed they'd get with him. So he would have to do that and still keep Donna out of it. And the amazing Mike Carhart, too, he supposed, although Ralph Blodgett would be collecting a bonus if Dane could pull that one off.

And there was Donna herself. Timothy believed that he lived the normal life of a single man in Manhattan, that he enjoyed no more than his fair share of the available women whose lives got briefly tangled with his own. But the one racketing around in the kitchen at his moment was a different breed of cat, an original so far as he was concerned. The girl was a contradiction, a riddle, and Dane knew that if he seriously tried to discover what made her tick he would become very much involved. So there was a decision to be made about that, too.

In his spare time he had to stop stumbling around with this Glines-*Info* business, stop getting sidetracked at every turn and start getting some answers. He ground the cigarette out, crossed to the shower and rejoined Donna ten minutes later, fully dressed.

"I suddenly feel very naked," she said, surveying him from head to foot. "In there I was a bride. Now I don't know what to make of myself."

"You haven't changed."

"But you have."

He shook his head, laughing. "This is my working face," he said and sat down to a breakfast that would have fed a squad.

"I guess I'll have to get used to all your faces," she said. He lifted his eyes to hers. "Won't I?" she asked.

"Donna," he said very deliberately, "these eggs are the best."

She smiled at him, touched his hand impulsively. "All right," she said. "I won't talk it to death."

"Let's see those negatives I found yesterday," Dane said, shifting the conversation easily. Donna went inside, came back clothed in a wrapper. She put the packet on the table.

"You looked at them?" he asked.

She nodded. "One of them is the picture of me with that gangster in the night club. Another one—it's hard to tell from such a small negative—but it looks like Mike and myself doing a scene in rehearsal. I don't know what the others are all about."

Dane took them one by one, held each to the overhead light and studied it. The first showed a man and woman, the woman in his lap, and Dane thought that the man was a Negro. If so, and if the woman was not only white but well known, then this was grist for *Info's* mill. He set that one aside, picked up another and whistled.

"What is it?" Donna asked.

"Some rehearsing," he commented. It was a picture of Mike Carhart embracing the girl in no uncertain terms. Donna was costumed in brief, theatrical step-ins, and with a more intimate backdrop painted in, the composite would appear to be quite different in *Info* from what it was here.

"A man gets paid for this work?" Dane asked.

"That one does," Donna answered quietly. "One fellow I know doesn't make a dime at it."

"Proving," he said in a casual voice, "that there are some things money won't buy." Timothy's hand parted the wrapper, came to rest unobtrusively on her lower thigh. It was a friendly gesture, as unprovocative as though he had put an arm around her shoulder. Even so, the warm firmness of her reminded him of the excitement she generated.

"You're a lover," she said. "All around the clock."

He broke contact with her, reluctantly, and brought his attention hack to Glines's cache of pictures.

"Tell me about this nightclub shot, Donna. How did Frank Carlo happen to sit down with you?"

"I don't think he did," she said. "It was a little place in the Village, one of those cellar clubs where the tables and the people are all crowded together."

"He wasn't in your party?"

"I'm sure he wasn't."

"Who took the picture?"

"One of the girls who come around," Donna said.

"Did she come back to sell you one?"

"I don't remember ever seeing her again. But it does seem strange, though, now that you mention it."

"This was a put-up job, honey. Somebody is going out of his way to give you a bad time."

"Barney Glines?"

"Well, he'd know all about Frank Carlo," Dane said. "He'd know he'd be poison to anybody in show business."

"But how did he get hold of those other pictures of me? How did he even know they existed?"

"Who does know about them?"

"Only a few people back home. Very few."

"Nobody else?"

"No one that I can think of."

"Then Glines is quite an operator," Timothy said, getting up. "I'll have to ask him about it."

"If you ever find him."

"If," he echoed. He left Donna's place then and went back to his own. Finding no police awaiting him there, he perversely put in a call to Lieutenant Graff.

Graff had bad news, which he delivered almost gleefully.

"The District Attorney just signed a complaint against you, buster. We're asking the Commissioner to revoke your license."

"That's hitting a little low, Graff."

"And I hope it hurts. But we'll talk business with you any time. Just come down here with your two playmates before eleven o'clock this morning and all is forgiven."

"So long, Lieutenant," Timothy said. "See you around."

Timothy hung up on the policeman, put in an emergency call to his lawyer, Marty Shea.

"Now what?" asked his friend wearily.

As he usually did, Dane gave the other man all the details of his latest trouble, omitting nothing.

"When," asked Shea, "do I meet this Donna?"

"When you've gone down to Centre Street and talked the Commissioner out of benching me."

"That could mean never."

"You think they've got me this time?" Dane asked.

"Well," the lawyer said, "I certainly can't defend you on the merits of your case. I *mean*, boy—hiding a material witness in a homicide, aiding and abetting an assault on police officers—"

"I didn't lay a hand on either one of them."

"You were there, kid. But what might help is that your friend Shea, and his friend Commissioner Ryan, are both from Notre Dame and will be marching together with the Loyal Sons of St. Patrick come March seventeen. That might get you off with a stern warning."

"Then I'll think no more about it," Timothy said.

"No. Just concentrate on your graceful exit when you've introduced me to Donna."

"Shea," Timothy told him, "you'd better get over the idea that I'm your bird dog." That ended the conversation, and having ducked the D.A.'s haymaker, Dane was free to concentrate on the other matter.

He left to see Barney Glines's client, Mr. Billy Tyson.

# 3

"You're crazy, aren't you, Larsen?" Detective Boros asked in a disarmingly friendly voice. "You're honest-to-god nuts, aren't you?"

"If you say so," the building superintendent answered tonelessly.

"The head doctors are going to sign a paper for you, aren't they? They're going to put you up in a nice place in the country, aren't they?"

"If you say so."

"So it doesn't make any difference, does it? You can tell us all about it and we can't do a thing. You got the laugh on all of us, isn't that right, Larsen?"

"I tell it to the television," Larsen said stolidly. "I tell the whole world the story of my life."

"Well there it is," Boros said, extending his arm to the television camera borrowed from the city station.

Larsen stared across the interrogation room into the center of the lens. He shook his head from side to side.

"A fake," he said. "You don't fool me with that fake. Take me to Radio City. Let Dave Garroway ask the questions. I tell him the story of my life. Everything."

Boros sighed tiredly, let his weary shoulders sag. For twenty hours, almost continuously, he and his partners had been on this off-beat homicide. Nils Larsen had been permitted to sleep, he was relatively fresh-minded, and now they had brought him from his detention cell for another session in the presence of the man from the District Attorney's office.

"That's how it goes, Cooper," Boros said, looking over at the lawyer.

"Larsen," Cooper said, "how did the King girl get into that apartment?"

"Ask me something new."

"Did you let her in?"

"She had a key. Mr. Glines give it to her."

"Did she use the apartment pretty often?"

"Ask me something new."

"Did she spend much time in there with Glines?"

Larsen's thin face split into a leer. "I tell you all about it on television," he said doggedly.

"Will you tell about the birthmark on her breast?"

"What?"

Cooper pointed to his own breast. "The star right here," he said.

"Sure," the prisoner said. "I tell about that, too. Everything."

"But you want to tell the truth when you're on television, don't you? You don't want the world to think you're a liar."

"I never told a lie to anybody."

"But the girl had no birthmark, Larsen. You know that."

"That's right, that's right. I know she had no mark...."

The Assistant D.A. and the homicide man exchanged a glance. Cooper began speaking again.

"You've been pretty rough on women all your life, haven't you, Larsen?"

"That's their story," the man said, his voice abruptly defensive, belligerent.

Cooper looked down at a typewritten card. "Assault," he read, "assault with intent. Rape, rape again." He looked up. "Twice you copped a plea, Larsen. So it wasn't just their story, was it?"

"If you say so."

"But you're getting old, aren't you?"

"You think so? I'm strong as a bull—"

"Then why didn't you rape Eloise King?" Cooper asked sharply.

"Who says I didn't?"

"The Medical Examiner says you didn't." Cooper turned swiftly to Boros. "Will you tell me why in hell we're wasting time with this character?" he asked with heat. "The city pays me to prosecute, for God's sake, not to defend."

"Okay, Cooper, okay," the Homicide man said. "But what should I do with him if he didn't kill the girl? Turn him loose?"

"Christ, no! Send him over to Bellevue for observation. Get his picture and his record on the Vice Squad's active file—"

"I want a lawyer!" Nils Larsen cried suddenly. "You don't push me around!"

"You'll get what's coming to you, mister," Cooper told him. "And as long as you stay in this town you damn well better walk on the tips of your toes. Slip once, Larsen, just look at a woman sideways, and I promise you'll spend the rest of your life in stir. And not the country club, you sadistic sonofabitch. Dannemora."

Boras beckoned to the uniformed policeman at the door. "Get his pedigree at the office," he told him, "then take him over to Bellevue on a hold-and-wait order." The policeman nodded, hauled Larsen out of his chair and took him out of the room.

"Where do we go from here?" Cooper asked Boros.

"Don't ride me," the detective answered, yawning against his will. "I've got a long day's work to put in on this thing."

"What other leads do you have?"

"We're trying to locate this Glines. We got him through Friday. He took the King girl out, dinner and a show, then brought her back to the apartment. She stayed there till about three, then took a cab uptown to her place. But Friday," Boros said, "was not so tough. That's because of the girl, who made herself easy to remember. Saturday is something else. Either Glines was trying to keep out of his regular spots or else it was just one of those times when a man goes left-handed on you."

"Dane," Cooper said, "gave our people the impression that Glines was out of town on a job. Something that was routine with him."

"Dane," Boros said, "is a cutie. He conned the three of us onto Larsen and it was five long hours later before we got wise."

Cooper looked impatient. "Where does he figure in this, anyhow? What's his angle?"

"I don't know," the Homicide man answered thoughtfully. "But I'm not especially worried about him."

"You're not?"

"No. Finding the girl dead caught him completely off base. I'm ready to go along with him that he was up there trying to recover some shakedown material from Glines. I also think it doesn't make a damn bit of difference who was with him—"

"That's strictly Homicide's point of view," Cooper said. "So far as my boss is concerned this guy Dane is thumbing his nose at us."

"Your boss is sensitive," Boros said. "I got a boot out of Dane, myself."

"The hell with him," Cooper said. "Now, let me try an idea I've got and see what you think."

Boros covered a yawn with his big hand.

"Besides the girl in the tub," Cooper said, "there was also a very thoroughly searched bedroom. So there must have been something up there worth looking for, right?"

"So?"

"So the girl worked for Glines. We know that she had a key to the apartment and used it regularly—"

"They shacked up, Mr. Cooper," Boros said with a straight face.

"As you say. The point is, the girl probably knew quite a bit about Glines and his business."

"She probably did."

"And with her being murdered up there, and the ice ransacked, that business could have been blackmail, couldn't it?"

"It sure could," Boros agreed. "And that's the reason two men are going through Glines's office right this minute."

"Well, why the hell didn't you say so?"

The man from Homicide laughed. "Come on," he said. "I'll buy you some coffee."

## EIGHT

"You can send Mr. Dane in," Billy Tyson told his secretary, and the intervening seconds were like so many eternities, to be got through somehow. This is how it is going to be from now on, he realized dismally. The waiting, the awful waiting.

But when the tall, dark-haired man appeared in the doorway, Tyson found that he was able to smile, and speak the platitudes of greeting and wear the disguise of the man everybody loved.

"Come in, come in," he said. "I've been expecting you."

Dane lowered himself into an armchair, admiring the comfortable, pine-paneled office and the framed, autographed pictures of the famous faces that hung in profusion on the four walls. The reception room held even more, and while he waited there for the agent Dane had been impressed with the warmth of the sentiments on each portrait. Now he regarded the man himself, found a plump, apple-cheeked type, a model of that congenial little guy who picks up a conversation with you in any bar.

But this wasn't a bar.

"Ralph Blodgett," Tyson was saying, "thought we might be able to work together on this thing. Sort of put it all into one package."

"I just wonder," Timothy said, "if Barney Glines would go for that arrangement."

"I don't understand …"

"It's his job," Timothy explained. "He's been on it for some time, hasn't he?"

"Well, yes. Yes, he has."

"How did you come to hire Barney, Mr. Tyson?"

Tyson looked surprised. "I don't think I really know how— Your name is Timothy, isn't it?"

"Yes."

"I don't know how we picked Glines, Tim. He'd done some work for theater people and somebody suggested him."

"Who?"

"I couldn't say just who. It simply happened that we hired him."

"How close is he to telling you who gets the magazine out?"

"Frankly," Tyson said, "I'm not very happy about his progress. The whole committee is a little concerned about him."

"You mean FAST?"

"That's what we call ourselves. But Glines is moving anything but, if you follow me."

"Who are the other members of FAST, Mr. Tyson?"

Tyson looked over his shoulder, turned back with a laugh. "I don't know any Mr. Tyson," he said. "If you want me, I'm Billy."

"Who are the other members of FAST?" Dane asked again.

"That's a pretty touchy question, Tim. It's gotten out that I organized the group, but the other fellows want to stay anonymous." He shook his head worriedly. "Once this thing breaks, you know, the publicity is going to be blinding."

"I guess it will. The last time you talked to Glines, Mr. Tyson, what did he have to say about his progress?"

"He was pretty evasive."

"Where is Glines, Mr. Tyson?"

"Where is he? I haven't the slightest idea."

"Didn't he tell you last Friday?"

"No. He didn't say anything last Friday."

Dane leaned forward in his chair. "That's what bothers me. How you knew he wouldn't be in his office yesterday—"

"*Know?* I don't know anything...."

"But you suddenly stopped calling him. All week long you were on the phone; two, three, four times a day. But yesterday you didn't try to reach him at all."

"I've just been too busy."

"Where's Barney, Mr. Tyson? Is he out of town? Hiding? Is he dead or alive—what?"

"I don't know where he is. As God is my judge."

Dane's hand went inside his jacket, came out holding the nightclub photograph of Donna James and Frank Carlo. He laid it on the desktop and watched Tyson's expression.

"Glines found out who publishes *Info*," he said. "He went to work for them on certain stories, then branched out into a private shakedown of his own. He tried to extort money from the girl to keep this picture out of the magazine."

"That's terrible," Billy Tyson said.

"And you didn't know about it?" Dane asked. "You weren't suspicious of him at all?"

"I told you we weren't happy about his progress …"

"And you have no idea where he is?"

"None."

Dane got up abruptly. "Then I guess we can't help each other very much," he said.

"Gosh, Tim, I hope you're not blaming me for anything Glines might have done."

Timothy looked down at the man, felt the tug of his personality and instantly rejected it.

"I'll be seeing you, Mr. Tyson," he said.

"You'll keep our group in touch, won't you?"

"You produce your group," Dane told him, "and I'll explain what I think is going on."

"Hey, hold on, fella. You're implying something I don't think I like."

"I'm implying that you're FAST," Dane said flatly. "Or at least you think you're fast."

"Now wait a damn minute ...!"

Dane had turned and was striding toward the door.

"Listen, Dane, you're making a big mistake."

The door opened and closed, and Tyson sat staring at it, his whole body trembling. Finally he picked up the receiver of his private phone and dialed a number.

"Frank?" he said into it, his voice barely audible. "There's trouble. I've got to see you right away."

## 2

Timothy picked up Billy Tyson as he exited his office building five minutes later, surprised not only that his flagrant fishing expedition was showing results, but that the agent was making things happen this quickly. No finesse, Dane thought, remembering how the man had shown panic around the edges in their brief conversation.

Dane leaned forward in his seat, spoke matter-of-factly to the cabdriver. "The one we want is in the tan overcoat," he said.

"The fat little guy flagging a hack?"

"That's him."

"This is going to be just a quiet tail, isn't it?"

"Absolutely."

"Otherwise that finnif ain't worth the headache."

"All we're going to do," Dane assured him, "is have a ride."

"Well, here we go," the cabbie said without enthusiasm, moving away from the curb and expertly using a Madison Avenue bus as a cover between himself and the taxi Tyson had entered.

Three blocks later they turned west, crawled with the traffic, almost lost each other when Tyson's driver beat the light crossing Fifth. Then were faced with an abrupt decision when the lead cab suddenly swerved to a stop at a hotel just beyond Seventh Avenue.

"Keep going," Dane told his man. "Turn into Eighth and drop me."

"You want me to wait?"

"Not with your clock running I don't."

The hackie shrugged, set the flag up. "I'll wait," he said.

Tyson was nowhere in sight as Dane recovered the distance on foot to the hotel, and he could not know that Frank Carlo was already inside the place. It would have made a difference, seeing the hoodlum; would have filled in the picture of what was now just a puzzling jigsaw. But whatever he was, Timothy was not clairvoyant.

He was not especially happy, either, as he stepped into the lobby. This was not exactly the Waldorf, where a man could move unnoticed, get the lay of the land and plan the thing. This was a dump, a fleabag, and whatever he did would have to be done right now.

"Where did the little guy in the tan overcoat go?" he asked the clerk, still not knowing about Frank Carlo, wondering if the man behind the desk shook so from the palsy, or what.

"Cop?" the clerk asked in a hoarse voice. "You—a cop?"

Dane squinted at him. "Sure," he said. "Sure I am."

"Room two-ten."

"Don't you go anywhere," Dane told him, cop-like, making his way to the staircase. But he did not stop at the second floor. He continued on up, four more flights, then came out onto the flat, snow-covered roof. He turned toward the front of the building then, took up a place at a parapet overlooking the street below and resigned himself to wait in the freezing cold until Tyson left again and he could examine Room 210 at his leisure.

In the room, a frightened Billy Tyson was having a hard time convincing his partner that the business should be liquidated.

"He's on to us, Carlo. We've got to quit—get out of town…."

"I'll take care of him," Carlo said. "Forget that 'out of town' business."

"You can't take care of everybody!" Tyson said desperately.

"I say I can. Now let's drop it and start talkin' business. Where's the stuff you got for the next issue?"

"We've got to stop—"

"Show me what you got," Carlo ordered and Tyson got a suitcase from beneath the bed and opened it. Inside were a dozen pieces of artwork that had been made ready for the engraver, and these Carlo examined piece by piece.

"This one oughtta sell." he said. It was a layout, across two boards, and featured Donna James, Mike Carhart and the show called *Solo*. The nude snapshot was there, censored by panels, as well as the rogues' gallery picture. Blown up from the actual prints, they looked fuzzy and indistinct—but no less incriminating. A different love scene from rehearsal was used, but as Dane had guessed, the figures were superimposed over a shot of a bedroom, complete with whiskey bottle and half-filled glasses. In the upper righthand corner of the layout there was a curious open space, where something obviously had been pasted down and then removed.

"This where my picture was gonna be?"

"Glines had it there."

"The son-of-a-bitch. Now how do we turn all this into dough?"

"I don't know," Tyson said. "It was all Glines's idea. I never figured on blackmailing anybody—"

"You never figured on a lot of things, seems like. Well, who do we show it to? Who pays?"

"The producer is a man named Ralph Blodgett. Glines figured to make up a sample issue and let him buy all the copies."

"How many copies?"

"Fifty thousand," Tyson said. "At a dollar apiece. But we can't do it, Carlo. This detective is working for Blodgett. He's out to stop us—"

"He's the one gonna get stopped," Carlo said. He picked up the next group of pictures. "How much is this story worth?"

Tyson looked at the layout of the call girl, Lili Storm, the semi-pornographic pictures Glines had taken of her. He winced at the juxtaposition of Mickie Grayson's publicity photo.

"That's dynamite," the agent said nervously. "It's all a fake. There isn't a word of truth in the whole thing."

"It says here she tried to get a job on the show. Isn't that true?"

"It was a phony," Tyson said. "Anyone at all can go to an audition. But Grayson had nothing to do with her—"

"The hell with that. It'll cost them another fifty grand to kill it."

The agent looked sick. He was thinking of Fred Marsh, the network lawyer who had contributed to FAST, who had suggested he hire this Timothy Dane. He was thinking of a naked girl in a bathtub full of water. No jury would understand about that. No one at all would understand why he'd got out *Info* in the first place....

"Tonight," Carlo was saying, "you take this over to Jersey."

"I can't do it tonight," Tyson said. "I'm going to a rehearsal. I'll take it over there this afternoon."

"Don't try any more cute stuff on me," Carlo warned.

"I don't want to try anything," Tyson said. "I want to quit the whole business."

"Go on, beat it."

"What are you going to do?"

"Wait till you're gone," Carlo told him. "Then go after this Timothy Dane."

"Frank ..."

"Beat it."

Tyson left with his package, and from the rooftop a very cold and uncomfortable Dane watched him hail a cab and ride away. Then, grateful for the warmth of the hotel building, he made his way down to the second floor. He knew of no special need for caution as he moved, nor for any as he bent to the task of springing the uncomplicated lock in door number 210. The lock responded and he eased the door inward, followed on through and closed it. Dane knew one small moment of alarm just before Frank Carlo's gun butt dealt him a stunning blow at the base of the skull. He went forward with the impact of the thing, then seemed to genuflect. Carlo struck again at the semiconscious figure below him and Dane pitched full length to the floor.

Carlo turned him on his back, searched him swiftly. The wallet identified the tall man, and when he found the nightclub photo of himself, Carlo's face went cold.

First it was Barney Glines who had tried to make trouble for him with this goddamned picture. Now it was this one.

"All right," the killer said aloud to the unhearing Dane. "*All right!* You can have it just like him!" He pulled a chair over then, and sat and waited. Twice Dane stirred back to consciousness, and twice Carlo hit him viciously with the gun. Darkness came on, and now Carlo allowed him enough strength to stand under support and be half-carried, half-walked out of the room and down the stairs. The clerk watched their progress out of the hotel and did absolutely nothing about it.

Carlo pushed Dane into the back of his car and drove due east. He came to the dock area and made his way familiarly to the winter-deserted pier that housed the boats of a summer excursion line. Then, working at his leisure, he lashed Dane's wrists behind him with picture wire, bound his ankles securely and laid him face down on the floor of the car with a blanket over all. He drove again, north this time, gained access to the West Side Highway and continued on out of the city. Carlo dutifully stopped and paid one toll to cross the Spuyten Duyvil bridge, then another for the use of the Westchester County road. He swung westerly then, got onto the Bronx River Parkway unerringly, and exited that winding route via a little-used street that tunneled its way dangerously beneath the tracks of the New York Central railroad.

This was in a small village called Tuckahoe, now mainly a residential suburb of thirty-mile-distant New York, but once the site of some very productive marble quarries. Frank Carlo had been born in Tuckahoe, in fact, and his grandfather had been a part of the large immigrant labor force who had mined the marble. But though the rock ran deeply into the earth, shaft after shaft broke through to underground springs and quarry after quarry became filled to the very top with water. Pure, cold, crystal-clear water—but the absolute ruination of Tuckahoe's marble industry.

Children took to swimming in the quarries that first summer after the shutdown, but after an alarming number of them had struck their heads against the abandoned pipes and machinery underwater and drowned, the village barred their use by an ordinance. No fences were erected around them, however, merely signs warning of the danger. After that, Frank Carlo and another young hoodlum found a different use for the quarries—or at least one of them. It was in a very remote spot, in the center of what was practically a jungle of wild growing bushes and dense woods. The miners had pushed a dirt road through, but within three years nature had taken back most of it, making the place all but inaccessible. Except to Frank Carlo.

This was 1928, and Prohibition. The bootleggers sold their stuff in New York City a hundred different ways, but the best liquor—the honest Scotch and Canadian whiskey—came by rail from Montreal to White River Junction in Vermont. There it was generally loaded onto big vans, some going Boston way, most directed toward New York. But the outsize trucks didn't make the run directly into Manhattan. It wasn't because police protection wasn't bought and paid for, but because to block traffic on, say, West 52nd Street while a truckload of Johnnie Walker was delivered would be an outright thumb to the nose.

So the vans came partway, pulling into warehouses and garages in towns like Troy, Cohoes, Poughkeepsie, Stamford, and there the shipment was transferred to a dozen smaller trucks—pickup wagons whose side panels read "Laundry Service," "Acme Bakers," "Butter & Eggs." Frank Carlo knew all about the dodge. He also knew that the drivers on the Poughkeepsie run were fond of the coffee and waitresses at a particular diner on the White Plains Post Road in Eastchester, the township adjoining Tuckahoe. He knew because his sister Marie was one of the waitresses who accommodated the drivers in the tourist cabins next door to the diner.

Carlo and his gang would watch until Marie and her friend went inside and drew the shade. Then they would break into the pickup and loot it of as much as they could carry away. They peddled the liquor to the Elks Club and to local speakeasies, and because it was so much better than what these places were used to, the demand was high. Carlo met this by hijacking an entire truck one night, and that almost cost him. The truck was abandoned in Yonkers, but the mob traced it back to Frank Carlo and he was given a severe working over by way of a warning.

Carlo recovered from the beating, and during his convalescence figured out what to do with the delivery trucks once they were stolen and the liquor emptied out. Taking only a cousin into his confidence, he made off with three trucks in the course of the next six weeks. This time a rival mob was suspected, possibly from as far off as Atlantic City, or Philadelphia, because there was no sign of the trucks within one hundred miles of Tuckahoe. Armed guards went along after that, and the drivers were ordered to by-pass the friendly diner near Tuckahoe and come into the city along different routes. But whether they used Central Avenue or the Boston Post Road, whether they took their coffee break as far north as White Plains or south in Mount Vernon—whatever evasive action they took—Carlo & Cousin located them. Five more trucks were never seen again, along with the gunmen supposedly guarding them.

Marie helped with the guards, although she never did know what happened to them. All she had to do was engage the man in an interesting conversation, aided by a revealing neckline and tight skirt, while Frank entered the opposite door and jammed a loaded .32 against his neck. That was all Marie did for fifty dollars. Frank and Cousin Tony drove the guard away. Some were shot en route to the hidden quarry, some were still alive and conscious when they and the emptied truck were shoved headlong into the two-hundred-foot water-filled mine.

Needless to say, the mob then forbade *any* stop for any reason between Poughkeepsie and the Manhattan delivery point, but Frank Carlo continued to use the place over the years in his work of hired killer and to settle personal grievances. Cousin Tony, in fact, was down there, encased in cement. And so was Barney Glines, his body weighted by four concrete building blocks.

Now, tonight, Carlo emerged from the little tunnel beneath the railroad tracks and made his way to the quarry. And though there was a golf course nearby, and homes were clustered where once there had been nothing, this spot was still a wilderness in almost all respects. Indeed, there were families living within a quarter of a mile who were ignorant of its presence—and certainly of its peculiar use.

Approaching the hidden dirt road, he dimmed his lights and swung into it, heedless of the overhanging branches that raked the car from front to back, the deep ruts that threatened to rip out the chassis. And hardly had he left the paved street but he was lost from view. The foliage parted reluctantly, closed swiftly, and it was as though nothing had ever passed within.

Carlo halted the car at almost the exact spot on the quarry's edge where he had brought Barney Glines three nights before. There had been a difference that night, more time to plan it. A week, a week from the day Glines had braced him with the picture and actually tried to shake him down. He stood for a moment outside the car, looking down into the freezing blackness of the quiet water, and a smile curled his lip. *Shake down Frank Carlo....*

He opened the rear door, reached down, and with his hands under Dane's shoulders pulled him roughly out onto the ground. The bound man groaned, tried to roll over on his back. Throughout the trip he had alternately revived, then blacked out again. Pain was at a minimum, thanks to the numbing cold, but in his few moments of awareness he understood that he had come to a very bad situation. It took only the effort to move to realize how helpless he was. An expert had made his arms and legs useless to him. As hard as that, perhaps even worse, was the loss of physical strength, the drain on his energy. And with that, the will to resist whatever was being done with him.

He came to again as Carlo jerked him from the car and let him fall to the ground. He lay for a moment with his face on the hard crusted earth and then tried to roll over on his back. Dane was suddenly afraid. Not afraid that he was going to die, but that he wouldn't be able to fight against it.

Carlo opened the trunk of the car, worked the heavy spare wheel loose and got it down. He set it upright again and rolled it to where Dane was, then let it fall. He returned to the trunk, took out a large green sack, carried it back to the wheel and dumped out its contents of linked snow chains for the tires.

Dane made the rollover, found himself staring up at a figure who was familiar even in silhouette.

"Carlo?"

"Know me, hanh?"

"I know you. What is all this to you, anyhow?"

"Money, what the hell do you think? Now shut up and let me work."

Dane watched as Carlo forced the ends of two of the chains through the openings in the hub of the wheel. "Where's Barney Glines?" he asked.

"You'll see him in a couple of minutes. Give him my regards."

"What did he do? Why did you kill him?"

"Just shut up."

Carlo looked at what he had done and then changed his mind. He pulled back one end from each chain, crisscrossed them and reinserted them through the wheel. Now he seemed satisfied.

"It's that picture, isn't it?" Dane asked.

Carlo said nothing, only reached down and lifted him across the face of the wheel. Dane tried to twist his way off the thing and Carlo's fist slammed into his face. He must have kept trying, for the killer hit him twice more. Unconsciousness, almost a familiar phenomenon by now, engulfed his mind again.

Carlo finished his work in silence. Laying the two remaining chains over Dane's body, he secured them with wire to the two that passed beneath the wheel. Now he put one foot on the rim and pulled with all his force. The chains held, held with a promise that they would hold until eternity. Then he pressed his finger to the tire's valve, letting out the air and adding the weight of the rubber to the improvised coffin that was already heavy enough to sink to the bottom and stay.

Carlo rested from his exertions briefly, lighting a cigarette within the warmth of the car, contemplating the still figure of Dane and congratulating himself for the Carlo-luck that had put the man so completely in his hands.

*Smart guy, he thought. Started to figure about the picture. Him and Glines. Figured out that friggin picture.*

He tossed the half-smoked butt aside impatiently, got out of the car again and began to move the man and the tire to the water. There was, Carlo knew, a sharp incline at the edge of the quarry. A hard shove and that was all.

## NINE

The marquee lights spelled it out: "*Solo* with Sylvia Hall and Michael Carhart." Below that, with simple confidence, "Opens Tomorrow Night."

Donna James stepped from the cab, glanced at the lower message and felt a quickening of her heartbeat. *Opens Tomorrow Night ...!* It was getting to her, inevitably—the excitement of the theater, of being a part of it. The fear of the theater, the thousand darting worries that something she would do would ruin it for everyone. Show business was like nothing else. At all times you were on your own. At all times you were part of a company, a member of a team.

She walked away from the marquee, into an alleyway that held the stage entrance, and her steps carried her past a very colorful and busy-looking display poster for the new musical.

It was a painting, and the heroic, bare-chested figure of Mike Carhart dominated. On either side of him the artist had placed Sylvia Hall, capturing her stately, bosomy blonde beauty, and dark-haired Donna with her gypsy-like sex appeal. It was not as forceful a presentation of the basic story as a Roy Winkler would have done, but it was arresting.

"Ralph Blodgett presents *Solo*," the printed portion announced, and the names of the two principals appeared in letters that were about seventy-five percent as tall as the title. The rest of the cast, beginning with Donna, were named in much smaller type across the bottom of the poster. But a week ago Sylvia Hall had confided to Donna that she had seen the artist's suggestions for new posters that would go up after the show opened—and if the reviews were favorable. She said that the one Blodgett okayed called for *three* names directly below the title—and preceded by that all important word, *Starring*.

A week ago it hadn't made very much difference to the girl where her name appeared, or how big, or even if she played in *Solo*. But this evening, hurrying to the last dress rehearsal, everything that happened to her was assuming a tremendous importance. All at once she wanted to succeed very much, to become as important a human being in Timothy's eyes as he was in her own. After being pushed around almost the entirety of her young life, the girl who had been Dottie Jenkinson now felt the desperate need to *be* somebody, to have somebody be proud of her. It was new to want that, and very frightening.

A dozen thoughts chased each other through her mind as she entered the dressing room she shared with Shelley Bowers, a featured dancer in the musical. Shelley was a Texan, a natural redhead whose long straight legs and outsized bosom were in classic proportion to her six-foot frame, and now she lay full length on the divan, half-covered by a flowered kimono and contemplating the ceiling overhead very thoughtfully.

The girls exchanged greetings and Donna went immediately about the business of undressing. Suddenly her mood became subdued, for Shelley had swung to her feet, dropped the kimono unselfconsciously and had begun to sort out the rather intricate sections of her own Act One costume. The redhead was a throwback to some Amazonian female, and though Donna must have seen her like this on a score of other times she, was now viewing Shelley's figure through Timothy's eyes. In her imagination he had just walked into the room, unexpectedly, and in the inevitable comparison she had run a woeful second.

"What's the matter, honey?" Shelley Bowers asked in her altoish voice.

"You're the matter," Donna told her frankly. "You don't lose a fella very often, do you?"

"Well, no," the other girl answered. "Not very often. Why?"

"Gosh, Shelley, I don't know! I've met this guy, and if I ever lost him I don't know what I'd do …"

"You?" asked the Junoesque redhead. "A man wouldn't figure to let you get away."

"If he saw all that he would," Donna said and Shelley laughed aloud.

"What's funny?"

"You are, honey. Why, if I had a real man I wouldn't dare double-date with you."

"Do you mean that? Really?"

"But positively."

Donna looked closely at the other girl's face, then a bright smile broke across her own. "That's wonderful," she said. "That's about the best thing I ever heard."

The wardrobe mistress came in then and sewed both girls snugly into their costumes. Twice—once in New Haven, again in Philadelphia—the gyrating redhead had burst right out of hers, and tonight the seamstress took special pains with tinted fishing line. All three of them had fun about that, and when Donna was called for her first entrance she was as "up" as she would ever be for a performance of *Solo*.

And tonight's was the one that counted, so far as Ralph Blodgett was concerned. The producer still called it the last rehearsal, but the curtain went up tonight exactly as it would tomorrow, and from beginning to end it was the real thing.

Every seat in the theater was filled. Not by a "first night" audience of cold-eyed critics, noisy celebrities and half-tight politicians who made a snobbish career of attending premieres. These people did not support the theater, so Ralph Blodgett made of his dress rehearsal a kind of bonus for those who did. Persons had come to stand in line to buy tickets for his last hit, *Carnival*, and on certain days, chosen at random, their names and addresses had been taken. The same for those who lived in the Metropolitan area and had written in for seats. Out of the thousands of names collected, eight hundred had been picked in a blind lottery, and the eight hundred invited to attend the *actual* Broadway premiere of *Solo*.

True, this was a receptive audience, a risible one. Some, no matter how long they had planned for this night, arrived after the overture. Some, despite heavy medication, brought hacking coughs to compete with the actors on stage. And there were audible gasps when Mike Carhart's rippling muscles strode from the wings, rising applause when Sylvia

Hall finished her first ballad—and Donna James stopped all activity completely for nearly two full minutes in the midst of the second scene of the first act. The audience had been fully satisfied with the story line, the lilt of the music, the performances and the lavish outlay of scenery and beautiful girls. But they were not prepared for the sad happiness of not-quite beautiful Donna, the artless talent that made them demand she stand there and never leave the stage. Just stand there and let them look at her. Donna drank it in shamelessly, took nourishment from it, felt her ego balloon to the second balcony. She wasn't seen again until midway in Act Two, and Ralph Blodgett knew by then that the rest of tonight and tomorrow would be spent doctoring the book with the writers to correct that situation. *Solo* belonged to Miss Dottie Jenkinson of Tampa, Florida.

There was no producer's party after the performance, that would be at Sardi's tomorrow night, but Blodgett did invite a group for dinner which he warned them in advance would be a work session. There were Sylvia Hall, Carhart and Donna. The stage manager, the assistant director, the choreographer and the arranger. And Billy Tyson. Blodgett included the agent almost automatically, just as he had made sure Tyson's ticket was on the center aisle, and when he sat his guests around the round table at Tony's he purposely placed him between Donna and himself.

"Well, Billy," he asked him, "is the jury still out?"

"They never left the box, Ralph. Your worry now is, have you got a large enough theater?"

"It'll do us until spring. How was Donna?"

Tyson turned his head to the girl. "A star," he said. "Without qualification."

Blodgett leaned across to her. "A little different from riding in beauty parades, isn't it?"

The girl looked startled by the good-natured question. "How did you know about that?"

Now Blodgett was surprised. "Why, I guess we all know the story of how Billy found you, honey."

"What else do you know about me?" Donna asked, feeling the elation desert her swiftly.

"Why, nothing," Blodgett said puzzledly. "Nothing except that you're the most exciting thing on Broadway tonight." He looked around the table, caught Mike Carhart studying Donna as if he could taste her. "Do your serious drinking now," the producer said, signaling the waiter. "Because after the steaks we go to work."

"What else did you tell people about me?" Donna asked Billy Tyson.

"What I thought, Dottie—" He smiled away his lapse. "I'm afraid it'll be a while before I forget you're not Dottie any more."

"Does Mr. Blodgett know my real name?"

"Do I know what?" Blodgett asked, coming back into the conversation on hearing himself mentioned.

"That I'm Dottie Jenkinson."

"No, I didn't. Does it make any difference?"

"Yes," she said. "To a man named Barney Glines and this *Info* magazine."

"What do they think they're going to make out of it?"

"I can't talk about it," Donna said. "Not here."

"You're among friends," Billy Tyson told her in a soft voice. "You can tell Ralph and me."

She shook her head. "Timothy will tell you," she said. "He knows what they're trying to do."

"Speaking of Dane," Blodgett said to Tyson, "did you talk with him?"

"Yes, we talked."

"Fine. Between that lad and your outfit I think we'll get results."

Tyson nodded, but seemed preoccupied with what Donna had said. "What has Dane told you?" he asked.

"That someone is trying to ruin my reputation."

Even before the sentence was out, the knowledge came to the girl with an agonizing clarity. Not a suspicion, not a guess. Donna knew....

"No one would do that to you," Tyson said, and amidst all the turbulence within her mind his voice sounded thick, unreal. But very real were the remembrances, recollections dragged up from her subconscious. She thought of how famous Billy had made himself with her landlady in Tampa during the week he persuaded her to come to New York. Of the positive fact that Mrs. Fowler searched all her boarders' rooms when they were absent. She recalled, now, the question of parental consent for her going away. And her sorry answer that her mother and stepfather would never know she was gone. More, too, about her stepfather and her getting into trouble. Too much.

"Of course not," she heard Ralph Blodgett say. "Who'd want to do a kid like you any harm?"

"I don't know," Donna said, her eyes full on Billy Tyson's face. "I don't know." How could he look so harmless? How could he be so evil? She had to be with Timothy. Very suddenly she had to be with Timothy ...

"What's the matter, honey? Where're you going?"

"I'm sorry, Mr. Blodgett. I—I've got to leave."

"But you haven't eaten. We haven't talked over the changes for tomorrow night."

"I've got to leave...."

"It's delayed reaction, Ralph," Billy Tyson said with a smile in his voice. "I'll take her home."

"No!"

The whole table became starkly silent at the vehemence of the girl's refusal. Donna felt their puzzled glances impaling her.

"I'll take you home," Mike Carhart said, lifting his big frame from the chair. "My pleasure."

"Now wait a minute!" Blodgett protested. "Donna can be excused, although she's got one helluva lot of work to do tomorrow. But nobody else. The jackals attack that theater in exactly twenty hours, and by God, this is one time I'm going to do my own second-guessing! We have *work* to do, you guys and dolls."

Donna was flooded with guilt at his words. She was wanted here, she was part of the show. She needed Timothy, had to tell him what she remembered about Billy Tyson. But now she was needed. The personal thing could wait.

"Come along, Donna," Billy Tyson was saying, his fingers gripping her arm, pulling her away from the table.

"No. I've decided to stay."

"You go on home, honey," Blodgett told her. "Get as much sleep as you can get before we come around to hound you with new material."

"I'd rather—"

"Come along, Donna." His grip tightened on her arm.

"No! I want to stay!"

Her voice broke, hysterically, and then they were all around her, crowding her, making knowing, sympathetic sounds. The words "delayed reaction," "aftereffect," "needs a real blackout" kept bombarding her mind, causing confusion so great that blood rushed into her brain, made her feel almost faint.

"I'll take her home," she heard Mike Carhart say clearly, then Ralph Blodgett's blurred objection.

"You don't need me for anything," Billy Tyson said. "I'll take care of her." He kept leading her away from them, farther and farther away. And they thought she was ill, temporarily addled by the success of the dress rehearsal performance. What could she tell them, when everything she might say would only convince them that she was not herself?

The cold midnight air went through her body like a knife thrust, set her to shivering violently. The street, two full blocks west of Broadway, was dark and deserted on this midweek night, but instead of walking toward Eighth, where they might find a late-cruising cab, Tyson led her deeper into the West Side.

"No," Donna said unevenly. "Not this way." She tried to twist around, suddenly stiffened in his grasp as his thumb and forefinger pinched hard against the sensitive nerve above her elbow.

"Yes," he said close to her ear. "This way." They walked across Ninth, with the girl's left arm paining her exquisitely, the rest of her almost numb from the freezing cold.

"Please, Billy, please," she said but he hardly heard her. Tyson was scarcely aware of anything that was happening. From the moment in the restaurant when Donna had looked at him with such perfect clarity in her face, the man had acted purely from instinct. He must, at all costs, preserve himself. She must not, at any cost, reveal him. A simple, primitive drive—but now reason began to assert itself, he began to think about his predicament and not merely act on the solution.

But still the problem was with him, was right beside him. Could he explain it to her? he wondered. Explain the unexplainable? That for all his work to make her an actress, there was a counter-effort to destroy her? He had failed to make Barney Glines understand. All that Glines saw in the magazine was a lever to blackmail the rich and famous. Glines had not understood, and his greed had tripped him when he went to Frank Carlo for money and misjudged his intended victim.

But Donna might see why he had to do what he did. Perhaps there was even some predatory instinct hidden in her own personality, some need to tear down what a person has created. There was much more thrill in destruction.

"I'm not going to hurt you," Tyson said. "But I have to talk to you, tell you something that's very important. Will you go someplace with me and listen?"

"Yes," she whispered, nodding her head, ready to agree to anything now.

He turned back toward Ninth, and at the corner hailed a cab.

"Remember now," Tyson said as the taxi approached them, "you're going to listen to what I have to say. After that you can do anything you want."

"Yes," she told him again, but as they sat back in the seats of the cab his fingers were still clamped tightly to her upper arm, ready to apply their torturous pressure again if she appealed to the driver for help.

They came in a few moments to the hotel off Seventh Avenue. Tyson paid the hackie and hurried Donna inside the disreputable-looking place. There was no one in the lobby, not even the clerk. They climbed to the floor above and entered room 210.

And as soon as the door closed behind them, Billy Tyson knew that an explanation would be useless. Donna would only pretend to understand him, to sympathize. No sooner would he let her out of this room than she would betray him to everyone. He couldn't let her do that....

Donna turned and saw the insane verdict in his twisted face. She opened her lips to scream. His hands lunged at her, closed murderously around her throat, the thumbs jammed deep into her windpipe. Donna struggled with all the wild young strength in her body to break that death grip. Then the bed came up behind her legs, unbalancing her, and she fell over backwards with all of Tyson's weight forcing down.

## TEN

*One hard shove and that was all....*

Carlo edged his cumbersome burden to the brink of the inclined quarry wall. From deep in Dane's throat there came an awakening murmur, a blurred protest, and the killer listened to it and reflected on it. What, he wondered, was going through this one's head right now? How did it feel to be absolutely helpless?

And what did they think about, the ones who were still conscious, when the water first closed over their heads and pulled them down and down, always down? How long did it take before they died? He didn't believe those stories about their lives passing before them, their whole damn lives. Those who said that had come out alive. Carlo wondered about those that didn't. They couldn't breathe, they couldn't move, they couldn't do anything but die.

"*Jesus!*" He spoke the word aloud, mirroring his own morbid horror of such a death. For though he had improvised this use for the quarry, Carlo himself was a non-swimmer, a man with a nightmarish fear of the water. Perversely, the drowning of his enemies was much more gratifying than killing them any other way.

He paused and took a deep breath, watching the agonized straining of the man, imagining the same scene under the water. Carlo got down on one knee and laid his palms against the wheel for leverage. Now push, his mind directed. *Push!* But the impetus came from behind. Strong hands slammed against the small of his back, relentlessly, and he was catapulted over Dane's body. He clawed grotesquely at the air and his terrified scream split the night—to be choked off abruptly as he broke through the thin crust of ice on the water.

Carlo plunged straight downward into the fresh, unbuoyant, all-but-bottomless spring. His breath had been expelled with his outcry and, unthinkingly, he sucked the freezing water into his lungs. He tried to expel it, and in the next instant began to strangle. His descent halted, he began to rise, and with arms thrashing blindly his head appeared above the surface.

But only briefly. "Help me!" he tried to shout, but it was only a jumbled, croaking sound. The man who watched from the land plunged unhesitatingly in its direction, hit the water in a flat dive and found that his arms and legs were almost immediately paralyzed by the cold. He reached Carlo and grabbed for his hair to keep his face clear of the water. But Carlo was berserk. Both his arms enclosed the second man's shoulders and they both went under. Now, in that terrible darkness, their terror was equal. Sodden clothes and dead-weighted shoes added to their desperation, and driven from the second man's mind was all thought of rescue. On instinct alone he fought to be free of Carlo's frantic hug and to save his own life. Finally he wedged a forearm between their chests and with all his might pushed outward. They broke apart, and as one made his exhausted way to the quarry's edge the other, brilliantly, learned what it was to drown.

Dane could not see any of it, and what he heard was as unintelligible to him as the bare fact of his still being alive and conscious. None of the sounds, so plaintive and desperate as they were, had any clear meaning for him. But he did hear movement near him now, as if a man were crawling along the snow-covered ground.

Dane's voice came up to him through the awful quiet.

"Carlo?" it asked uncertainly.

"No," came the answer. Hands reached over to unchain Dane from the rim.

"Then who?"

"Packi." When the chain wouldn't give, he jerked it apart. "Who was it I pushed into the water?"

"Frank Carlo."

"Is he in this, too?"

"What do you know about it?"

"Can you stand up?"

"I don't know. I don't seem to feel my legs."

"Just cold is all," Packi assured him, helping him erect. "What happened to Carlo?"

"He's in there. Where you're supposed to be. What's it all about, anyhow?"

"First tell me how you got here." Dane tested his muscles, tried to increase the circulation of blood.

"I brought the letters up to the hotel where Ruthie's staying," Packi said. "I told her about you, about how I tried to kill you and then stood out there in the other office and heard you take the gun rap for me...."

"But how did you get here?"

"Ruthie remembered telling somebody else about the trouble I was in, about how she wrote to me all the time. She said she told him all her troubles—"

"Billy Tyson."

"That's the name. I got to wondering about him, trying to figure it out. So I tailed him all morning. Where he went, I went. You know what he was doing?"

"What?"

"Planting copies of that magazine all over town. I made a list of the places...."

"That's pretty nice work, Packi."

"Yeah. And then I got a bad jolt. You came up to see him. I didn't know how to take that one."

"What'd you do?"

"Well, you came out and got into a cab. But you didn't go anywhere. Then Tyson came out and you followed him."

"And you followed both of us?"

"Yeah. But after both of you went into the hotel, I spotted you up on the roof."

"The hell you did!"

"The hell I didn't. That made me figure you were after him, too, and I thought you could use what I'd seen. So when he left the hotel I waited around for you. When you came out of there," Packi said, "you were in bad shape. All I did then was follow the guy's car up here."

"That's all you did. Where are we, do you know?"

"Up in the sticks somewhere. Tuckahoe, the last sign said." He swung an arm around Dane's waist. "Let's get you to a doctor for that head of yours," he said.

"Stop by Carlo's car for a minute."

They went to it and Dane unlocked the glove compartment with the ignition key. Inside was his wallet, his wrist watch and a pint of whisky. Timothy pocketed his own belongings, uncapped the bottle and handed it to Johnny Packerd.

"Get warm on the inside," he said and Packi sipped at the liquor tentatively, returned the bottle.

"This is to you," Timothy said very seriously.

"Come off it," Packi protested. "Let's get to a doctor. You ought to see the shape you're in."

Dane put the bottle back and shut the compartment. Then he ran his fingers across the tops of both sun visors above the windshield and the one on the driver's side yielded a small card that had been fastened to it with a paper clip. It was a calling card of Billy Tyson's and Dane turned it over. On the back was another name—Charles Mueller—scrawled in pencil, and an address in Guttenberg, New Jersey.

"What have you got?" Packi asked.

"I don't know."

"Come on then. Don't you feel cold?"

"I don't feel anything," Timothy told him truthfully, and they made their way slowly to where Packi had parked the car. They got in and the motor started sluggishly. "Let's find the local law," Dane said.

"Do we have to?"

"Always go to them when you can, Packi. If you wait until they come to you it gets very complicated."

"Whatever you say." They drove out of that lonely neighborhood until they came to a main road. A filling station attendant directed them to the Tuckahoe Police Headquarters, and there, while a doctor made repairs to Dane's injuries, both men explained in tandem what had happened to Frank Carlo. For his own part, Dane volunteered nothing beyond the actual fact that he had lost a skirmish to Carlo in Manhattan and that Johnny Packerd had stepped in to save his life. And Packi, picking up the faint signal, was equally vague as to how he happened to be there when needed.

Timothy didn't expect to get by with just the skeleton of the story, but that was exactly what happened. The man in charge, a Captain Creamer, seemed to know so much about Frank Carlo's past escapades that an explanation of this one was unnecessary. Dane even got the idea that the local policeman was a little grateful to them both, as though there were something ancient and personal in the Captain's relations with Frank Carlo.

The real interest centered on the quarry. Packi led them back to it in a police car and, on their return, Creamer made arrangements to have it dragged immediately. The Tuckahoe police apparently had hopes of closing several puzzling cases from the evidence they recovered down there. Timothy and Packi signed their joint statement and were sent on their way with a clean bill of health.

"That didn't hurt, did it?" Timothy asked his newest friend when they were back on the parkway.

Packi gave a rare smile. "No," he said. "That was all right. That cop almost had me feeling like I'd done some good deed."

"What plans have you got for yourself, Packi?"

"None. I could probably change my name and take another shot at show business. But if I ever clicked somebody would remember who I was and what I did time for."

Timothy was watching him closely as he spoke, noticing the manner in which he handled the car.

"Having any trouble getting the stuff?" he asked him now.

"What stuff?"

"The snow."

"Snow? *Me?* You couldn't give me a pop if they were handing it out free on Times Square. Hell, I've even quit smoking tobacco."

"Just asking," Timothy said.

"Why?"

"Because I thought you handled yourself pretty well. Following Tyson without him knowing it, trailing a hood like Carlo in a car. Ever think of earning a living at it?"

Packi was silent for a long moment. "You mean working with you?"

"Yeah. I'll never be rich and famous," Dane said, "but I eat regular. And don't think you're being done a favor. You'll *work*."

"When do I start?"

"You went on the books this morning," Timothy said matter-of-factly. "Our client's a man named Blodgett and the job is to put the magazine out of business."

"I'm going to like that."

"So will your girl."

"I haven't got a girl."

"Just the same, it'll be a good idea to go have another talk with her about Billy Tyson—"

"You mean tonight?"

"And there's no overtime. Expenses, but no overtime."

Packi grinned now. "You're going to be a hard man to work for," he said.

They went on into Manhattan and Packi dropped him at the 53rd Street address.

"Your office is in the Paramount Building," Dane said. "I'll get the lawyer working on your license in the morning."

"My record will kill that."

"You don't know Marty Shea," Dane told him, and with a brief handshake the men parted. Timothy went on inside, to soak his ill-used frame in a tub, to dress again and have one hard one for the road. But when he left again he was armed, and mentally alert against any more blunders.

The car arrived from the uptown rental agency and he headed for the Lincoln Tunnel and the Guttenberg address across the Hudson. Quite without intent the route he chose took him past the theater where the dress rehearsal of *Solo* was underway. Silently, he wished Donna good luck.

## 2

"Ever seen this ugly mug before, Cooper?" Detective Boros asked blandly.

"Frank Carlo," the Assistant D.A. said. "Where does a picture of him fit into this thing?"

"Time will tell," the man from Homicide answered, laying still another print of the nightclub photo on the desk. "Now tell me who you think the girl in the picture is?"

"Don't know."

"I took it over to Bellevue," Boros said, "and showed it to our friend Larsen. He says this is the girl he let inside the apartment with Dane."

"Well, now. Dane covers up for Frank Carlo's girlfriend," Cooper said, almost sniffing the air for the elusive scent.

"You'd think that, wouldn't you?" Boros said. "But most probably not. This picture turned up in Glines's office, stuck behind a desk drawer. Then we turned up the camera girl who snapped it—"

"Christ, what a job, Boros."

"You might say that. What made the girl remember the occasion was that she got one hundred dollars for the negative. Now, she doesn't know Frank Carlo and she doesn't know the girl who seems to be sitting beside him. But she is sure," Boros said, "she is absolutely positive that they were not in the same party."

"Oh, hell...."

"Maybe not, maybe not. With a hole punched in that lead we went off in two different directions. Number one, identify the girl. She turns out to be a Donna James, a name possibly assumed, and she's an actress in the cast of a new show opening tomorrow. Also in the show is a broth of a lad name of Carhart." Boros smiled. "Your two detectives," he said, "the pair who work for Graff and had so much trouble pulling in Dane last night—"

"What about them?" Cooper asked defensively.

"They identify Donna James and Carhart as the two other people present. Graff wants to get out an immediate pickup, especially on Carhart, but I persuaded him to talk it over with cooler heads."

"Why? Carhart assaulted two officers—"

"But this show, *Solo*, is being put on by Ralph Blodgett. Your boss may not have mentioned it, but Ralph Blodgett is one of the very decent people in this town. If the District Attorney can help it, he's not going to embarrass the man." Boros held up his big hand. "So what have we got?" he asked. "We've got the possibility that this Glines operator maneuvered an actress into a picture with Frank Carlo. Object, shakedown. No?"

"As you said, a possibility."

"Okay. So the girl gets approached and hires Dane. Dane goes right to the heart of the problem, Glines's apartment. There, almost as he told it to us, he finds the place ransacked and the King girl in the bathtub—"

The telephone on Cooper's desk gave off a buzzing sound. The city's lawyer picked it up. "Cooper speaking," he said and then listened. "No, Captain," he said. "We have nothing out on him currently, but we'll have a man up there in the morning. Thanks for calling." He set the phone down.

"That was a police captain named Creamer," he told Boros. "Up the line in Tuckahoe."

"So?"

"So he has information that Frank Carlo might be dead...."

"No kidding?"

"Might be. He has to dredge a marble quarry to find out."

"Well, I'll be damned."

"Naturally," Cooper drawled, "a character named Timothy Dane reported the statistic. According to Creamer, Carlo was about to do the favor for Dane when help arrived."

"Carlo was doing mischief to Dane?"

"That's what the man just said."

Boros snapped his fingers. "Then Carlo got to Glines," he said, happy as a Homicide detective can ever get. "And Pat Herman was right!"

"About what?"

"The picture, what else? Pat knows Carlo's career like a book. He took one look at that nightclub photo and said it was trouble, trouble for Carlo."

Cooper studied the thing again. "Why?" he asked.

"Carlo is on parole," Boros explained. "The parole itself stinks, just like every other rap that killer never served. But there's a new setup over in Jersey. The Prison Commission that's in now would like nothing better than to trip Carlo on a parole violation. Something as simple as leaving the jurisdiction of the state, or frequenting a place that serves liquor." Boros tapped the picture with his forefinger. "That meant going back to stir for Brother Carlo. According to Pat, the man can't take prison."

"Interesting," Cooper said thoughtfully. "So he kills Glines on account of the picture. But if this call just now was the straight goods, why does he go after Dane?"

"I said before that we looked two ways when the actress and Carlo seemed unconnected. In Glines's office the boys also turned up some information on a magazine called *Info*."

"*Info?* I've got a folder full of complaints about that thing..."

"What have you turned up?"

"Haven't really gotten around to it. All we have is complaints, all anonymous. John Rowe and I went through two copies of it and couldn't find anything particularly criminal. Innuendo, double meaning—but, hell, stuff just like it goes through the mails by the millions."

"This rag wasn't meant for the mails, Cooper. It was a hell-raiser pure and simple, with Barney Glines as the star reporter."

"Now you start to make a lot of sense. Glines engineers a picture of Carlo and this ..."

"Donna James."

"Donna James. He starts to shake her down and she hires Dane. And then, or at the same time, he puts the squeeze on Frank Carlo?"

"It could almost be," Boros said by way of answering yes.

Cooper looked triumphant. "And you came all the way down here on this miserable night to tell me that Frank Carlo killed Eloise King?"

"No."

"*No?* What the hell do you mean, no?"

"I'm just a wet blanket and I know it," Boros lamented. "But Frank Carlo didn't do that murder. Even a hothead like Carlo develops a particular style. The killer was an amateur, Cooper. A very lucky one."

"We're not back to that janitor again?"

Boros shook his head. "Not his style either. A guy we'd like to talk to is named Tyson. Billy Tyson."

"Who is he?"

"An actor's agent. Glines was hired by Tyson to investigate the magazine, find out who was running it. The thing is, Glines was already out bird-dogging for *Info* by the time he was given the job of exposing it. The thing also is that this Tyson was in touch with Glines every other hour but quit calling him about the same time that Glines disappeared."

"Meaning that he knows something about where he is?"

"We'd like to talk to him," Boros admitted. "He lives in New Rochelle but he wasn't home half an hour ago. He left his office early this afternoon without leaving word where he'd be."

"Sounds nervous about something."

Boros nodded, smiling. "His last visitor," he said, "was Timothy Dane."

Cooper looked steadily into the policeman's face. "Dane is pretty good, isn't he?"

The Homicide man shrugged. "I don't know how good he is," he said, "but I never saw such a persistent son-of-a-bitch in my life." Boros pulled his misshapen brown fedora over his forehead. "Well, got to go find my partners," he said.

"Where are they?"

"Prowling the theater district. Trying to get a line on Tyson."

"Good luck."

"Yeah, sure," Boros said. "Good luck."

## ELEVEN

Finding Charles Mueller's address in tiny Guttenberg had been a bewildering job, especially since Dane was disinclined to ask directions or call attention to himself in any way. And when he did spot the two-story frame house he made a careful circle of the block and then parked above it with his lights out.

His first impression was that the place was empty, that no one was inside. But a street lamp across the way caught a strange reflection in one of the windows over the large garage, and Dane was surprised to discover that every window was very heavily shuttered. Then, by staring intently, a faint glow of light could be detected around the shutter edges. Just a sliver, but enough to convince him that Charles Mueller was a man who liked his privacy. Nor was Mueller without air, for now Dane made out the silhouettes of three different air conditioners protruding from the walls of the building. There was nothing special about that, except that this was not what Dane would have called an air-conditioned neighborhood. Timothy was in the act of stepping from his car when another, a sleek new Chrysler, passed him and swung into Mueller's drive. Dane had a glimpse of two girls seated in the front seat beside the driver, and now he reclosed his door and waited. The garage doors swung open and the Chrysler rolled on inside. The doors swung shut and it was as if nothing had happened.

He gave the Chrysler five full minutes to come out of there again, then crossed the street on foot to have a closer look. The ordinary thing, Dane knew, would be to walk up and ring Mueller's front doorbell, find out what the man's connection was with Tyson and Carlo, and let events run their natural course. But so much of the unordinary had been happening these past forty-eight hours that the tall man was strongly persuaded to engineer the future along a pro-Dane bias.

So, with the .38 transferred to his outside pocket for easy use, and keeping always within the shadows, he made a thorough scout of the secretive place. There was a door in the back, solid-feeling and unresisting to the tentative pressure he put against it. That left him with only the single casement window, a narrow piece set at knee level on the far side of the house. Timothy went around to it, knelt down and put his ear against the glass. It was quiet on the other side. Using the .38 as a hammer he punched a quick hole in the window and listened again. Still quiet. He cracked around the edges of the hole, got it big enough to put his gloved fist through and pushed the black metal blinds aside. A moment later he had the window unlocked and swinging back on its hinges. Dane went through the opening feet first and let himself drop softly to the cement floor of the cellar. It was dark here, and Dane merely stood and waited for the adjustment. It came, and with it the discovery that he was among a great deal of bulky equipment. His hand traced the outline of a photoengraver's camera. Nearby was an electrotyper; farther on a small press.

A sudden sound made him raise his eyes involuntarily to the ceiling. It was the sound of a woman walking across a bare wooden floor in high heels. Then a piece of furniture was being moved, and within moments there was a great deal of activity overhead. What Dane wanted to do was stay right where he was and examine this compact little plant at length, but the sensible thing was to find out what he had to contend with from above. He made his way slowly to a staircase, and at the first landing he was able to look over a partition into the garage area where the Chrysler was parked. Assuring himself that it was empty, he continued on up until he came to a door closed against him.

*Be open*, he silently wished and it was. The handle turned in his hand and the door swung inward. This was a narrow corridor, darkened, but from the right came a great deal of light, powerful white light that was diffused for a wide area over the ceiling. It was all quiet to the left, and Timothy headed toward the lighted place, the sound of voices.

They came from a room, but not a conventional room. The walls, for one thing, stopped some six feet short of the ceiling. And they were sectioned off, hinged like the wild walls of a motion picture set. Timothy glanced above to a platform that itself looked down into the room. On it were two brightly burning kliegs. He continued on down the corridor, and as he had guessed, a ladder led aloft. He climbed it, then followed a narrow catwalk that brought him back to the platform.

"No, no, no!" said a man's voice; thick, guttural, heavy with German accent. "Turn to the camera!"

"Like this?" asked a girl.

"More so. Good! Now you, the blonde—come closer in. Now hold it. The blonde, smile. Now hold it...."

Dane edged out onto the platform and gazed down at the tableau below. The two girls, one a vivid redhead, the other a platinum blonde, lolled naked and inviting against a background of palm trees and sea. A brassiere and panties were tied to a pole and made to flutter in the breeze of an off-scene fan. Also off-scene, lounging boredly in a folding chair, was a man Dane recognized as Frank Rossi, the art dealer. Taking a picture of the girls was a gross, baldheaded man on a stepladder that raised him level with the propped-up camera.

"We got it," the cameraman said in his harsh Teutonic tones. "What's next, Mr. Rossi?"

Rossi pulled a slip from his breast pocket. "I got a customer for a peep shot. She's lying down in the bathtub and he's glamming her from the upstairs apartment."

"For that I use the platform—"

"The platform's taken," Dane announced, not needing to raise his voice. There was pandemonium. Both girls scrambled to their feet, screeching, and dashed for their kimonos as though Dane had actually invaded their privacy. Charles Mueller turned so violently that his thick elbow sent the expensive camera toppling to the hard floor. Frank Rossi came to his feet with an anguished moan, made as if to dart for the door.

"Hold it, Rossi!" Timothy called after him. The man kept going. The gun in Dane's hand spat fire, the slug pounded into the doorjamb just as Rossi's hand touched the handle. He stood as if suddenly frozen, and all at once the room was very still.

"I didn't want you to leave without the girls," Dane said to the pornographer then. "Get into your clothes, kids," he told them, and they were so anxious to quit the place that neither bothered to don underwear. They pulled skirts over their hips, sweaters over their breasts, hustled into woolen coats and were ready to leave.

"Now you can open that door," Timothy called down and Rossi was the first one through. The girls fled after him.

"Who—who are you?" Mueller asked, his face gray. "How did you get in here?"

"Stop drifting underneath the platform," Timothy said. "Move back where I can see all of you." The fat man obeyed quickly. "Now shove that stepladder over. I'm coming down." The ladder was put into position and Dane dropped to it nimbly, then to the floor of the studio.

"Let's go downstairs," Dane suggested.

"What are you going to do to me? I'm not a well man. My heart isn't so strong—"

"Your stomach is. Come on, *move!*"

Mueller moved, leading the way back to the corridor. At the head of the stairs that led below he switched on a light, and now as they descended Dane had a very brilliant view of the setup.

"What are you going to do to me?" Mueller asked again. "You let Rossi and the girls go. They're in this as much as me. More so. I only do what my clients order."

Spread on the make-up table beside the photoengraver was the artwork of Donna James that Tyson had delivered that afternoon.

"What client orders this stuff? Carlo or Tyson?"

"Carlo? I don't know any Carlo. Mr. Tyson publishes the magazine."

"Did you ever figure what he did with it, Mueller?"

The man spread his hands. "It's just like all the other ones," he said. "It's not my business what anybody does with the things I make for them—"

"You made plates on this artwork yet?" Dane asked, indicating the one on the table.

"Not yet. What are you doing?"

"I'm the new editor of *Info*," Dane explained, stripping the photos with the short-bladed engraver's gouge. "We've decided to suspend publication. Any objections?"

"No. It's all right with me. Anything."

"Hang out a shingle, Charlie," Dane advised him easily. "Go legitimate and live longer."

Mueller nodded, and when Timothy had satisfied himself that he had destroyed the layout he started on past the man toward the stairs. Mueller's hands closed around a heavy metal bar and he swung it viciously at the back of Dane's head. The fat man was vastly surprised in the next instant. The inviting target had ducked out of range, the club whooshed through resistless air, and then Dane's fist buried itself deep into Mueller's belly. His left hand chopped upward, flush against Mueller's jaw, and the man went down in an untidy heap.

"That's going to cost you," Timothy said, but it was doubtful if Mueller heard. Nearby was an extension telephone and now Dane dialed the operator. "Would you get me the Guttenberg police?" he asked her, and moments later was requesting some law. "I guess I want the vice squad," he said, "if you have one."

Two uniformed men and a Detective Sergeant Kovara responded. They entered via the garage Frank Rossi had left open in his haste and Dane laid out the operation very briefly.

Kovara looked down at the reviving Mueller in great consternation. "Him and me are lodge brothers," he said. "Who'd have figured him for making lewd art?"

"There ought to be plenty stashed around the place," Dane said. "And there's some fresh negatives inside the camera upstairs. The Manhattan squad will give you a hand picking up a dealer named Rossi...."

Kovara had his notebook out and Dane gave him the full name and address. "Appreciate it, friend," the detective said, "but I don't get your angle."

Timothy showed him the mutilated artwork. "Mueller's been helping some New York people spread a lot of unhappiness," he said. "Besides some miscellaneous extortion."

Kovara shook his head. "Right out of little Guttenberg," he said wonderingly. "Nobody in town will believe it."

"If you need me," Dane said, handing him a card, "I'll be available. Right now I'd like to get back across the river."

"You bet, Dane."

"And one favor, Sergeant. I'd like to keep myself out of it. Could you make it look like your arrest?"

Kovara cocked his head, then a broad smile spread across his face. "Sure," he said. "And thanks for that, too."

Dane walked away from that curious house with a certain swing to his wide shoulders, a bounce in his step. He knew he felt good because of the report he could make to Ralph Blodgett, but he was also aware of a keen anticipation in seeing Donna again. There would be time enough tomorrow to contemplate the mistakes. For now, his skull had ceased to throb, he felt loose, and it was as though there hadn't been a single foul-up during the entire job.

He returned to Manhattan almost exactly as he had come, doubling back from Broadway to park before the theater. The marquee was darkened now, and when he went backstage he was told that Blodgett had left. The doorman was not so certain about Donna James's whereabouts but directed him to her dressing room. A tall, warm-eyed, intriguingly dressed showgirl answered his knock with a highball in her hand.

"Is Donna James still here?" Timothy asked.

"No, Donna's not still here. She left with the elite, as they say."

"Do you know where she went?"

"You're the boyfriend, I hope," Shelley Bowers said impishly.

"Why?"

"Because Donna's a special friend of mine, and nothing's too good for my friends. You're not too good, are you?"

"No ..."

"Then come on in and have a drink."

"I think I'd better hunt up Donna."

"She's with Ralph Blodgett," Shelley said. "She's doing fine. Come on have a drink. I'm celebrating my landing a long-playing part."

"Show went off pretty good, did it?"

"Pretty good? Pretty *good?* We merely fractured an entire theater full of people, that's all. Here, hold my glass. I'll show you my second act dance. Back up a little."

"I'll catch the whole thing one of these nights. Any idea where Donna and Blodgett are?"

"What are you, anyhow, incorruptible or something? They went to Tony's. That's a block over and west of Eighth. Want me to go with you?"

"Suit yourself."

"You won't get me in the back of the cab and make an immoral suggestion, will you?"

"Nope."

"Then I might as well stay here. I'm waiting for my own john to come by, anyhow."

"So long," Timothy told her and left. He drove to the restaurant and went inside. A waiter led him to the private room where Blodgett's party was gathered and the producer greeted him enthusiastically, pressing a drink into his hand.

"Boy," shouted Mike Carhart across the room, "did you forget to duck!"

"What happened to you, Tim?" Blodgett asked.

"As Mike said—I forgot to duck. Where's Donna?"

"You missed her by ten minutes. All the excitement finally caught up with the girl and I sent her on home."

"That's too bad. I wanted her to know she can stop worrying about that magazine. It's all over, Mr. Blodgett."

"Well, that's wonderful!" Blodgett swung to the table. "You hear that?" he shouted. "We're rid of *Info* ...!"

There was a quick and happy response within the room. None of them had been safe from attack, all of them had awaited it defenselessly. Now Timothy found himself being congratulated noisily.

But Ralph Blodgett's voice came through.

"It's a shame," he said, "that Donna and Billy didn't stay—"

"Donna *and* Tyson?"

"Billy took her home. Why? What's the matter ...?"

Timothy was already turning, moving away swiftly.

"Dane! What's wrong ...?"

Mike Carhart caught up to him on the street. "Is there trouble? Is the kid in trouble?"

"Yes. You get to her apartment. If there's no answer, bust your way in—"

"Is Tyson mixed up with *Info?*"

"Right now he is *Info.* The last one left." Timothy slipped behind the wheel, and as Carhart hurried toward Eighth on foot the prayer was pounding through Dane's mind that the actor would find the girl safe in her own place. Dane's own destination was the hotel where he had had all his troubles, but even as he ran the red light and raced toward Seventh Avenue his anguished glance swept in all those things that accompany tragedy in the city: police cars turned in at the curb, the curious crowd that stands and watches, the blue-coated figures moving to and fro. Starkest of all, the ambulance waiting with its doors ajar. Dane remembered neither halting the car in the middle of the street nor pushing his way to the guarded entrance.

"Hey, buddy—you can't go in there!"

"Stop me." It was a murmur, unheard by the policeman. But the officer saw the strained face and Dane passed on through. More uniforms were bunched at the stairs, but they parted and the civilian went to the floor above. Now there was noise, actual shouting, and great confusion. That was the press, the irreverent photographers.

*"I gotta get one more good shot of her …!"*

*"C'mon, Lieutenant—for crissake!"*

*"… big story, damnit! The dame's an actress!"*

They stood in the doorway of Room 210, pushing and being pushed, swearing and being sworn at. Apparently they had arrived too soon in their radio-equipped cars. Apparently the almighty gods of Homicide West were demanding private use of the premises.

Dane started through. Strong fingers grabbed his forearm, turned him around. It was the detective, Boros, and he had reached out for Dane from a circle of reporters questioning him.

"I want to talk to you—"

"Later, Boros. Have you got Tyson yet?"

"Got him? Tyson is dead, Dane."

"Tyson …?"

The reporters came between the two tall men. Their voices clamored for information, demanded Dane's identification. Timothy looked steadily into Boros's face.

"The girl?" he asked. Boros could not hear the words but he read Dane's lips.

"She's inside," Boros shouted. "She's all right."

Dane spun like a fullback into the humanity blocking the room entrance, bored through it with the point of his shoulder and was abruptly inside, face to face with Boros's partner, Pat Herman.

"Where is she?"

"Next door with the doc. He doesn't want these newspaper wolves to get another crack at her."

"Can I go in?"

"You'd better. You're all she keeps talking about."

Dane went to the door that opened onto the adjoining room, glancing briefly at the sheet-covered form on the floor, at the third Homicide man, Carson, explaining something to a uniformed captain and an ambulance attendant. He pulled the door open.

"Timothy!"

Donna started to rise from the bed. The white-coated intern put both hands on her shoulders and eased her back.

"It was Billy Tyson, Timothy! He was the one—"

"I know. Did he hurt you, baby?"

"He went crazy. He said he wanted to explain something. He said that I'd understand. Then he put his fingers around my throat—"

"Easy," the young doctor told her. "Give the sedative a chance." He looked up at Dane. "She's had a bad time. I'm trying to get her to sleep."

Dane nodded, saw the blue-black marks on her slender neck where Tyson's hands had been.

"Try to sleep, Donna," he said softly, leaning down to press his palm against her cheek. "It's all over. *Info*, everything. All you have to do is sleep."

"Will you take me home?"

"Sure."

"Will you stay with me?"

"If you want me to."

"I want you to."

"Dane?" Boros called from the doorway and Timothy swung around. "Can you spare a minute?"

He nodded, said, "I'll be right back," to the girl and went back to 210.

"We need an identification of the corpse," Boros said, leading him to the sheeted figure. Carson pulled the sheet back from the face.

"Do you know him, Dane?"

"Slightly. His name is Billy Tyson."

"Occupation?"

"Actor's agent," Dane said.

"Okay, Captain?" Boros asked the uniformed precinct commander.

"Okay with me. Take him away." Another attendant joined the first and the re-covered body of Tyson was carried out of the place.

Timothy moved beside Boros. "Who got him?" he asked.

"Lou Carson. We split up, and Lou got a lead over at the Lambs Club that Tyson was probably at Blodgett's new play. He wanted to get a line on him, so he tailed him from the theater over to a restaurant—"

"Tony's."

"Yeah. Then he came out of the place hanging pretty close to the girl."

Lou followed them here and just did break in in time...."

"I had to shoot him," Carson said. "I never saw anything like it. He had her down on the bed and I couldn't break his grip. I beat on him with the barrel and he just kept squeezing harder. I knew the girl didn't have more than a few seconds left."

"You did what you had to do," Boros assured him. "Forget it now and go on home." He turned to Dane. "This job is about cleaned up, isn't it?"

"It is so far as I'm concerned," Timothy said, his attention on Lou Carson. "You did fine," he told the detective, extending his hand. Carson took it, nodding his head in acknowledgment of Dane's gratitude, then left. Boros was taken in tow by a reporter and Timothy returned to the next room.

The intern had his finger raised to his mouth. "Asleep," he whispered, coming to the door.

"What else does she need?"

"Very little. She's a pretty healthy specimen in case you don't know it."

"I know it."

"Somebody said she was an actress."

"That's right."

"You going to take care of her?"

"Yes," Timothy said and he thought he heard the intern murmur the word "Lucky" as he went past.

THE END

# The Root of His Evil
..................................................
## WILLIAM ARD

## CHAPTER ONE

That five-column picture buried in the fourth section of Miami's Sunday *Trib* was of more than passing interest to several people who seldom read a Florida newspaper, let alone the social notes.

The polite but concise caption read: VISITING LATIN DIGNITARY HONORED AT PALM BEACH BALL, and the five champagne toasting people in the photo were identified as Mr. and Mrs. Harland Burke, the hosts of the ball; Colonel Raphael Gomez, the guest of honor; and Mr. and Mrs. Luis Maximo. Colonel Gomez was further identified as Chief-of-Staff of his country's National Army, on a good-will visit, and Luis Maximo as the Consul stationed at Miami. The newspaper did not say—perhaps because such things are irrelevant to a Society Page editor, but nevertheless did not say—that Harland Burke was chairman of the board of the Burke Arms & Ammunition Corp.

*Photo by Preston* completed the written matter, and Mr. Preston was professionally pleased with the result, especially the highlights he caught on the Colonel's multi-medaled uniform and the symmetry of the raised champagne glasses, four of them extended toward the guest of honor, the Colonel modestly holding his own close to the top button of the royal blue tunic. Preston, wisely enough, had taken the picture very early in the evening (when everyone was still clear-eyed, and when there was still time to make the first edition), but if he had hung around the premises of the spacious Burke winter home, he would have got another shot of the host and his important guest that *Time* and *Life* would have bought at the premium rate. But that is hindsight and hardly justice to Mr. Preston who makes a very nice living on the Gold Coast without winning any Pulitzer awards.

As for Mrs. Burke's ball, that was the usual dull success most of them are. No one got really stinking, no one got pushed into the fountains, and every woman left with the same escort who'd brought her. The Luis Maximos, faced with the trip back down to Miami, got away in their chauffeured Imperial shortly after midnight. That began a general exodus, and at about one thirty Colonel Gomez bid his hostess a courtly good night and went upstairs to the room he was using for the weekend. An hour after that even the servants were asleep, and it was then that Harland Burke left his own bedroom and knocked very softly on Gomez's door. The Colonel had long since got out of the striking blue uniform, but surprisingly enough he was now dressed in a severe-looking black business suit, dark tie and civilian shirt. Burke, too, had changed from white tie and tails to gray flannel. Moreover, he carried a briefcase.

"I was afraid you'd gone to sleep," Gomez said in the crisp, American-sounding voice he had acquired at West Point—but hardly the tone of an officer and a gentleman with a generous host.

"Of course I didn't go to sleep," Burke said, bristling like a true board chairman.

"But you did have your good share of the whisky," Gomez told him rudely, and the accusation wilted Harland Burke.

"I'm perfectly all right," he protested. "After all, I'm expected to drink with my guests...."

"Is his car ready for us?" the Colonel broke in.

"It's waiting in the rear drive. We'll go down the back stairs and through the garages."

Burke led the way down the corridor, down the servants' stairway, through the garageway to a glistening black Fleetwood whose big motor purred expectantly. Two other men stepped from the shadows, large, menacing figures who loomed above the middle-sized Gomez and Burke.

"Which one is Burke?" asked a rough voice.

"I'm Harland Burke," he answered and a tiny flashlight shone on his face, lingered briefly and went out. "Gomez?"

"*Colonel* Gomez."

For all of that he got the flashlight identification. And something extra.

"Spread your arms."

"Spread my arms? Are you being ridiculous?"

"Hold 'em out wide."

"I will not!"

"Raphael ..." Harland Burke said plaintively, and Gomez darted him a stormy look. But then, despite an angry harrumphing, he lifted his arms from his side and submitted to a thorough search. His frisker removed a mean-looking sneak automatic from its holster at his belt.

"Now you," Burke was told and he submitted to a search that produced no weapon but relieved him of an expensive lighter.

"What are you taking that for?"

"We saw your catalogue, Mr. Burke. You make guns out of everything."

"Now why would I have a gun?"

"Why does your pal have one? Okay, get in the car." Burke started to obey. Gomez held back, truculently. Burke turned to him. "It's just the way Cashman does things," he said in a cajoling voice. "Try to humor him."

But the Chief-of-Staff of the National Army was no man to humor anybody.

"What am I doing with this trash?" he demanded.

"Suit yourself, buddy," the rough voice said irreverently and both of them moved toward the car.

"Raphael—this may be your last opportunity."

Burke's words had a catalytic effect. The Colonel squared his shoulders and marched briskly to the Cadillac, opened the rear door and settled himself inside with a great show of importance. Burke followed, found room for himself in the corner, and the black car whisked down the driveway and swung south.

Minutes went by, each second more uncomfortably silent. Finally, Gomez broke it.

"What did you say he was—this Cashman?"

"He's an entrepreneur," Burke said, and it was as though he didn't know what that was, either.

"How does he make his money?"

"He has—ah—various interests."

"Like what?"

"Well, he dabbles in real estate. And I understand he owns a very successful night club down in Miami Beach."

"The movement is gathering some strange supporters. What does your friend expect to get for his money?"

"I have never represented Cashman as my friend," Burke said quickly. "And as for what he expects—that's why we're going to meet him."

The Colonel grunted, lapsed into a brooding silence again. The high-powered car sped through the night, Route 1 practically its own private raceway, then slowed on the outskirts of Delray Beach and finally halted before a darkened and apparently empty roadhouse. The two up front opened the doors for their riders.

"He's inside," they were told, and as they approached closer to the place, a dim light could be seen through the drawn blinds. At a knock the door was opened. Gomez, Burke and the driver entered. The fourth one posted himself outside.

There were three others already there: the doorman, one who stood with arms folded across his chest at the bar, and the massive, vigorous-looking man seated at the round table in the center of the room. His attention was completely on Gomez, hawkishly, and there seemed to be an instantaneous contest of wills.

"How are you, Mr. Cashman?" Harland Burke said tentatively.

"Fine," Johnny Cashman said, never letting his gaze waver.

"I'd like you to meet Colonel Raphael Gomez. Colonel, this is John Cashman."

Cashman didn't stir from the chair. Gomez held his ground. From a distance of ten feet they looked each other over—the big, bluff, arrogant-faced American with close-cropped steel-gray hair; the squat, beady-eyed, black-haired, olive-skinned Latin with the trace of Indian ancestry in the flat nose and high cheekbones.

"Sit down, Colonel," Cashman said, and it was practically a command. Then, as if counseled by a more prudent thought: "Make yourself comfortable, *amigo*. It's a late hour to be on your feet."

Gomez winced at the patronizing *amigo*, but he moved toward the table. Harland Burke got there first, pulled out a chair deferentially for the military man, sat down in another.

"The hour is late," Burke said to both of them. "Suppose we get down to business."

"Fine," Cashman said, smirking broadly at Gomez. "I hear you're in the revolution business, Colonel."

"It's hardly a business," Burke said with a nervous glance at the easily combustible Latin. "Colonel Gomez is ready to lay down his life to liberate his countrymen."

"Yeah, sure," Cashman said. "But he wants me to lay down the money—"

Gomez's fat hand came down sharply on the tabletop.

"That's enough!" he shouted, shoving his chair back and rising. "Burke, you are a fool even to think I could associate with the likes of this insolent ass. We're leaving!"

"Sit down and relax, johnny," Cashman told him tightly. "Nobody leaves before I do."

"Please, Raphael," Burke pleaded. "Mr. Cashman is the key to all your plans. Believe me."

"Believe the man, Colonel, but don't get me down on you. You're here with your hand out, both of them, and if you're really serious about knocking your pal out of business, you damn well better treat the moneyman nice."

With a great effort Gomez got his volatile temper under control. He fished a cigar from inside his coat, lit it with a flourish and blew a cloud of blue smoke.

"Mr. Cashman," he said, "do you *really* have a million American dollars to spend?"

Cashman's square jaw jutted forward. "A *million?*" he echoed. "Who the hell's talking about a million?" The man's craggy, formidable face whirled to Harland Burke. "You said five hundred thousand. You said that would swing it."

Burke seemed to shrink. "There—ah—have been some—ah—

unforeseen difficulties," he stammered. "The—ah—Colonel's timetable has been changed. Events must move at a quicker pace. For my factory to meet the new schedule we have to work overtime, pay premium rates for everything connected with the operation."

"I checked you out, Burke," Cashman said. "You're the chairman of the goddamned board of a company that's hanging on the ropes...."

"That's an outrageous lie! Burke Arms & Ammunition is in first-rate shape—"

"You're in hock, brother. You need this deal to stay the hell out of jail."

"Ridiculous!" Burke protested, but there was too much worry and no conviction at all.

"That's very interesting," Colonel Gomez said, turning his gimlet gaze on the munitions maker. "I wondered why a man with such a show of worldly goods could grovel as you have. Well, now!"

"Get the price back in line, Burke," Cashman said. Burke shook his head. He relieved himself of a deep sigh.

"I am in debt," he said meekly. "The company is in trouble. But even at a million—with the quantities the Colonel wants, the speed-up—even at a million the profit is very small."

"Then you cut down," Cashman told Gomez. "Buy what you need for the job. Don't get fancy."

"Do not tell me my business," Gomez snarled at him. "I am Chief-of-Staff of the Army. I know what I need to defeat that army."

Cashman shrugged. "I've got half a million bucks to throw into this deal. I'm thinned out."

"And I must have what I ordered from Burke. To the last cartridge."

"Then it's up to you, pal," Cashman told the board chairman. "Cut your price or forget the whole thing."

Burke passed a slim hand wearily over his eyes.

"The best I can do," he said then, "the absolute minimum, is seven hundred and fifty thousand."

It sounded sincere, as though the man really meant it. Cashman stared at him sourly, stroked his beard-stubbled chin. Gomez inhaled on his cigar, sent another cloud of smoke into the room.

"It is possible," he said, "just barely possible, that I will have air support from a nation friendly to my cause. It is a dangerous gamble, but I may be able to reduce my requisition by a hundred thousand dollars. I would rather risk that than the chance of receiving inferior arms."

Cashman studied both of them, made up his mind.

"Then it looks like the Secretary of the Treasury has to dig up an extra quarter mil. How soon do you need it?"

"Within a week," Burke said eagerly.

"Oh, come on ..."

"A week, Cashman," Gomez told him. "There has been, as you call it, a leak in our plans. I still have the accursed dictator's confidence, but with every passing twenty-four hours I must take some new person of influence into my confidence. Some of my aides are already suspect ..." Another thought came to him and he turned to Harland Burke. "Which reminds me—what in the world possessed you to invite Luis Maximo tonight? He is not only the most suspicious man I have ever met but my greatest personal enemy."

"Agnes handled the invitations," Burke said defensively. "I suppose she thought that the Consul should be properly there."

"The man is a toad," Gomez said. "We must watch him very carefully ..."

"Okay, boys, let's get back to business," Cashman said edgily. "Settle these other little details on your own time."

Gomez eyed him distastefully.

"Perhaps that's a good suggestion, Mr. Cashman. Getting back to *business*, what exactly do you expect for your contribution?"

"You mean Burke didn't tell you?"

"No, he didn't," Gomez answered, and they both looked at Burke again, impaled him mercilessly.

"Well, tell him," Cashman said.

"I'm not—ah—completely sure what you do want."

"It's simple enough," Cashman said. "I'm buying the gambling in your country."

"*Una más?*" Gomez asked, leaning forward, so surprised that he lapsed unconsciously into Spanish.

"The gambling," Cashman repeated. "The bolita, the horses, the crap games on the docks, the tables in all the live spots—"

"But you're in real estate. I thought your interest was to develop property."

Cashman shook his head impatiently. "That real estate collar is my front with Uncle Sam. A tax dodge."

"But what is it you do? How do you come to have three quarters of a million dollars?"

"I'm a bookmaker. What the hell did you think I was?"

Gomez began laughing, so hard that he choked on his cigar smoke. "A *bookmaker!*" he said. "You take bets...."

Cashman came out of his chair to loom head and shoulders over the Colonel.

"I wouldn't take any bets on you right now," he said and Gomez lost his laughter.

"Gentlemen, gentlemen," Harland Burke broke in. "We're here in a mutual cause. Let's not lose sight of our objective."

"I'm never laughed at," Johnny Cashman said. "There's nothing funny about me or my business."

"A thousand pardons," the Colonel said with little feeling. "Just how would you go about 'buying' the gambling in my country?"

"I run an organization called East Coast Associates," Cashman said, settling down in the chair again. "We'd set up shop in your capital and run the games on a percentage basis. Say ten cents on the dollar."

"And how much do you plan to make?"

"Oh, I guess I'll get my investment back."

"You will? At ten cents on the dollar?"

"It's a risk, naturally."

"But what of those people already in control of the gambling?"

"You'll take care of the competition, *El Presidente*," Cashman told him blandly. "You'll lean on them."

"I see," Gomez said and thought about it for a long moment. Then he nodded his dark head. "All right, Mr. Cashman. We will work together. Burke will have his money within a week?"

"A week to ten days."

"Good."

Cashman walked them to the door, stood watching from the entrance as they climbed into the black Fleetwood and went speeding toward Palm Beach.

# 2

Cashman turned to the man who had never stirred from his place at the bar. "Did you hear him, Shag?" he asked, and there was a ravenous triumph ringing in his voice.

"I heard everything."

"Will I get my money back! Will I!"

Shag was short and round, serious-faced and spaniel-eyed—that placid, fiercely loyal type that the Cashmans always have hanging around in one capacity or another.

"You will, Johnny," Shag said judiciously. "But as of right now you're light a quarter million."

"I won't be," he said. "Not after I shake up a few delinquents." A sudden thought made him laugh. "I heard Stix Larsen checked into the Americana this afternoon. Get him on the phone, Shag."

"From here?"

"Why not? I own the dump, don't I?"

The other man walked around and behind the bar meekly, dialed the phone on the shelf below the register.

"Mr. Larsen's suite," he told the hotel operator. A woman answered the phone, her voice shrill with liquor.

"C'mon up, whoever you are!"

"Put Stix Larsen on the phone, please."

She giggled. "Stix is very, *very* busy. Aren't you, honey?"

"Tell him Johnny Cashman is calling," Shag said.

"He says to tell you Johnny Cashman is calling," she shouted. "Who the hell cares …?" But her raucous voice fell away at something unseen happening at the other end of the line. The next speaker was a man.

"This is Stix," he said nervously. "Johnny?"

Shag handed the phone to Cashman.

"How you doing, Stix?"

"Pretty good, Johnny. Took a licking in that goddam pro football. How're you, pal?"

"I'm in a box, hotshot. Got to pack you in."

"How much do I owe you?"

"You're on the books for seventy-five big ones, kid. You got hurt bad in the Rose Bowl, remember?"

"Christalmighty—is it that much?"

"That much? What's seventy-five G's to an operator like you?"

Larsen laughed hollowly. "Tell you what, Johnny. I want to get down twenty on the third at Hialeah Tuesday. The number five horse, Druid—"

"First send over the seventy-five," Cashman told him. "Then we'll do business on your horse."

"You can carry me till *Tuesday*, can't you?"

"No."

"You're all of a sudden, Johnny. I'm kind of strapped myself—"

"Get it up, Stix. Get it to me tomorrow."

"*Tomorrow!*"

"I only call once," Cashman said. "After that, watch out for yourself."

"Yeah, Johnny. Okay. I'll have it for you tomorrow."

Cashman cut the connection with a drop of his finger.

"Hamp Rohara's back in Tampa," he told Shag then. Shag made the cross-state connection, and when Cashman ended the conversation, there was another ninety thousand dollars promised for payment.

"Now call New York," he told Shag. "There's one particular sonofabitch I want to hit hard."

"The singer?"

"The singer. Karl phoned about him again tonight."

"He's bothering your girlfriend?"

"Making a nuisance of himself."

Shag dialed the long-distance operator.

"I want the Riviera night club in New York City," he said. "Johnny Cashman calling Mr. Buddy Lewis...."

## CHAPTER TWO

The entrance to the Riviera is on Broadway, but Dane's instructions were to use the stage door on Fifty-first, and he headed around the corner with a passing glance at the billboard advertising the night club's current show. Buddy Lewis was the featured attraction, and grouped around a big picture of the singer were the other acts: a trio, a magician, a long-legged dancer in the act of unpinning her skirt, and a line of silk-stockinged show girls.

The stage door was attended and, when Dane explained that he had an appointment with Buddy Lewis, he was escorted up a flight of stairs to the door of a dressing room. Without knocking, the attendant turned the knob and pushed the door inward, surprising a man and woman who were standing very close to each other inside the room.

"Forgot you two was in here," the attendant said, so impudently that it was plain he didn't care whether he was believed or not. "This fella has a date with Mr. Lewis."

The other man had put more space between himself and the woman and after staring at the doorman for a long, unloving moment he raised his eyes to Dane.

"Timothy Dane?"

"Yes."

"I talked to you this afternoon. Bernie King. Come on in." His voice sharp and direct, each word crisply spoken, bitten off. Physically he was of medium height, chunky, with a strong, square face and dark hair that was graying at the temples. He had identified himself to Dane on the telephone as Buddy Lewis's manager. "This is Karen, Dane, Buddy's wife."

"How do you do?" they both said, but only Dane smiled. Karen Lewis's face intrigued the tall man, made him think of a cat that is always a little hungry, never content enough to purr. She was a willowy type, small-breasted and all but hipless, with black hair that she wore straight and close-cropped.

"Buddy will be along in a few minutes," Bernie King was saying.

"You've caught his act, haven't you?"

"On television," Dane said, taking his quiet gaze from the woman. "Not in person."

King turned in his abrupt fashion and walked to the far wall. A panel was set in it and he slid it back. Dane joined him and found himself looking down over the nightclub floor. Buddy Lewis, slim and straight in a blue-black tuxedo sang energetically to a large semi-circle of solidly filled tables while the brassily pretty show girls paraded around him in cadence with the tune.

"That must be work," Bernie King said, "because he pays an awful lot of taxes on it."

"*Owes*," Karen Lewis said behind them and Dane thought he had never heard so much derision crowded into just one word. It seemed to echo around his head, dripping its poisonous scorn.

"Okay, okay," King said a little wearily. "We'll get the boy straightened out on that angle, too. But first things first."

Down below, Lewis finished the number and walked out from under the spotlight to enthusiastic applause. There was no encore. Instead, an MC came on, raised his arms over his head for quiet, then turned to his left.

"And now," he said, "for her final appearance at the Riviera this season—the indescribable Lissa!" A tom-tom began to beat a quick rhythm, nothing more, and the long-legged girl from the poster swept onto the scene, swept all around it lithely, with exquisite grace—and whereas a woman's face had caught Dane's lively interest minutes ago, now all his attention was for two luxuriantly curved thighs and as pleasantly shaped a derriere as he could remember seeing since summertime.

Then the panel in the wall was closed, without forewarning, and Bernie King turned him around by the arm.

"A word," the older man said gravely. "That belongs to Johnny Cashman, sequins and all."

"The gambler?"

"Gambler! He changes money. Yours. More about Cashman in a minute. You want a drink of something?"

"Thanks, but I just had dinner."

"I didn't and I would," Karen told Bernie King. With that he went in one direction, toward the portable bar; she in another, to Dane's side.

"So you liked Lissa?" she asked, her voice low, competitive.

"Nice-looking girl," Dane answered, not prepared for such intensity.

"And unspoiled, wouldn't you say?"

He looked quizzical.

"Just one of those sweet, wholesome bitches," Karen Lewis said, and Dane looked over the top of her head to the opening door. Buddy Lewis came into his dressing room, unsmiling, followed by a short, round, baldheaded man carrying a briefcase.

"You really belted them out tonight, kiddo," Bernie King told the singer heartily.

"How the hell would you know?"

"Karen and I had the best seats in the house."

"I bet you did," Lewis said, crossing to the bar and pouring whisky from a decanter into a tumbler. He sipped from it, savoring the bouquet, then tossed off the entire contents of the glass thirstily. He repeated the business, amid a strained sort of silence, then gazed over the rim of the glass at Dane.

"Is this the errand boy?" he asked.

"Timothy Dane, Buddy," Bernie King said. "The bank recommended him."

"Those grubbing usurers. He's bonded, I hope."

"Now, look," King said. "You're in a nasty little jam. Dane, here, is going to fix things. Let's all be nice and friendly …"

"How much you going to take me for, friend?" Buddy Lewis asked and Dane smiled at him, a wintry, wolfish grin that made the singer's tartness seem adolescent.

"You're one up on me already," he said quietly. "I don't even know what this is all about."

Karen Lewis laughed harshly. "What else could it be with Buddy but money?"

"You haven't missed any meals lately, have you?" Lewis asked, switching the attack to his wife with obvious relish. "Not down to your last monogrammed French pants yet, are you?"

"But I can't go near Bergdorf's, Saks or Cartier—"

"Try Macy's. Pay cash, pay less."

"Cash?" she echoed. "Seems to me I did see something called cash once—"

"Kids, kids," Bernie King broke in. "You're on camera." The little man with the briefcase cleared his throat embarrassedly and only Dane seemed unperturbed by the marital byplay. He enjoyed the rumpus, especially the woman's cold fury, the stiletto slimness of her high-fashioned body as she gave back as good as she got. That one, he decided neutrally, would make cohabitation a lively business.

Buddy Lewis was something of an oddball, himself. From the poster on Broadway and the glimpse of him on the nightclub floor, Dane had guessed he and the singer were of an age. But that was an illusion. At the close quarters of this dressing room, with its unflattering lights, Lewis's face was skillfully made up to resemble a man in his early thirties rather than his actual mid-forties. His steady gaze was also deceptive, because it could be broken, and even while it held fast there was a queer expression behind the eyes, as though some vital part of his attention was elsewhere—and elsewhere was a place where Buddy Lewis would dearly love to be.

But the nastiness was apparently sincere. The sneering, sarcastic, superego was no affectation. For some reason that Dane had yet to discover, Lewis considered himself pretty hot stuff.

Bernie King's commanding voice had worked a ceasefire and as Karen went to claim the drink waiting for her atop the bar, Dane glanced down at his watch, half restless, half bored, wondering what "nasty little jam" he was supposed to settle. Paternity suit? Divorce action? Statutory rape? Compromising picture on the verge of being peddled to a scandal rag....

"I mentioned Johnny Cashman a few moments ago," he heard Bernie King saying to him. King had taken a seat. "You identified him as a gambler—"

"Lousy crook," Lewis said, hoisting his third straight one in as many minutes.

King paused, annoyed, then resumed. "You ever had any direct contact with the man, Dane?"

"Nope."

"Know of any reasons why you'd rather not?"

"I like gamblers," Dane told him.

"Oh, fine!" Lewis said. "You say the bank recommended him?"

Against his better nature Dane found that now he was getting an edgy feeling about the singer. He put his hands behind his back, leaned his shoulders against the wall. That, as usual, relaxed the big man, restored his perspective of things, made him see the folly of anger.

"If I were you," he said easily to Buddy Lewis, "I'd keep my yap shut."

There was a peculiar, echoing quiet then. The singer's handsome under jaw fell open, his eyes blinked. His wife smiled.

"Say something, darling," she said, her voice husky with malicious enjoyment, but when her husband seemed about to speak out rashly, Bernie King overrode him.

"Goddamit, *I'll* say something! The bank did not recommend Dane, Buddy, they *insisted* on him. That is a condition of the loan. You can take it," the manager said crisply, "or you can leave it."

Lewis shrugged negligently, a broad, negative gesture designed to put him above and beyond all this. A movement of his shoulders beneath the extravagantly tailored jacket of the three-hundred-dollar tuxedo that tried to say he couldn't care less about Bernie King, Timothy Dane, a bank or the business at hand. It was their problem, not his.

"This is your problem," Bernie King said, obviously having been exposed to that shrug before. "I want to help. I think I am helping. But it's not me that Johnny Cashman has his hooks into, Buddy. It's you."

"Drink, anyone?" Lewis said facetiously, its smartness falling flat.

"Thanks," Dane said, pushing himself away from the wall, striding toward the other man at the bar. His contrariness was something he had never been able to explain to himself, this swift, unreasoning, about-face of attitudes, a purely instinctive siding with anybody in trouble beyond his depth.

Dane reached for a bottle of rye, poured out a sociable ounce-plus, added ice and water and pretended not to notice that Buddy Lewis was studying him intently. He swung around, the glass snug in his broad fist, and spoke to Bernie King.

"How much does Buddy owe Cashman?" he asked.

"Okay," King said, darting a nervous glance that touched all their faces, came to rest on Dane. "Okay. Two hundred thousand dollars."

Dane took another pull at his drink, took refuge in it for a startled moment.

"I heard you say it," he said then. "But how do you lose two hundred thousand?"

Buddy Lewis laughed. "You have to work at it," he said. "Gambling is not a game."

"Buddy worked at it," Bernie King said, "but he kept the details to himself. Oh, we all knew he was gambling pretty heavy—"

"To put it mildly," Karen Lewis said.

"You never have any trouble with the profits," her husband said. "It's the losses that annoy you."

"Not as much as they annoy your friend Cashman," she said.

"That's about the gist of it, Dane," King said. "Cashman is making threatening noises."

"He's stymied here," Dane said. "Gambling debts aren't collectible in New York."

"Miami is a different proposition. Cashman makes his own law down there."

"Then spend the winter in Arizona," Dane suggested, but Bernie King shook his head.

"That's the rub," he said. "Buddy has signed contracts for two long dates in Miami. If he doesn't sing there, he doesn't sing anywhere."

"I open at the Chez three nights from now," Buddy Lewis added.

"Which doesn't give you much time."

"Time for what?" Dane asked.

"To go down and see Cashman," King answered. "Make a deal with him."

"How much do I have to deal with?"

"One hundred thousand. It's absolutely all we could borrow, what with Buddy's tax headache."

"And the bank knows what the money is for?"

"The bank and the Fedelis Insurance Company. It's some bird there named Joe Spencer who tossed your name into the deal."

"He would."

"There's a Fedelis policy involved as collateral. This Spencer talks as if he wants Buddy to make quite a few more payments on it."

"That's Spencer," Dane agreed. "But what about Cashman? Does he know he's getting half his money?"

King shook his head. "Buddy didn't mention this little trouble he was in until yesterday. I'm afraid relations between our side and Cashman are a little strained …"

"Don't mind me," Karen Lewis broke in unexpectedly. "Tell the man about the pass Buddy made at that belly dancer—"

"Pass, hell!" Lewis protested. "We work in the same show—am I supposed to give her the back of my hand?"

"Cashman's watchdog threw you out of her dressing room."

"That's a miserable lie!"

"Twice, darling."

"Where are you from, anyhow? The D.A.'s office?"

"Cashman, for—Christ's—sweet—sake!" Bernie King said sharply. "Let's stick to Cashman." King was angry now, and his stormy voice silenced the combatants. The manager ignored them both, turned to Dane.

"Come on outside," he said. "Let's finish this in peace."

Out they went, into the corridor, followed by the quiet little man with the briefcase.

"The dancer is a complication," King said there, his tone low and confidential, worried. "From what I can make out, Cashman was willing to carry Buddy on the books indefinitely until he heard about the pass he made at Lissa. Then—*crunch!* Get it up in seven days or don't come near Miami—" King broke off to turn around and see what was distracting the tall man's attention. It was the selfsame Lissa, ascending the stairs to her own dressing room, enclosed in a blood-red silk robe that trailed to the floor. She was followed by a maid who held the various items of costume that had been discarded during the act and a burly, hard-faced character whose very manner of walking was a loud warning to beware, not to trespass.

And because of the red robe Dane was free to look at the girl's face, her nice-looking, nicely proportioned face with its wide-set eyes and good-humored mouth, all of it framed by auburn-colored hair that hung almost to her shoulders and twinkled to the lights from the ceiling overhead.

"Keep right on staring," Bernie King said in an undertone. "Ask that goon to clobber you good."

Lissa and the maid swept into the room. The bodyguard posted himself stolidly before the door that was closed at his back. There was nothing about him that interested Dane and he lowered his gaze to Bernie King again.

"Don't do it," King said. "Just for what you're thinking you're in trouble." He swung to the baldhead. "The envelopes, Felix."

Felix opened the briefcase, took out a thick manila envelope and a thinner white one. He handed them to King.

"Two hundred for you and a ticket on the train," King said, extending the white one. Then, almost reluctantly, he placed the thick envelope in Dane's hand.

"One hundred thousand dollars," he said with reverence.

Dane slipped both of them into his jacket.

"You said train?"

"The planes are booked solid. I laid out damn near double for your compartment. Now about the job. I have a reservation for you at the Golden Shores. When you get there call the office of East Coast Associates. That's Cashman's front. Tell whoever answers that you want to talk about Buddy Lewis's bill. What happens from then on is up to you. I don't even want to hear about it. Just make sure you get Buddy's markers, canceled by Johnny Cashman ..." He was interrupted a second time, looked around again in the direction of Lissa's dressing room. A dispute was aborning there, involving two fresh-faced, sport-jacketed youths loaded down with double armfuls of roses, light-hearted with liquor—and the surly, single-minded watchdog. They wanted to present their flowers in person, a natural enough thing, but he shook his head, said something tough out of the corner of his mouth. One of the lads didn't take him seriously, tried to reach around him to knock on the door. The bodyguard reacted swiftly, viciously. He drove his fist hard and deep into the boy's unprotected stomach, jackknifed his slender body and slammed him into the wall with a sickening sound. The second boy shouted something, defiantly, found himself jerked forward by the lapels, felt a thick knee jammed expertly into his groin.

He collapsed, clutching his middle.

"*Dane*—stay out of it!"

Bernie King's urgent command went unheeded as the tall man moved down the corridor, a kind of expectancy in his stride, eagerness. The thug swung to him, sized up the new competition knowingly and put a used-looking blackjack into his hand. There was keenness in him, too, as if the brief and easy violence had only whetted his desire to inflict some real hurt.

Dane saw that in the man's dull face and he smiled. Smiled and seemed to be walking gallantly and foolishly into a fight-finishing swipe from the murderous blackjack. His right shoulder dipped, telegraphing the punch, hiding the blurred motion of his left leg as he lashed it forward. The tip of his shoe struck the other man's shinbone, his heel ground into an instep. The thug screamed his misery and all forgotten was the blackjack. Now Dane straightened, threw the right hand, followed with a left that had shoulder and leverage behind it. The punch spun the man's head around, knocked him down and out against the dressing room door.

The door swung open and Dane and the dancer stood looking at each other a little foolishly over the body of her collapsible guard.

"Nobody should be that hard to see," Dane said then.

"What?"

"These kids have some flowers for you."

"Well, gee, bring 'em in. I'm crazy about flowers."

Dane turned away, helped her manhandled admirers to their feet, gathered the roses and stuffed them into their arms. They were both still badly shaken, ill-looking.

"Come on in," Lissa told them cheerfully. "You, too," she added to Dane, and there was a fine shade of difference in the two invitations.

Dane eased the unconscious man out of the doorway and was starting inside after the boys when Bernie King called his name sharply.

"What's the matter?"

"Oh, nothing! Nothing at all!" the manager exploded. "Move right in. A fat lot of help you'll be to us with Cashman!"

With that Lissa came into the corridor.

"What about Cashman?" the girl asked.

"Cashman? Who said anything about Cashman?"

"You did, Bernie." She swung to Dane. "What was he talking about?" she demanded, but King wasn't going to let him answer.

"Peace, doll," he said. "Let there be peace and no misunderstandings. Oh, Christ—now look who's with us again."

They all looked to the bodyguard, who was climbing groggily to his feet, moving his head around to clear the cobwebs.

"Let's get out of here, Dane," King said worriedly. "That ape won't stand still for you twice tonight."

Also worried was Lissa. "Maybe you'd better take those boys out of here," she said to Dane. "Karl is a very bad actor."

"Tell him to behave himself," Dane said reasonably. "Stop pushing people around."

"Tell him? If he'd do anything *I* told him he wouldn't even be here."

Dane considered that, saw she meant it. He stepped around her, walked to the hoodlum and closed his big hand on the man's upper arm.

"We just had a vote, Karl," he said quietly. "Everybody wants you to go home."

"*I'm gonna lay you open!*"

"Some other time, kid." The fingers tightened imperceptibly, enough to pinch the large nerve above the elbow. Karl's eyes shut tight, involuntarily, and it wasn't so much the paralyzing pain shooting through the right side of his body but the promise of what it could become.

"Pick 'em up, Karl, and lay 'em down," Dane said persuasively, guiding him to the stairs. He gave him a little push then, not hard, and Karl had to scramble to keep his footing. Halfway down the steps the hoodlum halted his descent and would have started up again until he discovered he would have to resume the argument one-handed. Dane apparently knew that, for he was already retracing his steps to the wide-eyed and waiting Bernie King and Lissa.

"Suckered him again, by God," King said. "You're a pistol."

"But what did you say to him?" Lissa asked.

"Just trade talk," Dane said, holding her eyes for a moment before swinging to King. "When does that train leave?" he asked him.

"In one hour. You better get packing."

"Train?" the red-haired girl said and they looked at each other again.

"You want to come along?"

"Dane!"

"I know, King. I know. This is Johnny Cashman's girl."

"Then why the hell don't you act like it?"

"Because she doesn't," Dane told him simply, grinning at Lissa. "Know anybody named Cashman?" he asked her.

The warm light went out of her eyes and she glanced away from him.

"Afraid I do," she answered. "Dane? Is that who you are?"

"Timothy."

They spoke as if they were alone, and Bernie King fidgeted under the heavy scent of musk filling the air.

"That hour is shrinking fast," he said out of his irritation. Dane nodded.

"I ought to be back in a week," he told the girl.

She shook her head. "I'll be long gone. Won't play New York again until next September."

"My luck," he said and King pulled him around.

"Your luck is going to get a lot worse if you don't lay off," King warned him angrily. "Go pack a bag and get on that train."

## 2

It wasn't a week that Johnny Cashman was likely to forget. He had thrown the hook into Buddy Lewis, and that had felt good. Stix Larsen had come up with the seventy-five big ones. That had been a good start on the quarter million extra that Harland Burke needed.

But late last Monday night Cashman had heard the first glimmering of the trouble. A harassed-looking Burke had driven all the way from Palm to the big house in Coral Gables—not trusting his bad news to the telephone—and told him that the Colonel had come a cropper in his own country. The munitions man had seen the Latin off on his plane in the morning but had been unable to phone him all afternoon.

"Then I got a call," Burke said. "From Luis Maximo."

"Who?"

"He's the Consul here in Miami."

"Oh, yeah. Gomez doesn't like him."

"It's very mutual. And Maximo seems to have won their long battle."

"If you've got something to say," Cashman told him impatiently, "for crissake say it!"

"Maximo knows our plans," Burke said. "He told me that the Colonel was arrested as he stepped off the plane. He also threatened me—told me to stop interfering in their affairs. He told me to pass the warning along to you...."

"Are you telling me the deal is off?" Cashman demanded. "That Gomez queered it?"

"I'm reporting everything as I know it...."

"You boobs! You pair of stupid, goddamn jerks!"

"Now, wait a minute, Cashman—"

"*Wait?* I've been waiting for a setup like this my whole life. Don't say 'wait' to me."

"This is a blow to both of us," Burke said. "I need that order desperately."

"Peanut money," Cashman said scornfully. "I'd have done that much four times every year."

"Really?" the financier asked. "Well, listen. That isn't our only market. Nicaragua is in ferment, there's talk of revolution in the Dominican Republic. You and I, Cashman, could go into this thing on a large scale. Almost all of South America is restless—"

"You and I," Cashman repeated. "A kind of road show?"

Burke nodded eagerly. "The possibilities are limitless. Costa Rica, Argentina—why we might even find customers in Bermuda and Nassau. The English government is in no shape—"

"Get lost," Cashman told him. "You're going off your rocker."

"I've never been more serious in my life," Burke said with the desperation of a man going down for the last time. "There's millions to be made out of the present world conditions—"

Cashman's dark scowl stopped him.

"So long, little man," the gambler said. "Pleasant dreams." Burke had left him then, but early the next morning—Tuesday—he had been on the phone.

"I've been in touch with our friend," he said, new hope and excitement crackling along the wire. "His supporters helped him escape."

"Good for them," Cashman said with no enthusiasm.

"He's set up headquarters in the mountains. He wants to make a formal declaration of war ..."

"What the hell do I care?"

"What do you *care?* He's got to have the—the merchandise we talked about."

"And how are you supposed to get it to him?"

"They're in complete control in the south. His forces control the big port. He's been promised air support for the safe delivery of the shipment."

"I'll think it over and call you back."

"Speed is essential," Burke said. "I must get word to him quickly."

Cashman broke off the conversation, spent the rest of that morning brooding over the proposition. Even the first plan, with the Colonel controlling the situation as the army boss—even that had been loaded with risks and unknowns. Now it was riskier still—throwing all that money to some ragtag mountain army, getting the guns to them through the back door.

And then had come the call that thickened the Irish in him, made up his mind.

"My name is Maximo, Mr. Cashman, and I'll be brief. Do not get involved in any attempt to help the traitor Gomez. He is accused of a grave crime against my country, and anyone—anyone—who continues to support his crimes will be dealt with very harshly."

"You sound worried, pal. Gomez got you on the run?"

"Gomez is living out his last hours. He will be flushed out of his rathole before nightfall."

"The way I hear it, he's running his own show in the south."

"He runs nothing. Stick to the things you know, Cashman. Good-bye."

Cashman sent for the reliable Shag, dispatched him to Palm Beach with word for Burke that he was back into the deal and a down payment of three hundred thousand to get the wheels moving. That was shortly after noon. At about six o'clock, when he was having his first Martini before dinner, the bomb came through the big picture window.

It burst through the thin plate glass, rolled still smoking across the white rug, kept rolling beneath the outsized divan near the piano and exploded. Cashman was lifted bodily out of his deep-seated chair and thrown approximately six feet away. The Filipino houseman, who was in the act of leaving the room, was catapulted into the foyer. The divan disappeared, several hundred fragments of the piano were scattered everywhere, an entire wall was gone and a hole three feet wide was blown through the oak parquet flooring.

It was the bomb's final roll, the momentum that carried it under the sturdily built divan, that saved Cashman his life. For though he was dazed and incoherent when Shag found him thirty minutes later, the only damage seemed to be shredded clothing and a nosebleed. Shag got him to a bed upstairs and the doctor came to check him over for any internal injuries.

During the examination Cashman revived considerably.

"Keep what happened to yourself," he told the doctor. "I don't want it in the papers."

"Whatever you say. But whoever did this ought to be punished severely."

"I know who did it, Doc. And they'll get theirs. How about the neighbors, Shag? Anybody nosing around?"

"Didn't see anybody, Johnny."

"How's Ricci?"

"He says his arm's busted. The doc's going to fix him up at the hospital."

"Good. Now go out and rent me another house. Bud Linder will have a furnished one in a quiet neighborhood. But don't use my name. And I want an unlisted phone."

Within two hours he was moved out of Coral Gables and into a thousand-dollar-a-month place in Hollywood, some twenty miles away.

But lest Mr. Luis Maximo mistake his intentions—and in keeping with the Cashman style—an eight-man task force in two panel trucks set out just before dawn to punish the Consul's country. The Consul was waiting for them, in force, but at the wrong places. He expected an angry counterattack at the consulate in Miami, at his private residence in Miami Shores, or both.

Cashman's troopers went to the docks. Because he controlled the numbers business pier-side, banked the payday crap game, made book on whatever bet any stevedore wanted to lay—for all that he knew as much and more about what happened inside Port Miami than any man who made his honest living there.

So he went to the docks. On one pier they were challenged by a watchman who took a nasty clubbing. On one of the freighters just inbound they rudely broke in on the love-making of the third mate, the only man aboard, tossed him into Biscayne Bay and then hosed down the still unloaded cargo of sugar with a thousand gallons of salt water. A sister ship carried a hull full of rum—five hundred cases—and they demolished that valuable shipment with their axes. That, and some miscellaneous vandalism to the ships' passenger appointments, concluded Johnny Cashman's retribution for the bomb hurled through his window, and the raiders went home.

That gave the Miami papers a little local color to go with the wire service story on Colonel Gomez's defection across the way, although Consul Maximo pooh-poohed the suggestion that the rebel boss hiding out in the southern mountains had any real support in the States. Nevertheless, Maximo was recalled to his capital Wednesday afternoon to report on Cashman and Harland Burke in person. Also present was Roberto Alazar, the former head of the secret police who now served his government as Consul General in New York City. Maximo and Alazar compared notes, got their instructions and flew back to their posts Thursday morning.

That same day Johnny Cashman put the bee on Buddy Lewis a second time, made his intentions so crystal clear that the singer dumped the matter into Bernie King's lap. And forty-eight hours later Timothy Dane was packing a bag for Miami.

## 3

As usual, there was the problem about the gun.

The way Bernie King had laid it out, this would be an uneventful assignment—overnight on the train, a possible stopover in Miami tomorrow night, back in New York the next. For that he threw one extra shirt into the bag, two changes of underwear and an unopened fifth to reduce the unnecessary expense of drinking in the club bar.

But what about the gun? There it lay in the bureau drawer, the snub-nosed Detective Special, oiled, loaded, ready to go. Ready to go where?

Not to Miami, not for the work Bernie King was ordering. He was not committing an unfriendly act. He would not have to shoot his way into the office of East Coast Associates to settle Buddy Lewis's debt.

And transporting the money fifteen hundred miles to Cashman? How much risk was involved? Who besides the interested parties knew he was going south as a courier and not just another sun worshiper?

Nobody knew, Dane decided and shut the bureau drawer. What that did was to spare him a lot of dreary, time-consuming meddlesomeness by people who seemed to live for no other reason than to suck a man dry of all the personal and confidential information he owned.

What Dane meant was that he would have to report directly to both the Miami Police Headquarters and the Dade County Sheriff's office as soon as he set foot in the land of sunshine. They would finally let him carry the damned .38, because Florida reciprocated his New York State & City license to carry one, but not before he had carefully filled out a gross of forms, been fingerprinted, photographed and submitted to an exhaustive grilling in both places that was one third belittling, one third demeaning and one third threatening. He would have to sit and listen to every city, county and state ordinance relating to the bearing of concealed weapons and the severe restrictions laid upon "said unofficial law enforcement persons offering their services for hire and at the specific direction of private citizens."

Then, in the event he didn't get the subtle hint that he was not as welcome as some three million other winter visitors, he would find his hotel room searched every hour on the hour and a team of glowering, crowding plainclothesmen clumsily dogging his every move. That's why Dane didn't want the gun.

He was closing the bag when the telephone rang. "Yes?"

"Am I speaking to Mr. Timothy Dane?" It was a clipped voice, careful of the enunciation. It was also intimidating.

"Yes."

"There are two ways to exit your apartment, Mr. Dane," the voice said. "If you leave by the front door on Fifty-third Street, you will note a car parked there. The hood is raised and a man is looking inside, as if there were engine trouble. There isn't, Mr. Dane. That man is armed, and so are the three sitting in the car."

The voice on the phone paused, as though this was a script and Dane had been cued. Dane said nothing at all, let the dead silence hang.

"Mr. Dane? Are you there?"

"Yes."

Another pause. Then, "If you leave by the way of Fifty-fourth Street, through that dark basement, climbing that high fence, you will find four other men in the next yard. Perhaps you won't find them, Mr. Dane. But they will be expecting you, and they are armed."

Once more his caller stopped speaking. Dane still showed no curiosity, and when the voice spoke again it was definitely annoyed with him. "So just stay put, Mr. Dane. You're not going to Miami after all."

The receiver clicked in Dane's ear, but though the next sound should have been the dial tone, instead there was a kind of vacuum. There was no trick to disconnecting a telephone providing you were that close to the box. Someone obviously was, and the man he had just heard from probably wasn't kidding about it.

Out of the drawer came the .38 and into his topcoat pocket. He went out of the apartment very quietly, easing the door shut behind him and leaving the lights burning inside. As the stranger had said, he could go out via Fifty-third or through the basement and eventually to Fifty-fourth. Instead, Dane went straight up—up three flights of stairs and onto the roof. Across the roof then, over a low parapet, and across the roof of the adjoining brownstone.

So far so easy—but now the operation became abruptly interesting. There was another roof to be crossed, but because of some legal difficulty, or some long-forgotten argument, the builder of the next house had left an eight-foot separation. It was a paved alley, but that was four stories below and Dane's problem was to negotiate it up here.

He tossed the suitcase over, heard it land softly on the tarred floor, and lightened himself of the topcoat, jacket and shoes. They joined the bag on the other side and for just a moment the tall man poised on his own ledge. *You're seventy-four inches*, he reminded himself. *On the tips of your toes, arms outstretched, maybe ninety-four.* All it took, then, was a mere two-inch thrust. Four, to play it safe.

He went, as a racing diver does, outward. But he had overshot it, come in too low, and his right hand, grabbing for a hold on the opposite ledge struck instead and found no purchase. Pure reflex sent his left arm shooting up. Three fingers hooked onto something solid, held all one hundred and ninety pounds of him the way they will when life and death are in the balance.

His right hand, feeling a little numb, got its hold and Dane paused for one deep breath before pulling himself to the safety of the rooftop. Fully dressed again, with the .38 a comforting weight in his pocket, he crossed the tops of three more houses then went down flights of stairs almost identical with his own. He left the building as naturally as he could, swung east toward Fifth Avenue without a betraying backward glance. No one shot at his broad back, no one interfered. He hailed a cab, and from the back seat took his first look back down Fifty-third. Sure enough, there was a car parked before his apartment. With the hood raised to lull the suspicions of any curious cop.

Dane stretched his long legs, struck a light for his smoke. Conned again, he thought. Bernie King had given it to him like an expert.

## 4

All through their five minutes with Lissa the two college boys found the girl gay and vivacious, supercharged with the breathless ingredient called glamour and almost painfully more beautiful close up than she had been from their table at ringside. They left the dressing room in a kind of perfumed haze, not realizing they were being shooed out, completely unaware that hardly a word that was spoken was really heard by the dancer.

She'd tried to listen to them, tried to be gracious and entertaining, but her mind was elsewhere, restless and unmanageable. And when they were gone she prowled the room deep in thought, unmindful of the maid who had started the water running in her bath, who had helped her out of the robe and was divesting her of the remnants of her costume.

She came back to her surroundings after the warm water closed around her, relaxed her as nothing else could. The awakening was punctuated by a loud banging on the door.

"It's Karl," the maid reported fearfully. "He wants to come in!"

Lissa jumped up in the tub, grabbed a towel and wrapped herself in it even as the door's lock was being sprung. Seconds later Karl pulled the screen apart and stood on the threshold of the bathroom, his ugly face dark and raging, a gun gripped tight in his fist.

"Damn you, get out of here!"

"Where is he?"

"Gone. Get out!"

"Gone where? I'm gonna kill that sonofabitch!"

She could believe it, looking at him. She could also believe that his murderous mood could be turned into something else, directed at her.

"How do you think this is going to sound to Johnny?" the girl asked with more self-assurance than she felt.

"The hell with Johnny! This is between me and that wisenheimer …"

"I'll be seeing Johnny in Miami. Don't forget that."

His expression changed, as though he were just remembering it.

"When's that plane leave?"

"Nine tomorrow morning. You'd better get out of here, Karl."

"I'll find him before then," he said, almost to himself. He turned and hurried away, and for many seconds Lissa and the maid stared at each other in silent relief.

"Someone ought to warn that fellow," the maid said then. Lissa nodded, stepped from the tub and quickly dried herself. She shrugged into another robe and went to the telephone directory. There were two listings for "Dane, Timothy," one at 1501 Broadway, another at West Fifty-third. She dialed the first and there was no answer. She tried the second, got a strange clicking sound and then the return of her own dial tone. When she dialed again the same thing happened.

"The poor guy didn't pay his bill," Lissa told the maid sympathetically. "I'll get dressed and go over to his place."

"I'd better go with you, honey."

"No, you stay here by the phone."

She dressed herself simply in a knitted suit, applied a minimum of lipstick and was enroute to Dane's place in a matter of minutes. The cab pulled up behind a car having engine trouble and she told the driver to wait.

Dane, of course, didn't answer the door. He was, at that moment, contemplating the chasm four stories overhead. But there was light shining inside the apartment so Lissa pressed the bell a second time, a third.

Not only broke, but deaf, she decided. Or dead? It wasn't possible that Karl could have beaten her here. Karl, so far as she could remember, didn't even know his name.

"Who are you looking for, Miss?" a soft voice asked, startling her badly.

"The fellow that lives in here," she answered. "Timothy Dane."

"I'm sure he's in." The speaker was a slim, dark-complexioned man of medium height. Lissa found him polite enough, but somehow ominous-sounding. "Call through the door," he suggested. "Identify yourself."

Lissa knocked on the panel.

"This is Lissa, Timothy. I have something to tell you."

When there was still no response she looked at the man who had, strangely enough, moved back several feet from the doorway.

"I guess he's not home," she said.

"But the light is on." Now there was an anxiety about him, a note of alarm. "Call to him again. Tell him you must see him."

Lissa frowned. "Why is my business so important to you?"

"Mine is the important business," he said curtly. "Call Mr. Dane."

"Call him yourself," she said, walking around him and on down the hallway. But he didn't call to Dane. Instead he knelt at the keyhole, and Lissa couldn't figure that out at all.

She was still wondering about it as the cab pulled away and started back to the Riviera. How many of them were looking for Dane, anyhow? More important to Dane, how many did he know about? She went back over some of the things Bernie King had said, the very definite worry about some business with Johnny Cashman. And a train that was leaving in an hour.

Well, if he was going to see Johnny that train left from Penn Station. "Skip the Riviera and drive to Penn Station," she said. Lickety-split." The cab switched direction, and with each passing block Lissa found herself more troubled about that character hovering outside Dane's apartment.

The girl suddenly sat up straight in the seat. "By golly," she said aloud, "I am worried about him." The frown appeared on her pretty face again and she shook her head impatiently. The last thing she wanted this year was another romance. The way she went at them it was too damn nerve-wracking.

Penn Station seemed unusually jammed tonight, beautifully confused, and as she stood in the slow-moving line at the information booth it seemed that the hour must surely be gone. So she left the line and struck out to find the Miami-bound train on her own. It was there, on Track 36, but the gatekeeper was passing no one through without a ticket. Lissa detoured, gained entrance through a baggage gate and stepped aboard the waiting train.

"When do you leave?" she asked the first conductor she met. He pulled the inevitable gold watch from his vest pocket.

"Six minutes," he said, smiling as most men did when they were brought this close to Lissa, seeming to want to put all other important affairs aside and prolong the meeting. But the girl had no time to spare. She hurried off toward the Pullman section to deliver her warning and get off the train again.

"I'm looking for a tall fellow with dark hair," she told a porter. "Is he in this car?"

"What kind of space does he have, ma'am? Berth, room …?"

"I don't know. But his name is Dane and he's tall. If you had him, you'd know it."

"I guess I don't then."

She went through the next car, the next, repeating her questions, adding to the identification that Dane had "nice eyes" and "a lazy voice"—but finding no porter who'd seen such a one tonight.

"All aboard!"

Lissa was in the middle of a car when she heard that stentorian warning. Heard it at the same time that she saw a porter approaching from the other end carrying a bowl of ice cubes and a single glass. She watched him knock on a door of a drawing room and enter a moment later.

"*All aboard!*"

She started to swing around toward the nearest exit, hesitated, then began walking swiftly to the door of the room. She didn't stop to knock, just turned the handle and pushed. The porter pulled the door from his side simultaneously and her entrance was graceless but effective.

Dane glanced up from his magazine. "Hi."

"Hi, nothing. Good-bye. I wanted to warn you that Karl is very mad. He's got a gun."

"No kidding?" It was as though she had told him it was beginning to snow outside. "Is he on the train with you?"

She shook her head. "There's also somebody acting creepy around your apartment."

"Smooth talker?"

She nodded. "Don't tell me he was a bill collector?"

"No," Dane laughed. He turned his head to the porter, who was listening to everything attentively. "Bring another highball glass, will you?"

"Not for me!" Lissa protested. "I've got to get off this thing."

Dane looked past the window shade. "That's too bad," he said.

"Yes," Lissa said vaguely. "Well, so long again."

"So long." He stood up. "Thanks for taking the trouble."

"No trouble." The porter had the door open for her and she left the room.

"Did that lady say there was a gunman on this train?"

"No," Dane said and the porter went out. Dane mixed a drink then, took it to the seat and raised the shade. He was finishing it fifteen minutes later when there was a knock on the door.

"Come on in," he said and Lissa opened it again.

"I can't get off."

"I know."

"But that's ridiculous. I haven't got anything with me. Just the clothes on my back and five dollars."

"I'm loaded," Dane said. "How much do you need?"

"Enough for a ticket, I guess. What's the next stop?"

"Philadelphia."

"Damn, I would pick the express!"

"Well, have a drink," Dane suggested easily. "You've got about an hour and a half ride."

Lissa nodded. What she wanted most of all was to sit down. There was something compelling about the size of him in this small compartment. She sat on the edge of the bed.

"Water all right?"

"Fine."

He made it informally, in the washroom tumbler, handed it over.

"Take the chair," he said.

"This is comfortable. This is fine."

Dane lowered himself into the chair, put his legs out in front of him. "I knew a dancer once," he said. "Called herself Dolly Dawn."

"Oh, sure. Dolly's in Las Vegas this winter." She sipped lightly at the drink. "Know her very well?"

"Professionally."

"Oh? Exactly what is your line?"

"Investigation, some of the time. The singer called me an errand boy."

"I hope you're not investigating Johnny Cashman."

He looked at her for a moment, then shook his head. "Nope. Just bringing him something."

"It must be money. That's Johnny's one and only interest."

"Everybody tells me it's you."

"That's what everybody tells me, too. I even read it in the newspapers."

Dane got up, freshened his drink.

"Who was that character at your apartment?" Lissa asked abruptly, making her mind quit its speculation about those shoulders.

"Don't know that one," he said, and thought about the near miss atop the apartment. "I'd like to meet him, though."

"Some life you lead, people chasing after you all the time."

"Imagine it's a lot like yours. How's your drink?"

"I'll fix this one," she told him, slipping from the bed, crossing to where he stood by the wall table. "A girl sized one." It was considerably less whisky than Dane had poured, much more water. But when she had it stirred, she didn't seem to know what to do with it, except stand there holding the glass before her. And the longer she stood the more confused she got, while a crimson flush spread along the curve of her throat and into her cheeks.

"Say something quick," she said.

"I like your face."

"No."

"What's wrong with it?"

"Everything. Talk about your wife. All the children."

"I wish I could."

"Tell me about that man I met tonight. What does he want from you?"

"Cashman's money."

Lissa blinked. "What?"

"According to him I should have skipped this ride."

She remembered her highball, drank from it and eased back toward the bed. She sat down again, crossed her legs, smoothed the tight-fitting skirt over her thighs. Anything to avoid meeting that steady gaze, to keep the boat from rocking. "Is it a lot of money?"

"I think so."

"Ten thousand?"

"Times ten."

Now she looked up at him, had to. "But that's impossible."

"It sure is."

"You've got a *hundred* thousand dollars?"

"For your boyfriend."

That brought a smile to her face, an enigmatic one that he was not meant to understand.

"In a way, I suppose, you're working for Johnny?"

"In a way," Dane agreed.

"So am I."

"How's that?"

"He bought my contract from Bernie King." Again the smile, as if she were enjoying a private joke. "Johnny Cashman is my manager."

"That's nice for him."

"Isn't it?"

"When is the contract up?"

"It's what is known as a life sentence," Lissa said, shifting her position on the bed. "At the time I thought I was getting the big break. That was a year ago, when I was just another clothes horse in the Copa line. Bernie King has a fabulous reputation and I couldn't see how I could go wrong, lifetime contract or not."

"Isn't there any clause about the paper being sold?"

"It never entered my mind. Three months ago—I was playing the Trocadero in Hollywood—Bernie introduced me to my new manager."

"You'd never known Cashman?"

"You can believe this or not," she said very quietly, "but I hardly know Johnny Cashman now."

Dane came over to her. "Your glass is empty."

"So it is."

He took hers, refilled them both and brought the new drink back.

"For somebody you hardly know," Dane said, "the joker seems to have you pretty thoroughly managed."

"He's anything but a joker. I'd hate to have him walk in here right now—" A sharp knock on the door at that moment held the girl frozen.

"Come in," Dane said, moving slightly so that he stood between the bed and the door. It was opened by the conductor.

"Tickets please."

Dane went to his topcoat, got his and handed them over. The conductor examined them, punched the ones on his run and turned to Lissa. "The lady's getting off at Philadelphia," Dane said. "What's the fare?"

"She has no ticket?"

"She came down to the train to deliver a message. She couldn't get off in time."

"But Philadelphia is a boarding point, not a discharge. I can't issue a ticket …"

"Then let's pretend she isn't even here," Dane said, handing the man a neatly folded five-dollar bill.

"That's probably the best solution for all of us. Just be sure," he warned Lissa, "that you get off there."

"I promise."

The conductor went out then and Lissa stood up from the bed very deliberately.

"You weren't worried at all, were you?" she asked. "The door was unlocked. There wasn't much I could do about it."

"But it could have been Cashman, or Karl—anybody. You just got between me and the door and that was that."

He grinned at her. "You're making me sorry it was only the conductor."

"And what would you do? Claim your reward?"

"I sure would."

The redhead's gray-green eyes roamed his face from chin line to hair top and back again. She sighed deeply, decisively.

"Lock the door, Timothy," she said in a soft voice.

"Really?"

"And pull down the shade."

Dane turned to do as he was bidden, heard Lissa move into the washroom. The tall man undressed himself leisurely, not taking his great good fortune for granted—and not beholden, either. What would be, would be, not because of him but to him. He switched the light out.

Lissa came back to him naked.

"Timothy?"

"What?"

"You are kind of in love with me—aren't you?"

A wonderful laugh poured out of him, filling the small room with its happiness, scattering the last remnants of strangeness between them.

"Kind of," Dane said and pulled her down to him.

## 5

"What's happening?" Lissa said lazily.

"The train is slowing down."

She put her lips against his ear. "Did we do that, too?"

"Philadelphia did it. We're pulling in."

"You said an hour and a half. It can't be."

"Time flies," Dane said. "Sometimes."

"But that means I have to go."

"Or stay right where you are."

"I can't," she said, swinging her feet to the floor. "I'm not even moved out of my dressing room at the Riviera."

"Where do you play next?"

She looked over her shoulder at him. "Don't you know? I open tomorrow night at Cashman's club in Miami."

"Well that's fine."

The girl shook her head, stood up. "No it isn't. That's his town...."

"You know what I think, Lizzie?"

"*Lizzie?*" she echoed, laughing. "What a name!"

"I think this Cashman has graded himself up. He's got the whole bunch of you believing it."

"I believe it because I've watched what he can do. He's rough, Timothy, and he wants his own way." The train had slowed down even more. "Golly, I gotta run!" she said and swung abruptly to the washroom, presenting Dane the same view that had intrigued him so much at the Riviera. The train was braking to a full stop when she came back again, fully clothed.

"You're wonderful," she said a little breathlessly and kissed him.

"But you don't want to see me in Miami?"

"It would show, darling. I'd be a dead giveaway. Maybe in New Orleans. I'll be there around Mardi Gras. 'Bye, Timothy."

"So long," he said and she was gone. But the scent of her lingered on in the small room and even as he strolled to the shower the memories were falling into line. Lissa was some girl.

And as he stepped back into the room, his middle wrapped in a towel, the door burst open and there she was again.

"That character—he's on the train!"

"Karl?"

"The other one. I got off and saw *him* getting on. I didn't know what to do."

"Where you going?"

She turned in the doorway. "I'm getting off again."

"Too late."

"Oh, *no!*"

"Baltimore next stop."

"And how long is that?"

"Couple of hours. After that, Washington. Then Norfolk."

"But I just can't, Timothy. No clothes, ticket—anything."

"Don't worry about it."

"And what about you? What are you going to do?"

"Well, I liked what I was doing before."

"I mean about him!"

"He's got to come to me if he wants the money bad enough."

"Apparently he does."

Dane nodded. "They're well organized," he agreed. "They had to fly a plane to catch this train."

"What do you mean, *they?*" the girl asked in dismay.

"There's a flock of 'em. At least eight that you probably didn't notice at the apartment."

"You mean that car that was parked—? This is terrible, Timothy!"

"I'll get dressed and have a look around," he decided. "You stay here and mind Cashman's goods." He got into trousers and an odd jacket. "Tell me what he looks like," he said then.

"He's about up to your shoulder," Lissa told him. "A kind of Latin type with a thin mustache. He's wearing a black overcoat and one of those black banker's hats."

"Okay. Just lock the door after me and open it for nobody."

"That thing you slipped into your pocket—that was a gun, wasn't it?"

"Don't worry about that, either. The smart thing for you to do is crawl into that sack and get some sleep."

"*Sleep!*"

"Don't forget that you're working tomorrow night."

"If I ever get off this train."

"You will. See you in a few minutes."

"Please take care of yourself, Timothy."

Dane left the room, listened for the click of the lock, then began a walk-through of the long train. It was asleep, car after car of it, and nowhere in evidence was there a man answering Lissa's description. He came to the deserted observation lounge and stood there, waiting. If they were going to take him at all this was the time and the place. But they weren't, and Dane started back to his own room. He had covered about half of the return trip when a tremendous shock went through the body of the train. It was the hydraulic brake, applied without warning, so suddenly that each car seemed to buckle toward its own center, sway precariously on its rails.

Dane was nearly rocked off his feet. Then he caught his balance and began moving swiftly to where Lissa was. Now sleeping was at an end. There were shouts of alarm, children's voices crying out, anger, confusion and fear. And all the while the train was shuddering to an emergency halt.

He and the various employees of the railroad were the only ones with any destination or purpose, or so it seemed, and when he reached the end of his journey he found the door still locked.

"Open up, baby," he called to her but there was no response. He hit the panel again with the flat of his hand. "All clear, Lizzie. Open the door." That should have reassured her but it didn't. He looked to see he was having company, a trio of angry-faced conductors bearing down on him.

"What in hell is going on?" asked the head man, his blue sleeve blanketed by gold service bars. "Who threw the switch in this car?"

"I don't know that, but I want this door opened in a damn hurry."

His own conductor put a passkey in the lock, turned it and threw the door wide. The inside looked as if a tornado had twisted through. A shambles.

"Lissa!" Dane shouted into it. "Lissa!" But she wasn't here. There was no place where she could hide, or be hidden. The conductors had converged on the box that held the emergency handle. It was disengaged, guilty-looking, and the sight of it made the sharp blade of betrayal twist inside Dane's stomach.

"This is your space?" the head man demanded. He nodded. "Who pulled that handle? What's the meaning of this mess?"

"Somebody was looking for something. It wasn't in here, so she decided to get off the train altogether."

"She?" the man asked, but something one of the other conductors said floated into Dane's thoughts and caught hold.

"What did you say?"

"I wondered why anyone would go to the trouble of locking the door after them."

One stride and Dane was at the adjoining door, pulling it open effortlessly. Lying on the bed of the other room were two women, one frail and elderly, the other Lissa, both bound and gagged by a past master. To his credit, Dane went first to the old lady, let the conductors free the voluptuous redhead.

But then Lissa came to him, threw her arms around his shoulders and began talking and crying at the same time.

"Easy, baby, easy. Everything's all right."

"… came right through the other door. Four of them…. Grabbed me. I couldn't even scream I was so scared…."

Her companion seemed more miffed than frightened. In a voice of controlled anger she ticked off the various indignities that the railroad was going to pay for, and dearly. From the old lady's account there was a knock on her door shortly after the train left Philadelphia. A man with a polite voice identified himself as the conductor. She opened the door to him and his politeness vanished. His three companions put a gag in her mouth, trussed her hand and foot and deposited her on the bed. They used her key to go into the next room and returned with Lissa, who apparently had fought more furiously than she'd let on.

The four of them then went next door and began a complete search. From her place on the bed she saw the one with the polite voice pull the emergency handle. The four of them fled via her room.

The conductors heard her out, patiently, then left to get their train rolling again. Dane took Lissa back into his room.

"Now you see how us smart operators handle things," he told her ruefully. "Sorry I let you in for that."

"Don't say it, honey. If you'd been here there'd have been somebody shot."

"They were armed?"

"And how they were."

"Funny-acting hoods," Dane said, more to himself than the girl.

"Funny?"

"The way they hit and run. All the elaborate planning. Then they get next to pay dirt and they blow it like a bunch of kids."

"You mean they don't have the money?"

"Nope."

"It isn't in the room?"

"Look—don't ask so many questions. I had a few bad seconds when I wasn't sure what the score was."

"*Me?* You thought *I'd* searched for it?"

Dane smiled pacifyingly. "It's a nice bundle," he said. "A hundred thousand of them and not a nickel's worth of tax." He'd said it and he was immediately sorry. It hadn't struck Lissa as either light or particularly funny.

Her eyes showed hurt and quick anger. She turned away from him.

"Now wait a minute, Lizzie. The whole thing's over and I was wrong."

"You sure were! And don't call me 'Lizzie'!"

"Speak low," he said. "The neighbor."

"But you actually thought it was me! I suppose I went to bed with you just to lull your suspicions …"

"Ah, come on now, Liz—"

Her eyes stopped him. Two shafts of blazing light. The silence between them sizzled.

"Lissa," she said dangerously. "My name is Lissa."

"Okay, Liss—sah," Dane told her, and he had plainly had enough tantrum. "I should have been here, I wasn't, I goofed it and I'm sorry. But anything that went on from there was anybody's natural reaction."

"There you go again! You're still not sure that nice lady isn't my accomplice. We tied each other up …"

The conductor didn't knock, just opened the door.

"You were supposed to leave my section at Philadelphia," he said accusingly to Lissa. "I was wondering where we'd met."

"I'm leaving *right now*," she said, marching to him and past him.

"Baltimore," he said firmly. "No more special stops."

"I'm not asking for privileges," the redhead told him with a regal air. "Just a place to sit until Baltimore."

"Well, you can stay here—if you get off there."

"Thanks, but no. I'll take a box in the baggage room."

"Stay here," Dane said. "I can stretch out somewhere in the men's lounge."

"I wouldn't think of it," she said, scathingly. "My kleptomania might break out again."

With that she walked off, swinging her nice hips, and after a lingering gaze the conductor looked back to Dane with man-to-man sympathy. Dane had another five-spot ready.

"Do what you can for her," he said.

"We're jammed, mister. There might be a seat in one of the coaches."

Dane was left alone then, to wonder how it had happened that she had been made so mad, to justify his own part. Neither one of them, he decided, was right or wrong—but there was a disaffection and now he realized how late the hour was, how good it would be to sleep.

Instead he mixed himself a strong drink, pulled at it for fifteen minutes. Then he left the room, made his way forward to the coaches. He found her in the last one, seated in a kind of drop seat just in front of the water cooler. She sat erect in it, but her eyes were closed and she was dozing. Very carefully he opened her purse, slipped one of his own hundred-dollar bills into it, snapped it shut again. He went back to the room and slept the sleep of the contented.

## CHAPTER THREE

And how Dane slept. Slept past the breakfast calls, damn near through lunch, and when he did leave his room the train was halfway through South Carolina and Lissa was no longer aboard.

"She left us at Washington," the conductor reported. "Said something about making her plane connection there and flying to Miami."

"Any kind word for me?"

He shook his head. "What I did, though, was slip those two bills you gave me into her purse. Didn't want a girl like that stranded in a strange town."

Dane heard the man and reached automatically for his wallet. The redhead, he thought dryly, was getting to be more than he could afford.

"No you don't," the conductor said. "I only took those bribes of yours on loan. Wanted to make you look good in front of your lady friend."

They both laughed at that, and even though it was on him, Dane was willing to be the butt if it spared another ten dollars.

"What I'm here about, though," the conductor said then, "is that funny business last night. The train stopping."

"Oh? What's the story?"

"Don't know. But a couple of railroad detectives got on at Washington. They'd like to talk to you after you've had your lunch."

"Sure," Dane said, and when he returned to the room he was joined there by a pair of quiet-spoken, alert-eyed men.

"We're Bennett and Shead," one of them said crisply, extending his hand. He was wiry, sandy-haired, all business. Shead was blockier, square-jawed. All business. All three of them sat down.

"The company wants to apologize for the incident last night, Mr. Dane," Bennett said.

"I don't blame the railroad for anything that happened."

"You say that as though you do blame someone else."

"Well, sure. Whoever broke in here."

"What did they take?"

"Nothing."

"What were they after?"

"Money."

"It must be a sizable amount," Shead said.

"It is."

"And they must have known you had it."

"They knew. In fact, they made a pass at it before I left New York."

"How much money is it?" Bennett asked and Dane paused.

"That's a little delicate," he did say, smiling into their serious faces. "You see, it doesn't belong to me. I'm delivering it to somebody."

"We're not from Treasury," Shead said.

Dane looked surprised. "I didn't think you were …"

"Then why not tell us the amount?"

"I guess it's because I think it's none of your business."

Bennett broke into the exchange. "It's really not that important," he said. "Who did you say you were delivering it to?"

"Wait a minute, boys. Let's get all the cards face up."

"What do you mean?"

"I mean that this room was gotten into last night by four characters. They pushed a couple of women around, stopped the train and got away. But all you want to know about is what didn't happen to some money that belongs to somebody who doesn't concern you."

His visitors were expressionless and unruffled.

"We just like to dot all the i's," Shead said. "But let's get back to what you say is pertinent. Who were these four characters?"

"I don't know."

"But you think they're the same ones who brushed with you in New York?"

"Yes. I also think they're spending a lot of their own money to get at mine. It had to be a chartered plane that got them to Philadelphia."

But though that still struck Dane as being curious, it seemed to be information they had already come to some private decision about.

"How long do you plan to stay in Miami?" Shead asked.

"Until my business is finished. Why?"

"Because something might turn up. Where can we reach you there?"

"You can't reach me there," Dane said, getting to his feet. "What the hell is this all about?"

They regarded him narrowly, critically, and at a signal from Bennett they both stood up.

"We're trying to be helpful, Dane," Bennett told him. "It's a policy of our company."

"You just might be overdoing it."

"We might at that," Shead admitted. "Take care of yourself in Miami." There were no parting handshakes and the railroad's detectives left the room. In the corridor outside they were joined by the train's anxious-looking head conductor.

"There was a call for you," he told them. "You're to get in touch with your office." He led the way to his own little office and Bennett gave the number to the radio-phone operator.

"Three one thousand," answered a second operator crisply.

"Extension five."

"Harrison speaking."

"Joe Bennett, Arthur."

"At long last," Harrison said. "Where've you been?"

"This bird on the train likes his shuteye. We only just got finished talking to him."

"What does he have to say?"

"As little as possible," Bennett reported. "He told us he was carrying a good amount of money down to someone in Miami. But then he got touchy as hell about it. Wouldn't say how much it was, who gave it to him or who it was intended for. George and I beat it before he started asking us questions."

"Well, he seems to be clean enough. He's a New York City private detective and on the up-and-up. But clean or not he's still carrying money to our friend Cashman. And Señor Maximo can't let that happen."

"He says they made a swipe at it back in New York."

"Anybody hurt?"

"We couldn't go into it, being railroad employees. As it is he's got the wind up."

"He doesn't know anything about Maximo, does he?"

"No. What do we do now?"

"Stay with him on the train, find out where he's staying. Brown and Keller are flying down to Miami. Turn him over to them and come on back up here."

"But, Art, it's cold up there. All that ice and snow."

"Ah, you're breaking my heart. See you both in the morning, bright and early."

For Dane, the rest of that day was uneventful, without a single attempt on his life or his goods—and though he saw Shead and Bennett from time to time they merely nodded to each other but didn't speak. The sun went down, as the newspaper predicted it would, and after a very good steak Dane found himself with nothing better to do than observe the flat Florida real estate between Jacksonville and Miami.

It was ten o'clock when they arrived in Playland and half an hour later when he was checked into the Golden Shores. Bernie King had done well by him, a two-room suite, and from there he called East Coast Associates.

"My name is Dane," he told the man who answered. "I'm down from New York to settle Buddy Lewis's account."

"Hold on a second." The second lengthened into a minute, nearly three. "Where are you now?" he was asked then.

"The Golden Shores."

"Wait there. You'll get a call."

Dane waited, for the duration of one cigarette, and the phone rang.

"Yes?"

"Am I speaking to somebody named Dane?"

"Yes."

"You've got something for me?"

"If you're Cashman."

"I'm Cashman." It was a strong voice, sure of itself, overbearing. "How much have you got?"

"One hundred thousand. But I have to bring back all the markers you're holding."

"What does that welshing sonofabitch take me for?"

"You could do worse than fifty cents on the dollar," a Dane said reasonably. "Money is tight."

"Tell me something I don't know."

"All right. To raise the hundred Lewis went into hock up to his ears. This is borrowed on his insurance."

"It sure is," Johnny Cashman said, and his laughter was a metallic sound carrying coldly along the wire. "But he's also lucky."

"How's that?"

"I'm pinched for ready money myself. Bring it over to the Surfside Club and my boy will pick it up."

"He'll have Lewis's paper?"

"Sure, sure." Cashman hung up in his ear.

A cab carried Dane across the Seventy-ninth Street Causeway to the beach, then south on Collins through a maze of traffic and finally to a stop before the magnificently lighted Surfside Club. He paid his fare and glanced up at the marquee. "Opening Tonight" it read. "Lissa."

The club itself was small, smaller by half than the Riviera, but its size gave it an intimacy and Cashman had spared no expense decorating it. On the elevated bandstand a five-piece group held forth and as Dane made his way to the bar a trio of very pretty brunette sisters came on from the wings to begin belting out the winter's hit songs.

"My name is Dane," he said and the bartender nodded.

"Mr. Cashman called. I'll point out Shag when he gets here."

"Good."

"Drink while you're waiting?"

"Some rye and plain water." The drink was made, but when Dane put a bill down the bartender shook his head.

"You're Mr. Cashman's guest."

"Well, fine. Tell me, did Lissa arrive all right?" The man's eyes became suddenly bland and distant. "You—ah—know the lady?"

"Yes, I know her."

"And you know Mr. Cashman?"

"Only to talk to."

"Well, let me tell you something. Don't ask me anything about Lissa. Ask him." Dane glanced in the direction the bartender indicated, fully expecting to see good old Karl. But the burly citizen holding up the wall beside the register was another version, though every bit as surly and implacable-looking as the original.

"How many of those things does Cashman own?" he asked and the bartender winced.

"Don't talk like that. Especially not to me." He left Dane for another customer and stayed away. Dane swung around to watch the energetic trio, and though they were something less than the McGuires, he and everyone else in the packed room enjoyed them. And the sister in the middle seemed to enjoy Dane, for when a fast-talking comic took over the floor, she popped up on the stool beside him.

"How's the big town?" she asked him.

"Cold. How's Miami?"

"Live. Vacation?"

"Going back in the morning." He signaled the bartender.

"That's too bad," she said.

"Yeah. What'll it be?"

"A stinger, Russ," she told the barman. "And vouch for me."

"What?"

"Tell this good-looking paleface that I'm not hustling a drink."

"Margie sings here," he told Dane earnestly. "She's a singer."

"A damn good one," Dane agreed. "Mix me another, too."

They arrived, and she lifted the cocktail glass, clinked it against his highball.

"Cheers, *amigo*."

"Compliments of the boss," Dane said.

"Really? You're a friend of Cashman's?"

"Never met him."

"Oh." She sipped at the pale brown drink. "Well, it's too bad."

"What is?"

"That you're going back in the morning," she explained, leaning toward him in her theatrically low-cut gown.

"Margie, it's a crying shame."

"But the night is young. We've only got one more show to do...."

All at once there was only her voice speaking. Then it stopped, and they were both aware of the expectant hush stirring throughout the room. The comedian had departed. The floor was deserted, dark. Music came into that void, slowly, an Indian rhythm, underscored by a huge, resonant kettle drum.

That was a sound Timothy Dane had heard only once before, a compelling tom-tom beat, but he remembered it well. A battery of red baby spots cut the darkness with dramatic suddenness and a voice spoke through the public address speakers.

"Ladies and gentlemen," it said, "for your pleasure the Surfside Club presents—Lissa!"

She seemed to materialize out of nowhere. The floor was empty one moment, completely dominated the next by a tall, perfectly proportioned girl who stood before them barefooted, her head lowered demurely, her body clothed in a white slitted skirt and a beaded white halter. Her auburn hair hung in shimmering waves to her shoulders.

Dane looked at his long-legged, redheaded friend. She, too, was well remembered.

The music had quit, all but the tom-tom. Now it began again and she swayed to it. The tempo accelerated, revolving blue and white lights mixed with the crimson. She reacted with a kind of frenzy, primitively.

The music built to a climax, stopped just short. The white skirt fell away. The drum had never stopped its beat. Now it was insistent, demanding, and she danced to it with wild abandon, passionately. Once again the music rose to a near climax. The halter came off.

After that, nothing. Complete and utter silence in the room while everyone contemplated a flawless nude. The white spots went out, the blues. The drum began its tom-tom, the other instruments joined in. Her head came up, eyes closed, and her naked hips undulated. There was only one light on her, dimly. The drum began to roll, its sound filling every corner, swelling out. Without warning it stopped. At the same instant the G-string dropped, the single spot went out and the whole club was plunged into pitch blackness.

For a count of three there was not a sound in there, not even a drawn breath. Then some happy soul at ringside revived.

"Wow!" he said. "Holy Toledo!"

The applause came, waves of it. The lights went back on but Lissa had made her naked getaway under the cover of darkness.

"You still with us, old boy?" the dark-haired Margie asked Dane and he turned to her.

"What happened, anyhow?"

She laughed at him. "Just hold on to me," she said. "The first shock will wear off soon."

"That's some act, isn't it?"

"I don't know where the gal gets her energy from," Margie said. "She flew in only late this afternoon, went right into rehearsal for two hours—and her wardrobe maid told my sister she hardly slept a wink last night. Can I have another stinger?"

"You bet," he told her and waved to the bartender.

"I only talked to her for a few seconds," Margie went on, "but she seems like a nice kid."

"Very nice."

"I wouldn't make any plans, though. The word is that Mr. Wheel'em-Deal'em Cashman has an exclusive contract."

"So everybody says." Dane turned from her to the bartender. "Where's our boy?"

"Should be here by now."

"Has Cashman come in?"

"No."

"He doesn't watch the show?"

"No," was the brief, guarded answer and the new cocktail was set down.

"Let me use your phone," Dane said, and the man produced one, plugged it in. Dane dialed the East Coast Associates again, but this time there was no answer. He set down the receiver, frowning, and noticed that everyone was looking expectantly toward the far end of the bar.

Lissa was coming toward them, dressed very simply in green, the red hair piled atop her head and fastened with a green scarf. The bodyguard fell into step as she passed the register.

Dane stood up from the stool, his eyes and the girl's locked tight.

"Hi," he said, but there was no greeting in return as she slipped onto the high-backed chair. The bodyguard stopped short, his expression shifting from surprise to worry.

"What are you doing here?" Lissa asked Dane then, her voice low and agitated.

"Your friend is sending someone to meet me."

"Johnny told you to come to the club?"

"Yep. You know Margie, don't you?"

Lissa turned to the singer, nodded to her. "Your act is very good," she said politely.

"Thanks. I'm glad we don't have to follow yours. That was terrific."

"Understand you missed your sleep last night," Dane said innocently. "I don't know how you can do it."

"Neither do I. Can I have something to drink?"

"The lady takes the same as mine," Dane said, and the bodyguard shoved in between them.

"Mr. Cashman won't like this," he said gruffly. Dane straightened his body and Lissa immediately reached across to him, fastened her fingers urgently on his wrist.

"No," she said. "Please ..."

"Come on," the guard ordered. "Let's get back to the place."

"Take your hand off her arm," Dane told him very quietly.

"Don't, Timothy. Don't...."

"Take it away," Dane said again, and the men looked at each other steadily. The hand came away. Lissa stood up immediately.

"Good-bye," she said. "Thanks for the loan." She reached into the neck of her dress, withdrew a tightly folded bill and pressed it into his hand.

"Where are you staying?"

She shook her beautiful head.

"Let's go," the guard growled, putting his back to Dane. "Before there's big trouble in here."

Lissa nodded obediently to the command, but her glance lingered in Dane's.

"You sure?" the tall man asked. "Just say the word...."

"I'm sure." Her eyes moved briefly to take in the other girl, came back to him. "Have fun, Timothy," she said and walked away.

"Lissa!"

For a moment his voice almost stopped her. Then the guard crowded in behind and she kept moving.

"Well, now," Margie said. "Intrigue at the Surfside."

Dane still looked in Lissa's direction, watched until she was out of sight. He turned, his face a dark cloud.

"Who the hell is this Cashman?" he demanded. "Where do I find him?"

"Easy," the singer warned. "We're not used to hearing that name taken in vain."

"Why? Is Cashman the new god? Where does the bum live?"

"Not so *loud*, handsome. Nobody knows where Cashman lives. He hasn't even been around the club for two weeks."

Dane swung his wrathful attention on the barman, oblivious to the startled alarm of the customers all around him.

"Get your tinhorn boss on the phone. Tell him to get Shag over here in five minutes. Then we'll get a few things straightened out...."

The bartender was shaking his head from the start. "Mister, don't get me involved in your troubles, will you? *I* can't call Mr. Cashman."

"Then call Shag, dammit."

"Can't call him, either."

"Shag Wilson?" Margie asked. "If it's all that important to you, I'll call him." She pulled the phone toward her, dialed, listened, put it down again with a shrug of her shoulders.

"Busy signal," she said.

"Oh, fine." He took out his cigarettes, impatiently, handed her one and lit them both. She took his hand, cupped it in both of hers.

"Unwind yourself, handsome. Make do."

"What?"

"A girl's a girl. Johnny Cashman doesn't have them all fenced off."

She said that and for the first time Dane looked at her as a personality, not just some character floating irrelevantly around the fringes of his own problems. He saw her now as a slim and willowy girl, wicked-eyed and knowing at twenty-five, looking for a good time all the time—and to hell with tomorrow.

"Let's try Shag again," he said. She did, shook her head again.

"Still busy."

"What an organization. Anybody know where he lives?"

"Up in Bal Harbour."

For all his anger Dane laughed. "The hoods?" he asked. "Now they live in Bal Harbour?"

"Don't be a snob, handsome. These are changing times."

"They sure are. Changed by Johnny Cashman."

"Hey—where you going?"

"Slumming," he said, moving toward the exit. "Up to Bal Harbour."

"Well, wait for me."

"You've got another show to do."

"Not for two hours. And you don't even know where Shag lives." She came off the stool, caught up with him and left on his arm. The doorman hailed a cab and when she'd given the driver the address, she settled herself close beside Dane in the back seat.

As the taxi drove away, another man came out of the Surfside Club. He was slightly built, quietly dressed, inconspicuous. Hardly noticed, too, was the slight signal of his head that set a dark blue Ford in motion toward him. He got in beside the driver.

"That was our boy," Harry Brown said and Fred Keller nodded.

"Where's he off to?"

"To see somebody named Shag in Bal Harbour."

"What's the matter with your voice?" Keller asked.

"I'm doing well to talk at all. You should have seen what that girl did in there."

"What girl? What'd she do?"

"Lissa," Harry Brown said reverently. "And after that she came out to the bar, walked as close to me as you are. I'm telling you, boy—Waterloo, Iowa, was never like this."

Keller sat silently behind the wheel for a few moments.

"Next time," he said then, "you can wait in the car."

"I guess that's only fair," Brown agreed. "What is it this guy from New York is supposed to be doing?" he asked.

"Making a money delivery to somebody named Cashman."

"But we're not supposed to stop it?"

"No. Harrison said to stay out of it, just keep track of the money itself."

"What's the money for?"

Keller shrugged. "You know the boss," he said. "He feeds you just so much of a job at a time."

"The cab just swung left."

"I got him. Tell me more about this gal that unhinged you."

"She's a bomb, Fred. Total destruction. And all the while this drum is going *boom*-boom-boom-boom, *boom*-boom-boom-boom...."

"All the while *what?*"

"She's taking her clothes off. And after she was finished she came right to the bar ..."

"Naked?"

"Oh, hell, no! What do you take her for?"

"I don't take her for anything. What'd she do at the bar?"

"Got involved with our guy up ahead. Damn near started a fight with some mug. Then she went back to her dressing room."

"Isn't she the one that got in the cab with him?"

"No. That girl is part of a singing act."

"But didn't Joe Bennett say he'd only gotten into Miami tonight?"

"That's what he said. But this guy has a kind of a style, I'd guess you'd call it. Big, good-looking bozo. Makes you think of John Wayne, Joel McCrea—that type."

The girl in the cab ahead was thinking similar thoughts. "*Relax*," she told him. "Let yourself go."

"But not too far. Right now I'm working."

"At what? What do you do?"

"As little as I can get away with."

"Seriously."

"Insurance."

"Shag wants insurance?"

"Sure."

"Sell me some," she suggested. "Make your pitch." She folded her legs up under her, let the skirtline stay hiked above her sheer-stockinged knees.

"The wrong time," Dane said. "Wrong place."

"I know a right place. Let's skip Bal Harbour and turn around."

"I wish I could."

The cab had turned off Collins into a darkened residential road.

"What was that number?" the hackie asked.

"Four twenty," Margie told him. "It's in the next section." Some minutes later the cab slid into the curb before a small bungalow. Lights shone dimly behind closed blinds.

"You stay here," Dane said, getting out.

"Shag is harmless. He tries to act like Cashman, but he's really just cute."

"You stay here," Dane repeated and approached the little house. He climbed the short flight of wooden steps and touched his finger to the doorbell. There was a delay and then it was opened by a man dressed to go out.

"Shag?"

"What do you want?"

"I'm Dane. Where you been?"

The other one seemed confused. "Been?"

"Cashman said you'd meet me at his club with the markers."

"Oh. Oh, yes. You're Dane?"

Dane bent closer to him, looked to see if the man was drunk.

"Cashman did call you?"

"Of course. Come on in, Dane."

Dane went inside the place and the door closed behind him.

"You brought the money with you?"

"You've got the markers?"

"Yes. Be with you in a minute." He went to the back of the house, via an archway. He returned.

"Now," he said, holding a sheaf of notes. "We'll trade."

Dane hit him, hopefully. Hit him flush on the chin, felt that sweet-shot feeling travel the length of his forearm. The man went down immediately and Dane, still hopeful, reached for the notes. A door squeaked and a dark shape slid toward him from the foyer closet. Another came through the archway. Each of them carried a knife, at hip level, the honed-looking blades tilted upward and straight at Dane's ribs.

Dane, for no good reason, picked on the first one, went at him aggressively. Defense became offense in an instant as Dane launched a full-blown, football-style kick at the knife and the hand holding it. His foot met the target, but more rewarding than the anguished scream was the sight of the knife flying free, the sound of it bouncing off the ceiling.

Dane wheeled then, found out too late that he had made a serious miscalculation. The other one should have seen that the odds had been suddenly shortened on him, should have been at least surprised enough to hang back. Instead of that he was charging headlong as Dane was turning into him. Dane's right shoulder caught his attacker a glancing blow, enough to deflect the path of the upswinging knife a vital two inches. Even so the razor-sharp blade passed viciously into his body, grazed bone and went hilt deep.

Dane closed down hard with his elbow, desperately pinning the knifer's wrist, holding him fast while he chopped three times at the face below him. The fingers gave up their grip on the knife handle and the man sagged to his knees, glassy-eyed. Now it was Dane holding the knife against himself, moving slowly but purposefully toward the bathroom. He switched on the light there, found a small roll of cotton in the cabinet. Then he eased the knife out of his side again, plugged the cotton into the lips of the wound and soaked the whole area with Listerine.

The blood still gushed out of him, staining the cotton a deeper hue with every beat of his fast-pumping heart. He substituted a fresh wad, felt a telltale giddiness in his head. Next his legs were going to go rubbery. Dane knew that—and knew there was something he had to do before they picked themselves up out in the other room and came in here to finish him.

## 2

Back in the Surfside Club when Lissa had turned and walked away from Dane, she had talked and acted with much more decision than she felt. She had even had to stifle an impulse to glance at him over her shoulder, knowing that that would bring the tall man to her side and touch off a battle royal.

So the girl had kept going, on into the richly decorated dressing room that Johnny Cashman had provided especially for her. It was an apartment in itself, that room, with a divan that opened into a bed, an electric stove, icebox—all the comforts of home. This was the star treatment, a goal achieved, but right then the redhead would have traded even for that noisy, drafty place she used to share with eleven other showgirls at the Riviera. Provided Johnny Cashman went with the deal and Timothy Dane was waiting for her after the last show.

She considered Margie's prospects for the night, remembering the interlude she had shared.

"What are you thinking about, honey?" the maid asked, looking up from her paperback.
"Philadelphia."
"If a place made me that sad," the woman said, "I'd start thinking about somewheres else."
"They all make me sad. Miami most of all."
The telephone buzzed softly and the maid answered it.
"Yes?" she asked. Then, spiritedly, "Yes, sir, she's right here."
"Who is it?" Lissa asked.
"Who else?"
The girl took the receiver. "Hello, Johnny."
"Well, don't be so enthusiastic, baby. What's wrong?"
"I'm tired."
"Well, that's different. I thought maybe you didn't like the dressing room I fixed up for you."
"It's beautiful."
"Sorry I couldn't get down for the show. Got some business that's tying me up."
"I heard."
"You heard what?" he asked her sharply.
"That you haven't been to the club for a week or more."
"Oh," he said, vaguely. "But there's no reason why you can't come up here."
"Up?" the girl repeated. "Up where?"
"I've—ah—moved, baby. Temporarily."
"Are you in trouble?"
"Somebody tried to kill me," Cashman said. "Threw a bomb into the house."
"Good Lord!"
"Shook me up, that's about all."
"Who'd throw a bomb at you, for heaven's sake?"
"Some screwballs," Cashman said. "Trying to squeeze me out of a deal."
"But that's a terrible thing, throwing bombs. Did you have them arrested?"
Cashman laughed, as if that was naïve. "No," he said, "I didn't. A thing like that you hush up. Don't want to give any other bums ideas. But forget that. How about coming up after you're through tonight?"
"I'm awfully tired," Lissa told him. "Practically out on my feet."
"That's one of the things I want to see you about. Karl says you kind of kicked over the traces last night." There was menace in his voice now, the talent he had for making her afraid of him.
"Did Karl tell you what somebody did to his traces?" she said with a

note of defiance.

"No, he didn't. But what happens to Karl isn't important to me."

"You've got to stop it, Johnny. Stop with these damn bodyguards—"

"They're for your protection, baby. I don't want anybody bothering you—"

"I can take care of myself. I always have."

"No you haven't, Lissa, I took you away from Bernie King without any trouble at all."

"That's a contract. I'm talking about me."

"But you and the contract are the same thing," Cashman said very deliberately. "And don't you forget it. Tell Benny to drive you up here after your second show." Just as he had earlier with Dane, he hung up abruptly on Lissa. The girl stood looking at the phone almost as if she could see a face in it.

"Now what?" the maid asked sympathetically.

Lissa shook her head. "I'm going out," she said, a little desperately. "I need some fresh air."

"Want me to come along?"

"No. I've got to get alone. To think."

"You won't be alone. What's this new one's name, do you know?"

"Benny," Lissa said, opening the door and stepping out. Benny was right there.

"Where we going?"

"*I'm* going for a walk along the beach. Alone." Benny shook his head.

"This is a soft job," he said. "I wouldn't want to lose it the first night." Lissa glared at him, fought down an angry reply and walked quickly toward the performers' exit. It was a starless night, and the moon over Miami hung low in the eastern sky, sending a shimmering, silvery ladder between it and the unusually quiet Atlantic surf.

"What a night," Benny said.

"Oh, shut up!" Lissa told him, close to tears. What a night it was—for that sloe-eyed brunette out in it somewhere with Dane. But the brunette wasn't with Dane, she was stepping out of a cab that had just wheeled up to the stage door. And one glance at the other girl's frightened face told Lissa that something was very wrong.

"What is it? What's happened?"

"I don't know," Margie said thinly. "I don't know...."

"Where's Timothy?"

"Back there."

"Back where?"

"At Shag's place. He went in and then there was a fearful racket. A man came out with a knife in his hand. His face was all bruised. I've never seen anyone so wild-looking...."

"You left Timothy there?"

"He was a crazy man—a fanatic...."

Lissa went past her in a blur. "Take me there," she told the cabbie.

"Not me, sister. That's a police call ..."

"What's the address?"

"Four twenty Carlouel Road."

"Hey!" Benny shouted. "Where you going?" But the long-legged Lissa was already thirty feet gone, running boy-fashion into the parking lot. By the time the heavy-bodied hoodlum had gotten underway, she was already behind the wheel of the milk-white El Dorado, gunning the motor to life. She backed out of the spot reserved for J. P. Cashman, spun the front end around in a maneuver that brushed Benny aside, then roared out onto Collins and north to Bal Harbour. Lissa was no expert driver, not even a good one, but tonight she was on the side of the angels—three miles through Florida's tourist-jammed east coast in not too many seconds more than three minutes. She made the turnoff on screeching tires and rocked the big Cadillac to a halt before number 420. When she got out of the car she was running....

For Brown and Keller it had been a curious quarter hour. Keller, an expert shadow, had moved behind the cab with lights cut, parked all unseen a block from 420. They had both advanced on foot and stationed themselves in the darkness to see what developed.

They were hardly there when the racket of the furious fight came to them.

"What do we do?" Brown asked.

"We stay out of it."

"But it sounds like a lot of them."

"That's his lookout," Keller insisted.

Then, as suddenly as it had begun, it was quiet. Until the door flew open and the knifer charged down the walk threateningly. The cab took flight and the man ducked back inside.

"Christ Almighty, Fred!"

"Harrison said—"

"To hell with Harrison!"

"Then let's go," Fred Keller said, as anxious as his partner to take a hand. They rushed the front door, found it locked against them, then fanned out on either side of the house seeking entry. In their hands, as though part of them, were businesslike .32 revolvers.

A voice in there gave the alarm.

"*Policia! Vamonos!*"

"*... no tengo el dinero!*" came a fainter shout from the bathroom.

Harry Brown shattered the glass of the rear porch door with his gun butt, reached in to release the knob lock and entered the place. A figure appeared before him in the kitchen, uttered a brief curse and fled the other way. His two companions joined him in the living room, all yelling at each other, then crowded out through the front door. Brown started after them.

"Let them go!" Keller commanded at his back.

"*Go?*"

"They said they didn't have the money. That's all we care about." He was the first one to find Dane, lying on the bathroom floor in a pool of his own blood. He knelt down, felt for a pulse in the temple.

"Dead?"

"Not yet. Better call an ambulance."

Brown went in search of the telephone, came back a minute later.

"It's a damn party line," he reported. "Somebody's got it tied up."

"And he hasn't got the money on him," Keller said worriedly. "We're in a mess."

"Too late to go after them now. What can we do for him?"

"He's coming to again. Hand me that cotton."

Brown reached out for the box on the bathtub ledge, abruptly stopped and looked toward the commotion outside the house.

"Now what?"

"We don't want company," Keller said, rising to both feet and moving through the door. "Come on!"

Brown followed him out the back way, then around the side of the house to a window whose blind wasn't completely lowered.

"Well, I'll be damned!" Brown murmured a moment later.

"What is it?"

"That's her—the girl from the night club...."

Lissa sprinted up the walk, went through the opened doorway oblivious of her own safety.

"*Timothy!*"

There was no answer. She crossed the living room, passed under the archway, cried his name again. A groan answered her and she swung toward the bathroom.

"*Timothy!*"

"Stop ..."

"You're alive!"

"... screaming. Get the cotton."

"Oh, darling ...

"Cotton."

She spied the box, but when she pulled a handful loose, a tightly folded manila envelope spilled out with it. She let it lie, dropped to both knees beside Dane.

"The cotton," she said. "What do I do with it?"

"Envelope there?"

"Yes," she told him and he sighed deeply.

"Hold the cotton tight against my left side. Where it's bleeding. Keep holding it." She did that, followed along with him as he carefully pushed himself upward, tested his legs and found they'd hold him.

"I think it's congealing," Dane said then, shakily.

"What happened to you?"

"Walked into a knife. Pulled a blackout."

"She said he was a crazy man."

"Who said?"

"Your date. Miss Runout Powder."

He grinned down at her, wearily. "Not you, though. Not old fearless Liz. How did you ever get rid of them?"

She shook her head. "I didn't get rid of anybody. The place was empty."

Dane didn't understand. They'd had him cold, but for some reason he was not only still alive but the envelope was safe.

"Let's get out of here," Lissa was saying. "Before that Shag character comes back."

"Shag?"

"Wasn't he the one who tried to kill you?"

"Shag is the one they did get."

"What?"

"He's in the bathtub. Behind the shower curtain."

Her head swung slowly toward the drawn plastic curtain. "There's a—dead man there?"

"He was supposed to meet me at the club," Dane said, going forward under his own power, reaching down to pick up the money. "Supposed to get this for Cashman," he told her.

"Timothy, take me out of here, will you?"

He did, turning her around, moving her out of the room, his fingers kneading her back to quiet the trembles just beginning.

"But why is he dead?" she asked hollowly. "Why do they throw bombs into people's homes …?"

"Bombs?"

"That's what they did to Johnny. What is it all about?"

Dane said nothing as he guided her through the late rumpus room. He saw that the sheaf of markers were gone with the killers and he had the very distinct recollection of at least two of them coming into the bathroom after him. At least two of them because, as they roughly searched him, he had heard them speaking....

*Speaking?* He was certain that he heard two voices. Positive. But what he wasn't at all sure about was what they had said—and now it came to him that they hadn't been speaking English.

Then he had gone under, from the shock of the wound, the too-sudden loss of blood, and there was a gap in his memory until the sound of Lissa calling his name woefully. And she said the house was empty.

Dane closed the front door behind them, started down the walk to the waiting Cadillac.

"Oh, oh."

"What?"

"That was a police cruiser just went by," he said. "Walk natural, let me take the wheel." He opened the car door and she got in. He went around to the other side, slid into the seat and switched the ignition. The long sleek machine pulled away from the curb unhurriedly, rolled down the dark street. The cruiser paused at the next corner and Dane was forced to pass it.

"They following us?" Lissa asked.

"No."

"Why are we worried about the police? What have we done that was wrong?"

"It's going to be messy," Dane explained. "I don't want you brought into it."

"Where are we going now?"

"First I want to pick up some things at a drugstore. Then you can drop me at my hotel...."

"St. Francis is only a little way from here...."

"I don't want to get mixed up with any hospital," he said. "My big problem is to catch up with Cashman."

"To tell him about Shag?"

"To tell him to collect his damn money. Enough's enough."

"I don't see why Buddy just didn't mail him a check," Lissa said and Dane laughed in spite of his troubles.

"Check is a dirty word in Cashman's business," he told her, then eased the car into the curb before an open drugstore.

"I'll get what you need, Timothy."

"Good. Some gauze bandages, a roll of adhesive and a strong antiseptic." She made the purchases quickly and they drove on down Collins and back across the causeway to the mainland. Then they were at his hotel, and so far as Dane had been able to tell no particular car had followed them here.

"I'll come up with you," Lissa suggested. "Help you bandage that cut."

"Don't you have to get back to the club?"

"Yes," she said, looking at him steadily. "But if I do go over there now, I have a feeling I may never see you again."

"In that case you'd better help me with the first aid."

The same cruiser that Dane had fretted about made Brown and Keller delay getting back to their own car. For several minutes they even worried that they had lost track of Dane until Keller spotted the hard-to-conceal white El Dorado at the drugstore. They followed it over to Miami, and with Brown watching any further comings and goings at the hotel, Keller went looking for a telephone.

Keller came back a very glum man.

"You talk to Harrison?" Brown asked him.

"Yeah." He climbed into the car, sprawled with his chin touching his chest.

"What's the matter with you?"

"Harrison was a *leetle* peeved with us."

"What'd we do?"

"We interfered," Keller said. "We boy-scouted ourselves right out of this job."

"For crissake—didn't you tell him the guy was being killed?"

"I told him. Then he told *me*. The private detective from New York is expendable. Even as you and I. The only thing that counts is to keep track of the money and stay out of sight." Keller's voice had descended to a growl. "Hell," he said, "I couldn't even guarantee where the money is."

"I never figured Harrison was such a cold proposition."

"He's not. He's a very talented guy."

"Then what's he so tough about?"

"Somebody's putting the pressure on him," Keller said. "There must be something a little sticky involved."

"And we get the hook. Did he say when?"

"Not the hour and the minute. Just tomorrow—'*as soon as two people I can count on*' fly down here. The man's words exactly."

"I've never been yanked before," Brown said.

"You'll get over it."

"But you didn't see her dance."

"I didn't what?"

"The dancer—Lissa. I'd have liked to see her act one more time, and know what was coming."

"You're a free soul, Harry," Keller told him. "You probably won't mind Warsaw at all."

"Warsaw? Is that what he said?"

"No," Keller said. "But he sounded like it."

Brown thought about that and kept his silence for nearly half a minute.

"That's all right with me," he said then. "I'd still do what we did."

"Me, too," Keller said.

Another silence. Then: "I wonder what they're doing up in his room."

That made Keller laugh at his friend.

## 3

An attendant had parked the car for him, and it was only with the likes of Lissa striding beside him that a man in Dane's disheveled state could have crossed that spacious lobby unnoticed. An elevator carried them aloft and they went into the room. Lissa helped him out of his jacket, peeled the bloodstained shirt off his shoulders.

"Gee, I bet that hurts," she said, watching him soak it again with the alcohol.

"Give me two of those bandages," he said, and while he held them in place she taped the adhesive to his body.

"Now a drink," he said, "and the treatment is finished."

Lissa made them a drink, handed him the glass. "I hope it's strong enough," she said and he sipped it.

"Yes, indeed. Thanks, nurse."

She pulled his head forward, kissed him meaningfully on the lips.

"Anything else I can do for you?"

"You're doing fine. It's nice to be out of your doghouse."

"That was some jolt you handed me, sitting at the bar during my number."

"I didn't know you saw me."

"I couldn't catch your eye, darling," she said in mild reproof, leaning close to him. She had the tall man's eye now, had him speechless, overwhelmed by the sight, sound and scent of her.

"You know something, Timothy? You look like you're in love."

"You mean I'm not sick?"

"And you know something else? I say to hell with Johnny Cashman. You game?"

"Always was. But that reminds me—what's the number at the club?"

"Oh, fine."

"What is it?"

"I'll get it for you," she said half pettishly and crossed to the telephone. The hotel operator gave her an outside line and she dialed. A moment later she handed the phone to Dane.

"I want to speak to Mr. Cashman."

"Mr. Cashman is not here."

"Has he been in tonight?"

"No."

"Would you tell me where I can reach him?"

"I'm sorry, but—"

"Then you reach him for me. Tell him to get in touch with Timothy Dane at the Golden Shores. Tell him it's very urgent."

"I will." They hung up.

"Not there?" Lissa asked. She'd turned on the radio, switched off all the light in the room but one small lamp.

"No. What's his home phone?"

"I don't know."

"Really?"

"And truly. I've never had to call him about anything."

As she spoke she moved around, as she moved during her number, but more slowly, in smooth rhythm to the music. The music stopped and a pleasant-voiced disc jockey began talking briefly. He played another record.

"How do you like Lili St. Cyr?" Lissa asked him out of the blue.

"I've never seen her," Dane said.

"You're kidding!"

"Nope. I've heard she's good."

"Good? The best. And certainly the most gorgeous figure around."

"Makes you look pretty sad, does she?"

"Oh, I guess my legs are all right. And where I sit down. But my breasts are all wrong."

Dane laughed.

"They are," she said. "I wish they were smaller. About thirty-six."

"Sure," Dane said. "You don't think Cashman would be in the book do you?"

"Not in his business. Timothy, mix me a drink, will you? Like the first one we had together on the train."

He went to the dresser where the liquor was, but he kept the mixture lighter than she'd asked for. While he was doing it, Lissa was telephoning—and then something odd happened. The record ended on the radio, and when the disc jockey spoke again it was directly to

Lissa.

"Doll-baby," he said happily. "How are 'ya?"

"Fine," the girl said, but of course only he and Dane heard that. "How have you been?"

"Terrible, up till now," he said to her and countless thousands all over Miami. "I'm talking to Lissa, friends," he said, remembering them. "Lissa is only the most beautiful girl in the world. You still there, doll?"

"Still here, Bobby. I want you to play something for me."

"You bet. And I'm going to catch you Saturday night. Doing the show from the Surfside lounge that night."

"Wonderful."

"Listen, you night hounds—you do yourselves the biggest favor of your life. Come down to the Surfside Club on the beach and get an eyeful of Lissa. What did you want to hear, honey?"

"I'm in the mood for love."

"Are you stating a fact, or making a request? Because I can close up this radio station in nothing flat …"

She laughed at him. "Can you play it soon?"

"Soon as we dig it up. It's not exactly a rock tune."

"I know. Thanks a lot, Bobby."

"For you, anything, Lissa. Anytime. 'Bye, doll."

The doll set the receiver down, walked to where Dane sat with the drinks. She lowered herself contentedly into his lap.

"What were we talking about, Timothy?"

"You were telling me what terrible shape you're in."

"Oh, it's not as bad as all that."

"No, it isn't."

"Except, like I say, for my bosom. Don't you think so, Timothy?"

"You want my honest opinion?"

"Yes."

"Lizzie, I think your chest is terrific."

"Ah, you're sweet."

The telephone rang.

"Upsa-daisy," Dane said.

"They'll hang up."

"That's what I'm afraid of." He rose from the chair, lifting her bodily, dropping her informally into the cushion and went to the demanding telephone.

"Dane speaking."

"Johnny Cashman. Where the hell is Shag?"

"That's it. Make with the hardrock."

"What?"

"Your business phone is bugged, bigshot. Shag never left home."

"Slower, friend, slower."

"Your—contact—man—is—dead. You hear that all right? I waited for him at your club. He didn't show and I went up to his place. They beat me to him...."

"'They' who?"

"If *you* don't know, Cashman, then we are in trouble. But there were three of them. They must have caught Shag as soon as he opened the door. There was a trail of blood right from there to the bathroom. I damn near gave them your money before I spotted it...."

"You ran into them?"

"Yeah, I ran into them."

"But you've still got the dough?"

"And they have the markers."

"So what?"

"So what? No markers, Cashman, no money."

"The hell with that!"

"Maybe so, but it's the arrangement I have with Bernie King."

"Listen to this, buster—I need that money *quick!* You pack it up here—" His voice broke off in mid-sentence. "You get it to the East Coast Associates office first thing in the morning," he finished and Dane laughed.

"No night delivery? I don't blame you. They're slick little bastards, and I think you know all about them."

"I don't know a damn thing."

"Then what are you hiding for? This is supposed to be your town—why don't you collect your money without all the bushwah?"

"Butt out, Dane," Cashman said in the voice that made wild beasts cringe. "This is my town. Which brings us to something else. I got word you almost made a nuisance of yourself with the redhead. Don't come into my club again. Don't come near my girl again.... What are you laughing about?"

"Nothing," Dane said, smiling still. For while the man talked into one ear, the girl was nibbling the lobe of the other and drawing his arm around her waist.

"Hang up," she whispered.

"Stay away from her," Cashman said. "I'm not kidding...."

"*Hang up*," Lissa whispered more urgently, guiding his big hand up and along her ribs.

"Dane? You still there?"

"Still here," he said, disconcerted; then let his arm fall away. "I came down to deal for Buddy Lewis's bad debts," he told Cashman in a new voice. "I've got his money. You get his markers. That's my business with you. After that we'll talk about anything else you think is important." He slammed the phone down, swung around to Lissa. She had backed away, stood looking up at him now wide-eyed.

"What's your problem?"

The girl backed off another step. "What?"

A wide grin split Dane's face. The laughter he had been bottling inside him burst like uncorked champagne.

"You're not angry?"

"Why should I be?"

"But the way you acted—the way you talked to Johnny. Why, you big faker! I was afraid to take another breath...." She came toward him again. "But you really shouldn't get him down on you," she said.

Dane brought her in close. "He told me not to do this."

"Did he?"

"Or this."

Lissa sighed, held onto him. "Tell him to mind his own business," she said huskily.

"Listen—isn't that the song you ordered?"

"I can't hear a thing. Kiss me like that again."

"What about the song?"

"Who needs it?" she said and Dane picked her up off the floor, carried her with him to the darkened bedroom.

That was as far as he got with her. The room's buzzer sounded and he set the girl down.

"You're certainly not going to answer it," Lissa said, getting directly in front of him. "Not at a time like this."

"I was half expecting a visit."

"Not that scaredy-cat singer?"

"The cops."

"Cops?"

"The car you drive isn't exactly inconspicuous, kiddo. Not even in Miami."

"You mean they've found Shag? They think we killed him?"

"Something like that."

The buzzer had been pressed twice more.

"Stand aside," he told her. "And stay in here." He went to the door.

"Who is it?"

"Police officers. Open up."

Dane opened it, found himself staring into the muzzle of a foreign make automatic.

"Back away, Mr. Dane. Keep those clever hands in front of you." This was the voice on the phone in New York, the mustached, black-coated Latin type that Lissa had described on the train. He crossed the threshold, alone.

"Where are your friends?"

"They are licking their wounds," he said in his precise tones. "But this is a peaceful visit, even a friendly one."

"Then you can pocket the gun," Dane suggested.

"Perhaps I can. We'll see." His dark eyes looked beyond Dane. "Why not have the young lady join us? I would enjoy seeing her again."

Lissa, who had been peeking into the room stepped out. From their visitor's face he really did enjoy seeing her again, seemed mesmerized by that gently undulating, ungirdled figure crossing the floor.

"How do you do," he said suavely, white teeth flashing in a smile.

"Don't *'How do you do'* me," Lissa told him, coming to stand close to Dane. "I remember how you were the last time we met."

"My deepest apologies," he said. "It was a matter of timing that made us so brusque. A car was waiting at a certain place with very definite orders." He smiled at Lissa again, glanced at Dane. "Why don't we all sit down and make ourselves comfortable?"

"Why don't you put the gun away?" Dane suggested again.

"We'll see," he said again. "First let's take seats." Dane lowered himself into the couch. Lissa stayed nearer than his shadow.

"I hope your wound isn't too painful, Mr. Dane."

"Shag doesn't feel his at all. That was pretty rough."

"Only because the man was so unreasonable. Now you," he added with a sidelong glance at Lissa, "obviously have a great deal more to live for."

"You're darn right he has," the redhead told him. "Why don't you go home?"

"I will be gone in a matter of seconds."

"If," Dane said.

"If what?" Lissa asked him.

"If I give him Cashman's money."

"*Pre*cisely."

"I don't think Johnny will like that," Lissa told them both very simply.

"*Pre*cisely," Dane said, mimicking the other man rather well.

"But what do we care," that one said, "what the pig of a Cashman likes or doesn't like?"

Dane smiled at him. "Can't please everybody, eh?"

He nodded. "*Pre*— Exactly my feelings, Mr. Dane. Now then. I have with me what seems to be a great number of IOU's signed by Mr. Buddy Lewis, the entertainer." As he spoke he slipped them from an inside pocket of his topcoat. "And you, Mr. Dane, have Mr. Lewis's one hundred thousand dollars." He leaned forward, laid the markers on the low table between them. "Put the money there, Mr. Dane, and we have a bargain satisfactory to everyone."

"Except Johnny Cashman."

"Except the despicable Cashman. The money, please."

"No deal."

His eyes widened at the curt turndown, then narrowed and lost their mock-friendly luster.

"Now it's you who are being unreasonable."

Dane got to his feet and the venomous little gun came up sharply.

"Who the hell are you, anyhow? What's your angle?"

"I like you seated, Dane."

Dane grinned. "There—I knew I could make you drop the 'Mr.' Now let's cut through the rest of the act. You're no trooper, you're not even connected with the rackets. But you are goddamned well-connected and you apparently think you own some kind of immunity to the homicide law ..."

"I warn you to stop moving around ..."

"Most any law, as a matter of fact," Dane continued. "You tap any telephone you want, you rob trains, stop them when it suits you, arm yourselves, impersonate police officers. And sell what doesn't belong to you." Dane looked down at the man. "All that and murder," he said. "Who do you think you are, mister?"

"I am a simple man doing a simple job. Give me the money, Mr. Dane."

"That, too. The money. You're spending as much as you hope to get...."

"As I *will* get." Now he came out of his chair, flourishing the gun dramatically, as though to show that the weapon gave him not only equality with the big man but superiority. "You," he said with intensity, "are a stupid man, acting stupidly." His angry face swung swiftly to Lissa. "Your choice of men is very poor," he told her almost jealously. "It's time you were educated."

"Time I was *what?*"

"Stand up, *roja!* You're leaving with me."

"Sit tight, honey," Dane said quietly. "The *roja, amigo*," he told the other man, "isn't involved at all."

"I beg to differ. As Cashman told you on the phone, he considers the beautiful lady as being very important. As I can see with my own eyes, she has a value to you." Those same eyes roamed the girl from head to toe. "Also to me," he said. "She is very much involved with this business."

"But she's not going anywhere."

"We'll leave it to her. Sweetheart," he said familiarly, "I want you to take a little trip with me. It will be very interesting...."

"No."

"In that case I am going to kill your lover before your eyes—"

"He's bluffing, Liz."

"Whether I'm bluffing is the chance you take," he said, concentrating on the girl. "This is a very modern gun in my hand. It makes less noise than a pop of a cork. I tell you that, and let you decide what to do."

"Timothy!"

"He's bluffing. If he was going to shoot me, he'd have done it when he came through the door."

"No, I came to negotiate. I came in friendship. I was very rudely rejected. Now my terms are emotional. You will hand over the money, here and now, or you will pay it as ransom—"

"That's for the birds," Dane said, scowling down at him impatiently. "If you're going to shoot, for crissake, shoot—"

"No!" Lissa cried. "Stop talking like that!"

"Easy, honey, *easy*. This is a con man. But it's all ten-twenty-thirty stuff ..."

"I will count three times," he said. "Then we will see how *el toro* looks with a bullet between his eyes ..."

"No, no! I'll go with you!"

"You're not going anywhere with him," Dane said.

"One," the man counted.

"Don't take a step, Liz," Dane told her. "If you do, I'm going to call his bluff myself."

"Two."

"Timothy—*please!*"

"You're not going with him...." Dane repeated.

"Three!"

Lissa screamed—but both Dane and his avowed assassin had heard the other sound, the buzzing from the door. Dane smiled into the man's stunned face, smiled in relief, because at the very end he had seen the gunman's knuckle whiten on the trigger, known that he had made a foolhardy gamble.

But there was that beautiful buzzer, sizzling away insistently, and in answer to Lissa's woebegone cry came a hand—pounding on the door panel.

"I vote we answer it," Dane said.

"All right—but I tell you this sincerely. Provide me cover or I will shoot my way out of this room."

Dane believed him, nodded his agreement. He went to the door, opened it gratefully.

"Police," said a granite-jawed, gray-eyed plainclothes man. "What's going on in here?"

"Police?" Dane echoed. "Who sent for the police?"

The cop brushed by him, left his partner to block the exit.

"Was that you who screamed for help, lady?" he asked Lissa.

The girl looked at Dane, at the man sitting nonchalantly in the chair, his hand pocketed, holding a loaded gun.

"I don't need any help," she said.

"Then why did you scream?"

She lifted her shoulders in a shrug. "Just felt like screaming, I guess," she said, her face as foolish-looking as the words she spoke.

The detective frowned, whirled on Dane.

"Who owns the white Caddy?"

"What white Caddy?"

"Kid me not, bo. A white El Dorado that was parked in front of Four twenty Carlouel Road, Bal Harbour, and turned up in the parking lot downstairs. A guy about your size and a so-called beautifully built redhaired woman left it with the attendant one hour ago."

"What do you mean—'so-called'?" Lissa said defensively and Dane laughed at her femaleness in the face of everything else that was going on in the room.

"Funny, hanh?" the cop growled. "Couple of thrill killers." His eyes stabbed the man in the chair. "Who are you?"

"My name is Diaz, officer. Manuel Diaz. And I know nothing about a white Cadillac."

"What was the lady yelling about?"

"I don't know that, either."

The detective at the door spoke then. "Where'd you pick up that wound?" he asked Dane.

"I fought like hell for it."

"And then you killed him."

"No," Dane said, "I didn't."

"We'll take your statement downtown," the other one said. "Let's go."

"You are not including me?" Manuel Diaz said, and it was not so much a question as a statement.

"I guess not," the detective answered.

"Thank you," the dark man said politely and let himself out of the room. Dane put on a fresh shirt after that and the four of them left. On the street they separated—Dane and one detective in the Cadillac, Lissa and the other in a police sedan—to meet again in a spick-and-span interrogation room of the Dade County Sheriff's Bureau.

The man in charge introduced himself as Chief Deputy Genovar. Dane handed him a card, identifying himself as an investigator for the Fidelis Insurance Company.

"This is an informal inquiry, Mr. Dane," Genovar said then. "Do you object to having the stenographer?"

"Not a bit."

"Fine. I wonder if you'd give me an account of your time tonight?"

"How much of the night?"

"Oh, begin about nine o'clock."

"Well, at nine I was still on board the train from New York. We arrived about ten and after I checked into my hotel I went over to the Surfside Club on the beach. It was eleven thirty when I took a cab up to Four twenty Carlouel Road in Bal Harbour. It was about midnight when I left there and drove back to my hotel. That's where your men found me."

"I see," Genovar said, turning a pencil around in his fingers. "So much for your time. How about events, Mr. Dane, and people."

"One person I remember is named Fred Young. He works for the Yellow Cab Company and drove me to Carlouel Road...."

Genovar looked past Dane's head and nodded to one of the detectives. The man left the room.

"I also remember three men who were inside the house—"

"Three men?"

"Total strangers. We had a brief fight and one of them knifed me in the side."

"Is it serious?"

"I don't think so."

"What was the fight about?"

"One of them claimed to be the man I'd come to see. Actually they'd killed him before I got there."

"Then that leaves you out?"

"It sure does."

"And the ones we want to talk to are your three strangers?"

"I'd like to talk to them myself."

"What was your business with Wilson?"

"Who?"

"The murdered man that you came to see."

"I only knew him as Shag," Dane explained. "And I can't talk about my business with him."

The pencil stopped turning in Genovar's hand.

"I think you know better than that, mister," he said. "There's no such thing as privileged information when it hinders the investigation of a felony."

"Well, that's the legal view of it," Dane said. "But I've got to be more realistic than that."

"There's nothing more real than breaking the law, Dane."

"How about a man's reputation? I deal in confidences. I'm expected to keep them."

"An honest difference of opinion," Genovar said. "Luckily, we have our courts to decide who's wrong."

"You're going to book me?" Dane said gloomily.

"I deal in laws," the Sheriff's man said. "I'm expected to enforce them."

"What's the charge?"

"Ah, hell, no charge. Nothing that will hurt. Just hold you on protective custody as a material witness to a homicide."

"How soon can I have a hearing?"

Genovar looked across the room to where Lissa sat, looked back to the tall man and made a natural assumption about them.

"This is a friendly town, Dane," he said. "A place to have a good time. Why don't you tell me what your business was with Shag Wilson?"

"Why is it so important?"

"Murder is always important. But Shag Wilson—well, that means your real business was with Johnny Cashman ..." Genovar glanced in surprise at Lissa. "Did you want to say something, young lady?"

"No," the redhead told him quietly.

"Anytime we can brush Cashman with a homicide case," Genovar continued to Dane, "then it becomes the most important business in this office. So why not unload yourself?"

"Sorry, Genovar."

"Timothy—why don't you tell the man?"

Dane winced. Genovar spoke up immediately.

"You sound as if you know it yourself," he suggested.

The door opened and the missing detective returned, crossing to his boss, speaking to him in an undertone. Dane took those few moments to shake his head at Lissa.

"Your cab driver backs you up," Genovar said to him then. "I guess you're not a suspect."

"He can leave?" Lissa asked.

"Just as soon as you tell me why he went to see Shag Wilson tonight."

She looked to Dane for a release. He didn't give it to her.

"I can't."

"You won't like our detention cells, Miss—"

"Ah, come on now, Genovar," Dane protested.

"And I'm going to see that you spend considerable time in one. Until this case is closed."

"This girl's got a living to make, dammit! She hasn't anything to do with your case."

Genovar ignored him to concentrate his fire on the girl.

"I'm going to ask for an awful big bail, young lady, and in a case like this I'm going to get it. You could grow a lot older in that little cell …"

"Hooray for friendly Miami," Dane grumbled.

"Timothy …"

All through this he had been watching the girl's face, seen her eyes grow more doleful with each word Genovar spoke, her beautiful chin began to quiver at the prospects of life in the Dade County Jail. He was thinking, too, very vividly, of how it had been going between them back in the hotel room, the prospects there. Dane let go with a deep sigh.

"Lock us up," he told Genovar.

"Doesn't the lady have something to say about that?"

To Dane's vast surprise his girl was smiling at him, telegraphing their very private thing for everyone to see.

"What you say goes," she said, standing up and turning to Genovar with her arms extended. "Lock us up," she said to him.

"This is a mistake," he said. "I hope the two of you know what you're doing—" There was a noisy interruption, a loud knock on the door and then the door thrown open. Two men came in, one carrying a notepad and pencil, the other a Graflex camera.

"Hiya, Chief," the reporter said breezily, his sharp eyes sweeping all their faces.

"Creamer, gahdammit, get out of here!"

"When you've got Lissa? Please, Genovar, let's not play games—"

"I've got who?"

Creamer turned to the girl, smiling wolfishly. "How's Johnny Cashman these days?" he asked. "Haven't seen him around."

"As a matter of fact," Lissa said, "neither have I."

"Where do you want her, Jojo?" Creamer asked the photographer.

"Anyplace so she's sitting," Jojo said.

"How about the desk? You don't mind, do you, Chief?"

Genovar was still thinking about something else. "You're a friend of Cashman's?" he asked Lissa as the quick-moving reporter led her by the hand to the desk.

"He's my business manager," the girl answered and Creamer paused to jot that down.

"That's good, honey," he told her warmly. "Now just make yourself comfortable on that desk and cross those legs."

"More knee, please," Jojo said, aiming the camera. The bulb flashed. "One more," he called out automatically, reloading and dropping to one knee.

"What business does Cashman manage you in?" Genovar asked.

"Oh, brother!" Creamer cried, as if in pain. "You mean you really don't know who Lissa is?"

"I'm just a dancer...."

"Cross 'em the other, way, please. Great! Hold it. One more please...."

Genovar swung around to Dane, the forgotten man lounging against the wall.

"Don't tell me *you* work for Cashman?"

"Nope."

"Okay," Creamer said importantly, "let's get the facts. What's the rap, honey? Reckless driving? Scofflaw? Overexposed?"

"I'm just going to jail," she said. "I honestly don't know all the details...."

"But you had to do something. Come on, kid, you can tell me."

Lissa shook her head. "That's it—I didn't do anything."

"They're both being held in protective custody," Genovar said. "They're material witnesses in a homicide investigation."

"Hot dog! Who shot who?"

"Shag Wilson was stabbed to death about eleven o'clock tonight."

"By who?"

"We expect to make an arrest within twenty-four hours."

"Yeah, sure. Did you say it was a gang killing?"

"No, I didn't."

"Gang killing," Creamer said, busily writing. "Probably the beginning of a big gang war, right?"

"I didn't say anything about that—"

"Are you bringing in Cashman?"

"We're looking for him."

"Hiding out, hanh?"

"Call it what you want."

Creamer looked at Dane.

"Who are you, pal, and how do you figure in?"

Dane ignored him. "Let's go," he said to Genovar.

"Hold it, hold it," the reporter said. "I've got to get the story here—"

"Not from me you don't," Dane told him, and a flash bulb popped in his face.

"You'll be sorry," the reporter told him and Lissa stepped forward.

"Take it easy on him," she said to Creamer. "Timothy's just a real nice guy trying to get a job done."

Creamer's eyes grew progressively wider. "Does Cashman know what a real nice guy Timothy is?"

"It's all Johnny's fault that he's in this jam—"

"Wowie!" came the joyous cry and the pencil raced across the pad.

"How's that?" Genovar pounced. "You say Cashman caused Wilson's murder?"

"No," Lissa said, confused now. "I didn't mean that Johnny actually did it. I only ..." She looked at Dane, who was resting against the wall again, his eyes closed wearily. "I'm not going to say another word," Lissa announced. "I promise, honey."

"Say 'honey,'" Creamer said, "how about a nice clinch shot with Lissa? Make a swell souvenir. Go ahead, Lissa—give Timothy a big kiss...." The newspaperman suddenly stepped backward, partly because Dane had straightened from the wall, partly because of the tall man's expression.

"Listen, Chief, you better get the cuffs on that guy."

"No, Creamer," Genovar said blandly, "I think I've got a better idea."

"Nothing doing, Genovar," Dane said.

"What's going on?" the reporter asked.

"Dane here has a living to make, just like everybody else. I don't think the Sheriff's office ought to deprive him of making it. You're free to go, Dane."

"Oh, wonderful!" Lissa said happily, linking her arm through his. "Come on, darling."

"He doesn't mean us, Liz."

"Just you?"

"Hold that expression," Jojo said. "One more now...."

"We'll have to detain you, Miss," Genovar said with broad sympathy. "For your own protection. All right, Dane—you can leave."

"Send these clowns out," Dane said heavily. "You win."

"You heard him, Creamer," Genovar said. "Both of you beat it."

"And miss the confession? Not on your life!"

"Mitch. Jonesie," Genovar said and the plainclothes men moved on the reporter.

"By God, you're breaking the First Amendment! Right here in the gahdam Sheriff's office! Who do you think you're shovin'?"

"Watch the camera, buddy, watch the camera!" Then they were out and it was quiet in the interrogation room.

"I'm listening," Genovar said.

"Gee, honey, I'm sorry ..."

"Don't worry about a thing," he told her, then moved closer to the stenographer. "My client," he began, "owes Cashman a sum of money—"

"A gambling debt?"

"Now look, Genovar—"

"All right, all right. But the amount is pertinent. I want to know that."

"Substantial."

"How much?"

"Enough, I suppose, to commit murder for."

"We had a tourist killed last winter for seven dollars and thirteen cents," he said. "How much, Dane?"

"One hundred thousand."

"Well—that is substantial. Wilson was the pickup man?"

Dane nodded. "And when I went looking for him at his house, the three I told you about knew I had the money with me."

"Did they get it?"

"Not yet."

Genovar studied him. "You've got it with you now?"

"No."

"You didn't leave it in your room, I hope."

"No, I didn't."

"When are you going to deliver it to Cashman?"

"That's a tough one. As it stands right now I may have to lug the damn stuff all the way back to New York."

The Deputy's glance sharpened and he smiled. "Well, that's interesting. What is it that the mighty Cashman can't deliver to you?"

"I think I answered the important question. How about turning us out of here?"

"Okay. And don't worry about Creamer getting this. I think with his pictures, and that lively imagination, he'll have enough for page one."

The reporter was laying in wait for them, like a gadfly, and the photographer was still popping away as they drove off in the big El Dorado. Dane took the wheel, but he seemed more concerned with something beneath the seat.

"What are you looking for?"

"This," he said, slipping the now dog-eared Manila envelope from its hiding place into his pocket.

"I guess you're sick and tired of that thing."

"Liz, you said a mouthful. I've had it."

"What are you going to do?"

"Well, I could take it out to Hialeah tomorrow afternoon and bet it into a million."

"And *I* bet you could."

"Easy. Then I'd buy us a long, white motor sloop. We'd take the grand tour, kid. The long way."

"Oh, nice, Timothy. I'd like that."

"Or we could live it up. Fly charter to Monaco. Champagne for breakfast, break the bank every night."

"And those long afternoons."

"Those crazy afternoons."

She took his hand from the wheel, put it in her warm lap.

"But what you're really going to do," she said, "is take it back to New York."

"Probably."

"In the morning?"

"Unless Cashman comes up with some bright idea about those notes—what's the matter?"

"I just remembered something. I was supposed to see Johnny tonight."

"See him where?"

"The watchdog was going to take me."

"You sound worried," Dane said. "Maybe I'd better drive you over to the club."

"I'm worried about you more than anything. He's probably looking all over town for us right now."

"We won't be hard to spot in this thing."

"That's something else. This is his car.... What are you laughing at?"

"At poor old Cashman, the guy who runs things around here. If we ever get together he's going to have a lot to tell me about."

"That's what I'm afraid of."

"I know you are. That's why I'd better take you to the club …"

"No. I want to stay with you tonight."

"They know where I'm staying," he pointed out. "It won't be very peaceful there."

"Then let's go someplace else. I could sure use some of that peace and quiet."

They had been moving rather aimlessly on Biscayne, but now Dane swung west on N.W. Thirty-sixth in search of a "Vacancy" sign. They were out past Hialeah, on the Okeechobee road, before he found one.

"This is cute," Lissa said when they were inside the spick-and-span little motel room. "Just what I had in mind."

Dane had drawn the blinds, but he continued to stand by the window. The girl moved next to him.

"What are you looking at?"

"Not looking at anything," he said and that was true. What he didn't want to tell her was about the feeling he had for the last half hour that someone was looking at them.

Lissa moved to the light switch on the wall, made the room dark. When Dane turned from the window she had already taken off the green dress and was stepping out of a half-slip. Then she was naked, waiting for him, and the man thought he could hear the pulse-pounding beat of that drum again.

Along about dawn she stirred against him, mumbled sleepily. "What?"

"The peace and quiet," she said again. "Just what I had in mind."

## CHAPTER FOUR

"Wherever they are, get them," Johnny Cashman said in a coldly furious voice to the four gunmen he had summoned to the house. "And whatever you do to him," he added, pointing to a newspaper photo of Dane, "I want him still alive when he gets here."

They left, driving off in two cars, and half an hour later four more joined in the search. Cashman stayed in the house, paced from room to room, but always returning to where the newspaper lay spread out on the table. And though it only added live fuel to his already smoldering temper, the man could not resist reading and then rereading the front-page story.

Creamer had scooped the town with it, and the city-side staff had glommed nearly all of page one with Jojo's eye-filling shot of Lissa's beautiful legs, a scowling inset of Dane plus the colorful narrative that left nothing to the imagination.

DANCER AND N.Y. PRIVATE EYE GRILLED
IN KNIFE SLAYING OF JOHNNY CASHMAN AIDE

was the catch-all headline, and from then on the innuendo was shoveled on because the reporter had gotten from Genovar absolutely no information that linked Lissa and Dane with the murder. But Creamer did have a fine common denominator in the well-known Cashman and he splashed that name throughout, suggesting at least three improbable reasons why Shag Wilson was stabbed to death and attributing them all to either the Sheriff's office or that old reliable, "informed police sources."

Lissa was described as being "demonstrative" and "affectionate" toward Dane, while in his turn the man from New York was "surly," "tight-lipped" and "threatening." Creamer noted that they "left arm-in-arm for some undisclosed rendezvous, driving away in a luxurious white Cadillac whose license tag was issued to Johnny Cashman ..."

Cashman finally crumpled the offending words and pictures into a ball and flung it away from him. He went then to a telephone and dialed a Palm Beach number. Harland Burke answered.

"What do you hear from Gomez? How's he holding out?"

"One of his men arrived during the night," Burke said. "The Colonel must have the guns immediately. His army is growing restless—"

"Then send him the damn guns. I'm good for the money ..."

"It isn't a matter of promises, Cashman. My plant foreman called and said the men will not work another shift until they are paid ..."

"My God—are you that hard up?"

"Cashman," Burke said, "I am broke. Broke and desperate."

"What an operation I dealt into," the gambler growled. "All right. Get word to Gomez that the stuff is coming. I'll have the money to you today."

"Everything depends on that," Burke said. "I hope you're not letting any personal business interfere—"

"What the hell do you mean by that?"

"Well, this morning's paper seems to suggest that you're having some sort of difficulties," Burke said delicately.

"Well, let me tell you something, *partner*. Any troubles I might be having are tied up in this goddam rat race you and Gomez got me into. That sonofabitch running around with my girl just happens to have the last hundred grand you need."

"A murder?" Harland Burke exclaimed. "We're involved in that?"

"Don't cry on my shoulder, pal. You don't know what a headache is."

"But you will have the money today?"

"That's what I said. It's being collected right now."

## 2

"*El ciudad* is on the wire," the pretty little dark-haired girl said in Spanish and Luis Maximo nodded his long, saturnine face gloomily, picked up the telephone that was a direct line to the capital.

"Maximo speaking," he said, also in Spanish.

"This is Huerta," his caller told him with an air of crisp self-importance. "The President has just read the airborne edition of the Miami paper. He would like to know what in the name of hell you are accomplishing."

"My respects to *El Presidente*," Maximo answered perfunctorily, "but the situation is confused at the moment."

"Confused? *Caramba*, what do you think it is like here? That damnable Gomez grows more embarrassing by the hour. In New York they are even talking of intervention by the U. N."

"We are doing all we can," Maximo said, "to block Gomez from purchasing arms. It has come down to a delivery of a final one hundred thousand dollars. So far we have prevented that."

"This Timothy Dane—he is their agent?"

"He brought the money from New York. As Alazar said he would."

The man Huerta was being reminded of information that he already had, and now he bristled at having been called on it.

"Then why hasn't he been liquidated?" he said hastily.

"Alazar had two tries at him. I, myself, directed two more attempts to make him part with the money. But he is a professional courier, elusive. And now, of course," Maximo said with a dry laugh, "he is very much aware of our efforts."

"Is that what you want me to tell the President?"

"No, my friend. But you can tell His Excellency that I have been in close touch with Alazar in New York and that his man Diaz is working with me here. We have another plan which we think will work successfully."

"I hope so," Huerta said. "Both for your sake and the government's."

Maximo set the phone down and swung his swivel chair to the other man in the office with him.

"That was *Señor* Huerta, Diaz," he said. "*El Hombre* is not very happy with us this morning."

"The failure is all mine," the secret policeman said humbly. "I still don't know how Dane eluded me in New York."

Maximo waved his hand. "Just so he does not do the same in Miami. Now then—go on with your report."

Diaz nodded. "I was saying that for most of last night we lost him. It was natural to assume that they would come back to the hotel after their visit with the local authorities. But for reasons of their own they decided to forsake the comforts of the room there and go for a long ride."

"But you located them again?"

"Thanks to the white car," Diaz answered, "which was parked at a motel some ten miles west of here."

"The young lady is still with him?"

Diaz' eye fell on the picture of Lissa in Maximo's copy of the well-circulated paper. "*Sí señor*," he said with feeling. "She is very much with him."

Maximo looked at him sharply. "That doesn't sound impersonal," he said. "Or professional."

Diaz shrugged his slim shoulders, smiled thinly.

Maximo leaned forward on the desk. "You have a tendency, Diaz, to do more than what is expected of you."

"I was not personally involved in the accident to this Shag Wilson. My men tell me they were defending themselves and I take their word for it."

"Then you will also take *my* word for this—there must be more control exercised. You are not operating at home and you are not operating with the protection you are accustomed to."

Diaz smiled again. "But I thought you are protecting me, *Señor Consul*."

"So far as I am able," Maximo said and the secretary put her head in the doorway again.

"A call for Mr. Diaz," she said. "On number three."

Maximo pressed the third button, handed the receiver to the younger man.

"Yes," Diaz said, then listened. "Good," he said. "We'll proceed with the plan I gave you." He replaced the phone. "They are checking out of the motel," he told Maximo. "I must be on my way."

"Remember what I said," Maximo cautioned. "You are not at home. Use discretion."

"What will be, will be," the policeman said and left.

## 3

"I hope this is just a bad connection, Keller," said the clipped voice from Washington. "I hope I didn't hear what I think I did."

"You heard it, Mr. Harrison. We haven't got the slightest idea where Dane is."

There was a strained silence.

"You seem to be taking it pretty calmly, son. I like that attitude. No matter what befalls, keep smiling through—"

"I'm not smiling," Keller said.

"Well, that's too bad. And how is the other jackass doing?"

"Who?"

"I believe his name was Brown," Harrison said. "Or have you lost track of him, too?"

"Harry's right here."

"Good. Keep a firm hold on him. I'd hate to see a sterling team like that get separated...."

"You can have my resignation right now."

"Oh, no you don't! You'll come back up here and get fired like a man. But let's dispense with the amenities and get down to cases. When was the last time you saw Timothy Dane?"

"Last night," Keller said. "Almost nine hours ago. He went up to his hotel room with the girl—"

"You told me about that, remember?"

"Yes, sir. Then they came out of the hotel again with two men who turned out to be detectives from the Sheriff's office ..."

"I'm reading about that right now. Go on from when they left the Sheriff."

"Dane started back toward the hotel," Keller said, then paused briefly. "I figured he might be expecting someone would be following him by then so I—I cut off Biscayne and drove to the hotel by another route."

"And Dane never showed up?"

"No, sir."

"Where have you looked for him?"

"We split up at Flagler Street. I took everything south of there and the Beach. Harry took everything north—"

"Where are you now?"

"We got together again half an hour ago. We're west of town at the moment, out near Hialeah—*holy Toledo, there's the white Caddy!*"

"Is it Dane?"

"Yes, both of them!"

"Then get with it. And this time hang onto him no matter what else happens!"

Keller hung up. Brown already had the car started and they took off in pursuit.

"What'd Harrison say?" Brown asked.

"He said we were fired. He also said to hang onto Dane regardless."

## 4

The object of all this particular attention had been awake for some time. More accurately, he had never actually slept, not in the all-out style to which he was accustomed. As with most of his bachelor breed, Dane had never mastered the trick of sharing a bed with a woman. He felt constrained, contained, became aware of the size of him, the fragility of her, and just when he would have slipped into sweet slumber he worried about an arm thrown toward an empty pillow, poleaxing, instead, a pretty little nose. When it came to sleeping the big man needed room, and freewheeling.

Lissa, for her part, was apparently born conjugal. When love-making ended, the redhead slept. Slept beautifully, totally—but with a dogged, subconscious determination that she and Dane occupy the same part of the bed at the same time. She was a vine that clung tenaciously, a warm, three-dimensional shadow who made the bachelor wonder if he could get used to something like this, if he had maybe been missing out.

What Dane finally did was disentangle himself from arms and legs and get out of bed. A shower and a shave cleared the cobwebs, and while he dressed himself he watched curiously as Lissa maneuvered a pillow into position in her sleep and hugged it serenely. He went over and covered her then with the sheet, gave her behind an affectionate pat and left what Creamer would have called their love nest.

In the lobby office of the motel he bought the morning paper, sat down to read it while the operator cleared the line on the call he placed to New York. In a few moments he was smiling at the story, then laughing aloud at the picture of himself and the descriptive copy that set him apart from his fellow men.

The pay phone rang, and he went to answer it.

"I have Mr. Bernie King in New York," the operator told him. "Go ahead, please."

"What's up, Dane?" the manager asked. "You just caught me on the way to the airport."

"Where you going?"

"Miami, where do you think? Buddy opens Wednesday night at the Chez."

"I hope so," Dane said. "I'm still walking around with the hundred thousand."

"You're kidding," King said weakly.

"Completely fouled up," Dane admitted, "but definitely not kidding. Some other crowd moved in on Cashman and picked up the IOU's—"

"Oh, Christ!"

"I know. But they don't want Cashman to have his money and they're not fooling around about it. What do you want me to do with it?"

"My hands are tied," Bernie King said. "Both the bank and that insurance company friend of yours were very definite about getting the original markers back. You got any ideas?"

"I say let Cashman work out a deal with these friends of his. There's something else involved between them, some private argument."

"How do you mean?"

"What I mean is that it's a different proposition from the one we talked about in New York. Lewis called me the 'errand boy.' He was right, so far as we knew a couple of nights ago. But this has turned out to be one hell of a screwed-up errand you sent me on."

"You're all right, aren't you?"

"I'm bruised," Dane told him frankly. "There's been some shoving around. But that isn't why I think Cashman ought to come to us with the paper. He just hasn't leveled at all. It's a lot more involved than his getting sore at Lewis for a pass at Lizzie—"

"Who?"

"Lissa," Dane corrected.

"You're not fooling around with that, are you?"

"No, I'm not fooling at all."

"You're crazy if you are, Dane. You're just asking for trouble."

"That's not what I'm calling about."

"All right," King said. "Handle the money the best way you can."

"Where can I get in touch with you?"

"We'll be at the Americana."

That finished the conversation and Dane returned to the room. The pillow had apparently been unsatisfactory, for Lissa was awake, propped against the headboard and smoking a long cigarette. His appearance seemed to make a big difference.

"I thought you'd run out on me."

"Why would I do that?"

"I didn't go into any reasons. Where've you been?"

"Talking to Bernie King in New York."

"What does he want you to do?"

"He says stay away from you," Dane told her, sitting down beside her, lighting a cigarette for himself. "He says I'm asking for trouble."

"I can't recall your having asked for anything yet."

"There's a nice picture of you in the paper."

"Let's see." She took the folded paper out of his jacket pocket, spread it over her lap. Her expression was critical. "What in the world was I smiling about?" she asked then. "You'd think I was at a party instead of a police station. And look what they did to you."

"Just call me surly," Dane said. "What do you say about breakfast?"

"You mean you cook, too?"

"I mean get into your duds before you get eaten alive."

"Yes, dear," she said obediently, turning the sheet aside and swinging her knees past his head. She stood up, walked away from him purposefully then suddenly stopped and looked back over her shoulder. "You're not looking very surly at the moment," she said mischievously. Dane, caught in the act of admiring her all over again, laughed and came to his feet.

"Your best bet right now," he said, "is to get your clothes on."

"Yes, dear," she said again and continued on into the bathroom. She lingered only a few minutes in the hot shower, began to towel herself dry vigorously, then paused for a moment to wipe a portion of the steamy mirror clear and gaze at her reflection searchingly.

*It shows*, the redhead decided. *A dead giveaway. One look at your face, and you might just as well have been bedded in Macy's window at high noon.*

Life—if anybody asked Elizabeth Ann Miller—was worth living, and with that thought she marched directly to where Dane sat reading his sports page and kissed him enthusiastically on the lips.

"That's good," he said. "But please get dressed."

"Yes, dear."

Dress she did, not as matter-of-factly as she would have if alone but with a definite awareness of her audience. It was a calculated performance, a first-rate entertainment, and the man's appreciation was candid. He said as much.

"I'm glad you liked it," Lissa told him, smiling. "It's a new routine for me—putting things on."

"Make a fine act."

"Sure would. Except Lili St. Cyr does it so much better."

They went out then, Lissa to the car, Dane to pay the bill, and since the girl had no awareness of any possible danger she took no notice of the black sedan with the four men in it, the special radio-telephone antenna set in the roof. If she had, she might also have seen the man beside the driver making his hurry call to Diaz at the Consulate.

The sedan had moved when Dane arrived to drive the El Dorado, followed them discreetly to the roadside coffeeshop where they breakfasted sumptuously. They drove through Hialeah after that, past Keller and Brown, and were bearing left onto N.W. Thirty-sixth, with the *jai alai fronton* looming up ahead, when the attack came.

Dane assumed the black car wanted merely to pass him. Instead, it cut across his path obliquely. Reflexes made him spin the wheel and the power steering responded quickly—too quickly. The Cadillac left the road and lurched into the soft, sandy shoulder. The sedan halted abruptly, blocking them and all four men piled out, came at them on the run.

"*Timothy, don't!*" Lissa cried, trying to grab his arm. But Dane had already decided to meet the charge on foot and he swung his door open, stepped to the ground. Two of them met him head-on, hit him simultaneously on each arm with wicked looking blackjacks. Dane lashed out furiously, but the paralyzing pain shot up through both shoulders in an instant. He launched a kick at the man on his right but the other tormentor slipped around behind and dealt him a stunning blow just below the ear. Bright lights shot through his brain, the world outside was a shimmering haze. Lissa was shouting for help.

Dane lowered his head and charged blindly forward. His shoulder struck a man's chest and the man bowled off his feet. The one at Dane's back was beating a murderous tattoo on his body, and all the while Lissa kept calling to him. Dane whirled, his arm extended like a club, and the wild, roundhouse swing landed flush on the mouth and nose of his attacker. Dane couldn't see any of it, could hardly make his legs move, and he stumbled around the front of the car toward the direction of her voice. But the more he staggered forward the farther away she seemed to get. Dane's left leg gave out beneath him and he slipped helplessly to one knee. That's when they got him good.

It had happened very suddenly. It was all but over before Keller and Brown could get out of their own car and intervene. That was their natural impulse, to help, but through both their minds ran the stern warning from Harrison to stay out of it. And though they wanted to prevent what was being done to the girl, their orders were explicit about sticking to Dane and the money.

An unsatisfactory situation to be in, but their presence on the scene made the two who were searching Dane break off and run to where the other pair were forcing the unwilling Lissa into the car. Brown started after them, unmindful of Keller's shout, and for his attempt caught a nasty swipe of a blackjack alongside the temple. The sedan sped off down N.W. Thirty-sixth.

"You all right, Harry?"

"God, those things pack a wallop," Brown answered shakily. "What's going on, anyhow?"

"I hope to hell Harrison knows. I sure don't. Come on, let's get back to the car."

"We can't just leave the guy lying there...."

"No, dammit, but we've got to. We'll phone for an ambulance down the street then follow along. At least he'll stay put for a while in the hospital."

Brown nodded glumly, no happier than the other man with their roles, and followed him to the car. A siren arrested their attention and a Dade County patrol car swerved to a halt beside the Cadillac. A lone policeman got out, surveyed what at first glance seemed to be another accident, then advanced to the unconscious victim and knelt down to find a pulse.

"Hold it there!" he told Brown and Keller. "Where do you think you're going?"

"This has nothing to do with us," Keller said. "We're just driving by."

"Did you see what happened?"

"Didn't see anything."

"And you were just going to drive off again?"

"We were on our way to call an ambulance."

"Both of you?" the policeman asked caustically, moving toward his car, reaching inside for the phone. He identified himself to the dispatcher and asked for quick assistance. Then he returned to the worried-looking Brown and Keller.

"Let's have a look at your driver's licenses."

"Now wait a minute—"

"Your licenses."

They produced them, handed them over, and the policeman transcribed the information to his own report sheet.

"When did you arrive from Washington?" he asked then.

"Last night."

He walked behind their car, noted the 'E' tag and wrote it down.

"In town on business or vacation?"

"Vacation," Keller said.

"Where are you staying?"

"One twenty-five, North West Seventeenth Street. Apartment Four A."

"How long do you plan to stay in Miami?"

"That's—ah—indefinite." The siren of the ambulance could be heard in the near distance. "Listen, officer, we've done absolutely nothing wrong. We have no idea what happened to him …"

"I'm going to have to hold both of you."

"*Hold* us?"

The siren grew louder, more insistent. The faces of Brown and Keller became more anxious.

"What in the world would you hold us for?" Brown asked.

"I want Sergeant Rowe to hear your story and see what he thinks of it. Go sit in your car and wait."

The ambulance arrived and the interne made a brief examination on the spot. He looked up curiously at the policeman.

"We were told it was a smashup," he said. "This fellow's been beaten unconscious."

"How bad is he?"

"We'll have to X-ray him. He's sure been hit a lot of times." While Dane was lifted onto a stretcher the county patrolman went to the Cadillac. He returned carrying Lissa's small purse, walked with it to Brown and Keller.

"There was a woman in the car. Did you see her?" Keller looked at him, shook his head slowly. "We didn't see anything."

"Okay. Follow me into town."

Keller was watching the doors of the ambulance closing.

"Suppose my friend goes with you," he suggested rather urgently, "and I take the guy's car to the hospital for him."

"The car is staying right here until it's been photo'd and dusted—"

"Then I'll ride with him in the ambulance."

"Why all the sudden concern?"

"There ought to be somebody to watch out for him?"

"He's got Dade County watching out for him. Let's go."

It was late, anyhow. The ambulance was already roaring off toward downtown Miami. Keller fired his engine, fell in behind the police car.

"Did you ever see such lousy luck as we've been having?"

"Really snakebit," Brown agreed.

"Well, it's your turn to call Harrison. I'd rather rot in jail than have to tell him after this development."

"What I'm worried about is that dancer. That's a rough bunch she's with …"

"Don't think about it," Keller told him. "There's nothing we can do."

"But it was outright kidnaping."

"There's nothing we can do," Keller repeated, slowing for a red light. "You damn fool—where you going?" he suddenly shouted. Brown had thrown his door open. Now he was running, his body bent low. The patrolman was out of his own car in the next moment, also running, unholstering a formidable .45. All Fred Keller could think of to do was lean down on the horn ring, hard, and that was sufficient. The already rattled policeman, thinking he was being run down, whirled toward the sound. By the time he had collected his wits again and turned back, the fleet-footed Brown had turned the corner and was gone.

## 5

"Liz? You okay, Liz?"

It was a woman's soft hand that had passed across his forehead and a woman's soft voice that answered close to his ear. But not Lissa's.

"I'm your nurse," the woman said.

"Where's Liz?"

"I'm sure she's all right—"

"Where is she?"

"I don't know. No—you must lie still."

"Where am I?"

"You're in the emergency room of Miami General. We're going to move you upstairs in a few minutes."

"Why? What's the matter with me?"

"You have a severe cranial concussion, that's what's the matter with you. You're also suffering trauma and a deep knife wound that should

have been treated surgically when it occurred."
"But what about Liz?"
"The police want to talk to you. They'll be able to tell you what you want to know."
"Send them in."
"The doctor wants you to rest first. I'm going to give you a nice shot right now."
"Oh, no you're not." Dane started to rise from the emergency room table. The nurse pushed him firmly back.
"You must lie perfectly still," she insisted.
"I've got to get out of here...."
"That's impossible. The only thing you *have* to do is lie still."
His hand went to his eyes, swept off the protective bandage covering them. "No wonder it was so damn dark in here ..."
"Stop! You have to keep that on!"
He blinked at the bright spotlights shining down, pushed himself to a sitting position. They had stripped him to his shorts, laid the rest of his clothing negligently across a chair on the far side of the room.
"Please lie down!" said the nurse. "You're a sick man!"
Dane was crossing toward the chair and the nurse fled out of the room, a trim-figured young blonde who had been dealing with too many fragile vacationers and assorted hypochondriacs. Dane was belting his trousers when she returned with a white-jacketed staff doctor and a uniformed policeman.
"Here, here," the doctor said importantly. "None of that."
"Got to go, Doc."
"Go? Good Lord, man, you're in serious condition. I don't want any movement at all for at least twenty-four hours!"
"I feel lousy," Dane admitted, "But it just can't be helped."
The doctor was shaking his head vigorously. "Absolutely out of the question. Impossible. If I have to, I'll sign a restraining order and put you in the prisoners' ward. I'll see you in a straitjacket before I let you walk out of here."
"Better do what the doc says," the policeman said and Dane focused his eyes on him. Everything seemed hazy.
"Where's the girl that was with me?"
"We want to talk to you about that later. Now get back on the table like a good boy." The cop moved in on him, crowded him. Dane's glance went past his shoulder.
"Behind you," he said, reaching out to turn the man around.
"On the table, buster...."
Then the nurse saw them, the four of them in the white jackets they

had gotten somewhere, and she shrieked a warning that was too late to protect the policeman from going down and out as a blackjack flashed expertly across the crown of his cap. Another intruder clapped his hand across the nurse's mouth, a third backed the startled doctor into a corner with an intimidating .32.

"Get dressed," the fourth one told Dane. "Can you walk out of here?"

"I can walk." He put on his shirt, buttoned it, slipped his arms into the jacket.

"Let's go," the speaker said crisply. "The doc and nurse in front, you in the middle. We mean business. Don't fool around."

They left the room in the order directed, making a strange processional that was somehow not out of place in the corridor of a large hospital. Even the elevator operator showed no curiosity as he took his unusual assortment of passengers down to the main floor.

Through the lobby then, out the door and down to the waiting car. Sweet and simple, with Dane wedged in the back seat, the doctor and nurse left standing foolishly on the sidewalk, the car losing itself in the downtown traffic. The doctor broke immediately into a run, reascended the stairs in two bounds and phoned the police from the desk of the startled receptionist.

"This is Doctor Prochaska at Miami General!" he shouted. "A patient has just been kidnaped...."

"Slow down, slow down. What did you say happened?"

"Four men, armed men, just marched in here and forced a seriously injured patient to leave with them. I've got the license number of their car."

"You'd better not be kidding, Doc," the desk sergeant warned him. "What's the tag?"

"It's a New York plate. The letters LH, numbers nine eight seven."

"What make and model car?"

"A dark blue Cadillac. This year's."

"Who's the patient?"

"Man named Timothy Dane. He's suffering shock and a bad concussion. You fellows brought him in a few hours ago...."

"Accident victim?"

"My God, man, don't just sit there and ask meaningless questions! Intercept that car. Bring Dane back here."

Two short blocks from where the policeman was taking the call, the New York-registered car was swinging into the East Coast Railway's parking area and Dane was being smoothly transferred from the stolen Cadillac to an undistinguished Buick bearing a Florida plate. The gunmen had quickly unfrocked themselves of the hospital garb enroute and the change from one car to the other was made without notice in the busy place. They left Miami, headed twenty miles north to Hollywood.

## 6

Luis Diaz left the Consulate with high expectations. Until this morning he had been working under instructions from his superiors, attacking the courier directly to prevent delivery of the money. And until now they had been successful, but only in a negative fashion. Dane was in Miami, and so far as they knew he was still trying to pay over the one hundred thousand to Cashman.

But this morning they were going to settle this problem Luis Diaz's way, and because of the distinctive Latin flavor to his plan the man felt very much at home with it and confident. The excitement, though, the expectation, came from the prospect of dealing with the redheaded girl under much different circumstances. Their first meeting on the train had been necessarily brief, under the pressure of a tight timetable. Their next brush, in the hotel room, had not only cast the secret policeman in a bullying role but resulted in considerable chagrin when he'd had to exit from the place so ingloriously.

This third encounter, the one he was hurrying to now, would be quite another matter, Luis Diaz promised himself. His destination was the docks, the warehouse there which his government leased from the city, and one of his own men was waiting for him.

"Garcia will be along very soon," Diaz said. "Keep an eye out for him." It was a large building inside, fairly new and rather crowded now with a wide array of cargo awaiting shipment. There was one very large crate which held the new bulletproof Lincoln for *El Presidente*, a smaller one for somebody else's Thunderbird. To kill recalcitrants and put down rebellion there were boxes and boxes of the latest arms and ammo—incongruously facing an equal supply of polio vaccine and antibiotics to make loyal citizens safer from death. Along one whole wall, piled nearly to the high ceiling, were American cigarettes, American whiskey, Kleenex, television sets, air conditioners, baseballs, fur coats, film—a sample slice of Americana that helped spread the good life week in, week out, year after year.

Diaz noted it impersonally, his mind on something else, and made his way up the stairs to the office. These were spacious quarters, an apartment really, providing an around-the-clock headquarters for protection of the valuable goods stored in the building. Diaz went in without knocking and the man behind the desk rose nervously.

"Señor Diaz?"

"Sí."

"I have the Consul's instructions," the warehouse manager said then, obviously uncomfortable in the same room with any of the infamous secret police.

"Then I advise that you leave immediately. Above all, not a word to anyone that we are here. This is very important government business."

The frightened man nodded, put on his hat and departed. Diaz crossed the office, opened the connecting door and looked in on the simply furnished bedroom. Beside the bed was the very efficient alarm system, an electronic setup that responded with a great buzzing and flashing of lights to the most sensitive impulse it received. Gone were the dreary nights when a watchman had to prowl round and round, punching his clock endlessly. Now he came into this comfortable little room, threw a switch, and a brain and eyes far more alert than his took over. Break the wireless signal at any of a hundred strategic places and a would-be thief found himself bathed in floodlight overwhelmed by a piercing siren. At the same time an alarm was sounding in the office of the private security police and the armed guard inside the building was ready and waiting.

It was very interesting, but the man Diaz was studying the room with something else in mind. He went back to the office, tried out the swivel back chair, found it more comfortable than the one he had at home. He got up from the chair and wandered into the bedroom again. He stopped before the small mirror on the wall and admired his face from a variety of angles. He smiled urbanely, with eyebrows knitted. He smiled sincerely, eyebrows raised. He frowned, scowled, then looked menacing.

That was the repertoire, and tiring of it he began to pace between the rooms, restlessly, anxiously. Then his solitude was broken by a disturbance from down below.

"Gently, gently!" he called in Spanish to the men who had just arrived with Lissa and were struggling to make her mount the stairs. "That is no way to treat such a beautiful woman," he added in English for the girl's benefit.

"This one is not so fragile, *amigo*," he was told. "She is a cat." They pulled her along with them.

"*Qué es el hombre*, Dane?"

"We cracked his head for him."

"Badly?"

"Who knows?"

"Fool! Didn't I tell you how to handle him?"

"You weren't there, Luis. He's big and he's rough."

"Against four?"

"It took two of us to take the woman."

That focused Diaz's attention on Lissa and he gave her a blended smile—half bland, half ingenuous.

"You have not been too badly treated?" he asked in her language.

"Oh, *no*," she said, brushing the hair back from her forehead, pulling her dress straight over her hips. "You've all been just wonderful. I want to get back to where they left Timothy."

Diaz brought his eyes back to her angry face.

"You're going to be my special guest for a while," he said.

Lissa shook her head. "I'm not going to be your special anything. I want to go back to Timothy. He's terribly hurt."

"Then he doesn't need you. Step inside, *roja*."

"Whatever that '*roja*' is, I don't like it. And I'm not stepping inside anywhere...."

"Bring her," Diaz said curtly, and with each arm imprisoned the girl was forced into the office. "Sit down," Diaz said, and when she hesitated she was pushed into an armchair. "You're acting very badly," he told her.

"*I'm* acting badly ...?"

"Like a child," he said. "I expect you to behave as a woman." It was bluntly put, and Lissa looked up at him for a long moment, calculating his strength, looked around at all four of the other men in the room with her. She had been furious until now, desperately worried about Dane—but with each second that ticked off she was beginning to know fear for her own self. Diaz recognized it immediately, watched it grow, knew the heady feeling of power it gave him.

"Get me the Golden Shores Hotel on the phone," he said and one of his men jumped to it.

He dialed, handed the instrument over when the connection was made.

"Has Mr. Timothy Dane returned?" Diaz asked. "No? Well then, leave this message. Tell Mr. Dane that his friend is very anxious to see him again. What he should do is check the package at the newsstand in the Fontainebleau. A Mr. Garcia will pick it up in an hour. Tell him that—exactly one hour." Diaz broke the connection, smiled down at Lissa. "We seem to have sixty minutes to get to know each other better," he said. "Let's go into the other room."

"Ah, no—you wouldn't do anything like that...."

"It doesn't have to be an ordeal," Diaz said. "I am at heart a very gentle man."

"Then why not forget what you're thinking? Just let me go."

Diaz shook his head. "After today I will never see you again, *roja*. All the rest of my life I would think about you, wonder about you. That would be an intolerable way to live." He turned from her abruptly, his thin face set, and strode toward the connecting door.

"Luis...." He looked back over his shoulder at Garcia, surprise in his glance.

"What?"

"*Amigo*, this is your private affair. I will go now, *por le favor*."

Diaz shrugged.

"I also," said another.

"All of you get out. Get out!"

As he spoke he moved swiftly toward Lissa, pulled her out of the chair.

"You are making a mistake," Garcia told him. "This is not professional."

"No, *hombre*. It is a private affair—as you said."

The four of them stood there irresolutely, as though they might interfere. Then Garcia turned to leave the office and they all followed, like sheep. Diaz slammed the door behind them, locked it and pocketed the key.

"Inside," he said to the girl. "There has been entirely too much talking."

## CHAPTER FIVE

Though the road beyond Ojus was comparatively open, as against the slow going along Biscayne, the driver of the Buick kept the needle just inside the speed limit and did nothing else to distinguish himself in the flow of traffic. And Dane, for all his impatience to be elsewhere and doing, had to be content to stare moodily at the passing scenery and bide his time.

The man didn't delude himself about the situation. As irked as Cashman might have been because of their failure to do business together, this morning's newspaper had more than likely pushed him beyond the point where nothing else mattered but giving Dane his lumps. And Dane could even sympathize with Cashman's wounded pride except that it was wasting so damn much time. He had a very real foreboding that Lissa could not afford to have them settle their argument at her expense.

And underscoring everything else was the lousy condition he was in physically. It went beyond the walloping, ceaselessly pounding headache, the hot pain along his ribs. He felt battered generally, run-down and weary, and the prospect of being delivered to another free-for-all was not appealing. What to do about it? Pick a fight right here and get punished some more? Throw himself out onto the Dixie Highway?

"Who's got a cigarette?" he asked instead, and the gunman on his right obliged. Then, "How the hell far we going?"

"The longer it takes, buddy, the better off you are." But in a few minutes they were at Harding Circle, then bearing due west on Hollywood Boulevard. On Park Road they made another turn and finally pulled into the driveway of an imposing house.

"Out," Dane was told, and he was crowded out of the car and up into the house itself. Down a spacious corridor then, past several large rooms, up a half-flight of steps and halting at last before the closed door of the rooms where Cashman ate, slept and handled his varied affairs. A gunman knocked and was told to come in. He pushed the door open and Dane was shoved inside the room.

Cashman had been watching their arrival from a window. Now he turned, leaned his butt on the sill and laid his hands palms down on either side. It was a relaxed enough pose but Cashman, somehow, managed to appear belligerent, menacing.

"Where is she?" he asked bluntly, his voice deep and penetrating.

"With them."

"Them *who?*"

"Whoever's been trying to keep us from getting together."

Cashman came away from the window. "You yellow sonofabitch!" he snarled, and a pulse jumped wildly in his temple. "What'd you do—hand her over to save your own lousy neck?"

"That's about it. Now let's get her back safe."

"I'll worry about her, goddamn you!" He held out his hand, demandingly. "Give," he ordered.

Dane looked into the stormy face below him, shook his head.

"The markers," he said and Cashman's fist struck him on the side of the mouth, jolting him around.

He struggled to free his own hand but strong arms held him fast.

"Give," Cashman said again, eyes blazing furiously.

"Don't have it …"

Cashman hit him again in the face, then in the pit of the stomach.

"Where is it?"

Dane shook his head. Cashman's fist smashed against the bridge of his nose.

"*Where?*"

"… markers …" Dane mumbled, his voice blurry through the blood thickening if his mouth.

Cashman stepped back, hit with all the force of his powerful shoulders. Dane slumped forward, unconscious.

"Search him," Cashman said. "Take him apart." The telephone rang on the desk and he went to answer it.

"Yeah?"

"Harland Burke, Cashman. The news is very bad."

"Now what?"

"The Colonel has been captured. His army has surrendered."

"How do you know?"

"The government radio just announced it."

"They'd say that anyhow. They're conning us...."

"No" Burke said dismally. "Gomez, himself, spoke during the broadcast."

"He *what?*"

"I imagine they gave him amnesty. A revolution down there is run under a special set of ground rules—"

"Well, where the hell does that leave me?"

"I've been thinking about that," Burke said, coming to life. "The fact is, I have some very confidential information about a situation in Costa Rica. My contact there is a very talented and ambitious young captain named LaGordo. Best of all, it wouldn't take quite so much to finance a change in government—"

Cashman slammed the receiver down in the other man's ear, swung to the activity over the prone figure of Dane.

"You find it?"

"He's clean, Johnny. Nothing."

"What is it around here?" Cashman raged unreasonably. "Can't anything go right?" He strode to where Dane lay, glowered down at him. "So this is what she goes for?" he asked, tilting Dane's face with the toe of his shoe. "Scratch the bastard."

"What?"

"Knock him off."

"That's kind of rough, Johnny," the gunman protested.

"*Rough?* Do you know what this bum cost me? You got any idea?"

"What's a babe mean to you? Hell!"

"Who's talking about her? On account of him I just blew the biggest deal I ever got next to. Now take him out of here and bust him for good."

"How?"

"I gotta draw you pictures?" Cashman exploded. "You don't know what to do? You got a whole friggin' ocean out there. Put him in it."

The four of them looked at Cashman balefully, then around at each other, finally down at the troublesome, faintly stirring Dane. The money they took down each week from East Coast Associates was plentiful and regular. The work—mostly collections and occasional intimidation—was agreeable and mentally untaxing. Being on Johnny Cashman's payroll was riding the gravy train, deluxe. Being off it meant a return to scrambling for a living, hard labor and lean pickings.

Without a word spoken among them they hoisted Dane to his wobbly feet, moved him out of the room and out of the house. Back in the car again they held a conference.

"He said the ocean—what about it?"

"The trick is not to weight him down too much. And cut him a little."

"Cut him?"

"Sharks. Anything in the water that's bleeding it's like they can smell it."

"But we got to keep him until tonight."

"And then heist a boat."

"I know a place on Haulover Beach that's quiet. We can take him there now, plug him and wait till it's dark enough."

"We got to watch ourselves."

"Hell, yes, we got to watch ourselves. Where'd you say to take him?"

"Haulover Beach. There's an old equipment shack there the county never uses until the summer. We can bust in and nobody'll ever know the difference."

They drove off then, with a much-recovered but helplessly ineffective Dane pinned down in the back seat. Now the route was east, toward the ocean, then south for a quick six miles until they were mingling with the tourists' cars inside the Dade County Park named Haulover Beach. The knowledgeable one directed the driver to the unused summer maintenance building and they hustled Dane inside.

"Who does it?" was the question asked then, the very important question on all their minds.

"We flip," was the answer and they plucked coins from their jackets, spun them into the air and let them fall.

"I got a head."

"Heads."

"Tails."

"Tails here."

They spun the coins again.

"Heads again."

"Same."

"Heads here."

The fourth voice was silent and the other three looked sharply at his coin.

"Tails," came the announcement. "You win, Charlie."

"Win what?" Charlie asked plaintively. "I never *killed* nobody all my life."

"You win, Charlie," he was told again. "You got a beef, tell it to Cashman."

"But you guys are with me? You'll help dump him in the ocean?"

"Sure, sure. But first you shoot him."

"And for crissake don't make a mess."

"Hey—where you going?"

"Outside, Charlie. It's best all-around you don't have anybody actually see it."

"Keep the noise down," another told him. "Shove the gun tight up against him." Then the three of them went out of the shack and Dane's reluctant assassin faced him glumly.

"What do I look like, Charlie? The hot seat?"

"Ahh, shut up."

"It doesn't hurt much when they hit the switch. You only think it's going to."

"Shut up."

"Cashman's really slipping, you know that? He's being sandbagged— and you're the fall guy."

Charlie had the gun in his hand and was staring intently at Dane's chest.

"They don't hurt you much up at Raiford, Charlie. One good jolt, that's all. Unless you got too much hair."

"What?" the gunman asked, his free hand going involuntarily to the dark stubble of beard on his face.

"The hairy ones sizzle for a while. And you heard about that accident up in Sing Sing last year?"

"What accident?"

"The jolt stopped his heart," Dane said glibly. "The doc called him dead. Only he wasn't, and they buried him that way."

Charlie's tongue licked his dry lips.

"I ain't going to no hot seat," he said and Dane laughed at him.

"You think my outfit's ever going to let up on you?"

"Outfit, hell. You're a private dick."

"Is that what Cashman told you?"

"That's what I read in the paper."

Dane only looked at him, an enigmatic half-grin on his face.

"You're all by yourself," Charlie said. "Nobody'll even miss you ..."

Dane suddenly cringed, threw his arms up as though to ward off some object coming at them from above. The gunman hunched his own shoulders, instinctively, swung toward the unknown danger. Dane closed in on him, rocked the other man with the hardest right hand he had left to him, wrenched the gun loose a moment later.

"Back away," he told the hurt, dazed Charlie. "Get to the other side of that door." When Charlie was where he wanted him Dane pointed the gun to the ceiling and fired once. The explosion echoed and re-echoed in the small closed place and almost immediately the door was thrown open.

"For crissake, Charlie!" the arrival shouted furiously then blinked foolishly at Dane and the gun in his hand.

"Inside, Buddy. Bring your friends."

He came into the shack but the other two had been warned. One of them pulled the door closed from the outside. That was a stalemate, the time-consuming situation Dane didn't want. He aimed the gun directly at the door and fired again, hoping the racket would either scare them off or focus some kind of attention on the shed.

"You're something, you are," the second man told Charlie disgustedly. "Wait'll Johnny gets ahold of you."

"To hell with him. I'm going back to L.A."

"In a box you'll go back. Oh, what a stupid jerk—" His voice broke off abruptly as the door swung inward. Dane braced to trade shots, just did manage to hold off when he saw that the other two were moving inside with their hands raised to their shoulders. Herding them was not a uniformed policeman but a youngish-looking civilian wearing a rumpled suit and a look of painful uncertainty. Dane, with a grateful glance, had the curious impression that the other man was not at all happy to be here.

"Glad to see you," he told him.

"Skip all that and come on out of there," Harry Brown said.

"Will do," Dane said cheerfully disarming his recent captors, filling his pockets with their weapons. "Let's go," he said then and the pair of them left. "Where's your car?" he asked.

"Up the line. But let's borrow theirs."

"Whatever you say. But why?"

"Because I had to steal mine, that's why," Brown said miserably. "Oh, brother, what a mess I'm in."

"You drive, will you?" Dane requested, climbing into the rider's seat and leaning back gratefully. Brown turned over the engine and they drove away.

"Got a smoke?"

"Don't use it," Brown said.

Dane sighed. "Who are you, anyhow? What mess are you in?"

"Skip the questions, Dane."

"But you know who I am?"

"I know you can get into more trouble than anybody I've ever seen."

"But where do you figure?"

"Just skip it."

"If you're in trouble about stealing a car," Dane said, "I met a fellow last night in the Sheriff's office—"

"I don't want anything to do with the Sheriff. Good Lord!"

"Listen—have you been following me around?"

"That's a laugh."

"Were you there when I got run off the road a little while ago?"

Brown nodded his head.

"Then you saw them take the girl?"

"I saw them."

"What was the license number?"

"1E3605," Brown answered, and it was as though the number was burned into his mind. "That's a rental tag, isn't it?"

"Yes."

"Get to the nearest phone. We'll see who's using that car."

"What do you mean, 'we'?"

"Suit yourself. There's a pay booth. Pull over." Brown slid the car to the curb and Dane got out slowly and stiffly.

"Here, I'll do it," the other man said, coming around from his side. But they crowded into the booth together, one working with the directory, the other making the calls.

## 2

"That news is wonderful," Luis Maximo said gravely on the diplomatic phone to his capital. "Extend my congratulations to *El Presidente* and the glorious victory of our arms...."

"Yes, of course," his boss, Huerta, said in a dry voice. "But now that the revolution has been put down, it is very important diplomatically that we treat the entire episode as of no real consequence to the government."

"I understand."

"Above all, there must be no incidents involving the Americans who were aiding Gomez. Dispatch the agent Diaz and the others home at once."

"Very good."

"I can tell you, Luis," Huerta said more warmly, "that *El Presidente* is not unaware of your loyalty, your vigilance and your devotion to him in this affair."

"*Gracias, señor.*"

"*El Presidente* will not let your patriotism go unrewarded," Huerta told him. "How would the ambassadorship at Buenos Aires suit your abilities?"

"*Señor*, I am overwhelmed. It is a dream come true."

"*Bueno*. My regards to the *Señora* Maximo, and advise us as to the speedy departure of Diaz. I am sure that the American State Department is aware of our activities. It behooves us now not to cause our good neighbor any further embarrassment on his soil."

"My feelings precisely," Maximo said, new timbre in his voice. The conversation ended then, and the dedicated man pushed himself away from the inexpensive desk, crossed the room meditatively. *Buenos Aires*, he thought. *Señor Ambassador!* And after that? *You are not a young man,* he told himself soberly, then squared his sloping shoulders, inhaled a deep breath. *Not so old, either. And after the Argentine—Rio? London? Washington, itself?* He expelled the breath, relievedly, let the shoulders resume their comfortable set. That brought him back into focus, reminded him of what else Huerta had said beside the golden promise of the promotion.

He turned to the desk, flipped open his notebook of personal telephone numbers and dialed one.

The phone rang in the office of the pier warehouse and Diaz set down his glass, irritated at the interruption. The jangling bell destroyed the mood he had carefully created, broke the rhythm of what he had chosen to think of as a graceful seduction.

The bottle of Spanish Pernod had softened his original intentions to simply take the girl and be done with it. One hundred fifty-four proof it was, an illegal liquor in this country, and though Lissa had declined to drink any, the harmless-looking white stuff had spread its stultifying warmth through the man's bloodstream, inducing a kind of schizoid reaction that made him think of himself as someone urbane and charming, an irresistible lover; made him believe that Lissa would very soon want romance of her own will.

And Lissa had helped nurture the man's hallucinations. Once inside the room, with the exit locked against her, she'd switched from an attitude of resistance to one of forced gaiety, as if this was not the situation it really was but only an innocent tête-à-tête. She kept her distance from him, but made herself smile, chattered ingenuously about any subject that came to her mind or seemed to interest him.

Then, with Diaz about ready to press his suit peacefully, the phone rang.

"What do you want?" he asked abruptly.

"This is Maximo, Diaz. You have just been ordered to return home.

*Muy pronto.*"

"Return?"

"Your mission is suspended. The revolution has been crushed."

"No," Diaz said, his slim face tightening. "My plan—I must have more time—"

"I said that the revolution is put down. We have no more need for such desperate measures. Huerta has particularly asked for the swift return of your party to the capital."

"All right," Diaz said vaguely.

"Is the girl in your custody now?"

Diaz looked over at Lissa. "Yes. In my custody."

"Then you will release her at once," Maximo told him, and added, "Unharmed.... Are you there, Diaz?"

"Yes."

"I am arranging for the government plane to transport you within the hour. You will report to Brown's Airport without delay. Diaz ...?"

But the secret agent had dropped the receiver into its cradle and all that Maximo heard was the signal of the broken connection. He was replacing his own phone, worriedly, when the sound of angry voices came to him from the anteroom and the privacy of his sanctum was rudely invaded.

"*Señor! Señor!*" his secretary shouted in great distraction. "Defend yourself!"

Maximo stared at the tall, formidable, battered-looking *yanqui* filling his doorway, striding toward him, and wondered wildly what defense the girl had in mind.

"Where is she, mister?" Dane demanded. "Produce her fast."

"Who are you? What are you talking about?"

"I'm talking about Lissa. Where you got her?"

Maximo looked beyond the angry man, saw Harry Brown and took courage from the obvious nervousness on that one's face.

"This is an outrage," he said sternly. "Do you realize this is an invasion of my nation's territory?"

Dane leaned across the Consul's desk, put his face close to Maximo's and spoke very seriously to him. "Don't," he said. "I've been having a bad time with you Latins for two nights running. Putting the arm on that kid was too much even for Diaz—"

"Diaz? What do you know of Diaz?"

"I didn't like the way he looked at her last night."

"But how do you associate me with him?"

"Come off it! The car was rented out to this address. Where is she?"

The older man sighed, spread his hands.

"She is safe," he said. "I have just given instructions for her release—"

"She isn't here?"

"There is nothing to worry about."

"Where is she?"

"I assure you, *señor*—"

"Is she with Diaz?"

"Diaz has my strictest orders—"

"Where is Diaz? Where is the girl?"

"Come on, Dane," Harry Brown said from the doorway. "If the representative of his government gives us his assurances—"

"You didn't see this Diaz," Dane said brusquely. "He made one rough play for Lissa already."

"How is that?" Maximo asked, his voice sharp.

"He went after her last night. He ended up with egg on his face. I don't think he liked it." With each sentence, Dane's voice grew more ragged. Now his big fist slammed down meaningfully on Maximo's desk. *"Damn it—where are they now?"*

"At the city pier," Luis Maximo told him. "Go quickly!"

They left and Maximo dialed the phone again. He got a busy signal at the warehouse.

### 3

Diaz had set the receiver down, then, as an afterthought, left it off the hook. He turned toward the red-haired girl, and now the powerful absinthe was working on him very badly. The man was suddenly drunk, drunk and ugly in his thinking, and it was so coarsely there in his eyes, in the looseness of his mouth, that Lissa stood up from her chair as though a warning had been whispered in her ear.

She stood up and put the chair between them. There was no point now in pretending that he intended anything else.

Her fear of him made Diaz smile. It was a cold, humorless thing, jackal-like.

"We're leaving here," he said aloud, and if the words were dull and slurred there was still a definiteness about them, a foreboding.

Lissa shook her head. "I'm not going anywhere with you...."

"... my rooms," Diaz told her. "Let Maximo find us there." He crossed to the door, steadily enough, unlocked it and pulled it open. "Come on!"

"No."

His hand slid inside his jacket, came out holding a thin glistening stiletto that had been sheathed to his chest.

"No time," he said unsteadily. "No time for argument." He took two strides toward her, the knife at hip level, pointed hungrily upwards. "*Venite*," he said, slipping unconsciously into his own tongue. "*Venite!*"

The girl gripped the back of the chair. Visions of that razor-sharp blade slashing at her raced sickeningly through her mind.

She nodded her head slowly, as you do with someone as unstable as Diaz, and tried to walk toward the door with a natural gait. He fell in behind her, very close, and when she faltered once the knifepoint prodded her sharply above the waist.

They went through the door and descended the stairs to the warehouse floor, across that to the waiting car. "Get in," he ordered and while she moved to obey he quickly pulled on the counterweight that sent the warehouse's big door sliding upward. Lissa watched the man, her mind dejected, numb with fear of him. All at once the idea came to her and she rolled her window tight, depressed the lock button. Then the rear door was locked. She lunged across the seat, aware that he was racing toward the car. The button went down with a click. She raised herself to her knees, reached frantically for the last door lock. Her finger touched it, fumbled, and then the door was yanked open.

Diaz laughed at her, let himself into the car, and was still smiling as the engine started and they rolled out of the warehouse. He drove with his left hand. In his right fist was the slim knife, its wicked point piercing the thin material of her dress, barely pricking the flesh of her thigh. The girl wasn't in pain, but she knew she would be an instant after she made any move to get free of him.

They headed west from the pier, out Tenth Street toward N.W. Seventh, then south on Seventh toward the Riverside Park neighborhood. The car finally halted before a rooming house.

"Leave very slowly," Diaz said, "and go into the building. Remember that you're with a very determined man."

With the harsh warning echoing in her ears Lissa stepped from the car and crossed woodenly to the house entrance. It was dark inside, woefully quiet.

"Upstairs," Diaz said, pushing her ahead of him. They had climbed halfway to the floor above when they heard heavy footsteps descending.

*It's a man*, Lissa thought. *A big man.*

He came into view, a big man in a hurry. Lissa lifted her face to him, locked his glance and made a silent plea with her eyes. The man hesitated, his own expression curious, and looked beyond her to Diaz. "Good morning," Diaz said.

The man's face cleared and he nodded to both of them. "Mornin'," he said and passed on down the stairs.

"Your last chance," Diaz taunted at her back. "Now you have none. Move, darling."

At the top of the landing he directed her to turn left and walk the length of the gloomy corridor. He halted her at a door, unlocked it, shoved her almost possessively into the small room beyond. Diaz relocked the door, stood leaning against it in an unconscious attitude of triumph that was not lost on the girl who watched him steadily.

"There is very little time," he said.

Lissa shook her head. "Please...."

"If you want to leave this room alive," Diaz told her, "you'll do exactly as I say. Get undressed, *roja*."

## 4

Harry Brown drove directly into the warehouse, and the car was still moving when Dane leaped out, looked around him and made for the office. He mounted the steps and plunged inside.

"Lissa!"

On the threshold of the bedroom he stopped short. She'd been here. Been in this room recently.

"Where are they?" asked Brown, out of breath from the quick climb.

"Goddammit, I don't know. But that's her perfume." He whirled toward the phone, began dialing the Consulate for some lead when Brown tugged at his elbow.

"Another car just came in," he said and Dane put down the phone.

"Diaz?" called a voice from below. "Diaz, have you heard the news?"

Dane pressed Brown back against the wall, took a position just inside the opened door. They heard the man ascend the stairs.

"Diaz, the job is over—"

"You said it, brother," Dane told him, enclosing the man's neck in the bend of his elbow. "Diaz isn't here. Where would he be?"

"*Yo no sabe*," the man said, seeking refuge in Spanish. Dane wasn't having any. His forearm tightened and the man's eyes bulged.

"*Where?*"

"He has a room," the man gasped. "About a mile from here—"

"Let's go." The feet of Dane's guide hardly touched the steps as they returned to the floor below. "Get behind the wheel," he told him positively, slid into the seat beside him. Brown prepared to follow them.

"I'm not too familiar with this town," the man warned Dane.

"You'll find Diaz all right," Dane promised him grimly and they backed out of the building. The car moved into the traffic, tracing

Diaz's route along Tenth.

"What'd you mean, the job is over?"

"*El Hombre*—the president has put down the revolt of Gomez."

"So what?"

"So the funds you are carrying to Cashman are of no use anymore."

Dane stared at him, said nothing, and it all fell into place. A damn revolution—that was the little messenger job Bernie King had sent him on. And from the beginning, back at his apartment in New York, he'd had the queer feeling that he wasn't doing business with professionals. Fanatics, that's what they were. A bunch of hotheads playing cloak-and-dagger games …

"I think we turn here."

"You'd better think right, joe."

"We are not with Diaz in this thing with the girl. That is the only reason I am taking you there."

"Okay. But stay out of the way once we arrive." Dane said no more, but the threat was there. If anything had happened to Lissa nothing could save Diaz.

"Up ahead!" his driver shouted excitedly.

"What?"

"The rooming house—but the police are there."

They were, units from both county and city were drawn up haphazardly before the place. Then Dane saw the Miami Hospital ambulance and his heart sank in his chest

"What shall I do? The policeman is waving me on."

"Just stop," Dane said dully. The car braked quickly and Dane stepped out.

"This is police business, buddy," the cop told him. "Keep moving."

"Is there a man named Genovar here?"

"He's inside."

Dane brushed by him, and there was a dark look about him that kept the officer from calling him back. The inside of the place was crowded with policemen, in and out of uniform, and there were others strung along the staircase. Dane climbed the stairs unchallenged, came to a knot of worried-looking men gathered around the door of Diaz's room.

"Genovar," Dane said to one of them and the Chief Deputy looked up.

"Where did you come from?"

"What's he done to her?"

"We don't know for sure. She's still alive."

"Then let's go in …"

"Not if we want to keep her alive." Genovar took Dane by the arm, pulled him away from the door. "This is the situation," he said confidentially. "We got a line on Diaz for the Shag Wilson knifing. It's the damnedest, mixed-up thing you ever heard—"

"A revolution. The hell with it. What about Lissa?"

"Somehow he got her in there with him. Now he sounds like he's either drunk, doped or crazy—and he knows he's facing a murder rap." Genovar shook his head. "We're afraid for her sake to brace him."

A deep breath escaped Dane's lips as the other man finished. Almost immediately he stiffened, then started toward the closed door as Lissa's voice pierced the tense quiet in a sudden cry of pain. Genovar grabbed him by both arms, another man planted himself squarely across his path.

"You can't do it that way!" Genovar growled in his ear. Then, from beyond the door came Diaz' high-pitched, panic-edged voice.

"I'll kill her!" he screamed out at them. "Get out of here or I'll kill her!"

"Take it easy, take it easy," a uniformed police captain answered persuasively. "We only want to talk to you, mister."

"I know what you want! It's her life or mine!"

"Why don't you just come out like a good fellow?"

Lissa cried out again, sharply.

"She has three minutes!" Diaz shouted. "*Clear out!*"

Silence followed, ominously, and on all their faces was reflected the certainty that this time they were dealing with a killer who meant it.

"Do the doors in these rooms connect?" Dane asked, and Genovar shook his head.

"No," he said. "We've got nothing working for us. Nothing at all."

"Can you get me some rope, Genovar?"

"Oh, come on—"

"About twenty feet."

"For what? To lower yourself to the window? You'd be a sitting duck."

"If I did it that way. But suppose I crashed in—and you hit the door at the same time?"

"No good. In the second place you don't have time."

"If you get me the rope, I'll make time."

Genovar studied him for a moment, then gave orders to produce a hemp line about thirty feet long. Dane moved toward the door.

"Diaz? This is Dane."

"What do you want?"

"You know what I want. I've sent for Maximo."

"Maximo?"

"As soon as he gets here we're going to work a deal. Didn't you know you've got diplomatic immunity?"

"What?"

"You're working for your government, aren't you?" There was no answer. "Well—aren't you?"

"Yes."

"That's what Maximo says. He's coming over to take you out with him. Providing nothing happens to Lissa. That's not government business, Diaz."

"She'll be all right," Diaz said. "Unless the Consul doesn't arrive...."

"He's on his way. Why don't you let her out now?"

"No! I'll do only what Maximo tells me."

"Treat her right," Dane said.

"Nothing will happen to her so long as no one tries to trick me—"

"Timothy?"

"Yeah, honey."

"Don't take any chances," she pleaded. "He really means it."

"We know," Dane said and stepped away from the door.

"Do you think he'll stay put?" Genovar asked quietly.

"He's ready to believe anything up to a point. What's with that rope?"

A deputy was coming down the corridor carrying a coil of hemp even as Dane asked about it.

"I'm going upstairs and one room over," he said, taking the line. "Lend me two men, and brother when you get the signal go in there fast."

"It's not going to work," Genovar predicted gloomily. "I'm not going to let you try it."

"I've fixed it now so you've got to," Dane said and walked away from him. Genovar watched the lonely-looking figure for several seconds, looked at the rope looped forlornly over his broad shoulder. He turned and pointed to two of his men, signaled them to go along.

The room Dane wanted was opened to him by a passkey. He opened the window, looked down and judged the distance to the floor below. Then he carefully measured out a length of the line, snaked one end of it through the legs of the bed, tied it securely to the grille of the wall heater. He fastened the free end around his chest with a running bowline.

"All set," he told the other two. "Somebody get down on the landing where you can see Genovar and this doorway. The other one stand in the doorway. Give me a ten-count after I'm out the window. Then flash the word."

"Ten fast or slow?"

"One-monkey, two-monkeys, three-monkeys," Dane recited, giving them the tempo. He went to the window ledge, straddled it and waited until the other man took his post on the staircase.

"He's there," said the one in the doorway.

Dane nodded. "Here goes absolutely nothing," he said and lowered himself out the window and down the wall of the house, counting monkeys as he went. At "five" the line was taut. He braced his feet against the wall, let his body hunch up into a tight crouch. At the count of eight he launched himself outward at an angle and aimed his outthrust legs at the windowpane of Diaz's room. He was in mid-air, shouting "Nine monkeys" aloud when he saw that he was going to miss his target. But there was no way to call off Genovar now. No way to bargain the killing Diaz out of one more chance for Lissa.

Dane would never know how he managed to contort himself so strenuously in the last remaining second he had left. And if he'd known beforehand that he had to do it, he could not have brought it off.

Strangely enough, inside the room itself there was a rare moment of calm. Lissa sat on the edge of the bed, huddled in a thin blanket that covered up most of her nakedness and Diaz stood nearby, half turned toward the door. Stuck in his belt was the small Italian-make gun that he had snatched from the bureau when the police had first knocked on the door. The stiletto lay on the table, where he had placed it to light the cigarette he was nervously puffing now.

His hand trembled and his eyes glittered unhealthily, betraying the dangerous state of his nerves, the tension that his liquor-dulled mind was unable to cope with.

He still couldn't believe that he was in such a situation. Nor could anyone who had ever known Manuel Diaz imagine that he could have maneuvered himself into a position from which there was no pride-saving way out. This was nightmarish, impossible, and he had reacted to it in kind—her life for his. Then had come the first words that made sense, Dane's solution of the whole unpleasantness via Maximo. "Diplomatic immunity." Magic words, the "Open sesame!"

He would have thought of it in time himself, but it was just as well to have the whole business negotiated out there. Maximo, however, should hurry. Then he would depart this hellish room immediately. Diaz did not wish to be present when Dane saw the girl's bruises.

He took a final drag on the cigarette and was lowering it to the ashtray when the whole window behind him gave way with a fearful crash. The man's taut nerves snapped with that and a wild shriek escaped his throat. The door burst open almost simultaneously.

Diaz snatched the gun from his belt and fired at the big form in the window. Three .38 slugs slammed into his body from the side, drove him to his knees. He pitched over headlong still gripping the little automatic.

"Are you hit?" Genovar shouted at Dane, but the other man didn't seem to hear him as he crossed to the mute and terrified Lissa. He leaned over her, lifted her eyes away from the dying figure on the floor.

"It's over, baby," he said gently. "It's all over."

"Get the doc in here," Genovar was saying. "The rest of you clear out. Come on, boys, give the lady some privacy."

Lissa at last focused on Dane's face, became conscious of a hand cupping her chin.

"Will you take me home, Timothy?" she asked simply.

"You bet." He went to the chair, gathered up her clothes, raised the girl to her feet and walked with her to the bathroom. "Put these on," he told her. "Then we'll get out of here."

Dane closed the door and joined Genovar beside Diaz.

"Well, it worked," the Chief Deputy said tiredly.

"But I wouldn't want to try it again. What are you grinning at?"

"If you'd seen me doing my rope trick," Dane confessed, "you wouldn't want to try it this time. What a damn fool stunt that was." He knelt down beside the agent and began calmly going through the man's pockets. Then he stood up again, looked to where the dark jacket was hanging very neatly and moved toward it.

"What are you looking for?"

"These," he answered, holding the package of IOU's for Genovar to see.

The police officer nodded. "What you went to collect from Shag Wilson last night?"

"Yep. How did you get a line on Diaz for that job?"

"You know anybody named Fred Keller?"

"No."

"Harry Brown?"

"Hell, yes, I know Harry. If you're talking about a stolen car, I'd appreciate squaring it for him...."

"I'm not, but it's interesting. A county patrolman picked up Keller and Brown for questioning about that *accident* you had out near the *fronton* this morning. Brown slipped away from him on the way into town, but he held on to Keller. You know who they are, don't you?"

Dane shook his head.

Genovar laughed. "They're C.I.A. agents. They work for Counterintelligence. When we got ready to book Keller and mug him he got on the phone to Washington. I spoke to some bird up there named Harrison."

"What was their angle, the revolution again?"

"Right. They wanted to find out who the Americans were that were going to supply the stuff to them. Diplomatic relations with a friendly country and all that hooey. Harrison told Keller to cooperate and that put us onto Diaz. Just one of those crazy breaks you get every once in a while."

Lissa came out of the bathroom, dressed, scrubbed-looking, even managing a flickering smile.

"You don't need us right away, do you?" Dane asked and Genovar shook his head.

"No. The two of you take it easy. We'll get a statement when the time comes." He glanced toward the motionless Diaz. "An inquest, most likely," he added laconically, then looked at Lissa. "If he does live, what charges will you press against him?"

"I don't know—kidnaping, I guess it was."

"Threatening you with a deadly weapon?"

"Yes, he threatened me."

"Anything else?"

"No," she said. "Nothing else."

"Good," Genovar said warmly. "That's real good. And say—my wife wants to come over to the Beach and see you dance. The story in the paper this morning really took her fancy."

His words had a just-right effect on the girl, brought her back to a world she knew.

"I'll be looking for you," Lissa said and left on Dane's arm.

# 5

It was late afternoon and the ringing telephone brought the tall man from the bedroom to answer it. He looked relaxed, rested, and there was an easy contentment in his stride.

"Yes?"

"This is the desk again, Mr. Dane. There's a Mr. Bernie King who'd like to see you."

"See me? He's down in the lobby?"

"Yes, sir."

"Well, send him up."

Within two minutes there was a knock on the hotel door and Dane opened it to a panicky-looking Bernie King.

"For the love of mike, Dane—what's going on down here?"

"A little of everything. What do you mean in particular?"

"After you called I saw a paper. Do you know you're all over the center spread of the *News?*"

"You mean Lissa is."

"I mean you are. They mentioned Johnny Cashman, mentioned him by name!"

"Is that why you're so excited? Cashman?"

"That's no reason, hanh? Listen—you got a drink in the place?"

"Sure," Dane told him, grinning at the other man's agitation. He laid open the partly packed traveling bag, lifted out the bottle and poured a generous portion into one of the hotel's tumblers. "You need ice?" he asked.

"I need strength," he said. "Gimme." King took the drink and tossed it off. Dane made him another.

"Holy Christmas," King said. "What a mess you got us in!"

Dane sank himself into a chair, lifted his long legs across the top of the coffee table.

"How do you mean, Bernie?"

"*Mean*, for crissake? I mean the redhead! I send you down here on a routine business deal, and you've got to completely foul us up by making a play for Johnny Cashman's girl. Don't you know yet that he's the big wheel?"

"How'd you come to sell her contract to him, anyhow?" Dane asked.

"I had no choice. Who am I to buck the likes of Johnny Cashman?" King walked to where the bottle was, replenished himself and turned belligerently to Dane. "Now let's rub your nose in it. How do you come to be sitting around in this fifty-a-day suite like the gahdamn King of Egypt? What are you doing to earn your money ...?"

Again it was the phone, cutting off Bernie King's sharp voice, and Dane rose unhurriedly to answer it.

"Yes?" he said, then listened. "I'm expecting him," he told the man at the desk. "Send him up." He returned to King. "You'll get a full report on this routine business deal," he said. "Plus all expenses and grievances."

"Expenses?" King said explosively. "Grievances? Sue me, Dane. Sue me in every court in the land. All you've done is chiseled yourself a nice trip to Miami. Took a vacation at our expense."

Dane laughed. "You're jealous of my tan," he said.

"The sun doesn't shine in night clubs. Now let's get down to cases. It's obvious you don't have the moxie to deal with somebody like Cashman, so let's have the money and we'll get somebody who can...."

There was a knock on the door and King looked that way nervously.

"Who's that?" he asked Dane.

"Cashman."

"*Cashman?*"

"Come on in," Dane called out and the door opened.

Johnny Cashman stood in the threshold for a moment, looking

strangely uncertain of himself, lacking his usual arrogance.

"I got your message," he said to Dane. "This is the fastest I could get back to town."

"How's my pal Charlie?"

Cashman shook his head. "I haven't seen him." He came inside, closed the door behind him.

"You know Bernie King," Dane said.

"Sure. How are ya, Bernie?"

The smaller man nodded his head cautiously. "Fine, Johnny," he said. "Sorry about all the trouble we've given you."

"Cashman's not mad at anybody," Dane said, shifting his legs comfortably on the tabletop. "As a matter of fact, he's still wondering why he's not talking to the State Attorney about an attempted murder charge."

King's complexion went a shade paler. "Murder?" he echoed.

"Twenty to life," Dane went on musingly. "A tough jolt."

"I lost my head, pal," Cashman told him. "Everything went wrong for me at one time."

"Maybe you ought to stick to bookmaking. Let the experts run the revolution business."

"Don't worry, I will."

"And managing talent isn't your line, either," Dane said, looking up into the gambler's face steadily. "Did you bring the contract like I said?"

Cashman reached into his jacket, brought out a folded document and dropped it on the table beside Dane's foot. Dane, in his turn, produced the sheaf of markers from his shirt pocket.

"Here you go, Bernie," he said, tossing them negligently to the wide-eyed King. "Buddy Lewis's love letters."

King looked at them in disbelief.

"Then everything's all settled?" he asked. "Buddy can open on schedule Wednesday?"

"Everything's fine."

"That's great. Great!" His face was suddenly beaming. "You're a real operator, Dane. From now on you get all my business." He smiled all around, backed toward the door. "I'll be looking for your bill," he said.

"Don't stint yourself."

"Don't you worry."

"'Bye." He was gone.

Then Cashman moved toward the door, his face thoughtful. He looked back.

"You did pretty good for yourself, didn't you?"

"How's that?"

"My hundred grand, my girlfriend."

"Life, Cashman. But you've got the money."

"Like hell I do."

"That white El Dorado is yours, isn't it?"

"What about it?"

"The package is under the front seat. I checked on the car and it's down at County Police headquarters."

Cashman stood there, looking across the room at him, finally accepting what he said for the truth. "Let's you and I play on the same team sometime," the gambler told him.

"Sometime."

"And when you see the doll give her my best. Tell her I'm going to set up shop in Tijuana."

"Good luck."

"Yeah, luck. So long, pal."

Then he was gone and Dane sat alone, smoking one cigarette and another. He glanced at his watch, stood up and went to the phone.

"Give me the travel service," he told the hotel operator. Another voice came on the line. "This is Timothy Dane checking back. Am I all set? Good. I'll pick up the ticket at the desk." He set the phone down, retraced his steps to the table and took the contract in his hand. He carried it into the other room.

"Wake up," he said and Lissa smiled, opened her eyes to gaze up at him languidly from the bed.

"I've been awake for fifteen minutes. Listening."

"Then I don't have to go over it." He dropped the contract onto the pillow beside her head. "There's the life sentence you signed."

"Does that mean I'm on my own?"

"From here on in," he said, "you call the shots."

"Come down here and tell me all about it," she invited.

Dane studied the offer for a long moment, shook his head sadly.

"I've got a plane to catch," he said.

"You're going back to New York?" she protested unhappily. "Where it's cold and dreary? Oh, Timothy—"

"Got to," he said.

"Why?"

"I left the lights on in my apartment," he explained. "Con Edison is burning up all the profit."

"When does the plane leave?"

"An hour."

"There's time," Lissa told him firmly. "There's plenty of time."

He started to shake his head again, but he was looking at her all the while and his head slowly stopped moving. He was remembering another time, between New York and Philadelphia. They'd had just a little more than an hour.

"You're right," Dane said. "There's plenty of time."

Lissa smiled again, closed her eyes so he wouldn't see the telltale mischief she was planning for him. But she knew, woman-wise, that the lights in his apartment were going to go on burning longer than he planned.

THE END

# WILLIAM ARD BIBLIOGRAPHY
(1922-1960)

**Timothy Dane series:**
The Perfect Frame (1951)
The Diary (1952)
.38 (1952; reprinted as *You Can't Stop Me*, 1953; and in the UK as *This is Murder*, 1954)
A Private Party (1953; reprinted in the UK as *Rogue's Murder*, 1955)
Don't Come Crying To Me (1954)
Mr. Trouble (1954)
Hell is A City (1955; reprinted as *The Naked and the Innocent*, 1955)
Cry Scandal (1956)
The Root of His Evil (1957; reprinted as *Deadly Beloved*, 1958)

**Lou Largo Series:**
All I Can Get (1959)
Like Ice She Was (1960; completed by John Jakes)
Babe in the Woods (1960; by Lawrence Block)
Make Mine Mavis (1961; by John Jakes)
And So to Bed (1962; by John Jakes)
Give Me This Woman (1962; by John Jakes).

**Mike/Danny Fontaine series:**
As Bad As I Am (1959; reprinted as *Wanted: Danny Fontaine*, 1960)
When She Was Bad (1960)

**Standalone Novels:**
A Girl For Danny (1953)
No Angels For Me (1954)
The Sins of Billy Serene (1960)

*As Ken Hamlin*

Guns of Revenge (1960)

*As Ben Kerr*

Shakedown (1952)
Down I Go (1955)
I Fear You Not (1956)
Damned If He Does (1956)
Club 17 (1957)
The Blonde and Johnny Malloy (1958)

*As Mike Moran*

Double Cross (1953)

*As Jonas Ward*

**Buchanan series:**
The Name's Buchanan (1956)
Buchanan Says No (1957)
One-Man Massacre (1958)
Buchanan Gets Mad (1958)
Buchanan's Revenge (1960)
Buchanan on the Prod (1961; completed by Robert Silverberg)

*As Thomas Wills*

**Barney Glines series:**
You'll Get Yours (1952)
Mine to Avenge (1955)

www.ingramcontent.com/pod-product-compliance
Lightning Source LLC
LaVergne TN
LVHW021811060526
838201LV00058B/3332